Heart of Stone

HEART OF STONE

John Haworth

CROSSWAY BOOKS • WESTCHESTER, ILLINOIS
A DIVISION OF GOOD NEWS PUBLISHERS

For Alison
with love and thanks

I will give them an undivided heart and put a new spirit in them; I will remove from them their heart of stone and give them a heart of flesh.

(Ezekiel 11:9)

. . . Yet Lord restore thine image, heare my call:
And though my hard heart scarce to thee can grone,
Remember that thou once didst write in stone.

(George Herbert: 'The Sinner')

*N*o one was surprised when I spent three years getting into scrapes in the wilder parts of the Middle East instead of doing conventional post-doctoral research. When the Christmas card from Damascus arrived on the mat they'd all say, 'That's Henry Stanwick for you; he's scared of boredom.' And they worried or prayed about me in the same way that they did about friends in intensive care and missionaries in Irian Jaya and fervently hoped that the cholera, the PLO and the Israeli airforce wouldn't get me. They didn't.

Then to everyone's surprise I came back to the UK and took a cosy little lectureship at a rather dull northern university. 'The boy's settling down at last,' they said, and I ceased to be the subject of either worry or prayer.

There was a revival of interest when I was given a grant to go to an isolated area of Madagascar for a summer to look at some exotic limestone scenery, but I came back with little more than some full notebooks and some striking photographs.

The opinion began to be aired, with some confidence (and a certain relief), that perhaps I had finally stopped getting into trouble. I began to believe it myself.

We were all wrong.

1

Miriam was picking up the mail from the porter as I came through the doors of the department. She gave me a brighter-than-usual smile for a wet Monday morning in January.

'Morning, Henry. There's an interesting one for you here. All the way from the States—Dallas! A big parcel too.'

'Thanks, Miriam. Here, I'll take it.'

I glanced at the sender's address and saw that Miriam was staring expectantly at me. I decided to satisfy her curiosity.

'It's the in-house magazine of Exploco. I did an article for them.'

Miriam looked definitely unsatisfied.

'It's a part repayment for their grant. It feels like a dozen copies at least. I'll put one in the coffee room, but I'll have to read it first.'

After a brief conversation about her weekend I took the package and headed off down to the office. Sitting down without taking my wet anorak off, I gutted the package and pulled out the top magazine, the compliments slip fluttering to the ground. The cover photograph was instantly recognisable. Jagged peaks of white limestone stood proud against a blue sky, isolated from each other by deep shadow-filled cracks. In the middle ground, partially overshadowed by the rocks, sat a helicopter. The diminutive figure of the pilot could be seen, emphasising the scale. Overprinting the sky was the journal title 'Worldwide Reach' and a heading, 'Madagascar's Hidden Heart of Stone.' So it had made the main slot. Underneath

11

were the other headings: 'Exploco Drills Offshore Alaska', 'Louisiana Cooking', 'Treasures of the Prado.'

I opened it at my article. The photographs were stunning. A double-page spread and four smaller ones, well-cropped and sharply printed. You could sense the cutting edges on the limestone blocks. The contrast was good with rich, mysterious shadows and yet maintaining the gleaming whiteness of the sunlit pinnacles. There was little vegetation on any of the photographs, but what there was was dense and green. I held the centre spread at arm's length. It was very satisfying, eerie and dramatic with a sense of being remote and totally hostile. They'd done a good job with my slides.

The elation disappeared on reading the article. The heading was not what I'd written, but it was at least bearable: 'The Antsingy Pinnacles, Madagascar's Hidden Heart of Stone'. Underneath it, however, lay the ominous words: 'Photographs: Henry T Stanwick. Text: Howard B Whitsell.' I scanned the text with increasing dismay. They had thrown out my carefully written article and substituted their own.

The first paragraph set the tone.

> The island of Madagascar is a world apart. Separated from mainland Africa for millions of years, it lies in splendid solitude in the azure Indian Ocean. Within this world there lies a hidden realm of stone, known to only a few bold travellers and penetrated by still fewer. The fearsome Antsingy Pinnacles form a vast region of tortured limestone terrain, hideous and grotesque. Here Nature has etched, over countless eons, deep crevasses across a rock plateau to produce a scenery of awesome drama and savage beauty.

And so it went on. Image piled on metaphor, propped up by simile. 'Like some graveyard of giant broken teeth', 'where even the jungle's verdant tentacles have failed to grip' and 'the ultimate badlands country'. There were the obligatory references to alien terrains and lunar landscapes. A whole paragraph developed the idea of a geometrical maze or labyrinth of enormous proportions with a wishful reference to undiscovered Minotaurs and 'caverns measureless to man'.

Finally, in a fit of exhaustion Howard B Whitsell ground to a halt with the compulsory paragraph about Dr Henry Stanwick of England's Grantforth University being an expert in 'limestone landscapes' ('geomorphology' always has been a problem word). The article ended with the statement that Exploco had been glad to assist my research from their oil exploration base nearby. Then, presumably to appease those shareholders who wanted to know why their money was going to some wretched Brit, there was a fine little bit about 'who knows but that in ten years time this may be the terrain that Exploco will be drilling for oil in'.

I sighed resignedly. I'd been grateful for the grant and if they wanted to rewrite the article with every cliche in the book they had a right to. As I put the journal down I saw that the compliments slip had writing on it.

'Dear Henry, how are you doing? Here's the article. Sorry about your text. Howard was down in Madagascar recently and flew over your pinnacles. He thought they deserved a more dramatic text. I guess he knows the public. Cheers, Melvin.'

Underneath was a PS: 'Incidentally, we are relinquishing the concession.' So that was the end of my free trips there.

2

The Tuesday that I received the telex was only the second day of the new term. It was a hectic day even by the standards of Grantforth's overstretched, understaffed geography department. Two of the lecturers were down with flu, the secretary's word processor was stricken by the silicon equivalent and half a dozen irritable students had found that they had conflicts with the forthcoming fieldtrip. Through the large quantities of greasy, condensation-prone plate glass that clothed the geography building it was all too possible to see that the grey moistness that had covered the campus since the New Year had not lifted. The only colour was provided by the orange waterproofs and yellow boots of the students.

I was just about to leave my office to snatch a cup of coffee when Miriam stuck her head around the door.

'Henry, there's a telex for you over in the library. I'd have gone to get it myself, but it's chaos in the office and I'm waiting for the repair man.' She looked despairingly at me. 'You can't fix the machine, can you? You're so good with computers.'

I shook my head sadly. 'Sorry, Miriam, I've already hit it for you—only don't tell the repair man that.'

Miriam disappeared looking disconsolate and vaguely cheated, as I decided to forego the doubtful pleasure of coffee and pulled on my anorak.

As I splashed cautiously over the uneven paving stones I thought vaguely about the telex. The only recent one had been about a last-minute change to a conference at which I was due to speak, but that had been unusual. The wet, stained concrete of Memorial Library looked particularly depressing in the darkening afternoon. I squeezed past the chattering students who were reluctant to venture outside and, ignoring the defaced notice 'No Coats or Bags in this Library', walked over to the issue desk.

There were two students in the queue, posing the old etiquette problem as to whether to push in front on the basis that a lecturer worked here and had rights, or whether to stand patiently in line. The problem hadn't been helped by the fact that these days you couldn't be certain they were students. The new maths lecturer was twenty-four and by all accounts looked five years younger. Fortunately the librarian recognised me and turned my way.

'How's things, Anne?' I said, moving to the front. 'There should be a telex for me, or so I'm told.'

'I'll check. Yes, you're in luck: Dr Henry Stanwick, Geography. I hope it's worth getting wet for.'

I took it from her, scattering raindrops from my sleeves over someone's inter-library loan form, and with muttered thanks and apologies mixed together retreated beyond the queue.

I pulled out the flimsy sheet and gave it a quick glance. It clearly demanded more attention, so I moved further out of the way of the students, leant against the wall and went through it again. Below the usual codes it read: 'Greatly appreciated your article on the pinnacles of Madagascar. Am hoping to arrange a visit there and would welcome your advice. Passing thru UK Jan 24-26. Is a visit to see you possible? Please telex reply asap. Best wishes, Tim Vaughan.' The telex was from Houston, Texas.

I began to flesh out the sparse detail in the telex. This Vaughan had read the pretty picture article. He had money and was probably bored with shooting the Grand Canyon and climbing Mount McKinley. He had access to Daddy's office telex and having obtained the university number he had decided to try and pick my brains. Well, I couldn't object: I had

15

been glad of the money, the various grants had been super, but they hadn't covered all the costs of the fieldwork by half. I had my diary with me and checked the last week in January. On the whole I was free during the dates mentioned. A Computer Users' Committee meeting was marked, but I could give that a miss if need be.

I decided to respond to the telex there and then and save another wet walk over. My entry into the telex room was clumsy in the extreme, resulting in a near-collision with a short dark figure standing by the door. He looked up over his piece of paper.

'Welcome, Henry. Welcome to the Tower of Babel. Look at this gibberish I get; meaningless, meaningless, meaningless. Look at it.'

The telex that Abie Gvirtzman was holding was certainly that. 'What is it, Abie; Yiddish?'

'Maybe you are right; or perhaps a Hebrew telex machine with a Gentile operator. Anyway, Henry, what brings you here, eh? Another trip to Tierra del Fuego?'

Abie was lecturer in Inter-Testamental Studies and seemed to revel in being what he termed 'this place's token Jew'. We had occasionally talked about serious things, but mostly had brief bantering conversations in passing. We disagreed about Middle East politics where Abie refused to see any merit in anything that even hinted at dialogue with the Arabs over the future of the State of Israel. We were also more curiously divided over religion. Abie was a dogmatic atheist while I held (at least intellectually) to a Christianity which, while it didn't mean very much to me, I was reluctant to throw away. Despite this, and the fact that he was some twenty years older, we were firm friends.

'What have I got, Abie? I've got a message from an American gentleman who loved my picture article on that pinnacled limestone region in Madagascar so much he wants not only to go there, but to meet me as well. A sucker for punishment.'

16

Abie grinned at me, showing bad teeth.

'Oh yes, I saw your slides. A horrible place. Made the Dead Sea look cosy. I'm surprised even you could be dishonest enough to market it as a holiday resort.'

He picked up the proffered telex and scrutinised it over his glasses. His expression changed. He slowly shook his head and stared at me; his eyes were distant, remembering or seeing something else. He half-sighed.

'Henry, I don't like it. There's something about it that stinks.'

I was taken aback for a second. A response about him ruining my Trans-Atlantic fan mail came to me, but I cut it out for friendship's sake. After a pause I ended up saying a pathetic, 'Well, maybe. We'll see.'

Abie suddenly focused on me and his tone lifted. 'Actually, I must dash; back to those glorious Maccabees.' Then his voice darkened again. 'Take care, Henry, take care.'

'Bye, Abie.' I could hear the note of puzzlement in my voice. I shook my head slowly after his sombre departing form and began to fill out the telex sheet.

The next few days were busy, and I gave little thought to the telex message or to Abie's curious comment. Indeed, when we met by chance in the Staff Club he didn't even refer to it. On Friday afternoon I was packing some work away for the weekend when the phone rang. It had the distinctive faint crackle of a very long distance line so that even before I heard the voice I was all attention.

'Is that Doctor Henry Stanwick?' It was an American voice, northern USA with no real hint of drawl.

'Speaking.'

'This is Tim Vaughan. Henry, I got your telex. I'd just like to confirm that we can meet on the 25th. Perhaps I could take you out for lunch. That'll be a week Tuesday, I think.'

'Hang on, Tim, while I check.'

I managed somehow to find and open my diary without dropping the phone.

'Yes, no problem, it's a quiet day.'

'Henry, I was wondering . . . would it be possible for you to show me some more photographs of the pinnacles, slides or prints, say, after lunch? Only if it's no trouble, of course.'

His voice was gentle and agreeable without being soft. In fact there was a definite precision in the tone; it was the voice of someone used to asking straight questions and getting straight answers.

'That shouldn't pose any problems, Tim. I'll set up a slide show.'

I paused. 'Tim, are you serious about visiting this place?'

'Sure am, Henry. It looks really fine. In fact I'm going to be asking you some questions on logistics when we meet. I'd really appreciate some input from you on that.'

'I'll see what I can do.' I wondered briefly about the sort of thing he wanted.

'Sounds good, Henry. Look forward to seeing you soon. I guess I can find my own way to you. I'll be there around 12.30. Should be good.' The phone was put down.

I headed off home, read the bills, watched the news, and it was only when I was phoning someone to invite them round for Sunday lunch that a thought struck me. Somehow Tim had got hold of my phone number. Careful thought suggested that it might not be too hard, given time and determination. The US phone service could probably have given him the university number and they would have eventually put him through to me. I concluded that whatever else he was Tim Vaughan was determined.

3

The next day, Saturday, was the Hensons' annual January party. Despite Scottish blood and upbringing Alec Henson professed a disdain of Burns, and lamented over the national antics on Hogmanay. 'Och, I'm a verra reformed Scuit,' he would joke, with an accent he'd long since all but lost. Nevertheless he seemed to feel some racial necessity for a January party of sorts.

My relationship with Alec and Viv Henson was complex but affectionate. I'd met them at the local church which I attended for a number of reasons, some of which I couldn't fathom myself. I'd found them an attractive, helpful couple with a good deal of tolerance. The chief complicating factor was their elder daughter Tina, with whom I was going out. It was not a very intense relationship because although we got on well together at a number of levels there was always something between us. The whole thing was currently stalemated into an affectionate ambivalence that could go either one way or the other but never did. Part of the problem was the entire family's religious enthusiasm which steadfastly refused to stay locked up between Sunday services and could just as easily emerge in supermarkets and theatres. It was all very civilised; I mean they didn't hand out tracts, shout 'Hallelujah!' or ask the bank manager if he was saved, but nevertheless Jesus was always there ready to leap out at you. I didn't argue against it. I knew what they were talking about and could even speak the same language. Auntie Maggie, who had looked after my brother Andy and me for ten years after Mum and Dad's death, had been that way inclined and had encouraged a similar 'lively faith' in us. The form of it all had rubbed off on me; the substance on Andy.

It was in fact a phone call from Andy that interrupted the process of getting dressed for the Hensons' party. He taught biology at a school in Cyprus, hadn't managed to call at the New Year, and was making up for it. We exchanged news of acquaintances and distant family members. After some minutes he suddenly said, 'By the way, big brother, did you know that James Erickson is leaving the school in the summer? He has just lost his father and feels it's time that he returned home to the US to look after his mum.'

'That'll be a loss,' I replied. 'He's George's right-hand man.'

'You said it, brother.'

He paused and went on in his usual bright, burbling manner. 'So we are starting to look around for a new Vice-Principal with responsibility for science and,' another pause, 'developing the Arab world links. I thought I'd better give you advance warning.'

I began to say, 'Of what?,' then realised with an unpleasant feeling in my innards exactly what he was implying. I spoke slowly, anxious to get an unambiguous denial.

'You mean you are thinking about me as a possible replacement for James Erickson?'

I wondered whether the stress in my voice could be detected in Cyprus. Andy's cheery reply was not what I'd wanted. 'Dead right, Henry. In fact a number of us are thinking of putting a formal letter to you.'

'But, Andy, I'm already on the advisory board. Doesn't that excuse, I mean rule me out?'

'That's one of the many good reasons why we want you, Henry.' The emphasis on the 'you' brought the unwelcome image of Lord Kitchener and his pointing finger to mind. Andy went on, heedless of the silence from my end.

'You taught here for a term, you know the culture and, besides, well, to be honest, we are moving academically up

20

market, to borrow a phrase. With Beirut down the drain again we are getting lots of Arab students, and they all want science 'A' Levels. It's tough, but what an opportunity! You've got the academic weight, Henry, and you've got the Arabic.' He spoke with carefree enthusiasm.

'Bad Arabic, kid brother.'

'No problem, brother. Anyway we feel that you are the right person.'

'And what does George think about it?' I was clutching at straws.

There was an innocent gurgle of laughter from the other end. 'It was his idea for me to call you and warn you.'

I gave in as best I could. 'Well, what can I say, Andy? You've caught me on the hop. At the moment I'm really not sure that I want the job. It's not something to be done lightly. I need to think about it.'

'Well, we're praying for you, Henry.' With some final pleas-antries he rang off.

I put the phone down slowly and sat down on the sofa staring at the gas fire. There was the sound of rain on the windows. The room seemed like an old friend, warm and comforting. So they were going to invite me to take on the job of Vice-Principal of St Paul's School. Indeed it sounded as if George Roumian was counting on me. I thought about the last time I had been there when a combination of misunderstandings and regional unpleasantness had made my absence in the Arab world desirable. I had taught 'A' Level Physical Geography for a term. I had pleasant memories to be sure; notably the curious but attractive blending of missionary kids, the offspring of businessmen and diplomats, and a sprinkling of Cypriots and Arabs taught by a dedicated and generally competent staff. There had been a growing intake even then, fuelled by the attraction of low fees, committed, honest teachers, and the relative security and tranquillity of Cyprus. The whole thing was steered, 'under the Lord' as he would say with emphatic and genuine modesty, by the dynamism of George Roumian. I had a great affection for George and owed him a debt of gratitude. He'd gone out of his way to help me when I needed help and he'd been very good to Andy. Now it looked as though that debt might have to be repaid.

'No way! Sorry, no way!'

The words seemed to echo accusingly around the room. The more I thought about it, the more impossible it all became. Reasons surged in one after another. For one thing there was George himself, impossible to dislike but a man who expected—and managed to get—total dedication to the school. I remembered him calling me at six one Saturday morning to tell me that he had decided to rearrange the library today and would I help? When I got there at seven-thirty half the staff were already there. He was a man who dreamed dreams that became others' nightmares, and I wouldn't have Erickson's excuse of a widowed mother to escape for a break.

More seriously it meant breaking up the life I had built here in the past two-and-a-half-years. Then, rootless and already an expatriate, I might have jumped at Andy's offer. Since then I had a house of my own, after ten years of flats, and good friends and tolerable neighbours. I had come to be fond of Grantforth for all its damp drabness. For the first time since I could remember, I felt settled. I had a future, a direction and relative security. I enjoyed my job and there was little doubt that I was at least competent in it and possibly better. Work was just fine, the papers were coming out, and the first two chapters of my book looked good. How could I give it all up for the insecurity, obscurity and poverty of St Paul's? What Andy hadn't said was that it would be a permanent break. I had managed to stay in Physical Geography all the way through my three years post-doc in the Middle East. Even then it had been tough to get back into the UK university scene. Now, with the deterioration in academic finances, it would be impossible. To leave my job to manage a school would be an irrevocable decision.

'No,' I spoke emphatically aloud. 'I want to stay!'

The phone rang. I half-expected it to be George Roumian himself.

'Henry, you are coming round tonight, aren't you?' It was Tina's gentle, concerned voice.

'Oh gosh, awfully sorry, Tina. I've just had the most odd phone call. . . . Oh, it's eight-thirty. Sorry, I'll be round imme-diately.'

As I drove thoughtfully over to the Hensons' in the cold, damp stuttering Beetle, Andy's phrase 'we are praying for you' ran round my mind in all its ambiguity. It had assumed all the charm of call-up papers in wartime, which was, I reflected somewhat sourly, exactly how George Roumian would see mat-ters.

4

As with all northern industrial towns Grantforth's better areas lie on the tops of the hills. Given the difference between my junior lecturer's salary and that provided by Alec Henson's directorship of a small specialist textile firm, it was inevitable that my journey was all uphill. I parked opposite their spacious late-Victorian house and ran through the chill rain up the long car-filled gravel drive. Viv answered the door with her habitual warmth.

'Henry! Welcome, you poor dear, you must be soaked. We were so worried that you were still working on your book down at the university.'

Her genuine affection made me forget my worries. I smiled at her, 'Honestly, Viv, I was being idle at home. I just forgot the time.'

She took my coat, still fussing over me. 'Henry, you need looking after, doesn't he, Alec?'

Mr Henson had appeared from the lounge carrying a tray of empty glasses, looking, as he always did on such occasions, the personification of benevolent relaxation.

'So you say, dear,' he answered without condescension and with a benign nodding of his balding head. He gave me a conspiratorial smile and a handshake of considerable vigour and affection.

He led me down the corridor to the lounge, his hand on my shoulder. 'Henry, good to have you here. You'll have been planning another trip to Mauritius no doubt?'

My voyages were something of a joke in the Henson household. Alec and Viv's annual trips to Skye were the limit of their travel inclinations.

I played him along, 'Sorry, Alec, that was last week. It's Mozambique this and Moscow next.'

'Well, all these outlandish places sound the same to me. Anyway, come in, there's still some food left. Besides I want you to meet the Grants. They're old friends of the family, and they've just retired from a Mission hospital in Burundi. A bit far inland for you, I think, but they're dying to talk to you.'

So much for Alec's claimed ignorance of geography, I thought.

In an area where the possession of wealth is generally flaunted in lavish and ostentatious decor I've always found the Hensons' house refreshing. Despite profuse but secretive giving, the Hensons made a practice of spending well and carefully on the house. Both Alec and Viv hated ornament and pretence in furnishings as well as life. The effect was a house which almost verged on the austere, but which everyone felt at home in. That night the main room looked superb. The lighting and decor was such that everything seemed browns and golds with subdued reflections in the dark, polished wood and leather-bound books. The room was just full enough of people that you couldn't hide in a corner and just empty enough that it didn't seem crowded.

One of the delights of Alec and Viv's parties was the mix of people. They cast the net widely in terms of class and age, and almost anybody could be there. The absence of alcohol and the presence of what had been described as a 'subliminal Puritanism' had deterred only a few. I, for one, could live with it. The general consensus was that neither feature stopped evenings at the Hensons' from being happy or merry ones.

The Grants were a frail silver-haired couple, gracious and diffident and full of questions about Madagascar. My ten weeks there seemed to them to be of much greater interest than their own forty years in central Africa. I caught sight of Tina, who gave me a warm smile and then disappeared, doubtless on some worthy errand, into the kitchen. At length we were interrupted by Mrs Lythgoe who wanted my advice on the best place for a church outing in summer. I managed to escape eventually to the buffet table and was helping myself when Tina turned up on the other side. Conversation between us across the table was proving difficult when she spotted someone with an empty glass. With an 'Excuse me, Henry, I'll talk to you later,' she moved away.

I stood there looking at her. There was little doubt that she was attractive. She was only a little shorter than me and her short, curly brown hair rested with a careful artlessness on a muted floral dress that contrived to be both homely and stylish. It struck me then that this combination of the genuinely polished but transparently natural was a strong element in the attraction she exercised on me. Any reservations about her face, which was perhaps too angular for accepted standards of good looks, were overcome by her force of personality. She shared her mother's concern for everybody, but it was an intelligent concern. There was no doubt that with Tina the head ruled the heart. This was doubtless fine for work like hers—she was a highly-valued junior administrator for the local Health Authority. I found it less attractive in our relationship where sometimes she could seem to be so cool and passionless as to be almost uninviting, even mechanical, and I occasionally wondered whether her heart hadn't given up in disgust. Yet every so often in a cuddle or a kiss the reins would slip, and although it was only briefly and tantalisingly, it nevertheless reminded me that there was flesh and blood and even passion underneath. But what she felt about me was unclear.

I found it difficult to decide whether I wanted to marry her because I loved her or because I simply felt she would be a good person to marry. On other days I wondered whether I really wanted to marry her at all. The element of inaccessibility certainly added to the attraction, however.

Eventually, Tina seemed satisfied that everyone was being looked after and made her way over to me.

'So, Henry, how's it going?' Tina gave me her intent big brown-eyed stare which managed to convey enormous care and attention. I gave her the usual platitudes about work. She seemed to give them more careful attention than I felt they merited.

'Were you pleased about your article? Incidentally thanks again for the copy—Mum and Dad were fascinated.'

'You did tell them what had happened to the text? I wouldn't want them to think I was capable of that sort of prose.'

'Of course, Henry. Anyway, Dad has read your more serious stuff. He knows you can write better than that.'

'Actually, I was pretty fed up about it at the time, but I feel it's quite funny really. I had built it up to be something marvellous and look what happens. It's a pity about the errors but . . .' I shrugged my shoulders.

'Incidentally, neither you nor this American mentioned any people in the pinnacles. Aren't there any at all?'

'None at all, Tina; the impenetrable bits in Howard B Whitsell's epic were spot on. It's too inhospitable. The rocks are so sharp they'd cut bare feet to pieces. There's little water except from the one or two streams. Anyway, why go there?'

She looked briefly nonplussed. 'For hunting? For religious reasons? Maybe just "because it's there"? Human beings can be odd.'

I thought for a second or so. 'Well, there's little to hunt and it would be too easy to get lost. As for the curious Malagasy, I think exploration in such a desolate region is a hobby for those with full stomachs. Religious reasons? I've never heard of any. Rather the converse—they don't like it at all.'

Tina was interested. 'You mean they are scared of the spirits or something?'

'It seems so, but it's always difficult to tell with the Malagasy. Laurent would never tell me; he gets embarrassed about Malagasy superstitions.'

'Isn't he scared?'

'It seems not. He has this rather charming faith. He says, "Jesus protects me, that is enough." Laurent's theological vocabulary is limited, but it seems to suffice.'

'I think I'd rather see him and his family than your precious pinnacles.' She gave me a half-cheeky, half-concerned look. 'Doesn't it ever worry you that in your job the only role for people is to show how big a cliff is?'

I managed a smile and tried to bounce her comment back. 'Ah, that explains a lot. You're afraid of being a scale in one of my landscapes.'

'Perhaps I am,' she replied in her quiet voice and there was a smile there, but it seemed to mask some deeper concern. 'Anyway, talking of people, I really must go and help Mum.'

Which she did, leaving me to wonder whether or not I had stumbled on a deep truth about our relationship.

The rest of the party passed pleasantly enough. I chatted briefly to Tina's younger sister Debbie who was all set to go off to London to some specialist nursing studies. I talked to a number of people and heard some of Alec's hilarious anecdotes about his early life in Glasgow. It was nearly eleven when people began to drift off. I offered to give Tina a hand with the washing up, and it was no surprise to find that we were left alone in the kitchen with the piles of dirty crockery. Alec and Viv's philosophy of life stopped at paper plates, dishwashers or leaving it till Sunday.

'You said you'd had an odd phone call. You haven't been invited to a party by Miriam again?'

'No such luck. I mean, that's fairly easy to deal with. No, it was Andy, from Cyprus.'

'That was nice of him. They don't pay him a lot.'

'Hmm, that's another thing. No, basically he was warning me. My Middle East past is catching up with me; someone is out to get me.'

Tina's eyes widened, and she gently lowered the crystal tumbler to the draining board.

'Oh, Henry, who on earth. . . I thought that had all been sorted out?'

I felt embarrassed; Tina always took things seriously. 'Sorry, I'm being naughty—it's not that bad. Actually, thinking about it, it's worse—a lot more drawn-out. It's George Roumian at St Paul's. He wants me to be Vice-Principal.'

I felt tired, lonely and self-pitying. I leaned on the sink edge for a moment as though it would take some of the burden. I turned to Tina who was looking at me with concern. She nodded her head slowly, just like her father did.

'That's a lot to ask, isn't it?'

I stared out of the window. The rain had lifted and the lights of Grantforth twinkled. There was the promise of frost.

'Yes, it is, Tina. I'm only beginning to realise how much. You know I've no objection to doing things or to taking risks for a worthwhile cause. But it's a lifetime's service George wants. It's not just asking a lot; it may be asking too much.'

Tina said nothing, she just put her hand on my back. After a minute she said gently, with evident care, 'Henry, you don't have to decide tonight. Sleep on it. Think it all through. Pray about it.'

The reference to prayer was a typical Henson comment. I merely nodded in apparent assent; I'd never found prayer sorted out my problems. But then I wasn't really sure that I wanted to open a dialogue with God. Who knew what He might ask?

At that point Viv and Alec came in, and together we finished everything off just before midnight. Tina saw me to the door. 'God bless, Henry, and good night,' she said tenderly, giving my arm a squeeze which meant a lot.

As I walked out beyond the trees at the end of the drive I turned round. She was still standing there, framed against the light, watching. Alec had joined her and had his arm round her shoulder. Both raised their hands in a farewell wave that seemed like a benediction.

5

I didn't see much of Tina over the next week or so. We never really got time to talk beyond a few friendly formalities at church. I heard nothing from Cyprus, and began to hope that it was all a delusion of Andy's.

Midday of Tuesday 25th found me in my office struggling with a program on the computer. I greeted the firm rap on the door with an abstracted, 'Come in.'

'Hi. Dr Henry Stanwick? I'm Tim Vaughan.' A firm hand grasped mine as I rose from the chair.

'Take a seat,' I said, gesturing with a sweep of the hand to the battered armchair in the corner. I got up and turned my own chair away from the computer to face the visitor. He took off his coat and with a certain delicacy placed his thin briefcase against the wall. We weighed each other up. My first impressions were of a tall, lean man in his late thirties with a tanned face topped with short, pale brown hair that looked sun-bleached. There wasn't an ounce of spare flesh on him. He was clean shaven and immaculately groomed. If I hadn't been facing away from my desk he would have given me a compulsion to tidy my papers away.

Tim's suit was of the respectable grey colour that is commonly bought by impoverished academics who can only afford one suit. It would have done for most functions. The cut and fitting, however, strongly suggested that in his case economy hadn't entered into the equation. The shirt and shoes looked also to be the sort that aren't often seen in universities; at least not these days.

I couldn't place Tim; he wasn't the sort of playboy that I had been expecting. He looked controlled, even disciplined and there was no hint of dissipation. He gave me a grin which either reflected—or was meant to reflect—happiness.

'So this is your place, eh, Henry? Mind if I look round?'

He didn't wait for an answer and walked over to look out of the window. The view of anonymous halls of residence against a damp grey sky didn't detain him long. He scanned the book shelves and then nodded at the computer screen.

'What are you running?' he said, looking intently at the lines of code.

'I wish "running" was the word. It's still being written. Actually it's a program to simulate the weathering of a limestone block given certain conditions. I intend to try to model the shapes of our mutual interest, the Antsingy Pinnacles.'

He gave me a faintly quizzical stare. 'You mean it's really not a random pile of junk?'

'On the contrary; it obeys fairly well understood rules. A limestone formation is fractured under regional stresses and then exposed at the surface. Now naturally erosion starts at the lines of weakness and erodes back and down. The whole thing seems to obey fairly straightforward constraints. The angle of dip of the beds appears to be critical.' I realised I'd begun to give him a lecture and felt a bit silly. Tim gave me a disarming smile, but I felt the eyes scrutinise

'You academics are all the same. You live off enthusiasm. Actually it's interesting. I've come across other systems that appear random and chaotic to the outsider; but in fact they have their own internal harmony.'

He glanced at his watch. I noticed that the case and bracelet looked to be made of titanium.

'Talking of internal harmony, Dr Stanwick, how about you and I go eat someplace? Where do you suggest? The pleasure's mine, of course. I guess I'd prefer something quiet, but otherwise I'm not fussy.'

I suggested the Plough and Harrow, an old pub about ten

minutes out on the Anaston road which tends to be reasonable. It also has a view that doesn't overlook factories or wasteland and a menu that extends beyond scampi and chips. That seemed satisfactory to him, so I saved my program and grabbed my anorak.

'You can leave your briefcase here, Tim,' I said, noticing him pick it up. 'I keep the office locked when I'm out.'

'If you don't mind I'll take it with me. It's just force of habit. I've nothing of value in it.' He seemed to be momentarily put off balance.

I noticed as we made our way down to the foyer that Tim was in good shape. He had that fluidity and bounce in his movements that spoke of hard regular exercise.

I hesitated at the foot of the steps. 'Your car or mine, Tim? I'm afraid mine is a venerable Beetle.'

'That's OK, we'll take mine. I'm so rarely anywhere where driving is a pleasure that I like to hire something decent in the UK.'

'Something decent' was a large black BMW that could only have been a few months old. Despite its power he drove carefully and was scrupulous in obeying road signs and speed limits. His driving was revealing; alert, precise and of a text-book quality. His eyes never left the road. As we pulled out of the grounds he asked me how I'd got into 'the limestone scenery business.' I gave him the brief outline of how I'd grown up on the Carb Limestone in Yorkshire and had always had an interest. At university I'd decided I might as well specialise in it. I'd been fortunate in that I'd been able to follow it ever since.

The conversation continued in this vein until something happened that I wish I'd paid more attention to. We were following about twenty yards behind another car just where the road comes out of Grantforth and onto the moors proper. Suddenly the driver ahead struck a sparrow and it careered over the top of his car and landed—broken wings fluttering uselessly—on the road ahead. Without hesitation Tim twitched the steering wheel. The right hand wheel went directly over the bird. I grimaced and saw him watching me out of the corner of his eye.

'Well,' he said in a matter-of-fact voice, 'what would you have done? Left it to die slowly?'

'I suppose I would have dithered about it until it was too late to do anything,' I answered reluctantly.

'I'm afraid I've learned that it is sometimes necessary to be swift and severe.'

The Plough and Harrow appeared above the rise in the road and terminated that conversation.

It was an interesting meal. Tim and I found a corner table in the almost-deserted restaurant. The food wasn't a disgrace, although neither of us ate a lot. The conversation maintained a steady flow, but Tim did most of the leading. We soon touched on the reason for his visit. He was single and enjoyed travel. He'd 'done' most of the regular places; Kenya, the Himalayas, Australia and so on. These pinnacles looked so weird and new that he was instantly attracted. He paused and leaned back in his chair.

'I suppose it's because the place looks so alien, so unearthly. It may sound silly, Henry, but my generation grew up with the space programme. I watched it all on TV and hitched to Canaveral for Apollo 11. We all thought we'd get the chance to go to the moon and further. But I guess we're now all realising that it's the next generation that will do that.' He paused for a moment. 'If there is a next generation, that is.'

He took a mouthful of food and chewed reflectively. 'Apparently some guy in the States is making a big thing of it, "a neurosis affecting millions of middle-aged Americans." So your pinnacles are the next best thing. Besides, I spend a lot of time in the Indian Ocean. I always wanted to find out what happened in Madagascar.'

'Whereabouts in the Indian Ocean?' It was a natural question for a geographer, but as it came out I realised that it sounded a bit like an interrogation. Tim paused with his fork halfway to his mouth and putting it down reached into a hip pocket. He pulled out his wallet and with an enviably fluent motion of the fingers presented me with a plastic business card.

I read it carefully:
'Timothy R Vaughan
Computer Consultant (Communications)
New Technologies Inc
789 Richmond Boulevard, Houston'

Underneath were telex and phone numbers and some other codes for on-line computer-link up. Impressive as it was, it didn't answer my question. I looked up at him.

'Diego Garcia. A defence communications contract with the US Navy. And I've already told you too much.' It came out as three separate, awkward statements and almost sounded like a confession. I felt embarrassed. Tim seemed to discern my state and shrugged his shoulders.

'Well, it had to come out, but it's policy in the company not to let too many people know. It's amazing how frequently your house gets broken into once word gets out you are on a confidential defence contract. Strange women with foreign accents offer to buy you drinks, though.' He grinned widely, showing the inevitable perfect teeth. After a pause he went on.

'The other thing is that I hate the thought of some kook taking a crack at me because he thinks I'm military. There is a lot to be said for being a civilian these days.'

'I know what you mean; I've been in trouble in the Middle East on that sort of mistaken identity business and I don't want to repeat it.' Tim raised his eyebrows in interest, and I noticed there was a small curving scar between them.

'Did you now? Whereabouts?'

So I told him a bit about Beirut, Amman and Damascus and hinted that there had been a certain awkwardness that I didn't want to spoil my lunch by being forced to recount. He took it all in.

'Do you know the area?' I asked. I caught him with his

attention elsewhere and it took a fraction of a second for him to recollect himself.

'Sorry? Oh yes. No, I mean I've only passed through. It's an area I'd prefer to avoid. I like to take my risks with Nature. Talking of which, let's get down to business.'

A little to my surprise he pulled out of an inner pocket a large leather pocketbook with a gold propelling pencil and a microcassette recorder.

'Now let me say a couple of things at the start, Henry. I'm deadly serious about going there, but I'm a thorough man. I don't want to go there and find I brought the wrong shoes or my compass doesn't work. I've found virtually no information on the area and very little of practical use on Madagascar generally. I've got a precise list of questions and I'd like precise answers. If you can't give them to me, don't make them up. Just tell me. If there is anything at all you think I should know, then give it to me. Assume I'm an idiot.'

He smiled in a reassuring but definitely un-idiot manner.

'Well, I hope that doesn't put you off?'

I told him it didn't, which was in fact true. I've always been a bit dismissive of those people who end up risking the lives of rescue teams because they didn't take crampons or only brought the road map. Tina tells me off for it and I suppose she's right. But I was impressed by Tim's thoroughness. He started the tape recorder.

'OK. I arrive at Antananarivo Airport. What are the formalities I'm likely to undergo?'

Half an hour later as we drank the last of our coffee I was still impressed. Daunted by the onslaught, but still impressed. From the airport at 'Tana he had kept relentlessly and logically on. Weather, daytime and night-time temperature, diseases, suitable clothing, poisonous plants and animals, medical facilities, communications, the police, roads. Details of the pinnacles he said would wait till he had seen my maps and photographs. He asked little that had anything to do with cost. He didn't seem terribly bothered about Malagasy customs or lifestyle except as far as they would affect him. Most answers simply elicited a grunt and another question. As a teacher I couldn't help but wish my students had the same zeal for knowledge.

A number of questions seemed to be of particular interest to him. Was the pinnacle region as tough as the photos made out? The text of the article clearly couldn't be relied on. I said that while not strictly unique, it was as inhospitable a terrain outside the polar regions that I'd ever heard of or seen described. He looked unconvinced. 'I've seen some pretty tough going in Nepal; some of those gorges are unbelievable.'

'Tim, let me give you some idea of how tough it is in those pinnacles. From the edge I walked in with Laurent, the Malagasy who was with me. I estimate we got maybe a hundred and fifty yards in. There and back I don't suppose took us less than five hours of non-stop effort.'

He looked at me for a moment.

'OK, next question; what medical supplies would you take?' And so it went on. Eventually he asked one question with, it seemed, a particular intensity.

'The article says this place is uninhabited. Hype or fact? Are you sure of that? Absolutely no Madagascarans—what's the word—Malagasy?'

I must nave looked puzzled because he continued. 'What I mean is, there isn't much point mounting an expedition with a fanfare of trumpets on how difficult your objective is if at the end of the day you find that people have been happily living there for centuries. A bit like Columbus discovering America. As the man said, the Indians didn't even know they'd lost it. So that's why I'm keen to know if it is genuinely uninhabited.'

'It's absolutely uninhabited. It's uninhabitable in fact. There is nothing to live on, and the people don't wear shoes, so they'd cut their feet to ribbons. I suspect, too, that you'd probably end up insane if you were there for any length of time.'

'That's an interesting comment. What do you mean "end up insane"?'

It was an awkward question; it probably would tell him more about me than the pinnacles. Tim didn't look the sort to be swayed by atmosphere, to jump at shadows. He looked as unlikely a case to be bothered by the place as anyone. I thought back to those unscalable stone walls with only the high river of blue sky to remind me of the real world out there, and turning round to see hostile, threatening grey rock on every side. Even in this restaurant, with its piped music and its comfortable chairs and a view for miles, I could almost feel again something of that horrible fear of being lost forever that had come over me briefly in that place.

'It's a weird spot, Tim. I've only penetrated the edges, and I did that in company. It may simply be me, but I found it disturbing. There are a number of factors that come together to make it a bit odd. Your perspective becomes very limited. We call them pinnacles because that's what they look like from the sky. When you're in there you realise that it's not really about peaks at all, it's just intersecting crevasses. Other than the sky you can rarely see more than thirty feet.' I paused. Tim seemed to want me to go on, so I did.

'It's terribly easy to become disorientated. You are so busy watching your hands or your feet and you turn round and the rear view is the same as the front. Did you ever as a kid go into one of those hall of mirrors places at fun fairs where every direction is the same, and it's all reflections and it stretches on forever, and you walk round a corner to get out and it's just the same? Well, the pinnacles are like that. Only they are real. You think, did I take a right turn or a left at the last junction? And you start sweating, because you know that if you panic you will never get out.' I stopped suddenly, feeling that I might be coming over a bit neurotic.

'It sounds like you had a hard time,' Tim said gently. I didn't feel I'd convinced him though. I had a thought. I picked up a paper napkin and borrowed Tim's pencil to draw a rough grid pattern. 'Here—you asked for facts. Let me give you some rough figures. The pinnacles are a series of eroded blocks. You walk down in between them. They are on average, say, ten to fifteen metres long, then you get a gap of a metre or so and another one. So, in travelling a kilometre you would pass perhaps sixty blocks. The fun is that they aren't lined up straight and some crevasses become impassable. So that's sixty intersections minimum where you'd have to make a decision. And this is the best case. Of course, if you have to make a detour you'd increase that enormously. The main area of the pinnacles is about ten kilometres by five wide. Tim, this is quite a maze to get lost in.'

I rolled the pencil over to him with the sort of satisfaction you get when the worked equation on the blackboard comes out to the right figure.

Tim sat quietly for a moment, his right index finger caressing the side of his cheek as he thought it through.

'Excellent, it sounds like a real challenge. Finished your coffee? Good. While we drive back to the college I want you to give some thought to this idea. Don't answer it now.' He switched off his microcassette recorder and closed his leather pocketbook. As he got up from his seat with the bill he turned to me.

'Henry, I want to do what I'd guess no one has ever done. Walk right into the heart of those pinnacles and out the other side.'

6

We started the drive back in silence. I was thinking over Tim's remark. It was just on the sane side of lunacy, but despite the difficulties and hazards it held a certain attraction.

Tim switched on the radio for the 2 PM news. It was a particularly doleful array of international disasters and crises. At the end of the headlines Tim turned it off abruptly with a shake of his head and a faint 'tut.' He gave me a glance out of the corner of his eye.

'Henry, doesn't the state of the world worry you?'

I was caught a little off balance and hesitated. 'In what sense, Tim?'

'Well, I guess I feel like we are going to hell in a handcart. I think that the whole outfit is in danger of getting out of control. To use the computer image, I worry about the system crashing. I think it's only a matter of time before the whole card house, the whole political-ecological-military creation goes down.' He paused suddenly. For the first time I felt there was a hint of some concern, some emotion, in what he said. His views seemed another nail in the coffin of my idea of him as the carefree global playboy.

'I see what you mean. Yes, of course it does. It should worry anyone, I'd have thought.' My response sounded hesitant and laboured.

He was silent for a minute. The new bungalow estates on the edge of Grantforth passed by us.

'Henry, do you play any games on that machine of yours?'

I was rather taken aback at the shift of the conversation.

'Not much. Some bad chess—partly a case of lack of time and money; partly because I've not been impressed by what I've seen. Why do you ask?'

'A friend of mine in LA has been developing what he thinks will be the next generation of games. You're familiar with the two extremes of games software: the single floppy disk deal and the multi-user version where you communicate with a mainframe?'

'And build up massive phone bills?'

Tim nodded. 'Precisely the problem. Yet the single disk, stand alone deal is too limited. What this friend of mine has developed is the concept of what he calls a mainframe interaction system. It's a sort of hybrid between the two. The idea is you buy a disk, or a couple of disks, and play the game on it. The game has a supervisory program on it—let's call it an overseer. Then after, say, ten hours you call up the mainframe. The overseer passes on in a few fragments of code a report of what you have done so far. The mainframe then calls back and alters the disks according to its evaluation and adjusts the game as it sees fit.'

'I'm intrigued by the concept, but doesn't it still take up a lot of phone time?'

'Not if the software at both ends is written properly. You see, the mainframe doesn't actually rewrite the entire program, it just changes building blocks within it. With a fast transmission rate he figures the whole program can be modified in the most drastic manner in two minutes.'

'Mmm, I see. Give me an example.'

'See, Henry, let's say you purchased an aircraft simulator program. You spend a week playing around flying the Cessna around the local strip in perfect weather. The overseer might decide that you are ready for a change. You load the program, call the mainframe, and it reads the report and reorganises the disk. Now when you play the game it's a seven-forty-seven over the Alps. It's a beautiful concept. The whole thing is almost infinitely variable and totally open-ended. You can build in new problems for the advanced player or learning routines for the weaker. Any bugs in the software can be checked. Also—and this is real neat—the company gets feedback on how much the game is played and what works and what doesn't. You'd actually be able to say that 79.6 percent of users learned to fly, or managed to complete the maze, or whatever. So version two would be much improved.'

'It could have some real educational uses as well.'

'Of course. The game thing is simply the easiest way to get the process started.'

I was genuinely impressed with the idea, although I doubted how many people here had the necessary modem links for their computers.

Tim went on, his voice quietly enthusiastic. 'Of course, there are some snags to be worked out. The problem is, the whole concept is so complex that you don't want to start it and find that everybody calls the mainframe at six-thirty on Friday night. There are some trial versions going the rounds.'

He stopped speaking to negotiate a badly parked brewery lorry in a narrow stretch of road. He gave me a quick, intense look and continued. 'You'd probably find it pretty stimulating. If you're interested I can get you a free copy. All you'd have to do would be to check into the mainframe every so often. My friend would be glad of the feedback. You don't even have to call the States as we have the master program up and running on a machine in London—although the hours are a bit limited and it's a version one-point-zero program. Are you interested?'

I gave it some thought and couldn't see any snags, so I said I'd be glad to. The whole concept seemed to have such potential that it might be useful to get in at the early stage. It was just a pity that what clearly had great potential for a teaching tool was going to be marketed first as a game. We were still discussing trends in computers as the BMW pulled into the university. Tim's knowledge was impressive, and he had some interesting ideas about the way things were going in machine communication. It crossed my mind that if Tim Vaughan did get into trouble in the pinnacles, lack of intelligence wasn't going to be the reason.

7

We went into my office and closed the door. Tim was the first to speak.

'OK, Henry, let's have the verdict. I guess you think I'm crazy?' He leant back in the armchair and clasped his arms behind his head. His air of nonchalance seemed superficial.

'Well, it's not as simple as all that, Tim. I find your idea quite attractive. You are also the sort of person who might just carry it all off. However, I think I have to say that it's simply not on.' I paused for effect. 'I'd expect you to go in, but not to come out again.'

Tim's expression didn't change, but he gave me a faint nod to indicate that I was to continue.

'For one thing there is nothing on the other side. No villages, no roads, no airstrip.'

'So I'd have to go through and come back?'

'Exactly so: at least doubling your time and your food supplies. No, my verdict is negative. In fact I'll be honest. If you decide to give it a go I'd feel obliged to put something in writing on file to the effect that I'd warned you.'

Tim weighed the words and gave a little laugh. 'It's all right—I've got no dependents to sue you, Henry. Still, I'm glad you don't leave anything to chance. Anyway, let's see your slides and then we can kick around some ideas.'

It took an hour to show thirty slides. Tim kept relentlessly pursuing his quest for information. Every question was meaningful.

At length the lights came on. I unrolled the topographic

sheets and we bent over the table. Tim assimilated them quickly, and I was surprised how little of the French cartography I had to explain. He asked for some photocopies of critical areas and while he started on the air photos I got them done in the busy departmental office.

I came back to find Tim's gold pencil still moving rapidly across the notebook. Air photo numbers, map scales—everything was recorded in fine neat script.

Finally, and rather abruptly, Tim seemed to have had enough. He sat back in the chair, stroking his cheek with his finger. 'OK, let's play it this way. I'm going to go through these pinnacles. I'm not easily put off.' He spoke quietly but with a determined tone. 'Given that that decision is not open to discussion, what do you suggest to ensure I get back in one piece?'

The thought crossed my mind that I ought just to show him the door before I ended up with his blood on my hands, but his assurance and self-confidence won the day.

'OK, but don't say I didn't warn you. Your main problems could be solved by a slightly larger party. You'd fly out to Antsalova with a lot of dehydrated food. Get some locals to cart it to the pinnacle edges. You'd make a cache inside and a further cache halfway in. You'd then go to the opposite edge and back as fast as you could with a minimum of kit. An increased number would also help ensure that if you did break a leg you'd have a chance of getting out.'

Tim had his notebook out and was writing down a few words. He looked up at me. 'Please continue.' It came out as an order.

'Well, my next point would be, how good is your French?'

'Sorry, Spanish and some Russian. Will that be a nuisance?'

'Yes—you'll need someone to translate for you, especially with the gendarmes at Antsalova. You'd need someone like Laurent, the Malagasy I took; he was a gem. He'd also do the wheeler-dealing for you.'

There was a pause, the pencil hovering over the paper.

'Point taken. Now how am I going to avoid getting lost in the middle?'

'The trick would be to mark the route you'd just come along with indelible marker pens at each junction. As you leave a junction an arrow would point back consistently on one side, say at eye height. It would need discipline, but it could be done.'

Tim made a few more notes in his tight economical hand-writing and closed the book firmly. He tucked it away inside his briefcase.

'Good.' He spoke with an air of finality. He got to his feet and picked up his coat.

'Well, Dr Stanwick, Henry, a real pleasure. You've given me some food for thought. I'm much obliged to you. How much do I owe you for your time?'

I was a bit taken aback. Consultation is rather rare in my field. I shrugged my shoulders dismissively. 'Really, you bought the meal and I've enjoyed sharing an enthusiasm with you. Forget it, Tim.'

He grinned and reached inside his jacket pocket. 'I thought you might say that. Anyway, I see no reason why you shouldn't get something approaching what I'd charge for half a day.' I glanced at my watch and was surprised to see it was four-thirty already. Tim put an envelope on the table. As I got to my feet he reached out and shook my hand firmly.

'Henry, great meeting with you. I'll be in touch. Don't bother to see me out; I can find my own way. I've already taken up enough of your time.'

He gave me a last smile and left, closing the door quietly but firmly behind him.

I opened the envelope. There were twenty new ten-pound notes. In some consternation I tucked them into my jacket pocket and decided to check the afternoon mail.

In the gloomy office Miriam was beginning the long drawn-out business of closing down for the day. She looked up from the envelopes and the franking machine.

'Your American gone, Henry?'

''Fraid so, Miriam; an odd character; wants to go to Madagascar for his holidays.'

I picked up my mail and glanced through the circulars and library reminders.

'Well, he seemed nice to me. He certainly had a high opinion of you.'

I stopped shuffling the envelopes and looked at her. I had developed a rather distant attitude to Miriam ever since it had become apparent that she wouldn't mind being Mrs Stanwick. This frequently resulted in my being either unintentionally rude or missing out on some important item of news. I felt I was in danger of the latter now.

'I'm sorry, Miriam, I was miles away. When did you talk to him?'

She gave me what could almost have been a flighty look. 'Really, he was fifteen minutes early and he said he didn't want to disturb you, so he stayed here. We had quite a pleasant chat. He was very interested about the department, and especially you.'

She caught my glance, and her round face coloured slightly. 'Well, we just talked generally. I didn't say anything that wasn't true. So there.' I felt she was tempted to stick her tongue out at me.

Curiosity got the better of me. 'What did he ask about?'

'Shan't tell. All right. "How long had you been here?" "Did you have a heavy work load?" Stuff like that.'

She hesitated. 'Actually, he didn't really ask a lot of questions. I mean he said things like, "I suppose Dr Stanwick is kinda popular?"'

She gave a good imitation of a southern drawl, but it was totally unlike Tim's much fainter northern accent.

'To which you said, I was the life and soul of the department, the fount of all wisdom and an endless fund of anecdotes.'

'Don't be silly. I said you were very respected and how the students liked you.'

'That was nice of you.'

'All part of the job; they call it Public Relations.'

'Thanks. What else did he ask about?'

Miriam seemed to remember something and started to colour. She began to fidget with the envelopes. 'Well, if you must know he asked about your publications. Did I have a list of them? He was ever so polite, Henry.'

'So what did you do?' I wasn't aware there was a listing of departmental publications under author.

Miriam dropped an envelope in her nervous shuffling. When she stood up after picking it up she turned to me with an air of defiance. 'So I gave him a copy of your CV.'

I was incredulous. 'You gave him a copy of my CV! I mean, it's not just my bibliography, it's my life history.'

Miriam shook her head in irritation. 'Really, Henry, it doesn't say "confidential." If you're ashamed of it then I suggest you take all the copies now and issue them yourself!' It was the tone of voice that successfully intimidates students year after year, and I decided I didn't have the nerve to pursue the matter further.

'OK, Miriam, doubtless there's no harm done. Still it's a bit curious.'

I picked up my mail, wished her good night, and left the office. That night over tea I thought about the matter, and I eventually concluded that Vaughan had simply wanted to check that I really knew what I was talking about. As for Miriam's breach of etiquette, I wondered what I would have done in her shoes if I had been faced with someone of Vaughan's charm and looks. When I thought about it like that, I didn't feel I could be too annoyed about it.

8

Tina was away that weekend visiting an ailing relative in Leeds. Not that it made a great difference to my life. Our relationship was such that we didn't spend more than an evening a week together. So I spent Saturday on the book and visited some Arab friends on Sunday afternoon.

Monday morning was cold and windy. I was trying not to get marmalade on the newspaper when the mail arrived. As I picked up the single letter I resolved for the tenth time to get a new draft excluder for the front door. A glance at the envelope lowered my temperature even more. The stamps proclaimed a Cyprus origin and the faint typewritten address was an unmistakable indicator of St Paul's School. No one is more reluctant to buy new type-ribbons than George Roumian.

In a mood of defiance I propped the envelope against the cereal packet and glared at it while I finished my cold toast. Only then did I open it.

There was a single sheet of headed school paper covered on both sides by a large, energetic and determined flowing script. George began with some school and family news and only at the end of the first side did he mention how sorry he was to lose James Erickson. He went on to say how this left a gap in a critical post at a difficult time. He was anxious that I should consider the possibility of being James' replacement. Although unable to make a definite offer to me just at the moment, he hoped to be able to extend a formal invitation shortly after Easter.

He finished in his usual style: 'Henry, things here are going so well. We have a lot to be grateful for. On almost every front we are seeing the fruit of much prayer. But we must persevere. Night cometh when no man can work. But he has set before us an open door! Hallelujah. Remember us in prayer as we do you in ours, Yours in him, George Roumian.'

I put the letter down on the table. The whole thing was almost outrageous. I liked George and his wife Sevan a lot. I believed what he was doing to be worthwhile, and the job he was offering was one of real importance and considerable challenge. Cyprus too was one of the pleasantest parts of the world to live in, and Andy (who was almost my only family now) worked happily at the school already. But to give up everything here to go and help him? It required an awful amount of commitment. Far more than I had. In some turmoil I got up and walked to the window. Condensation obscured the view across the estate. I wiped the glass and looked out. Clouds moved speedily across the chill early-morning sky, driven relentlessly by the easterly wind.

But as I toyed with the idea of simply writing a note of rejection to George my heart sank. The thought of refusing George anything was almost impossible. I seemed to be trapped. For a minute I felt as impotent and insubstantial as the fleeting clouds, blown hither and thither at another's wish.

After a minute or so of this gloomy meditation I told myself I was stupid, tidied away breakfast, and went to work. On the way I comforted myself with the thought that at least there was one mercy; a decision wasn't needed just yet.

That Thursday night I took Tina to the opera. It was a touring production of *Don Giovanni* ('in period costume'). People moan about Grantforth being a cultural desert, but it's not entirely true. It's just that there is a stubborn conservatism here. Music is tunes and that's the end of the matter. The last attempt to stage Mozart with concrete blocks and barbed-wire scenery didn't make it beyond the first night. They say that the *Rite of Spring* still hasn't had its Grantforth premiere. Well, I can live with that.

We arrived just before the curtain went up, as Tina had been working late at the office, so it wasn't until the interval that we actually got time to talk.

'How did the visit from your American go? Tell me about him.'

'Very charming. I think Miriam fancied him. He's tall, lean, on the right side of forty and doesn't wear broad check trousers. Lots of money; works on computer contracts for the US Navy; drives a hired, black, top-of-the-range BMW. Paid me outrageously for my time. What else did you want to know?'

Tina laughed at me affectionately, showing slightly crooked teeth. 'How about, what did he want with you? And incidentally, before you spend it all you need some new brown shoes and I think Andy's birthday is at the end of the month.'

'Ah, yes, right on both counts. What a pity.' I decided that perhaps it was about time I got someone to look after me. Then I remembered her question.

'What did he want with me? He's bored with life, he wants a trip through the pinnacles to liven it up.'

'By all accounts it would probably terminate it.'

'Possibly, but he exudes competence. He leaves nothing to chance, and he pumped me dry. I told him there was a poisonous vine and you know what he said?'

'What did it look like?' Tina sounded hopeful.

'No, what was the proper botanical name? I was quite impressed. That's the way to do things.'

A shadow of a frown crossed Tina's face. 'Are you going with him?'

'I hadn't even thought about it. He hasn't asked me. Probably if he *did* ask me I'd go . . . under the right conditions, of course.'

Tina gave me a searching look. 'It sounds like he made a big impression on you.'

'Perhaps. I suppose I'm naturally envious of someone who can apparently do what he likes and go where he wants when he wants.'

'But can he? Is he free or driven?'

There are times when I think that the legal profession lost a good lawyer in Tina, but I don't terribly care for being in the dock.

'Ah, I said "apparently," but point taken.'

'I must admit I can't see the attraction of risking your neck in the pinnacles. It seems a futile gesture.'

Unintentionally she had touched a sore point. Tina's world seemed to be solely Grantforth and people. On odd occasions I had thought that her viewpoint was so restricted that London lay on the distant horizon and beyond that was *terra incognita*, peopled by dragons and the odd missionary. Whether that was out of choice or fear of the unknown was something that was a source of concern to me. The prospect of marriage to someone too timid to travel beyond the British Isles was not a happy one.

'Oh Tina, really! Some people are like that. Vaughan's probably clocked up half a million miles in plane travel. He probably knows every airport from Amsterdam to Zanzibar. He needs a challenge.'

As always Tina took it well. She smiled gently at me and lightly touched my hand. 'Henry, I'm sorry. I can see you and he have things in common.'

That took me a bit by surprise, so I thought about it. 'Yes, there's some truth in that. We're both made the same way, prepared to give up comfort for a dangerous adventure. Maybe we both get bored too easily.'

At that point the lights dimmed, leaving us to Mozart and our thoughts. And in due course Don Giovanni ignored the call to repent and went to his appointed end in a satisfying display of flame and smoke.

After it ended we went out for a meal and by unspoken mutual agreement avoided mentioning Vaughan. Cyprus, however, came up and proved nearly as bad.

We were on the steak when Tina quietly raised the subject. 'Have you heard anything more from Cyprus?'

'Er, yes, I had a little note from George saying more or less what Andy said. Erickson is leaving and they would like me to replace him, for reasons best known to themselves. But he can't give me a definite offer before Easter, so it's all up in the air.' Although I hadn't intended it, I felt that my tone of voice clearly indicated that up in the air was where it should belong.

'For which you are very glad?' I could see Tina carefully scrutinising my face for any trace of feeling.

'For which frankly I am very glad. It will give me some time to think it over. Perhaps it will all clarify itself.'

She didn't say anything for a moment, but carefully took a sip of Perrier and looked intently at me. Here it comes, I thought. She's steeling herself for some devastating question. She was.

'Henry, what do you want to do with your life?'

I considered giving her a flippant answer about writing the definitive textbook on limestone weathering phenomena and living to overhear the reverential whispers of students, 'That's the Stanwick of *Limestone Weathering*.' I looked at her no-nonsense face and decided to give a more serious answer.

'I think I want to go on doing what I'm doing here. I like Grantforth and although I need to escape from it every so often, I enjoy teaching and research. I'm apparently good at it. I think it's worthwhile.'

'Is it really important enough to spend a lifetime on?'

I toyed with what was left of my steak before answering.

'Tina, I asked myself the same thing before I started my doctorate, nearly seven years ago, at Oxford. I asked old Simon Hughes about it. He was very frail then and enormously respected; partly because of his intellect, which was still as sharp as ever, but mainly, I suspect, on account of the fact he gave no-nonsense answers. I was scared stiff of him, but anyway I caught him one morning after chapel. He thought about the question and then he pronounced on it: "Hmph, m'boy, if the Lord thought it worthwhile to create limestone, then it's worth studying." So I said thank you and retreated as deferentially as I could. Just as I was going he called out, "Stanwick!" "Sir?" "But mark you, only studying well." And off he tottered.'

I think Tina had heard the story before, but I thought it worth telling again. It was the sort of tale the Hensons liked.

'But you don't think that in terms of priorities there are more important things? What's the tag, "the good is the enemy of the best"?'

I decided to try another defence.

'Tina, you want me to go to Cyprus, don't you?'

Even in the dimly-lit restaurant Tina's cheeks could be seen to flush slightly.

'I'm not saying that. That's your decision and I have no right to say anything on that account. But I am worried that it might be the right thing and by rejecting it you could . . .' Her voice tailed off. She suddenly breathed out heavily and forced a smile. 'Anyway, as you say, Henry, the problem hasn't arisen yet. And I'm sorry I seem to be inflicting wounds tonight.'

So we changed the subject. We debated the old issue of whether Don Giovanni was a tragedy or a comedy. Then Tina pulled a classic Henson mealtime ploy.

'Henry, let me put forward a motion for discussion. That damnation should not be treated lightly in art.'

I could see them all arguing over it while the food went cold and guests watched on in bemusement. Well, there were only two of us, but I decided to enter into the spirit of it, although it wasn't a chosen topic. Damnation wasn't a thing I cared to give a lot of thought to. Anyway, it was a spirited discussion and Tina was at her best and it cleared the air. It was virtually midnight before the manager's careful scrutiny of his watch made me decide to conclude the discussion in the best Henson manner with a summing up.

'Limestone weathering can be treated frivolously; cancer, yes; death, yes; sex, most definitely; but damnation of a soul, no.'

Tina nodded in agreement: 'With the rider that the Scriptural emphasis is always on the redeemed, not the lost. As with Don Giovanni, the damned never have the last word.'

'I suppose so. Motion carried.'

Half an hour later as I drove back from dropping Tina off at her home I tried, as often before, to make sense of our relationship. We seemed like two pieces of a jig-saw. There was apparently a shared conviction that we belonged together. But how? No matter how we tried, no match seemed possible. The pieces wouldn't, or couldn't, come together. Either they didn't fit after all, or there was something in the way.

9

After the first few days, that February turned out to be a bitter month. The wind blew straight at us from the northeast for three weeks. The days were beautiful, cold and clear, and the city glimmered and sparkled under the snow and frost. But the cold! It found every crack around the sash windows of my house. I took to eating meals in front of the gas fire and wearing a quilted jacket about the house.

On the second Friday in the month the promised games software arrived. I was too busy to do anything with it during the day, so I went in that evening to try it out. I went into my office at six in the evening and came out at midnight, tired and puzzled.

The next day Tina was due to come round at three and stay for tea. It was a habit we'd got into once or twice a month. Among other things it forced me to tidy the house up. That morning as I shivered around the house with the vacuum cleaner I was still trying to make sense of the game.

Tina was late, which was unusual. At half past three she turned up on the doorstep encumbered by carrier bags and looking as if she'd spent a month on an icefloe. Her face was pale, and she was shivering.

'Tina, you're frozen! Where's the mini?'

'The clutch has gone. Dad offered me the estate, but it's too big. I'm scared to drive it. I caught the bus up from town, but it was delayed. Oh, Henry, I'm sorry if I'm late.'

As I bundled her along the corridor to the lounge where the gas fire blazed, it struck me that that summed her up perfectly. Too timid to tackle driving an estate and more concerned about a possible hurt to someone's feelings than about the fact she was chilled to the bone.

I hung her coat up and put the kettle on for tea. When I came in she was huddled around the fire.

'That's better, I'm thawing out now. How are you, Henry, anyway?'

When the Henson females say that they mean it. She gave me a scrutinising look.

'You look a bit tired. Have you been working late on your book?' She spoke in a tone of mock scolding.

I poured her a mug of tea. 'A confession. No. I was playing a computer game—if game is the word for it—for six hours last night. And I spent another three wondering about it when I should have been sleeping.'

She raised her eyebrows. I noted the blood had come back into her cheeks, but her hands were still clenched around the mug as if hungry for the heat.

'I remember you saying that Tim had promised you something fancy. It was to link up to a mainframe, wasn't it?'

'That's right. Well, it is a bit odd and I can't put my finger on it. I'd welcome the benefit of your common sense.'

She laughed warmly at me. 'Go ahead, for what it's worth. My brain is still frozen.'

As I thought how to begin, it occurred to me that she looked very lovely. The setting sun and the glow from the fire highlighted her face perfectly against the dark green of her pullover and the gathering gloom of the room. Why couldn't we sort out our relationship?

'Technical oddities first. It's a long program, a lot of code, unless it's badly written, which I doubt. There's no copyright logo or any legal warning about copying anywhere, which makes it unique in my experience. There is no copy protection either as far as I know. I made back-ups with no problem.'

'So there's nothing to stop you making endless copies to give to friends? Or even to market? Very odd. Even suspicious.'

'Yes, I thought that too. I ran all the usual checks and backed up my files first. But it doesn't seem as if it's booby-trapped. No, I'm inclined to believe Tim's story. You see, it would make marketing sense to make the program free, but to charge for the updating by the mainframe. Anyway, it's sup-posed to be a prototype version, but that doesn't come over anywhere so far.'

'Well, now you have me intrigued, Henry. What does it do?'

'I'm coming to that. I won't give you all the details; that would take too long. There are no titles or credits. There's an opening paragraph that sets the scene. It's a parallel world to ours, and the technology, physical laws and the rest are iden-tical. Only geography and politics are different. You are a Naval Officer with orders to survey a series of communities along the edge of a continent. You have forty-eight hours to examine the first one. Your orders are to observe only. Not to interfere. So the game starts with you off the shore of the first settlement in a small boat. It's mainly text with some rudimen-tary graphics, mostly maps. You follow so far?'

Tina pursed her lips slightly. 'So there's no indication of what the whole point of the game is?'

'Exactly! There lies part of the puzzlement. No dragons to kill or aliens to blast. At any rate the first settlement is a large delta backed by high mountains. It took me half an hour to get ashore, through the barrier islands. Lots of hazards, currents and the rest. You have to decide where to land too. I landed as near to the main town as I could. Well, there is plenty of description, and by asking questions you can learn a lot more. The geography is interesting.'

'But of course.'

'No, I mean it. It's a self-contained world. The currents are such that no one sails from the delta, and the mountains behind are impassable. The river that created the delta has been dammed. This dam, which is massive, is all-important. It governs the water, stops flooding in the rainy season, and allows irrigation in the dry season. It also provides the only source of power through hydro-electricity. The other thing about it that becomes apparent is that it is the product of a technology beyond the scope of the present inhabitants of the delta. Quite intriguing, and in its way believable.'

'You mean it could work.'

'Well, the delta shape is all wrong for somewhere with strong currents, but the concept of being governed by water and fatally dependent on an inherited irrigation system is very plausible. There are some good Middle East parallels—the Nabateans for one.'

Tina grinned at me over her mug. 'Your erudition delights me. Continue.'

'Anyway, it took time for me to piece together all the information. The social system is rotten. There is a small ruling elite who live near the dam, but the rest of the population are peasants who seem to have a rough time of it. Well, eventually I decided to make my way from the port city to the citadel where the rulers live. Incidentally, there are some minor oddities about the game. It doesn't seem as if you can retrace your steps. For example, I passed an open door and a few minutes later I realised it might have led somewhere useful and went back. The door was there but closed. The most striking thing is that you don't seem to be able to restart at the beginning. There is no going back.'

'Sounds just like life. Perhaps the mainframe can restart it for you.'

'A good point, but there's been no indication of it so far. Let me continue. After about an hour's playing time into the game I got the first hint of what it may all be about. It turns out that the ruling elite are mining the mountains behind the delta and the process is gradually undermining the dam. There is a real risk of the dam giving way in the next few months.'

I paused and refilled my mug of tea.

'I am eventually asked privately by one of the elite, who seems concerned about the impending catastrophe, to help him avert it. Basically, and here I've spent a long time trying to sort out the issues, I'm faced with a number of options. Firstly to obey my orders and simply leave, or to stay and try to prevent the disaster. If I do stay, then there appear to be a number of further options: I could run a revolution against the elite; or try to convince the rulers to curtail their mining programme; maybe even try stopping the mining programme by force. A final option would be to try to find a way off the delta for the population. Perhaps over the mountains.'

'Mmm, I can see why you lost sleep. How much time did you have left?'

'Less than a day. In fact, I would have to have turned back straightaway to get to the boat in time.'

'I gather then that you decided to stay to help them?' There was a vague look of unease on Tina's face.

'Well, yes. I mean, it was an intolerable decision. But I felt that if there was an opportunity to save lives, then, well . . .'

'Duty could wait?'

'Maybe. Anyway, no sooner had I decided to stay and to try to persuade the rulers of their folly when I got a message that the program needed modifying in the light of my decisions. So I called up the mainframe, got lots of electronic chatter, and then there was a message on the screen: "Program ready for you to continue. Probability of you saving the delta is estimated at one in five." So at that point I switched it all off and came home.'

The room had become quite dark. I got up and put the light on and pulled the curtains across.

'So what do you make of it, Tina?' I slumped into my armchair and stared at her.

'Not much more than you do, Henry. You don't suppose you find it intriguing because it is more like the real world than the computer games you have played?'

'You mean, it's not simply action but also issues? True. Perhaps I've been playing the wrong sort of game. Perhaps I'm like someone brought up on nothing but war comics trying to make sense of *War and Peace*.'

'Mm, a helpful illustration. Supposing we didn't call it a game but, say, "problem solving exercises." Would that help?'

'Truer, Tina, but less marketable. But then there are some things like landing the boat that use totally different skills.'

Silence fell on us. An idea came to me slowly. 'Supposing, Tina, that what they are trying to develop is the game that can be tailored to the demands of the player. The bits I do well in will be more common in the next version.'

'The fatal objection to that hypothesis is that it doesn't ask you what you want.'

'Oh well, I give up. I suppose I shall continue in faith, trusting that the whole thing is meaningful; that it is not a random collection of incidents.'

Tina gave her happy little laugh. 'There we are, just like life again.' She put her cup down on the table. 'However, I hope the game is not going to have a bad influence on you, Henry. You're already absent without leave.'

I felt slightly uncomfortable. Recounting the game was a rather personal thing. 'Yes, I'd thought of that. I suppose it's the price necessary to pay for saving the people of the delta.'

Tina muttered, 'I wonder,' but it was more to herself than to me.

I decided it was time to eat and disappeared into the kitchen to transfer the house specialty from the freezer into the microwave.

After supper we listened in semi-intent fashion to some classical tapes and discussed a variety of topics. Cyprus and Vaughan were two topics that we skirted with care.

It was getting late when the subject of the summer came up. Tina asked me what I was intending to do.

'I've applied for a research grant to go down to Yugoslavia.'

'I thought you'd been there before?'

'Yes, but there's more to see. Anyway, I've got some ideas to test and it's the type locality for the karst type of weathering. I just hope college will come up with the grant.'

As I recounted it I realised that through whatever reason,

I had made no mention of even the possibility of moving down to Cyprus. 'Of course my plans may change. Anyway, what about yourself?'

'Well, nothing as exciting as any of your options.' The fact that Tina felt I had more than one option didn't go unnoticed.

'Debbie and I were planning to travel round Skye and other areas for a week or so. Then I have a week when I am involved with the church Bible school and then a long conference on "Health Administration—Towards the year 2000." Should be quite interesting.'

Whether it was the end of the day or the oblique reference to Cyprus that provoked me, I don't know, because I heard myself saying something that I'd always avoided.

'So it doesn't look like we'll be getting married this year then?'

There was a slight uncertain bewilderment on Tina's face. Then with a gentle but mocking smile she quietly said, 'We? I didn't even know you were thinking about it. Who's the lucky girl?' But neither her eyes nor her voice seemed to have heard the joke. I looked at her. Her eyes seemed to say, 'No, Henry, no, please don't ask me, please don't.'

I looked at my watch to hide my confusion and embarrassment. 'I suppose it's time to take you back, Tina.'

'Yes, Henry, I think it is.'

We drove back slowly along the icy streets with care. As I stopped outside the Hensons' I spoke: 'Tina, I'm so sorry. I didn't mean to say that.'

Tina was silent and half-opened the door. The cold clean air rushed in. As she got out she turned to me. 'Henry, I'm awfully sorry too.' She leant over, kissed me on the cheek, and was gone before I could think of anything sensible to say.

10

At church the next day Tina caught me at the end of the morning service. She looked pale and tired.

'Henry, are you in this afternoon? I need to talk to you. It won't take long.' She spoke quietly in a detached faraway manner.

'Certainly. I'm in all afternoon.' I tried to hide the unease that I suddenly felt.

'OK, I'll see you at half two. Thanks.' And she walked off in a subdued manner to the Henson estate car. Alec unlocked a rear door for her, and as she sat down he gently patted her shoulder.

'Trouble, Henry?' It was Alun Thomas, one of the deacons who kept a friendly eye on me.

'Probably, Alun, probably.' And I walked away without a further word.

Lunch tasted awful, the house was cold, and I felt miserable. Eventually half two arrived and the doorbell rang. Normally Tina rang with two sharp, precise rings, but all she managed that day was a single half-hearted buzz.

She wouldn't let me take her coat and just sat on the edge of the sofa in a precarious manner, as though ready to get up and run for it.

'Well, tell me all.' I was trying to be cool and ruthless about it, but my emotions were twitching and refusing to lie down quietly.

'Henry, I've been thinking things over. I mean our relationship, us, since yesterday.' Her hands were twisting the car keys on their chain.

'Haven't we both?' I said for something to say.

'I suppose we both let a perfectly good friendship drift into deeper waters than we meant to.'

My various emotional alarm bells were ringing loudly.

She went on. 'I suppose we, I, should have sat down and talked about where we were going and what the relationship was about.'

'Spit it out, Tina.' I could feel the stress in my voice.

She looked at me with a face that was pinched with resolution.

'OK. Well, Henry, to use a phrase we laughed over about Miriam, if there is a vacancy for a Mrs Stanwick I do not wish to be considered for the post.'

'I see.' It was a verbal noise while my mind went into a tailspin.

Tina went on. What she was saying sounded like a prepared statement. 'That being so, then it would be pointless,' she paused and swallowed, 'I mean wrong, to continue to go out with you.'

I recognised the logic, but it didn't make any sense. At least not where it mattered, not where it hurt. I thought about saying something, but I didn't think I could say anything without making things worse. Besides Tina had made her mind up.

She got up still twisting her keys. I could see she was wanting to say something. She moved towards the door and abruptly half-turned.

'You won't do anything silly, will you?'

'Like what? Throw myself off a cliff?'

'No, you idiot, I mean agree to take the Cyprus job. I mean . . . unless you're supposed to.'

'No, I dare say I'll survive.'

She paused and seemed to be on the point of coming towards me. Then she stiffened, turned to the door, and a second later I heard the front door shut.

I sat in the chair feeling sorry for myself for some time. Then I got up, put on my jacket, slung some boots in the back of the Beetle, and went up onto the cold deserted moors. There in the solitude things began to come back together again. I've never been much of a one for self-pity, at least not on more than a momentary basis. I reassured myself that it wasn't the end of the world, that I was still intact. I was even able to remind myself that I had had real doubts about the relationship. It came to me that perhaps she had realised that she had no deep affection for me; at least not enough to continue the relationship. Working out how much she cared for me had always been a problem—the female Hensons were so affectionate and caring to everybody that it was difficult to know how special you were.

At the top of Marton Pike I stopped and sat on Millstone Grit blocks at the foot of the rimy cairn, and gradually the gloom lifted very slightly. Then, cold and unhappy, I walked back to the car.

I went out to church that evening; partly out of habit and partly hoping to see Tina and to hear her say that it had all been a terrible misunderstanding. She wasn't there. I noticed out of the corner of my eye Alec coming in late. After the service he came over to me as I was getting into the car in the church car park. He put his arm on my shoulder and gave it a squeeze of affection.

'Henry, I'm awful sorry about the whole business. My heart bleeds for the both of you. Viv is terribly upset about it all too.' He shook his head. 'Remember, you're always welcome as a brother and a friend at our house. We'll continue to pray for you.'

He paused for what seemed a long time, and I thought he had something more to say. Then he shrugged his shoulders, looked at me and said, 'No, I shouldna meddle. I'm just a very foolish, fond old man and I'd best be gone.'

And before I could deny it he was off, leaving me to my thoughts.

11

That week was a busy one in the department, although I suppose I went out of my way to make work for myself. The whole thing with Tina was puzzling as well as painful. For the life of me I still couldn't work out why she'd so abruptly ended everything between us. It was true enough that we'd never sat down and said, 'Hey, this is getting serious, do we want it this way?' On the other hand the relationship had been pretty serious for quite some time. It seemed unlikely that my oblique and frivolous allusion to marriage could have triggered off what was by any standards a pretty drastic reaction. I decided that I just didn't understand Tina at all.

What with one thing and another it wasn't until Thursday night that I managed to get a chance to work on the game again. On starting it up I was a little surprised to find that there were no obvious alterations to it after the link-up to the mainframe. Following my previous decision, I made my way back to the citadel and the dam behind. I took an option of looking round the mining area and indeed found large-scale workings almost directly under the sheer face of the dam. The problem was compounded by the presence of a number of rival companies. Each on its own appeared to be being careful not to overmine, but the cumulative effect was a clear threat to the fabric of the dam. I resolved to try to talk with the rulers of the elite and made my way back to the citadel. The interview when obtained was brief and futile. The dam had existed for generations. Even in the remote chance of damage it was probable that ways could be found to repair it. Furthermore, there was no way the mining could be stopped. For one thing the mining companies had rights under law and, more seriously, the resources of the delta were so limited that they would only ever be capable of sustaining a small population at anything above peasant level. Even on this basis, constant, ever-deeper mining was necessary to provide enough metals for ploughs, water pumps, and to keep the delta functional.

I was warned neither to listen to, nor spread, the rumours about the dam on pain of imprisonment, and it was suggested that I had best leave the delta. On that note I left the citadel with no clear plan in mind.

At this point I got up from the screen, made myself a cup of coffee, and spent some time thinking about the program. With all its trappings of conventional games, there was something increasingly compelling about the game. There was a grim logic behind the social fabric of the delta with its awful vulnerability and blind greed driving it on to extinction. Despite the graphics, which tended to be merely adequate, and all the constraints of the program's limited vocabulary, whoever had written the game knew the real world and the mess that humanity could make of it.

I finished my coffee and began to go back to the dam with the hope of trying to talk to someone in charge of the mines. I was wondering which way to go when there was a knock on the door. Before I could say 'come in,' the door was pushed open and in walked Jim Barnett with his tatty jeans, grubby fisherman's pullover, and imitation fur-lined nylon anorak.

My feelings on seeing him were definitely on the negative side of mixed. Jim was a junior lecturer in chemistry and had arrived at Grantforth at the same time as I did. That, a bachelor status, and an interest in computers were the only things we had in common. Our only formal point of contact was the Computer Users' Committee where he and I frequently disagreed. Fundamentally, I distrusted him. For one thing he was notorious in pursuing his computing interests beyond even the vaguest definition of legality. Most of his software was illegally copied, and I had a strong suspicion that he was able to gain access to far more of the university computer files than he had any right to. I was wondering what he was doing over in Geography at nine on a Thursday night till I remembered that Miriam had mentioned that there was an attempted relationship going on with one of the more attractive postgrads. 'Attempted' was probably the word, as Jim was an even worse advertisement for the bachelor life than I was. At least I ironed my shirts.

Without waiting for an invitation he came in and sat on my spare chair. 'What a day! Students, students and more students. The only thing wrong with this place is it's full of students.'

'Well, Jim, they are why we are here, but I have some sympathy with your comment.' That was Stanwick code for, 'Actually, I disagree a hundred per cent in theory with your comment and a mere ninety-five per cent in practice.' I didn't feel like violent disagreement.

'Huh.' He pouted his lower lip forward in a distressingly ape-like manner. 'I'm not impressed.' His eyes stared at the computer screen, and a flicker of amusement crossed his face.

'Oho, what's this Stanners? Playing games, eh?' He got up out of his chair and leaned over the machine, staring at the screen. His hand groped in a full anorak pocket and came out with matches and cigarettes.

'I'd rather you didn't.'

'What?' He was miles away.

'Smoke in my room.' I tried to keep the edge out of my voice. Tina would have said that the commandment about loving your enemies is supposed to apply within universities too. I was a bit more pragmatic—I just didn't want a row. Jim looked at me as though I'd insulted him and put them back into his pocket.

'Well, what have we here, then?'

'It's a game that was given to me by a fabulously rich American benefactor.' Then I went on with a bit more seriousness to describe the program. He weighed it up.

'Pretty neat, the totally open-ended game. I suppose the ultimate goal is that you create a separate games universe and people get hooked. Then you up the mainframe charges. A good way of making some money.'

'So you won't be wanting a copy then?'

'Well, thank you, sir. A perfect gentleman. But I thought you didn't go into that. Weren't you trying to get us to buy 500 word processing programs only last week?'

'Not fair, Jim. Negotiate a licence was what I said. Anyway, this isn't copyrighted. It's not even protected.'

He looked puzzled for a moment and then gave a sneering grin. 'Got it. You know why it isn't copy protected, Stanners? You wait, you'll just be at the point where the girl's about to take her clothes off and the screen will come up with: "Please transfer 100 dollars to this account." Smart, eh?'

'Possibly. Anyway, if you get some disks I'll give you a copy.'

'You wouldn't have a couple spare, would you? It's pretty cold outside.'

'Sorry, Jim, we're on a tight budget here.'

He grunted and said, 'OK, be back in a sec,' and left abruptly, leaving the door wide-open.

I breathed out heavily after he'd gone and exited the game with the decision of how to approach the mines unresolved.

Jim was back in five minutes with a cigarette in one hand and a pair of grubby floppy disks in the other. He drew on the cigarette. I waved my hand to clear the air.

'Oh, sorry, I forgot.' He took a last puff and ground the butt under his heel on the vinyl floor. He saw my gaze, picked it up, and dropped it in the waste bin.

It didn't take long to copy the disks, and I gave him the brief sheet of starting instructions. He tucked them into a stuffed, shabby briefcase. I looked at my watch. It was nearly half nine.

'Well, Jim, I must go.' I switched off the machine, got up from the seat and began to put on my jacket.

Jim made no effort to leave, but stood by the door shifting

his weight from foot to foot. 'You don't fancy a drink do you, Henry? I know you're not one of the usual pub crowd . . .'

Suddenly, in a moment of awareness and conscience, I realised that Jim was lonely. The decision didn't take more than a fraction of a second. 'Sure, why not? You can buy me a pint.'

Jim smiled. It wasn't quite angelic, but it was a definite improvement.

So we went to a smoky, noisy pub, The Angel and Child, not far from the university, that I'd been in once or twice before. I managed to manoeuvre us as far away as possible from the juke-box, but avoiding the smoke was less easy.

Jim wasn't the company that I would have chosen, but it wasn't a bad hour. He didn't get drunk and he gradually opened up a bit. It turned out that he was in a real mess over this girl, and the whole thing was made worse by his egocentric viewpoint which made it all feed back on himself. One good effect of the problem with Tina was that I was in no position to be smug or patronising, at least not as far as his female problems went.

In fact the whole thing was curiously therapeutic. I've found it often to be the way that when you think you are doing someone a good turn they end up giving you more help than they received. That night was no exception. It helped me realise that things could be a lot worse and that self-pity was no solution. Whether it did Jim any good I do not know, but he was calling me 'Henry' instead of 'Stanners' when the barman called time.

12

Friday night of that week I spent at home. There was lots to do in the house and I felt I needed an early night. When the phone rang at nine I hurried to it hoping to hear Tina's voice.

It wasn't. It was Philip Ringwood, who worked with the Anglican church in the vast and troubled diocese of Jerusalem and Antioch. He was briefly back in the UK visiting his family and had taken the opportunity to ring me. We were friends from the old Lebanon and Syria days and had done a number of trips, visiting the archaeological sites together. He was quite knowledgeable on the area, and lots of books on the Phoenicians or the early church list his name under the credits, either for photos or advice. We still kept in touch sporadically.

The first part of the conversation was all news of acquaintances and their doings. Phil sounded happy in his single state, and I dodged his questions on my own marital situation. He passed on messages from old friends. I was particularly glad to hear about Raji and Sanaa Abdul-Malik. They were working in a tiny orphanage up in the Maronite heartland of Mount Lebanon. Things apparently were tough.

'Yes, quite a list of woes and tribulations. The local militia wanted to use the grounds for training exercises. The Syrians gradually get nearer. One month a scrap of wood, the next a villa. You know the sort of thing. Ain Mroueh also gets a bit of light shelling now and then.'

Phil spoke as the Lebanese do, treating shelling as if, like snow or rain, it was a meteorological phenomenon that one must live with.

'They are tempted to get up and go to Cyprus. Sanaa is keen; she has relatives and they are both very tired. Raji feels it would be wrong to go. Henry, that man is a saint.'

I ruefully reflected that indeed for many people the offer of a job in Cyprus would be heaven. I made a mental note to count my blessings.

Phil went on. 'Incidentally, talking of which—Cyprus—I have heard, I can't reveal my sources, that you are going to St Paul's to work with that other great saint, George Roumian.'

There was a pause. Phil never believed in asking direct questions. He just let people think he asked them. That way he got more of an answer.

'Really, Phil, that's very interesting. For the record, they have, as yet, made no formal offer to me and, as yet, I have not accepted it. Nor, to be honest, have I decided what I would do if such an offer were made.'

I tried to make my voice light and cheerful. 'Much as I'd like to do the antiquities of Cyprus with you, don't bank on it.'

'Mmm, yes. Well, I'm sure they will be making that offer. That George is quite a character. You know, Henry, you and George could be a good balance there. You'd complement each other nicely.'

'Thanks a million, Phil,' was what I said to myself. What I actually said was a bit different.

'I feel that working closely with George could be quite a task, Phil. One saint like that needs another to work with him. I'm not sure that I could handle it. Anyway, I'll give it a lot of thought.'

I wanted to change the subject and was thinking of something to say when Phil spoke again, even more hesitantly than usual.

'Er, Henry, on a different note—I don't know whether I should say this but, well, there have been enquiries about you.' The word 'enquiries' had a very considerable stress attached to it.

'Sorry, Phil, I don't follow. The school knows all about me.'

'No, no, not the school. No, rather, through the Embassy.'

I was too surprised to say anything. Phil went ahead in a big burst: 'Yes, you know I have all sorts of business with the Embassy. Well, there was apparently an enquiry about you. General clearance sort of thing. It was a bit embarrassing because there have been a lot of changes in the last three years and your record was, apparently, ambiguous. No one there now knows you personally.'

I listened, appalled.

'Anyway, my name was linked with yours, so they asked me. Of course it's happened before. I mean, about other people. I dislike it all intensely, but someone has to give them honest information. I mean, they are capable of drawing all sorts of conclusions otherwise. Sometimes I'm able to clear the innocent. Which was your case.'

I could take no more. 'Hang on, Phil—am I supposed to be a past, present or future terrorist?'

'Henry, I wish I knew. As I say, I gave you a clean bill of health. But with a track record like yours it's easily open to misinterpretation. I mean you've stuck your nose in places that the intelligence boys didn't know existed. And that Jdeita business couldn't have helped.'

The phone felt cold and clammy, and something seemed to be crawling down my spine. 'Oh dear, that again. Well, they have my statement on that. How was I to know that the best cave system in the Middle East was full to the ceiling with armaments?'

Phil made a vague cough. 'Well, Henry, you did make some effort to avoid the guards. If you ask me you weren't sufficiently grateful to the ambassador for his personal intervention at the very highest level. He hated having to talk to Pierre.'

'Phil, the complications from that piece of heavy-handed diplomacy have bugged me ever since. Because I wasn't shot by the Phalange, the Syrians assumed that I must be an Israeli agent. I had a couple of very unhappy interviews with the

Mukabarrat; those boys don't have very nice manners.' Even talking about it three years on made my stomach do funny things.

'Ah yes, I'd forgotten that complication. Of course, that may explain the ambiguity on your record. My understanding is that once one intelligence agency starts to sniff at you, then all the others think that something must be up. If you're totally innocent it's worse because you're not on anyone's records. They may also have been simply cleaning out the files. In the absence of facts, speculate. I shouldn't worry about it.'

With some final pleasantries he rang off.

The shadow that his conversation had brought didn't lift very easily. On and off over the weekend I wondered quite a bit about who was checking up on me and why. Tina was away, whether by accident or by design I didn't know, but I didn't see her on Sunday. The matter of the phone call seemed to be revealed on Monday morning.

Archie Turner, whose job of running the foreign students office clearly hadn't allowed for early retirement, called me over to his office after morning coffee. He and I knew each other quite well because I'd sometimes been called in to help with various matters to do with the Arab students. After a few cordialities he put on his reading glasses wearily and pulled a slip of paper out from a folder. 'Now, Dr Stanwick—Khalil Farah. Third year Civ Eng student.' He pronounced the name badly. 'Know him?'

I thought through the various Arabs I knew. 'Yes, I think so. Large chap. Yes, not well-liked, even among the other Palestinians. Once went to a party when he was there. He made some less than diplomatic comments about the British government.'

Archie scribbled something at the foot of the paper. 'So you didn't know him well?'

'Not at all. He took a dislike to me. Most of the guys I'm friendly with are a bit embarrassed by him.' I had a pretty strong idea what lay behind the conversation and continued talking. 'He's unlikely to be a terrorist menace if that's what Special Branch thinks. He's too obvious, very high profile. But I don't know; you can never tell.'

Archie sighed and looked at me. 'That's true enough. Thanks, Henry. They are probably going to deport him and your name came up. You are known to have Middle East links, as they say in the papers. Anyway, I thought I'd ask you. That's all.'

'No problem. A pity about his education, but he was a troublemaker. Too keen by far on the bomb and gun, but it was probably just rhetoric.'

'You don't seem upset.'

'Actually I'm not. Nor, I suspect, will most of the other students be from his part of the world.'

Archie shrugged in a tired way, tucked his piece of paper away, and that was that.

On reflection afterwards I considered that the fact that Khalil Farah was being investigated was a very convenient explanation of the enquiries into Henry Stanwick that had been recently conducted through Her Majesty's Embassies.

With hindsight it is unfortunate that I did not consider whether, in fact, it was a correct explanation.

13

The problem with Tina now returned to top priority and occupied my mind a lot. I managed to keep myself busy for the next few days, and that helped a bit. But I still found it hard to feel positive about the whole thing. It was all rather puzzling, and I was still incredulous about the speed with which the relationship had disintegrated.

Wednesday morning's mail didn't help my spirits. There was a letter from the university authorities rejecting the grant for the Yugoslavian field work. It was 'greatly regretted that they could not afford to support this work in the present financial climate.' It was a definite blow. I'd been rather looking forward to the Adriatic. I eventually decided that it had been a long shot anyway and began to think about alternatives. The trouble was that they all cost money.

In the afternoon I had a phone call from Tim. I presumed it was from the States as he didn't say, and I didn't ask.

'Hi, Henry. Sorry I've been slow to get back to you, but I've been busy doing some homework. I'm now in a position to make you an offer.'

I grabbed a loose sheet of paper and listened carefully to the distant voice.

'Just hear the whole package first and then give me your comments. I'd like you and your Malagasy friend to come with me on this pinnacles trip. I'll cover your airfare, and it won't be Aeroflot this time. I'll also pay your other expenses. On top of it all I'm offering you 5,000 US dollars and a thousand dollars for him. Half in advance, half on return. So far what's your reaction?'

I thought quickly. It sounded like an answer to prayer, except that I hadn't prayed about it.

'Interested, Tim, very interested. It's a very generous offer indeed. I'd need it all in writing before I agreed. But I'm very keen. What about dates?'

'I'm talking about getting a Monday, 13th June flight to Antsalova from 'Tana and getting out from there back to 'Tana on a Saturday, 25th flight.'

'I wasn't aware there was a Monday flight, Tim.'

There was a little chuckle across the wires. 'There isn't yet. But I've established that the Morondava flight can be rerouted to drop us off. It's not very expensive in real money. Still, glad to see you have your wits about you. We may need them before this is through. Anyway, check those dates.'

I squinted at my wall calendar. 'Yes, they look OK here. I suppose twelve days would do us from Antsalova and back. But only just. There's no slack in it.' As I said it I realised I'd used the word 'us.'

Tim's voice was quiet and even-toned. 'Nor is there meant to be. I'm sure you appreciate it'll be a tight operation. I want to get through and back safely and quickly. Any science you do is a bonus to the main goal of the trip. I want to play this safe. We will be stretched and I want no putting the whole thing at risk because of some pretty scenery. Understood?' There was no hint of malice in his voice. It was just an instruction that had to be obeyed.

I nearly said, 'Yes, sir,' but merely assented, 'Understood, Tim.'

'So will you join the expedition, Dr Stanwick?' He spoke with a note of wry humour.

'Are you sure you want me?'

'Henry, I inadvertently acquired your CV when I was over with you. You sound like you're a survivor. Yes, I want you. We can work together.'

'Well, in that case, provisionally yes. Fax the details over, and I'll telex back my agreement. I'll write to Laurent tonight. If he can't do it, he'll know someone who will.'

'Good enough, Henry. Now I've got some final odds and ends to sort out with you. You remember the spot where you landed the chopper? Is it the only place to land a decent-sized machine in? Also, would it be a good point to try to cut through the pinnacles?'

'Yes, it's more or less unique. We called it the Cricket Pitch because it's so flat. That's British humour, but it's comparatively level. As for heading through there, yes, it's a good place.'

'Anyway, there is the chance of getting a supply drop by chopper to your Cricket Pitch. I'm working on it. On that basis can you draw me up an accurate map of the projected route with scales and proper longitudes and latitudes. In standard English fashion please. None of this French degrees grad from a Paris meridian. Fax it over to Houston as soon as possible. Also, can you send with it your friend's name? Laurent, wasn't it? And his address. I may be able to pass through 'Tana over Easter and sort out the trip with Air Madagascar. I'd like to meet him if that was possible. Any other questions?'

There were lots, but they could wait. 'No, that's fine. Look forward to getting your fax.'

'Good enough. Ciao, Henry.' And the line was dead.

I sat for a few minutes in the office thinking it over. It occurred to me that perhaps I should have been more cautious, given it a night or two's sleep and thought it through more carefully. But I found myself arguing that it was necessary to be decisive in these things. Anyway, it surely couldn't be a coincidence that it should turn up on the same day as I got my rejection of the Yugoslavia grant. In fact, Tim's money would allow me to do both. Madagascar early in the holidays and Yugoslavia at the end. The opportunity to see Laurent had also played a part in my decision. He had been recommended to me by a mutual acquaintance, and he and I had become close friends. I remembered our farewell at the airport in the midst of the noisy swaying mass of passengers, relatives, and belongings at the check-in desk.

'Henry, my brother. It was good to meet you. God willing we may see each other again. God be with you and keep you.' Then a final hug and he had turned abruptly as if to hide his emotions and left, a thin insignificant figure picking his way gently through the children and suitcases into the darkness. It had either been a subtle manoeuvre, or an act of real charity on Tim's part to offer to take Laurent as well. A thousand dollars would certainly be more than he earned in a year in his teaching job. His father's salary as a pastor in 'Tana was probably tiny as well. I realised how much I looked forward to seeing him again.

I was wondering how the timing of the trip would fit into the Malagasy school year when a flash of inspiration struck me and sent me to the wall calendar. I had to give three months' notice to resign my position at Grantforth. As my yearly contract ran from 1st October, that meant that my resignation to take up the Cyprus job could be made right up until 30th June. I sat there looking at the calendar for several minutes.

The trip would provide the ideal time to think it all over. A last chance to see the best of limestone scenery. There, away from it all, I could make the decision. It would also give me the maximum period of time to think about the implications of my choice. If I did take the Cyprus job then, it would be the perfect way to end my career in geomorphology, allowing me to go out with a final flourish. There was a neat sense of drama to it all. I could see myself walking out of the pinnacles, looking back towards them, saying farewell, and then turning on my heel and walking away from them forever. Perhaps Tim would take a photograph of the great event to be subsequently captioned: 'Dr Henry Stanwick says farewell to the study of limestone weathering.'

It was an intriguing idea, but would it work out in practice? It would certainly be neater if I resigned earlier, but I was only down for one course in the autumn term and a replacement could readily be found, given today's job market. The real problem was whether or not I could persuade George to let me postpone a decision about taking up Cyprus till the end of June.

As I pulled out the airmail paper to begin to write to Laurent I wondered what Tina would think of it all. Then I realised that it didn't really matter any more.

14

I was booked on the flight out of Paris on the afternoon of Thursday, 9th June. What with getting exam marking out of the way I had left a lot to be done on the Wednesday.

Much of the morning was spent tidying up the office. As I cleared away the thick accumulations of computer printout I thought again about the 'delta game,' as Jim and I called it. In the past three months I'd only spent about twelve hours on the game. At first I'd got lost investigating the mines and then had made a forlorn attempt to try to get into some mining offices in the castle. I'd accessed the mainframe three times. Each time it had given me longer odds about saving the delta. As I unplugged the computer I decided that with odds now at twenty to one I might as well call it a day anyway. What was slightly perturbing was the fact that Jim had been very successful. Adopting a different, more ruthless strategy he had infiltrated the 'rulers' and had recently managed to shut down half the mines. That his carefully planned mine accident had taken twenty lives hadn't bothered him at all. Curiously, it hadn't seemed to have perturbed the mainframe either. When I'd last talked to him it was giving him even odds on saving the delta. Well, that was life, I thought. I just wasn't cut out to be that sort of a hero.

Finally, because I had deliberately left it to the last, I pulled out the Cyprus file. I went through the letters again in the forlorn hope of seeing some light. None came. The words of George's last letter caught my eye. After confirming that he could indeed allow me until the end of June to make a decision he ended with: 'Be assured, Henry, dear brother, that we sympathise with your difficulties. But, Henry, we do need you here.'

Was I going? I shook my head. The past few months had been a long drawn-out battle on that issue. There was an undeniable pull towards Cyprus; something somewhere in my mind was telling me that it was the thing I should do. I tried reasoning myself out of it; I used every argument that I could, but it was all to no avail. Whether it was conscience or something else I did not know; but there remained this conviction that I ought to help George Roumian. I just didn't have the strength of will either to take the job or to refuse it; so I had been unable to decide. For a time I had been so certain that I would take the job that I had repackaged the half-written book into three paper-length portions that I could get readily published with little further effort. Then in May I'd had a letter from the Karst Institute of Guiping, China, telling me they were keen to have me on an exchange visit if I could arrange some funding with the British Council. The thought of China with its millions of square kilometres of limestone scenery had all but determined the issue. For the past month things had been more or less in a cautious truce waiting for the Madagascar trip to sort them out. It seemed strange to look at the file and think that one way or another the whole issue would be resolved within a few weeks.

Finally I did what I knew I must do. I took out a sheet of headed paper and typed up my resignation notice, dated it 29th June, sealed it in an envelope and addressed it to Prof. It was the letter Prof had told me he didn't want to see. I had nearly told him that that summed up my feelings precisely.

I locked up my cabinets and left the office. I said good-bye to Miriam who was busy collating exam results. 'No forwarding address, Miriam. I'm totally out of reach from tomorrow.'

'Well, have a good trip, Henry. Don't get into any trouble.'

'Not likely, I've got enough already.' As I wheeled out of the office I wondered what she would make of that.

The next stop was Abie Gvirtzman's cluttered office. He was bent over an old book as I came in.

'Hey, Abie, you're reading it backwards.'

He gave a malicious grin. 'That's why I always know who did it first.'

He sat down at his desk, pushing a sheaf of papers to one side and leaned forward on his folded arms. 'Now, Henry, what can I do for you?'

'You know I'm off to Madagascar again?'

'Yes, I heard.' He spoke quietly. His face looked down at the desk.

'Abie, you don't seem very happy about it. You haven't been since the moment you saw the telex from Tim.'

He was silent.

'Come on, Abie, what is it? What don't you like?'

Abruptly he got clumsily to his feet and walked to the window, looked out briefly and then leant back against his overflowing bookcase, a stooped, dark shape silhouetted against the light.

'The whole thing is ridiculous, ridiculous.' He shook his head violently, like a horse trying to get rid of a fly. I watched bemused.

'Henry, you know that I am a rational man.' He spoke deliberately, almost as though between clenched teeth. 'I do not believe in a supernatural world. Not for me your demons, your Mazzaloth, your Shedim, your heavenly host and the whole ridiculous apparatus and paraphernalia that go with them. Nor even the stripped-down, bargain-basement Protestant faith that you pay token assent to. You excuse me, of course?'

I nodded, wondering where this curious outburst was going.

'Yet every so often I get a feeling from nowhere. No, more than a feeling, a compulsive belief about something. My father used to get it and his father before him and so on no doubt back to Abraham. A prophetic instinct.' There was a hint of contempt in his voice. He sat down.

'So something in your telex triggered my inherited irrational streak. That's all. A psychological quirk in an unbalanced Jew. All due to some wretched copyist's error in the DNA along the line. Some jot or tittle missing in the nucleic acids. That's all. And don't try and convince me otherwise.'

He paused for a minute and then, slapping his hands down on the edge of the desk, turned to look me in the face. 'There, I've aired my dirty washing. What can I do for you?'

I hesitated. Although part of me wanted to explore this new aspect of an old friend, I decided he had said all he would say. Besides I had business to do.

'OK, Abie. I have a decision to make during my trip abroad. I won't go into it. At any rate it is just possible that I may need you to perform a simple errand for me.'

I reached into my briefcase and pulled out the letter to Prof. I put it on the desk. Abie glared at it over his glasses.

'I understand you. The end of the month is the last date for resignations for next year. You are thinking of leaving Grantforth.'

'Thinking only, Abie. But I'm told the flights back may be overbooked. In that case, if I do make the decision to leave, I want to be sure it is carried out. If I am going to be delayed I will telex you to take that letter over to Geography. Hand carried; you know what I think about internal mail. Prof knows all about it. He will accept it. Reluctantly, but he will accept it.'

Abie picked up the letter gently by the edges. Twenty years of holding manuscripts showed in that single gesture.

'I will do this thing for you. But . . . Ach! Anything I say will be wrong.'

I thought of something. 'It may be that I can only get one telex or phone call out. So here's the telex code for George Roumian. I may ask you to telex him with, well, my acceptance.' I checked my diary and wrote the name and number down on a sheet of paper. Abie took it silently and put it with the letter in his desk.

He got up from his chair and shook my hand sadly and firmly.

'Go in peace, Henry.'

As I left the room he was standing by the window staring out at nothing.

The afternoon was spent in town and packing. I spent two hours in town buying the last remaining things on my list. Tim and I had already sorted out most of the major things, so it was just a few minor personal items. The rule we had adopted for Madagascar was to take everything we needed on the basis that you couldn't get anything there. At a camping store which stocks so-called survival gear I bought a large bushknife. Once or twice the previous year I'd had to make my way through the scrub on the edge of the pinnacles and found the need for something to cut the creepers and omnipresent thorny twigs, but it didn't warrant a real machete.

Quite a bit of the shopping was for Laurent and his family: a couple of bottles of vitamin supplements and some good paperback English dictionaries for his younger brothers who were just starting university. For Laurent's father I got some paperback commentaries on the Bible. For Laurent himself I bought a rather basic but solid shortwave radio. Laurent's mother and sister presented the biggest problem. With considerable trepidation and a certain hesitancy I bought some female underwear, having been reliably informed by a smirking engineer the previous year that it was an infallible gift for Malagasy ladies. Guessing the size was the worst part.

I normally enjoy buying presents, but this I found disturbing and depressing. It made tangible the vast economic gulf between us. With so many necessities being unobtainable in Madagascar, I felt guilty about taking them so little. How can anyone feel complacent about having friends who think a half-used ball-point pen is a luxury?

The last duty of the day before an early night was the most

awkward. I had promised to visit the Hensons before leaving. Over the last few months I had seen little of them, and my church attendance recently could only be described as spasmodic. At half past six I drove up the hill and found Alec in the garden tending the roses. Despite his gardening clothes he still looked dignified. His greeting was warm, but his words radiated concern and a certain unease.

'So you're off tomorrow? I wish you well. You are in a difficult position. But we will all be very glad to see you back in one piece. By all accounts it sounds a grand wee trek that yon American has lined up for you.'

'It won't be a picnic, Alec. But I have a certain faith in my Mr Vaughan. He does his homework.'

'I'm thinking your faith would be best placed elsewhere, laddie.' He spoke warmly, but there was no doubt of his meaning. I accepted his rebuke in the spirit in which it was given. One of the regrets I had about the breach with Tina was that Alec wouldn't one day be my father-in-law.

'At any rate you should go and talk to Tina. See me before you go.'

Tina was sitting in the lounge listening to the radio, her long legs curled up under her on the sofa. She got up as I came in. She smiled with genuine but restrained affection. 'Henry. Come in and take a seat.'

I suppose I had been hoping for some breakthrough. I realised there was going to be none. The wall that Tina had erected three months ago was not going to be dismantled now. In that time her attitude had never seemed to waver. Just once I had caught her watching me at church. When our eyes met she had turned away quickly, her face colouring.

Yet that evening, although there was no obvious thaw, I felt sure that her attitude concealed something more at depth. But perhaps it was wishful thinking.

She was keen to know the details of the trip that Tim and I had planned over our numerous telexes, faxes and phone conversations.

'And you're sure that Laurent is going to be able to come?'

'You sound as though he is going to be my chaperon at a particularly wild party.'

'Well, I don't know Madagascar, do I? Anyway, it will be good to have someone there you can trust.'

I thought about defending Tim again and decided against it.

At that point Viv came in and showed her solicitude for me by offering me all sorts of totally useless things. Was I sure that I had the right suitcase to take with me? She had a spare one that she'd found ideal to take to Edinburgh. It was well-meant.

As she left I caught Tina smiling genuinely for a second or two. Then she became all serious again. 'So you haven't made any decision yet, Henry? I know I shouldn't ask, but you've got less than a month.'

'No, Tina, I haven't. In some ways I've been postponing thinking about it until this trip.'

'And you will find time there to think about it.' It was meant as a statement, but it came over as a vaguely threatening question. As usual she had put her finger on a nerve spot.

'I think so. You see, Tina, I feel the problem is Grantforth. There I will be away from it all. Away from my cosy house, from my cosy office routine, from my cosy Henson friends.' As I said it, I wondered how true it was.

'One of whom has been less friendly than she might have been over the past few months.'

'Indeed.' I shrugged my shoulders. 'What can I do about that?'

There was silence. Tina looked uncomfortable.

'Well, I suppose I'd better go. It's the five o'clock train tomorrow morning for me.'

'Anything we can do for you? Mind the house, for example?'

'Thanks, no, it's all sorted out. The neighbours are going to keep an eye on the house. Abie Gvirtzman is minding things at university.'

'Good old Abie.' The Hensons knew Abie from an extra-mural course on Judaism he'd given that Alec had attended.

I got up from my seat, and Tina came with me to the door. Alec saw me and strolled up off the lawn. He called out to Viv that I was leaving.

In a minute they were all out on the doorstep with me, except for Debbie who was off horse riding. Alec spoke. 'I think it would be good if we had a word of prayer.'

Alec prayed for perhaps a minute. A good sincere prayer; sensible and warm-hearted. He prayed for safety on the trip for all three of us. He prayed for my decision about the future, and as he did I could sense him cautiously choosing his way around that particular minefield.

And so we parted. It was a bright sunny evening, the garden looked marvellous in its geometrical precision, but over us hung something impalpable. Something was not right and we all knew it.

15

As the 747 dropped below the early morning cloud cover on the approach to 'Tana I again tried, and again failed, to make any sense of the geography. Everything looked orderly, with the hills and little villages with their whitewashed churches. But what precisely was the order? The hills just seemed to lie here or there as they wished, obeying no known rules of geology. The little villages were similarly minded and lay scattered around as though seeded from heaven. The roads meandered aimlessly, here running across a paddy field, there around a hill. Even the distant city itself seemed nothing more than an accidental aggregation of a hundred villages.

As I thought about it and other similar problems I began to formulate a rule about Madagascar. The first reaction of the traveller expecting the bizarre and wonderful is disappointment. Everything seems more or less familiar. Then, as you think that it is all comprehensible, you look again and it has all disintegrated without warning into the grotesque, the lawless and the alien. I spent the time queueing to get off the plane thinking of illustrations of the principle.

I thought of walking through a stately forest of swollen baobab trees that was in every way African and coming out into a Polynesian beach scene of gabled huts and outrigger canoes.

Or the occasion when I'd been coming into the capital from the airport and had found the road blocked by a funeral procession with pall-bearers and bier. As I waited quietly and respectfully it had suddenly come over me that they were in fact taking the corpse out of the tomb.

Or the time I'd camped on an airstrip and had realised with horror that the friendly, civilised airport manager was offering me his twelve-year-old daughter as a gift for the night.

The rule even seemed to apply with the natural history. I'd walked over a landscape looking exactly like the Yorkshire moors after a dry summer and then over the rise of a hill found myself staring at an emerald swath of tropical rain forest full of plants out of palaeontological texts. Then there was finding in the rare and beleaguered fauna that what is manifestly a monkey isn't a monkey, the hedgehogs aren't hedgehogs and the wild cats aren't wild cats.

No matter how long you are in Madagascar it seems as soon as you think you understand something it undergoes some monstrous shift and turns into something extraordinarily different. Madagascar seems like an island that is passing through some episodic warping process so that everything is constantly changed, mixed or muddled.

The formalities at 'Tana airport were tedious and confusing. But despite the number of forms and the checks and the long lines of customs no one seemed annoyed or irritated. I can take a lot of entry rigmaroles and official paperwork when the temperature isn't above body heat and there is no evident threat of being machine-gunned by accident or design. Laurent was excitedly waiting for me beyond the customs desks with their happy, patient lines of Malagasy with their radios and black and white TVs. He had his suit on and looked smart and erect.

'*Salama tompoko*, Monsieur Laurent.'

'*Salama tompoko*, Dr Henry.'

We embraced and looked at each other. It was good to see him again.

'Welcome again, my friend. I have prayed that you would return, and the Lord has answered my prayer.'

Laurent's English had always impressed me in a land with so little evidence left of British influence. His father was taught by some of the last British missionaries and spoke good

English. Laurent had built on that by years of study and diligent listening to English radio programmes.

We walked out of the terminal to the school's VW van, talking. 'You look well, Laurent.'

'Yes, praise the Lord. I had some fever, but it has passed. And how are you, Henry? You look tired.'

'It's just the flight.' But my words didn't convince even me.

The Antsimonony School Volkswagen bus had always been of considerable fascination to me. I had picked up a passing knowledge of the VW bus over the years in the Middle East, and on any reckoning this model left the Wolfsburg factory in the middle of the 1950s. There was little left of the original maker's conception. Laurent unpadlocked the sidedoors, and I carefully packed my baggage to minimise the chances of it falling through the floor. Something—either a mouse or a cockroach—scuttled into a dark recess. Then with a roar, a lurch, and a cloud of smoke we were off.

Conversation of a civilised nature was only really possible when Laurent turned off the engine along the few downhill stretches on the road to the city centre. Even then, rattles, judders and a nasty metallic knocking broke through.

I asked Laurent how things were.

'How should I know?' He gave me a warm grin. 'You know Madagascar, it is very big. I know what happens in our street, but in Antsirabe, Tulear or Tamatave? Stories, only stories.'

There was a muffled explosion as he turned the ignition back on. Nothing seemed to fall off.

He shouted over the engine, 'Rice is short again, petrol is difficult, there was another cyclone in February. We hear of trouble in the south.' He shrugged his shoulders with the universal gesture of acceptance.

We were passing through a straggling village with its brown buildings of dried red mud and high roofs. Broad-faced infants played in the gutter, and Laurent swerved to avoid a wayward zebu. A crowd of school children clutching tattered notebooks waved and shouted at me happily.

Laurent was silent at the start of the next downhill stretch as we rolled down to the last open expanse of rice paddies. He looked serious.

'But, Henry, we do not complain. God gives us what we need.'

Then he smiled again at me happily and concentrated on overtaking a struggling Citroen van that looked like it had seen the Liberation of France.

The evidence of economic stagnation was everywhere. Half-finished concrete buildings and villas lay off the road. Those that were completed seemed to be trying to outdo each other in high walls, unclimbable fences and daunting metal gates. What could be seen of them suggested nothing more interesting than the standard western dwelling that occurs throughout the tropics.

Gradually the city became clearer, and against the cloudy sky I could distinguish the outline of the spires of the old Queen's palace. Laurent looked at me carefully.

'Are you well, Henry? You look like a man who carries problems.'

'The two worst a man can have, Laurent. Job and woman problems.'

'Ah well, at least it is not sin then.' His dark face wrinkled with wry amusement.

'Not yet, Laurent, not yet.'

Laurent gave me a thoughtful scrutiny and then concentrated on the road as we drove into the chaotic bustle of what was either the last village or the first suburb.

Petrol shortage or not, the traffic in 'Tana was as bad as I remembered, and my admiration for Laurent mounted as he avoided pedestrians and trucks with equal skill.

We swung up past the great edifice of the railway station, still pretending to be part of provincial France at the turn of the century. The main street was as busy as ever as Laurent neatly nipped in between a bus and a Chinese jeep. Then with a burst of acceleration and a few fluid swerves he brought the van to rest next to a battered Renault 4 in front of the Hotel d'Amiens.

'I have arranged for you to be here. It is not the Hilton, but it is OK I think.'

Laurent helped me carry the rucksack and the holdall into the gloomy hallway. There was a cluster of people at the desk. No one seemed to be doing anything. Laurent had a few words with the man behind the desk and came back to me. 'Good, I must get back to the school. I will come back tonight at five. Have a good sleep.'

He shook hands formally with me and left.

I called after him. '*Misaotra*, thank you, Laurent.'

The hotel wasn't much by European standards, being rather dirty and drab, but the patron tolerated my bad French and seemed glad of the business. He didn't even kick up a fuss when I refused to let him keep my passport. The only other occupants seemed to be some sort of Eastern European businessmen. My second-floor room overlooked the square and an overcrowded old building opposite, from which washing was draped. It wasn't too bad—the room locked, the sheets were merely off-white and patched, and the water came in both hot and cold forms. I locked my room door, drew the faded brown curtains against the sunlight, and my last thought before I fell asleep was, 'Well, Stanwick, here you are on a fool's errand at the end of the world.'

16

The next few days passed pleasantly. Although technically midwinter, the weather was mild enough in 'Tana for a thin pullover and a light anorak to suffice. The sun even shone much of the time.

On Friday Laurent was busy at school, so I took things easy and wandered round the market, absorbing the sights of the town. I managed to find some postcards and wrote a couple. On Tina's I couldn't resist putting, 'Wish you were here.' I meant it too. After lunch I walked towards the palace and stopped at the church of Ambotanakanga, which is a vaguely distorted realisation of every Englishman's idea of a parish church, and looked at the missionary gravestones and memorials. In the past I had found them in some way challenging, but today they seemed disturbing and accusatory. Faced with their dedication, my own indecision over Cyprus seemed highlighted. I left sooner than I'd planned and went back to the hotel by a circuitous route and read until Laurent arrived at six o'clock.

The Ranandrianosoas lived in the pastor's house attached to the old church at Antsimonony. Both house and church were built in the 1880s by the London Missionary Society. In Madagascar the architectural era between the reigns of wood and of brick (and later, concrete) was very brief, and the house is one of the few decent stone-built private dwellings in 'Tana. Although now in some disrepair, it was still a solid, noble building altogether appropriate to the ministry that it supported.

We were greeted by Laurent's mother who gave me a large hug and muttered something in heavily-accented French. Laurent's family, as I always called them to avoid use of the word 'Ranandrianosoa' too often, were of the Merina tribe, which is one of the more Asiatic of the many strains of the Malagasy. His mother still maintained some worn vestige of oriental beauty. She was joined by Laurent's father who gave me a beatific welcoming smile. He spoke slowly and quietly. 'Mr Henry, you have honoured us again. Welcome.'

His English preserved something of an older world of leisure, peace and dignity. It crossed my mind that Madagascar was perhaps not only the refuge of otherwise extinct animals, but also otherwise extinct manners.

A number of things should have marred the evening. Laurent's family were poor, and everything—clothes, furniture, and tableware—showed it. Everywhere I looked was some reminder of the awesome gulf between their standard of living and mine. The food too should have spoiled the evening. Doubtless purchased at a sacrificial cost, the stringy meat, beans and rice neither looked nor tasted very edible. The language barrier too should have served to trip up the evening. Only Laurent and his father spoke English well. Anne-Marie, a pretty girl in her mid-twenties, had studied in Moscow and had lost much of her school English. The two teenage boys and Laurent's mother seemed to understand only partially what I said and preferred to speak in French to me. A further problem should have been my own uncertain state; I felt in some way strung out midway between Grantforth and Cyprus, between denial and commitment.

And yet somehow none of it mattered. In fact the evening was a delight and its happy memory helped greatly in the days ahead. Everyone was overjoyed with their presents. To my considerable relief the ladies of the household greeted their gifts with a dignified but genuine happiness and with conspiratorial whispers to each other carefully wrapped the parcels back up again.

We all squeezed round the wobbly table and ate heartily. The conversation hummed along, and with the aid of some skilful and imaginative translation from Laurent everyone seemed to understand everything and we all laughed at each other's jokes. My French even seemed to be restored to an understandable level. Somehow the conversation stayed happy and peaceable, and even when the subject of poverty came up there was no bitterness or sorrow.

After the meal the boys and Anne-Marie stood and sang unaccompanied songs. Time seemed to stand still. Some songs they introduced, others they didn't. Some were hymns, others choruses. They sang beautifully and clearly with evident sincerity and enjoyment. I cannot describe the music; odd bars seemed to be derived from western hymns, but the best I can say is that I felt there was a fusion of African and Indonesian or even Polynesian elements. The Malagasy language with its enormous polysyllabic words must have imposed its own unique constraints on the music. If I understood the tone of the music, then it held no shallow Christian triumphalism, but rather contained within itself simultaneously sorrow and patient hope. The image of the four of them standing beyond the frail table lit only by the single feeble lightbulb and singing with a quiet joy lingers warmly in my mind.

At length Laurent walked down with me to where I could get a taxi. We strolled down the deserted streets in near silence.

'I hope you enjoyed the evening, Henry?'

I thought of a lot that I wanted to say and let it all pass. 'Yes, thank you, very much, very much indeed.'

I groped for a way to express it. 'At times like that, Laurent, I think I understand what heaven is like.'

The remainder of the weekend passed speedily. On the Saturday Laurent and I went down on the train to Antsirabe for the day. Sunday morning I went to church. Pastor Ranandrianosoa preached with vigour, and the large congregation flicked backwards and forwards through their Bibles following his long impassioned exposition. The Hensons would have been in their element, but the zeal seemed to mock me cruelly.

Laurent and I spent the early part of the afternoon visiting some of his student friends in their cramped rooms on campus. The warmth of the greetings was impressive and did much to counter the atmosphere of decay and gloom produced by the shabby rooms and the bare concrete floors with the worst cracks in the walls covered by faded posters or large handwritten Scripture texts.

Four o'clock that afternoon found us in the sanitised and marble-clad interior of the Hilton. Laurent was clearly uneasy, sitting on the edge of his chair and saying little. He looked as if he thought he was going to be thrown out.

Just after four Tim strolled over from the lift in immaculate jeans and a thin pullover carrying a folder. He smiled broadly as he saw us.

'Henry. Well, this is a long way from Grantforth; thanks for coming.'

He grabbed my hand and shook it with the manner of a professional politician. He turned to Laurent standing up diffidently a pace behind me. 'So, the famous Laurent. Good to meet you. I look forward to having you with us.'

Laurent took his hand, shook it and said simply, 'Thank you,' I felt he had only narrowly avoided saying 'sir' as well.

'OK, fellas, let's go grab a table in the bar.'

Tim got a corner table in the virtually empty bar and soon had us organised. He sat opposite us with his glass of beer in front of him and a sheaf of papers and maps from the folder. He seemed totally at ease, and I wondered if there was anywhere in the world where he would not have seemed at home. Well, the pinnacles might just be that place. By contrast Laurent, sitting behind his orange juice, seemed rather like an errant pupil in the headmaster's study. Being in the bar of the Hilton was clearly not his chosen form of Sunday evening entertainment. I stuck to soft drinks to keep him company.

Tim of course started the proceedings. 'We seem to be in

good shape. The flight leaves at nine-fifteen. You guys here by eight prompt. OK?'

'No problem, Tim,' I said. Laurent just nodded.

'Right, let's go over the whole thing. We hit the strip at Antsalova at around ten-thirty. Henry, then what?'

And so for the next two hours we went over the entire trip. We'd done it in parts over the phone, but this was the first time we had covered everything at one go. Laurent paid careful attention and said little except to ask me on occasions for clarification of some colloquialism. Tim didn't make life easy for him with a frequent use of slang and a tendency to speak fast. I admired Laurent for asking. I'd have been tempted just to nod agreement; but Laurent wasn't the sort to indicate assent to anything unless he knew precisely what it was he was promising.

Tim seemed to have contingency plans for every eventuality, and at the end of it all we couldn't see any obvious holes. It was a shame that the helicopter supply drop wasn't on, but I felt that had always been a bit of a pipedream anyway.

Tim invited us to stay to eat. I accepted readily, but I felt Laurent came more out of deference than desire. The food was excellent, but it was one of those occasions which demonstrated that there is more to a meal than food. Tim talked mostly to me, and his conversation with Laurent was curiously clumsy. He ended up saying such things as, 'How many brothers and sisters do you have, Laurent?' It was almost as if it was out of duty and that he had read in a textbook on man management that one should always express interest in the employees. Laurent was quiet and polite, and Tim didn't seem to notice that he was ill at ease. The thought struck me that Laurent looked a bit like Jeeves forced to eat at table with the Woosters, but I was certain that the social awkwardness was based on something far more subtle. During the sweet, Tim raised his glass and looked around at the marble, the wall hangings and the polished wood of the dining room.

'Well, gentlemen, let's drink a farewell to civilisation.'

Laurent and I raised our glasses of juice in a half-hearted gesture. I for one had very strong reservations about the virtues of this particular civilisation. What Laurent felt I could not read in his passive brown face.

As we sat in the taxi on the way back Laurent was evasive about his awkwardness with Tim. He merely said that Mr Vaughan seemed very polite and well-organised. I gave up, and decided that this was clearly one of those situations where Laurent was being a true Malagasy and nothing I could do would allow me to see beneath the surface.

I left him with the taxi and some money to pay the driver and got out at the hotel. It was just after nine and everything was quiet apart from the distant sounds of a radio. This part of 'Tana went to bed early, or at least conducted nocturnal business with the shutters closed.

The patron was sitting back in his chair listening to a radio and drinking beer out of a dirty glass. In the shadows of the hall a not unattractive pair of girls of an ancient profession giggled at me. I ignored them and went over to the desk. The patron reached over his shoulder, pulled out the key from the pigeonhole, and slid it down to me along the desktop with a great economy of motion. I wished him good night and walked up the stairs.

The second-floor corridor was lit only by a tiny bulb, and there seemed to be silence from all the rooms. The hall was so dark at the end by my room that I had great difficulty in finding the lock. I eventually opened it and walked in. A faint smell of cigarette smoke greeted me and for a second I wondered if I was in the right room. As I fumbled for the light switch I put my foot on something. It was soft and squishy. I froze and held my breath; then my scrabbling hand found the switch and there was light. I blinked at the scene.

The room was an absolute wreck. The rucksack lay inverted on the desk; a boot lay on the bed and the other in a corner; the floor was strewn with clothes from overturned drawers. I looked down. I was standing on what was left of a damp bar of soap. Next to it lay the shaving kit and tooth-brush. At the far end of the room the window was open and the curtains blew about slightly. I'd been burgled.

I swore aloud and didn't care who heard. I peeled the soap off my shoe and slung it into the chipped sink where it disturbed a spider busy investigating a sock.

I picked up a notebook from the bed, smoothed the creased pages, and sat down heavily. As I surveyed the devastation I congratulated myself that I'd at least taken one camera and my papers with me.

And yet. There was the other camera on the floor by the bed. I checked it and it seemed in working order. Curious, I thought. Then I realised that my film was all there too, although the cartons had been opened.

At the end of twenty minutes' careful tidying up, I was convinced that nothing had been taken. Everything had been gone over and thrown around, but that was apparently all.

I decided in the end not to call the patron. I didn't really want a summons to the police station at nine-thirty the next morning, and anyway it was all a bit silly. A burglary with nothing taken was a bit like 'a funeral without a body,' to use one of Laurent's expressions. I locked the door and blocked it with a chair and closed the window as tightly as I could. I lay awake for some time thinking about it all. Someone had been looking for something, but who and for what? Any Malagasy would hardly have left the camera, the compass and the first-aid kit with its locally unobtainable medicaments. I was starting to consider the possibility of some supernatural agency and wondering what the French for poltergeist was, when a thought struck me. I got out of bed and searched the room carefully again.

There was no doubt about it. The one missing item was the bushknife.

17

After the disturbing events of the night before it was a welcome relief to find that everything went well on the Monday. I got up early and took a taxi out to the Ranandrianosoas' house. Laurent's father answered the door, and while Laurent collected his things I handed over for safekeeping a holdall of the clothes I would not be needing in the pinnacles. Then, after fond farewells, we drove back down to the Hilton. The whole procedure would have been a lot easier if Laurent's father had had a car, but that was an undreamt of luxury. Tim was waiting. He had already loaded a taxi, and it was full to overflowing by the time we had all got in. I just hoped the plane had enough room.

Somehow it had, although the penalty was that we sat with rucksacks on our laps for the hour-long flight. The Twin Otter was full, and I didn't get a chance to take any photos out of the window. That was a pity because someone in Soil Science had asked me to get some good slides of the soil erosion which is, sadly, a Malagasy national speciality.

Shortly after ten-thirty we were shaking off the dust deposited on us by the departing plane and looking round the deserted airstrip.

'You sure this is the right place, Henry?'

There was more curiosity than any real doubt in Tim's voice. Fair enough, I thought, he's paid a small fortune to see spectacular scenery and he's ended up on something that looks about as dramatic as the Cotswolds and a lot less pretty. I looked at him and felt slightly pleased to see that the red laterite dust had stuck to the beads of sweat on Tim's face, giving him a bizarre form of freckles. For the first time he was beginning to look human.

'Have you got your binoculars? If you look over there you should see the edge of them.'

I pointed eastwards beyond the edge of the sandstone escarpment.

Tim dug into his own rucksack and pulled out a pair of large green German binoculars. They looked new. With the naked eye you could see the edge of the forest that marched north-south across the horizon like some defensive line.

'See the forest beyond this grassland? If you look down towards the south you should see the pale grey rock coming through. That's the edge of the pinnacles proper.'

He swung the binoculars along in a practised gesture and grunted.

After a bit he spoke. 'OK, if it's still as we planned I'll stick with the gear while you guys run on down to the village and get us some help.'

'You sure you don't want to see the sights of Antsalova, Tim?'

'Nope. I'll give it a miss this time round.'

So Laurent and I left Tim under a battered mimosa tree sitting on the baggage. A crowd of respectful children had gathered and were sitting about ten yards away. Laurent had a word with them and spoke briefly with Tim.

'Will they be all right?' I asked Laurent as we set off down the dusty road to the town.

'No doubt. I've told them to keep at least three metres away from the baggage.'

'What did you say to Tim?'

He looked a bit sheepish. 'I told him that they might be curious, but that they were very gentle.'

'I would have thought he would have seen that.'

'Perhaps, Henry, but I did not want him to misunderstand them. I'm afraid I do not really understand your friend. I hope I will know him better before we finish this trip.'

I felt he was tempted to say something else, but he didn't.

On the long dusty walk down I nearly told Laurent about my visitor the night before, but decided against it. I felt it would have upset him as he had found me the hotel, and anyway there was nothing that important lost by it. It took nearly three-quarters of an hour to walk into Antsalova, and we had gathered quite a crowd of children during the last half mile.

It might have been possible to be optimistic about Antsalova but for the evidence of the past. It was difficult to close your eyes to the rotting concrete buildings with their rusting corrugated roofs or the eroded French milestones under the eucalyptus trees. The tiny rundown office of the Gendarmerie had on its wall a yellowing poster version of the highway code for drivers. Although in Malagasy, the cartoons on it involved bustling city traffic of a France of the 1950s. In the hour we spent in Antsalova we didn't see a single car.

The two young officers there looked lost. They seemed to be administrative flotsam, washed up by the high tide of bureaucracy and now left behind as everything fell to pieces. Laurent laid on the charm with them, and they talked leisurely while I practised making the children laugh by pulling faces. At length an officer called a young boy in and sent him off running.

Laurent turned to me. 'No problem. They have sent for three men who will probably come with us.'

So we waited for a few minutes, and the boy came back followed by three men who seemed to be in their midtwenties. After a lot of haggling and sketching rudimentary maps in the dust there was agreement. The men hurried off.

Laurent came over to me. 'Excellent. I think they will do. They are coming back after ten minutes.' He paused. 'Ten minutes Malagasy time.'

He looked happy, doubtless very relieved at being able to get the men so quickly. 'Henry, I think it would be an idea to get something to drink for these policemen.'

So someone went and got four bottles of lemonade from

the Pakistani shopkeeper. It was outrageously priced, dusty, and had a curious aftertaste, but I quite enjoyed it. The gendarmes evidently found it acceptable. Eventually, after twenty minutes, the men returned and we all shook hands and said our farewells.

Tim was sitting where we had left him. He had not been idle. Three large rucksacks lay on the ground, and there was a pile of loose items piled in front of him. The children had edged only a fraction closer. Tim seemed to have adopted a policy of ignoring them.

'Everything OK? Great. Well, I guess you guys had better eat and then we will be off.'

This was a bit too fast for Laurent, who was still making introductions. The men gave a half-bow, and each in turn clasped Tim's hastily outstretched hand with both hands.

'This local handshake looks a pretty efficient way of transmitting disease,' Tim whispered to me out of the side of his mouth.

'Possibly. Actually I think we ought to give these guys some food too. They'll be able to carry for longer on a meal.' Tim agreed with a nod of his head, but there was a fraction of a second's delay.

It took half an hour to eat some of the dehydrated foil-packed items we had and to pack up the rucksacks. Everybody's bag was packed to capacity, and I wondered how the Malagasy porters would take the load.

Tim came over to me as I was adjusting the straps on a rucksack.

'What do we do about the trash?' He pointed to the empty foil packs piled up by me under the tree.

'Nothing, you just watch.'

I picked up my bag, walked away from the rubbish, and with a gesture indicated it was for the taking. There was a sudden mad rush from the children as they dived for the foil. In a few seconds the winners were running around waving their empty aluminium packs.

I glanced at Tim. He was genuinely nonplussed. 'Well, I'll be . . . That certainly is remarkable.'

'There's no waste here, Tim. Metal is rare.'

Tim stared at the children again and shrugged. Then he called out to Laurent and the porters. 'OK, troops, let's roll!'

Without waiting to see the results of his order he started walking along the track southwards. This caught everyone off balance and he was a full fifty yards away before Laurent had got his pack on. The three porters hadn't even got to the stage of working out which was top and which was bottom of their packs. Eventually, to the accompaniment of shouts from the children, we set off. I told Laurent to take a gentle pace and set off to try to catch up with Tim.

Within ten minutes or so the pattern had been set. Tim led the way, setting a good marching pace and periodically stopping to check his map or compass. Laurent and the three porters brought up the rear, plodding along at a more steady rate. I moved backwards and forwards between front and rear, trying to temper Tim's pace and keep an eye on the porters. Fortunately, the ground was easy as we kept to a gently undulating dusty track. The thin patchy grass either side of the road was already turning brown, although the rains couldn't have finished more than six weeks ago. The odd clump of trees here or there did little to relieve the rather monotonous terrain.

And so the afternoon went on. Each little rise we crossed showed the green smear of the forest edge nearer. Eventually the white rocks beneath them could just be made out to the naked eye, but it wasn't much to get excited about.

As the afternoon began to wane, plumes of smoke could be seen to the south and north of us as the grassland was set alight. Tim asked Laurent for the reason, and he explained that it was done by the farmers as it was supposed to help bring new grass for the zebu. Tim protested that it must wipe out the wildlife. Laurent agreed and said that in theory it was banned, but this was a long way from 'Tana, and anyway it wasn't easy to enforce it. Shortly afterwards one lot of fires was close enough to see the circling kites hovering to the windward of flames to pick up anything that tried to outrun the fire. I caught Tim staring and shaking his head in apparent sorrow.

The only other wildlife apart from two small lizards and a few birds were the notorious zebu flies. Discovering that however hard you slapped them they just came back, Tim rapidly evolved a method of putting his hand over them and rubbing vigorously. As he pointed out, 'They sure don't come back after that.' But he was very glad to hear that they were only found near cattle and shouldn't be accompanying us through the pinnacles.

Every so often we stopped for water and a look at the map. Tim seemed happy enough and was clearly pleased with our progress. Every time we stopped he went over to Laurent to check on the status of the porters. His concern wasn't over-sentimental, but it was business-like and there was no question of him pushing them too fast. At any rate sentimentality or affection was not a term that I had come to associate with Tim. It struck me that it would be interesting to know more about his family background. I didn't know, for example, whether he had ever been married. However, it also occurred to me with some force that trying to fathom out Tim Vaughan wasn't likely to be successful if I wasn't even capable of sorting out my own life.

One gratifying point was that the relationship between him and Laurent seemed to be thawing a little. I began to wonder if the problems had been as much to do with the setting in which the previous night's meeting had taken place rather than the people.

After a while Tim decided to break off the track and head south to the Beboka stream whose tortuous passage through the pinnacles we planned to follow. It was nearly five o'clock when we stood on the flat river bank above its muddy waters. As arranged, the porters took their leave and headed off to the village nearby where they apparently had relatives. They had promised to return at dawn. Tim showed Laurent and me how to put up the three tiny tents. We did that and set up the fancy water filtering unit for stream water while Tim started the cooking.

I was interested to see if Tim showed any evidence of being skilled in bushcraft. In fact Tim's performance here was perfectly adequate without being virtuoso. He decided to save on our precious fuel by lighting a fire, a feat he managed with speed and economy. Clearly his keenness for computers and technology hadn't caused the loss of some of the more basic skills of civilisation. It was encouraging; where we were going, bushcraft would count for a lot more than an ability to get two computers to talk to each other.

Darkness fell with its usual rapidity for those latitudes, and by half six it was pitch dark. In comparison to the amount Laurent and I ate, Tim consumed only a frugal amount of food. As we quietly sat drinking hot strong coffee around the embers of the fire I felt reasonably happy. We had made excellent progress, and none of the many things that could have gone wrong had done so. We stood within three miles of the edge of the pinnacles. Laurent had thoroughly vindicated my support of him, and there were signs that the relationship between him and Tim would turn out to be satisfactory if not fraternal.

At length Tim roused himself from an inscrutable reverie.

'Well, guys, congratulations. We've come a long way faster than I'd dared hope. In fact we are going to have to decide whether we can get through the first line of pinnacles by tomorrow evening instead of day three. At any rate, I'm going to walk round the campsite, take a look at the stars, and then crash out.'

He took his torch and set off through the grass to the top of the little rise. I turned to Laurent. 'You're happy, Laurent?'

'*Mais oui*, why not, my friend? I am here with you again. It is good.'

There was a certain hesitancy, so I prodded.

' But . . . ?'

There was a pause. 'I am uncomfortable about Mr Tim, Henry. I do not understand him. Perhaps it is simply that you are the only real foreigner I know well. You I understand—well, most of the time. You are my brother. Mr Tim I do not understand at all. Why is he here?'

'Laurent, I do not know. His story is that he is interested in exploring. But what drives him I do not know. Perhaps he wants to find something.'

'Or lose it perhaps.'

We fell silent as the torch came nearer, swinging this way and that. Rather to my surprise Tim did not return the way he left, but walked a complete circuit of the camp, stopping at intervals. Finally he returned to us.

'See anything, boss?' I called as he came into the circle of firelight.

'Nope, not a thing. Was I supposed to? No, just force of habit. I was once ambushed down in Mexico. I like to walk around a campsite at night.' He spoke to the dim figure of Laurent. 'So my friend, Laurent, no bandits here?'

'No, Mr Tim. Not now. I checked with the police. Maybe if the rice runs short this year.'

'I hope you're right. Incidentally, Henry, how come I don't see the stars clearly? I've seen better in Houston.'

"Fraid you got the answer this afternoon, Tim. The old slash and burn agriculture puts so much dust up in the atmosphere that things are generally poor for star gazing.'

'Great—seems like you can't win. Get industry and you have industrial pollution. No industry and you have agricultural pollution. Oh well, it's not my problem. At least not tonight. Night, all.'

Laurent and I followed shortly. The tents were very impressive. There was little headroom, but they weighed only a couple of pounds and were convincingly mosquito-proof.

Despite tiredness I lay awake for some time thinking about Cyprus and trying to sort out my feelings. There was no doubt that I was feeling very negative about going. The conclusion I came to before drifting off to sleep was that if nothing else happened on this trip to change my mind I would turn down George Roumian's offer.

18

The next morning I awoke stiff and cold, with condensation dripping down on me from the inside of the tent. I could hear Tim whistling something rather tuneless which sounded as if it had originated in an airport lounge. I crawled carefully out of the tent and slipped on my pullover. A thick mist covered everything, and there was dew on the grass. Laurent was tending the fire and, despite wearing everything he had, looked chilled.

Tim was concentrating on cooking breakfast and gave me only the briefest of grins before turning back to reconstituted omelette. I noted that he cooked breakfast as he seemed to do everything else, with care and dedication. He called over his shoulder to me.

'Good morning, Doctor Stanwick. I trust you had a good night. Breakfast will shortly be served.'

Breakfast and coffee fortified me a bit. Tim kept looking at his watch. It was seven o'clock and although the mist was still lingering, somewhere to the east over the pinnacles the sun had clearly risen.

'Hey, Laurent, where are your boys?'

Laurent looked at the mist. 'They may have got lost in this.'

'Lost? I thought they were experienced in the bush?' Tim raised a curious eyebrow.

The last word was lost on Laurent, and I felt obliged to speak. 'They don't live here, Tim. Anyway, this isn't Africa proper. There's nothing much to hunt and these guys don't do any stalking, other than the odd lost zebu. They don't have any tracking skills as such.'

'I guess I hadn't thought of that. Just as well we've got maps, eh?'

Just then there was shouting, and our three porters came running down through the thinning mist. 'OK. Let's get the camp packed up.'

By nine o'clock the mist had lifted and the sun was burning on our backs. I was still feeling stiff, but the proximity of the pinnacles was encouraging. Whatever lay ahead, it would be more than straight foot slogging. We walked on the edge above the river to avoid having to battle through the trees that hugged its banks. It grew warm. For some time we dropped down below a low ridge and could see nothing ahead. Eventually we left the river and began slowly to climb it. I was so busy watching my feet on the stony ground that I almost walked into Tim who had suddenly stopped. I looked up and caught my breath.

There, lying out before us, lay the great stone fields of the pinnacles. A few hundred yards ahead the abrupt dark line of trees began, rooted in the first cracks of the limestone. Behind them, as the cracks broadened, the trees thinned out, growing ever more precariously only on the tops of the intervening blocks. Beyond them was a region which stretched into the misty distance where no soil remained. There rocks alone endured, standing in bare, grey, naked spires and towers. As the eye focused, it could be seen that each jagged block was made up of pinnacles, each in turn made of smaller spires. Although I had seen similar views before of this region, it still produced a powerful effect. The whole thing was as if some power had given the rocks life and they had grown into infinitely multiplied copies of pine trees, producing what the Chinese called so appositely a 'stone forest.' In this light the impression was of something weird but benign. I had a faint suspicion that in different lights and positions that impression might well be changed.

'I'm impressed, Henry. I really am. That place is something.'

There was a trace of genuine awe in Vaughan's voice. Was it tinged with misgiving?

'Still want to do it, Tim?'

He paused and scanned the horizon. 'I tell you, Henry, I'm sure glad I decided not to do it on my own.'

We took a brief break while he took some photographs. His camera equipment was in keeping with his binoculars; expensive, brand-new and well-chosen for the trip.

We loaded on our packs again and cut southwards, parallel to the fault that so abruptly ended the limestone. Tim was plainly anxious to waste no more time. I guessed that he was keen to try to make it through the first line of rocks to the flat area we had designated the Cricket Pitch. I could only speculate about the path to it along the tortuous trail of the Beboka stream. My feeling was that we would be pushed to get through the first line of pinnacles before nightfall. If we failed to do that, then finding a dry site with enough space for three tents and full packs in the narrow crevasses was not going to be easy.

It was nearly eleven when we moved down through the trees and long spikey grass into the stream valley. We rounded a corner on the sandy river bank and suddenly ahead of us, framed by tall overhanging trees, the river valley ended.

Cutting across the path of the stream was a great wall of pure pale-grey limestone the height of a two-storey house. It was rent from top to bottom in three places to give dark fissures from which creepers issued. In front lay a sprawled pile of loose blocks, the smallest of which was car-sized. From the foot of this mass issued water in a number of small tired flows. The effect, even in bright sunlight, was daunting. I tried to ignore the impression of four colossal broken teeth that came to mind.

The noise of heated Malagasy made me turn round. Laurent was apparently trying to appease the porters who were speaking to him with some force. I went over to him. All I could understand was him repeating the Malagasy negative, '*Tsia, tsia.*' He caught my eye.

'Henry, they want to go. Can Mr Tim pay them off now?'

I called Tim back from his photography. 'Tim, the locals seem to have had enough of our company. I think we should just pay them off now.'

'Sure, I didn't intend taking them any further anyway.'

He called out towards the animated group. 'Hey, Laurent, what's all the fuss?'

Laurent seemed too busy placating the men to answer Tim's question, but whether that was an excuse or not I do not know. In a very short time the porters had piled the three rucksacks up on the sand bank. Tim counted out the crumpled green 500 Malagasy franc notes, and amid what seemed profuse expressions of gratitude they turned and disappeared from view.

Laurent seemed confused about their reasons for getting upset. Eventually we got it out of him that they had thought that we were taking them on in beyond the stone wall.

Tim looked at me and nodded knowingly. 'Well, what an unadventurous lot. Still, it encourages me to believe that any cache of supplies we leave around in there will be safe.'

After washing the sweat off our faces in the stream we sorted out the rucksacks. The plan was that we would store one with the supplies for the trip back to Antsalova. The remainder of the supplies we would carry in three overfull rucksacks on to the Cricket Pitch where we would make a base camp.

We sat on the sandbank under the shade of the overhanging trees and had an early and rather hasty lunch. Then, carrying the spare rucksack between us we set off. Scrabbling over the polished fallen blocks was not easy with the extra load, but we did it, and within a few minutes we stood in front of the wall of rock.

'Well, Tim, your first decision: right, left or centre fissures?'

'Centre, I think.' He spoke thoughtfully. Then with a faint, vaguely ceremonial gesture he turned round briefly to us and the green, living world behind us. 'Well, gentlemen, here we go.' And he stepped into the fissure.

Cautiously we followed. The central crack was wide enough to take a man with a rucksack and it ran straight. The cool dampness of the crevasse was refreshing. Despite the trees overhanging high above, the cleft was not particularly dark; indeed it was rather restful after the glare of the strong sun. A short way ahead a brilliant shaft of light penetrated the crevasse. A few yards in I turned round and gave a brief backwards glance at the framed fragment of river and the innocent green of the trees. Then Laurent tugged on the spare rucksack and we moved on.

The walls were polished smooth. We were able with some care to keep our feet dry; wet soles on smooth rock wouldn't make for a good grip. We kept moving on. After about ten yards the height of the walls above us rose, and the sky became only a thin band of blue some thirty feet above us. The crevasse lightened rapidly, and we were out into sunlight. But not open space.

It was the first junction. A five-foot-wide crevasse running north-south intersected ours forming crossroads. Despite its width it became blocked either way within yards, although there seemed to be other avenues off. High above us stood the trees in every direction. The sense of being enclosed came upon me.

Tim spoke first. 'I feel like a rat in a trench. Which way now, Henry?'

'Nowhere yet, Tim. Lecture time from Dr Stanwick. Let's sort out the rules for this.'

I spoke firmly and decisively. I'd been thinking about this for months. High above us a kite flew across the crevasse. I took off the creaking rucksack from my back and pulled out a thick red marker pen.

'OK. As soon as we leave a crevasse we stop and turn round and make an arrow marking the way back. Thus.' I made a simple arrow pointing back down the crevasse we had come from. 'About eye height on the right-hand side of the avenue we came along. We always do it. There are no exceptions, never!'

I paused for effect. 'I suggest that each day someone is appointed as responsible for marking and someone for double-checking him. We just cannot afford to forget. As a safety check the remaining person should keep a very simple sketch map of the direction taken.'

I pulled out a field notebook and began at the top of the first page. Vaughan was leaning back against the wall of rock and watching carefully, his blue denim baseball cap tilted back on his head.

'Nice stuff, Henry. It seems you want to get us back in one piece. Better than a ball of thread anyday.'

Along one of the lateral branches we found a large crack about five feet off the ground and stowed the spare supplies, after having wrapped the whole bag in polythene.

Then, laden only by our own rucksacks, we set off again. The next hour was astonishingly frustrating. We advanced up one crevasse to find it narrow out into nothing. Tim suggested we scale it. He tried to climb, but found that a few feet above the sandy crevasse base the limestone ceased to be waterworn and smooth. Rather it became scalloped with minute sharp ribs that threatened to cut careless hands to pieces.

We retraced our steps and tried another avenue. This one ended in a near-circular pit open only to the blue sky. Again we had to return along our path. Tim was continuously looking at his watch and working out the rate of progress. It was pretty desperate. He looked at me with a frown.

'My guess is we haven't made more than a hundred yards in from the edge in an hour and a half. I don't see us making it to your Cricket Pitch before sunset.'

'Tim, this stuff is unpredictable, at least to me. I'm working on it though. But we could easily get a long straight stretch and double our distance in ten minutes.'

'Well, let's hope so.'

To my relief so it proved. We got into a large fissure that kept going for a hundred yards or more. Eventually it started to become slightly filled in, and the vegetation began to give us problems.

'Tim, this is leading us too far south. We must keep parallel to the stream or we'll never get clear tonight.'

As I spoke there was a raucous grating noise from the trees above, and something white and doglike jumped across the skyline. Laurent spoke. 'Sifaka.'

Vaughan glanced curiously up, his face sweat-stained. The smooth polished man in a 500-dollar suit who'd visited my office six months ago was becoming hard to recognise.

'The large white lemurs, Tim.'

'Well, I missed them, but I guess we'll see them again. I suppose you're right, Henry, about turning off; this stuff is more disorientating than I thought.' He spoke curiously slowly as if absorbed in something else.

The next hour brought slow but steady progress. I wondered if we were getting better at recognising the signs of the dead-end fissures and avoiding them. One encouraging sign was that we were encountering more water, suggesting that we were getting closer to the main stream. This brought its own problems. Increasingly we found ourselves having to wade along the bottom of water-filled crevasses. At one point we came to a ten-yard stretch where the way was blocked by a pool of water of unknown depth. Tim waded in and was thigh-deep in sand and water before he gave up.

At about four o'clock we stopped by unspoken agreement and sat down on a tiny patch of dry sand. There was no need to worry about shade now; the sun angle was such that only the trees thirty feet up on the tops of the blocks were in direct sunlight. The result of our deliberations was that if we did not find a way through in the next half-hour we would be forced to bivouac overnight where we could.

We went on. Tiredness hung heavy on all of us, and

increasingly we stumbled and slid against the walls of rock. The shadows gathered. Once I forgot to mark the turning we had come out of and had to go back twenty yards to do it. Tim came with me to double-check; a procedure I felt rather unnecessary, but I didn't argue.

Then, finally, as we were about to give up, the fissure ahead suddenly opened up. Beyond it was a vista of a broad sandy river bank and a bare scrubby knoll behind it. In contrast to the view of rock walls that had faced us all afternoon, it seemed a blissfully unlimited perspective.

In this last stretch the crevasse was flooded, and we had to wade in knee-deep water. Out of the crevasses we sank down on the river bank. Laurent said something in Malagasy which didn't need translating; it was clearly a prayer of thanks.

As I had remembered the place from the brief helicopter landing last year it was a pleasant spot. Compared with what we had been through and doubtless would go through it was positively idyllic. The westwards-flowing river here looped into a sizeable meander as though reluctant to enter the last line of the pinnacles. It was even large enough here to swim in if you had been so minded. The river bank formed a broad crescent-shaped sandy expanse the size of a tennis court. To the north and south lay a scrubby wood which ran rapidly up to cliffs of limestone.

Eastwards the sands passed up on to the rocky rise we had glimpsed from the fissures. Only by the standards of the pinnacles could it even have jokingly been termed a cricket pitch.

I had expected Vaughan to put the tents up immediately despite the yellowing light that foretold the imminent plunge into darkness. He didn't. Rather he called me over.

'Henry, I want to check out the sand here for any tracks before we trample all over it. Wanna come?'

'Tracks? Like what?'

He looked slightly evasive. There was a slight flicker of the eyelids. 'Heck, if we are going to cache our supplies here we want to be sure that there is nobody else around.'

An outrageous thought crossed my mind, and I threw it out instantly; things were tough enough without thinking stupid things like that. I forced myself to think about something else. 'OK. I'll come. I want to watch out for crocodile tracks, especially around something we'll use as a washing place.'

Crocodiles share the persecuted status of all wildlife in Madagascar, but they do turn up in even the most isolated pools, and it doesn't hurt to keep an eye open for signs of their presence.

The light was fading rapidly when we returned. There were lots of tracks of birds, small reptiles, and small mammals, but nothing that indicated the presence of crocodiles. Or of other human beings.

As I lay in my tent that night in the brief quietness before sleeping, I found it somewhat disturbing that the three of us were cut off from the rest of human society by the maze of stone we had been through. It wasn't helped by the realisation that our safe return hinged on the recognition of almost insignificant markings on those vast rock walls.

What really disturbed me was the thought that I had had on the sandbank about Tim which had come back in all its ugliness. I tried to tell myself it was simply the effect of the day's efforts or that it was a psychological response to the threatening landscape. But however hard I tried to exorcise it or reason it away, it would not vanish.

Could I be absolutely certain that all Tim Vaughan's discipline and precision did not just cover some deep-seated mental instability?

19

Next morning my doubts had vanished. I woke to find both Laurent and Tim up and washed. The sun was already beating the mist away from the river bank.

The campsite was a mess. The rucksacks and supplies lay scattered here and there and the drooping tents showed the signs of being pitched hastily under darkness. To my surprise Tim was limping slightly.

'An old football injury—I must have pulled it yesterday and it's stiffened over night. It'll be all right if I can rest it a bit.'

After a leisurely breakfast in the shade of a tree we sat around and talked over the plans for the route ahead. Two choices presented themselves: to cut straight across the pinnacles along the shortest point or to follow the meandering river. Both had their advantages, but we concluded that there was too little data to make an accurate assessment. Eventually, we somehow agreed that Laurent and I would check out the start of both routes. In the meantime Vaughan would sort out the food into that which we would cache here and that which we would take with us.

So at about ten Laurent and I set off from the camp. It was pleasant to walk with a light rucksack. Our first move was to stroll to the rubbly and rock-strewn top of the flat-topped rise that made the Cricket Pitch proper. To the west we could look across to the wall of pinnacles through which we had come. From the limited height of our vantage point we could not see beyond them. To the south and east the jagged spires began again in apparently endless lines of tortured shapes a few score yards away. Northwards the course of the Beboka could be briefly followed upstream before it was lost in the jumble of rock.

The effect was strangely exhilarating in the bright clear morning light, giving an irresistible impression of being in another world. It seemed that Laurent and I stood alone on a small island of turf in a frozen grey ocean of stone breakers. With this view I could see that my technical prose for the article hadn't really done the place justice. It did indeed seem 'a heart of stone.'

We walked down to the river to try our first foray beyond the Cricket Pitch. We had to push our way through spikey shrubs and tall grass to get down to the edge. The river had cut a gorge at this point, and we stood on the rock banks some twenty to thirty feet above the deep, quietly turbulent water. This was no straight-sided gorge, but rather one where great rock pillars cut across and inter-fingered to give the stream a tortuous zig-zag path. Beneath the stone walls the water flowed deep and swirling. Here and there were deep shadow-filled cavities in which leaves and small twigs spun endlessly. I'm a dull soul really when it comes to landscape and not given to Wordsworthian frissons over daffodils and vernal woods. But this was an odd place, and it felt darker and more mysterious than the mere elements would suggest.

Laurent and I backed off some way up the flanks of the slope and finding reasonably flat and smooth rocks sat there quietly in the sun. Small brown lizards scuttled away across the sheer faces of the gorge, oblivious of the sheer drop into the swirling waters beneath them.

We looked at the way ahead to the east. While the gorge was clearly impassable here, at the bottom level it looked as though it was relatively short-lived and that within a few hundred yards upstream we would be into a broader valley. I turned to Laurent.

'Well, Laurent, what do you think?'

'Maybe it is not possible this way.' He peered along the

gorge. 'Besides, Henry, one slip on the edge of such a valley and . . . *c'est fini*. But maybe it can be done.'

'You are doubtful that we should try to go ahead with this foolish business?' It was meant as a question, but it came out as a statement.

Laurent looked uneasy for a moment, and then he gave a deep smile. 'I am being stupid, my friend. I am very glad to be here with you and to be doing this. I believe it is the right thing for me.'

Whether it was my imagination or my conscience I do not know, but I felt there was a definite emphasis on the phrase 'for me'.

'So you think we should set up a business, eh? Laurent and Henry; guided tours round the pinnacles?'

He laughed with a clear honest laugh. 'No, no, my brother. I think I will do this now, once, but I do not feel it a calling, a vocation. No, I have a real job to do. This is some help for a friend.'

I noted that he hadn't mentioned the money. It occurred to me that he probably would have come without that anyway. 'Laurent, will you stay at your school?'

There was a shy secret smile on his face. 'I think so. I did not tell you in 'Tana but I was given an offer of a new job this year.'

'Doing what?'

'An American mission wanted to start a work here— medicine and education. They wanted a Malagasy Director. Anyway, it was interesting but not right. I refused it. My mother nearly hit me, but what could I do?'

Laurent seemed to find the whole thing wryly amusing. I didn't.

I found a small pebble and threw it across into the gorge. I could well guess the battle: a job in dollars, foreign travel, a house, even a car.

'A difficult decision.' My voice came out gruff and harsh.

I was beginning to feel that there was unfair pressure

being put on me. My own decision was tough enough without this example of saintliness to follow. I decided to change the subject. 'What do you think about Mr Tim?'

Laurent's face assumed a look of impenetrable blandness. 'I am afraid I do not have a good feeling about Mr Tim.' He paused.

'Continue.'

'He seems a funny tourist. I think he is false. In what way I do not know. I do not think he is a danger to us, though. To himself maybe.' He spoke with pauses between the sentences.

I thought for a moment and shrugged my shoulders. 'What evidence have you got?'

'None, my friend. Except . . .' Laurent showed a trace of embarrassment. 'You remember I have told you how before I was converted I used to be in a gang. First football and then the kung fu foolishness. Then I never trusted anybody. Mr Tim is the same. He watches you all the time. Me he ignores.'

If I had not been feeling vaguely irritated with Laurent for being so virtuous I might have paid more attention to his observations. Instead I dismissed them.

'He's an American, Laurent. I never understood them anyway. In fact I don't really understand myself. Your problem, Laurent, is that you are too straight. Your honest Malagasy soul doesn't understand the rest of the world that has problems.'

I didn't mean it to be a rebuke, but I suppose that's what it must have come out like.

He paused, looked at me rather oddly, and then spoke quietly. 'Perhaps, you may be right.'

At that point I decided it was time to head on, so we got to our feet. To the west we could see Tim limping around the camp. I waved and called and he turned and waved nonchalantly back. We walked up the river for about an hour. It looked possible, but there were obviously going to be some difficult parts where it would be necessary to climb up and cut round through the pinnacles. It was a relief to know that we had some climbing rope with us, if only to hoist the bags with.

We stopped eventually in the shadow of a house-high cliff over which the stream flowed. Where the water splashed over, the damp had given rise to blocks of green moss on which a host of small butterflies hovered. During the rains the river would have been spectacular here. Now, only two months into the dry season, it was already withered to a fraction of its recent strength, and there was only enough for a good shower.

After lunch we set off back down the stream and at the edge of the Cricket Pitch cut off to the south to try to assess the possibility of a direct route through the pinnacles. In every respect it was even more spectacular than the stream route. Instead of the water-smoothed masses of the stream valley, the surfaces of these spikes were irregular and scalloped with sharp edges that threatened to gash fingers. Each great limestone block seemed like an enormous flint knife, and here too the crevasses were different from anything we had met before. They were narrower and wound about more so that being at the bottom was even more oppressive. In places the crevasses were so narrow that twenty feet above you could have stepped across them while the floors of the clefts were mostly a rock groove—so restricted that it threatened to grip the ankles. What did give rise to great concern was the way the crevasse floor would suddenly drop down to another level anywhere from a foot to ten feet below. In one dark narrow spot there was no visible evidence of how far below us was the next level. A dropped stone rattled down for over a second.

Much of the time we were in cool, humid shadow. Above us there was little to see beyond interminable walls of stone except the stream of blue sky or the miniature matterhorns of the pinnacle peaks. Climbing up for a view was beyond question.

We hadn't gone more than fifty yards in, a mere two junctions, before Laurent was looking at me as if to say, 'Do you really want to go on?' I ignored his glance and pressed on.

At the next junction I paused in some unease. Was I still going in the right direction? I checked the compass. There were two possible cracks I could take. As I weighed up the merits of each I found I was turning round frequently. Why? I asked myself. The answer was plain; to be sure Laurent was still with me. Not that he was likely to run off. After a minute I gave up.

'OK, Laurent, let's get out. This is impossible. We could wander here for months.'

There was a nasty moment on the way back. For a few long horrible seconds I couldn't find the red marking arrow. We must have somehow taken a wrong turning. I could feel my heart beating. I turned round, but the grey walls rose above and behind. I began trying to think of strategies to get out, but at the same time I could feel my intellect being engulfed by a rapidly rising tide of fear. Just as I felt my mind beginning to give under the weight of panic Laurent pointed out the red slash.

In a few minutes we were out into the sun, and the open roughness of the Cricket Pitch felt very good. I gave Laurent a gentle slap on the back and grinned at him.

'Well, that settles that, Laurent, my friend. I think we will take the river route. It may be tough, but I do not think we can get lost.'

The panic had had one good effect. It had washed out of my mind any resentment against Laurent. The causes of my annoyance with him seemed trivial in comparison with being stuck in the labyrinth.

Tim was lying out in the shade when we arrived. He got to his feet to welcome us. His stiffness seemed to have all but gone. 'Great to see you guys. I'll just have tea on now. How'd it go?'

Over tea we discussed our plans, and Tim—rather reluctantly I felt—agreed that perhaps the river route would be best.

'Anyway, I haven't been idle. I've sorted out all the food into what we will need for the next stage, and that leaves a surplus we can cache here to use on the way back out.'

Tim gestured carelessly to four piles of plastic-wrapped packages under the tree. Three to take with us, one to cache here. It didn't look like a great surplus to me, but I suppose it only had to do us a day or so.

Laurent got up and hefted the packages in turn. Vaughan was watching him carefully. 'I spent some time redistributing the load; I hope it's to your satisfaction.'

Laurent gave him a peculiar look and nodded. 'It is good. No, I was just thinking how much all this weighed. We are not used to this sort of food. It is remarkable. But I suppose we need water for it all?'

'Yup, that's the problem with dehydration. Can't keep too far away from water. Anyway, what do you fancy for supper?'

While Tim was down at the stream edge refilling the water-filtering unit, I saw Laurent walk over to the rubbish pile. I pretended not to notice as he picked up two used torch batteries and stuck them in the pocket of his tattered trousers. I felt embarrassed and half looked away. Out of the corner of my eye I watched as he carefully emptied his torch of batteries and replaced them with the two he had picked up. He switched the torch on and cupping his hand round the lens he squinted at the feeble gleam. He seemed satisfied and, pulling them out, stuck them in his rucksack. I thought unhappily that this about summed up the Third World; we throw away without a thought what is still valuable to them.

We ate well that evening—a leisurely meal around a proper fire. Here, away from the burning grassland, the stars seemed clearer. At dusk, great fruit bats could be seen flying slowly out from some hidden lair in the trees on their inaccessible heights. We sat or lolled on the sand while Tim told stories of camping expeditions he'd been on. Alaska, Nepal, Kilimanjaro, the Andes. It was rather a monologue, but it was interesting and it was pleasant to hear him talk. He seemed to have genuine affection for wild places, but he remained the same low-key Tim.

I thought to myself that there was no passion in it all. My mind was wandering as I listened in the flickering firelight. I wondered if Tim had made some strange satanic bargain where he could see all the kingdoms of all the world if he forswore passion.

Suddenly, I realised that even as I was thinking about it Tim was talking with anger and bitterness. 'That was twenty years ago. Then the state built a new road. What happened? You guessed it! Everybody and his wife came up in their Winnebagos. Soon you couldn't move for motels, flashing lights, drive-in cinemas, retirement homes. There were so many trippers they had to build a dam and a power station. Oh, and an airstrip so they could fly over the wilderness and ruin what peace was left. I went back once ten years ago and swore never again. Now I won't go near the place. It's ruined, finished. The elk are gone. The bears live off the trash. The people were just greedy. They thought they could have their cake and eat it; that they could keep a wilderness and yet market it. So they let everybody in and they've ended up with a glorified wasteland. So much for the twentieth century.'

I looked at him. He caught my glance and stopped in full flood. 'What the heck. Ain't no point in getting worked up about it all. I guess it's time for bed.'

As he strolled down to the stream, brushing his teeth with vigour, I reran his monologue in my mind. Something was familiar.

'Hey, Tim, that place you were talking about; the place they ruined. Sounds like the delta in your friend's computer game.'

'Sorry, Henry, I don't follow. What delta?'

'The game you sent me. That has a threatened place in it; ruined by greed and stupidity.'

It was difficult to see Tim's face in the gloom. It seemed vaguely discomposed. 'Oh, is that what it's about now? That's Eric. He's always tinkering with it. He'll never market it at this rate.' He paused. 'No, I think any similarities are purely coincidental.'

But as he strolled back to his tent I had the strongest impression that they were not.

123

20

Physically the next three days were not easy. The river meandered, braided itself between blocks, and on two occasions seemed to disappear totally underground. Twice we left the gorge to try to cut through the flanking pinnacles in an attempt to strike eastwards. Each time involved several hours of slow single-file walking along deep narrow crevasses. Although we were rigorous about marking our path and managed to make progress eastwards, it was generally admitted to be an unpleasant business with full packs. The effort of watching every footstep, and the necessity of ceaseless vigilance against losing our way, contributed to making the trekking particularly tiring.

By a combination of providence and skill we managed to escape any injuries worse than cuts and grazes from the limestone edges. Rather to my surprise the psychological effects of the trip were more disturbing. Curiously, it wasn't the people; against my worst fears the three of us worked together very well. That was doubtless due, I thought, to the sheer physical effort of going through the pinnacles, suppressing the personality problems that had threatened to surface. Certainly the relationship with Tim was now one of a shallow—but workable—level of conviviality. There was still much that remained unfathomable, but in the midst of this rock jungle it didn't seem to matter. Laurent, too, seemed more at ease, although once or twice I caught him giving Tim unobtrusive scrutinising glances.

No, it wasn't the personalities that I found disturbing, but rather the place. I have always felt particularly immune, even possibly insensitive, to atmosphere. Perversely, that is an attribute that you need in physical geography. To be able to distance oneself from the landscape and to view it dispassionately is a necessity. Yet after a couple of days of nothing but the grey limestone slabs and after negotiating crevasse after crevasse, I had to admit that the place was getting to me. It wasn't simply the ever-present threat of panicked disorientation that afflicted me. It began to be more exotic than that. At least once I felt with absolute certainty that the laws of space and time had been suspended and that we were in a labyrinth that knew no end. The irresistible belief settled on me that the whole world was nothing except these stone corridors and junctions, with their dead, winter-sky colour. Fields and houses, sea and snow, roads and cars became vague concepts that the mind could find no grip on. All was hard unyielding greyness. I tried to counter it, with only partial success, by staring at the prosaic but definitely real image of Laurent's pack and head bobbing along gently ahead of me in the permanent half-light of the crevasse's bottom.

On another occasion, bringing up the rear of the party, I became gradually certain that we were being followed by a fourth person—if person it was. I found myself turning round sharply, half-expecting to catch a glimpse of a shadowy form trailing us in the gloom. I never did. I kept telling myself that it was a well-attested psychological phenomenon known from similar situations worldwide and that I should keep a tighter grip on myself. In this case I tried to exorcise the fourth man by the speculation that the mind could only handle so much monotony of colour and shape before it began inventing things to fill the sensory void. In practice it still didn't help. This particular illusion of a fourth man was so persistent that I eventually mentioned it to Tim and Laurent when we stopped for lunch. In the broad sunny junction, with the three of us sitting together talking, it sounded silly, but neither Tim nor Laurent laughed.

In fact it seemed that Tim was affected by the pinnacles in a similar manner. Once or twice he seemed to be definitely disorientated, and he managed on occasions to get his north and south confused. It's an easy trick for the visitor to the southern hemisphere, but given the perils of a wrong direction in our stone maze it gave rise to a quiet unease.

On only one occasion did Tim's behaviour give real cause for concern. Tim was leading, followed by me, with Laurent bringing up the rear. The section was very tight, and progress at times involved wriggling to get the packs through the crevasse. In fact, at the point where the incident occurred it was so overhung that we were virtually on all fours to get under the rock.

Suddenly with a cry of horror Tim leapt backwards at me, and I tumbled over into Laurent. It was a nasty moment, a tangle of wriggling packs and bodies in that narrow claustrophobic space. On every side was unyielding stone. I felt I couldn't breathe and that I had to break free, but movement in any way was impossible. Eventually, just as I was going to yield to the temptation to panic, we somehow disentangled ourselves. We edged back a few feet to before the overhang and leaned back against the crevasse sides, breathing heavily in the gloom. We were all in disarray, and Tim was clearly very unhappy with life. His lower jaw moved as though it had a life of its own and his face was pale and sweat beaded. He swore repeatedly as he tried to wipe his face.

'Spider, size of my hands . . . right on my face. . .' He shuddered. 'Sorry, you guys, but that was the mother of 'em all.'

Another pause. Then he seemed to get a hold of himself and said, 'Let's try another route. It scooted into a hole before I could hit it, but I'd rather not try that way. Sorry about that, but it was the stuff of nightmares. At least mine, anyway.'

'Sure, Tim. Those things can give a nasty bite too. Anyway, this is too narrow for comfort.'

126

Laurent nodded agreement and motioned for Tim and me to pass him—a difficult manoeuvre. As we started to set off again I noticed that Laurent was squatting, checking his pack straps in such a manner that he could see up along the overhang to the point where Tim had got to. Then Laurent turned, gave me a secretive, rather mystified look and we set off. Later on, on our own, he spoke of the incident.

'I saw no spider, Henry. I saw no sign of its net either.'

'It's "web," or sometimes we say "cobweb." Interesting, but something scared him. He seemed pretty panicked by the whole thing. Still, I'm not personally overenthusiastic about snakes . . . even your harmless Malagasy ones. Curious though. I've never seen him panic like that before. He seems pretty highly strung underneath all that surface cool.'

And we left the matter at that.

Of the wildlife we saw little. In the heart of the pinnacles there was little life by day, although the stream revealed a little more. The most attractive were brilliant blue kingfishers that seemed just like the British ones. Or at least as pictured in books; I couldn't remember ever having seen one close in the wild. The nights were accompanied by strange noises that defied identification. Once we met a twelve-foot-long chequered boa constrictor that the Malagasy call a 'Do.' I commented that I had read that it is widely revered.

'Some Malagasy reverence it,' said Laurent with an emphasis which left no doubt of his position with regard to the worship of reptiles.

In the end it took us the best part of three days of travel to get through to the other side of the pinnacles. Sunday afternoon saw us clambering slowly and stiffly out of the river valley. Tim pushed his way carefully through a final line of spiny bushes and stopped.

'Henry, Laurent, we've made it, we are through.' His voice held little emotion. A trace of tiredness, of relief, but any elation was absent. What struck me as curious in retrospect was the absence of any note of anti-climax either.

We scrambled up to join him. To the west against the setting sun lay the tormented blocks and peaks of the pinnacles, the clefts between them filling up with sooty shadows. In this light it looked like the skyline of a destroyed city with ruined, half-melted towers and spires. Beyond them could be seen the low smooth hills around Antsalova from which dirty plumes of smoke arose. I turned to the east. There the coarse grassland rolled in gently undulating terrain up to the plateau edge beyond. By any normal standard it was a harsh, rough landscape, dominated by a miserable brownish grass and strewn by boulders of torn-off limestone. Here and there embattled tree clumps stood. Compared to what we had gone through, it was a pastoral delight.

We lay down on the surface of a smooth stone slab, and there was silence for a minute. As I stared up at the sky my mind went over the past few days. 'Tim, we did it. Congratulations. Well within the schedule too.'

Tim raised a blue denim baseball cap up from off his face and looked across at me. 'Yup . . . well, I figured we could. Leastaways the credit should go to you largely, Henry. I'm sure glad I had your company. Both of ya.'

Then he paused briefly and went on, almost as if to change the subject. 'Well, let's take some photographs for the record and get on and pitch camp. Sunset isn't going to be any the later out here on the hill.'

As we pitched camp I thought about Tim's curiously muted response to getting through. In the end I decided that he had finally realised that it was at best a rather vague, subjective triumph. Ten miles to the north and we could have walked through the pinnacles in a day. Four hundred yards to the south of our route and we would probably never have made it at all.

It felt good to camp in the open that night; to look around and see no dark silhouettes of rock encircling us. After coffee I strolled out down to the crest of the hill and looked across the pinnacles. There was a faint waning moon which gave enough light to show the pale teeth of stone gleaming hungrily.

I sat there for some time looking over westwards. Whatever illuminated the town of Antsalova at night was inadequate to be seen from this distance. Nevertheless it, and its airstrip, lay there. In a week's time we would be through it and I would be on the flight to Paris and London. From tomorrow I would be going back. And I was still without any real decision on how I was going to spend my life.

I could half-hear a little cynical dry voice in my mind. 'Well, Henry, a pretty mess, eh? You've been running from this for the past six months. You've gone to the end of the world to get away from it, but it's coming to the crunch now. Still no decision?'

My little voice paused for effect. 'Not very impressive, eh? No wonder Tina gave you up. You're indecisive. Fatally so. If you try to drift through life you know what happens? You end up on the rocks.'

I tried to think of a withering counterblast but none came. After some minutes of this Laurent came over and carefully sat down near me.

'Can I help, Henry?'

'I'm afraid not, Laurent. It's a decision I have to make about my future. It's not an easy one. I haven't really explained it to you, I'm afraid.'

I wasn't really sure I wanted to. He sat silently for several minutes. I suspect he was praying.

'No, Henry, it is not a thing I can advise you on. I think you know the facts well enough. I think your problem is perhaps not that you need more knowledge or advice, but obedience. And that I cannot help with.'

If I'd have said it, it would have come over as a rude piece of crassness, but somehow, coming from Laurent, it was difficult to take offence.

He got up, clapped me gently on the shoulder, and with a gentle 'Good night, my brother' was gone.

Eventually I gave up and went to bed. As I lay awake in my tent for a while, I felt that it really did look like I was going to have to say sorry to George, Cyprus and St Paul's. Tina wouldn't like it. But then she had forfeited any say in the matter by her hardheartedness. Besides, she wasn't infallible. She had been uneasy about this trip. My last thought before falling into a deep sleep was that we had certainly proved her wrong on that point.

21

Although it took only two days to get back to the Cricket Pitch it seemed longer. The careful marking of our way through paid off on the way back. Only rarely were we in any doubt about our path. With lighter packs and time in hand we made regular detours to explore particularly interesting corridors. I felt that I had, in large measure, fulfilled my terms of the contract with Tim, and he seemed happy to sit around while I made notes.

There was a lot to see. I made lots of rough sketches and shot off several rolls of film. With my eye now attuned to the scenery I was beginning to pick up all sorts of shades of variation and difference in the weathering patterns. The enormous diversity of weathering within a basically identical rock unit was remarkable. Even to the untrained eyes of Laurent and Tim the scenery evoked awe and wonder. For example, along one avenue we came across a line of tumbled pinnacles, each two-storey block toppled against the others like bleached and dissolving dominoes. Along another we found ourselves in a corridor where the walls had been undercut to give a series of small caves. Had we been so minded they were large enough to explore, but none of us, least of all Tim, seemed at all interested in what he termed, to Laurent's mystification, 'spelunking.'

In places the flora showed a matching bizarre streak. In particular, the etched tops of the pinnacles were often the site of wonderful bulbous and leafless tree-trunks clad in a spiny silver skin and looking as though they had only the vaguest relationship to the rest of the plant kingdom.

Despite these wonders we were becoming increasingly tired. It showed itself in many ways. Our starts in the mornings became later, the decisions at the junctions became slower, and the tents were pitched in an increasingly sloppy manner. My notes became poorer and towards the end of the day became almost illegible. As we headed westwards in our meandering fashion the conversation turned increasingly to the outside world and what we were going to do there.

Tim was keen to get back to his machines. 'I've thought up a way to solve a long-standing problem we have with interfacing two machines.' He gave a wry, almost embarrassed smile. 'Long-standing in our business means that it's been a pressing problem for six months or so. But if we don't do it soon the systems will be obsolete.'

He paused, and when he spoke again it was almost in a confiding tone. 'Actually, it's one reason why I come on these trips. It disengages your mind totally from problems. When you get back to them the chances are that you hit them from a different angle and find them soluble. But that apart, I reckon a cold beer, a non-rehydrated steak and a genuine shower wouldn't go amiss.'

Laurent's plans were simple. He had relatives on the east coast he wanted to visit.

As for me? Well, I said little beyond stating that I hoped to go to Yugoslavia to look at limestones. Vaughan gave me his look of faint bemusement again.

'And that's a holiday? Henry, let me tell you, I have seen enough limestone scenery to last me several lifetimes.'

Eventually, late on Tuesday afternoon, we came out of the river gorge to see the gentleness of the Cricket Pitch and the campsite. Everything was as we had left it, and there was no trace of any human visitation.

As we sat around the fire that night we discussed the plans for the next few days. Tim lay sprawled out on the sand, propped up by his rucksack. To judge from his physical attitude, he was relaxed. His voice, typically clipped and precise, gave little indication of his frame of mind.

'OK, today's Tuesday. We need to be at Antsalova for the 10 am flight Saturday morning. Agreed? I'm anxious to minimise the time I spend near the strip; not that I've got anything against the town.'

He looked reassuringly at Laurent. 'But I'm happy just to walk straight onto the plane. So I figure we leave here on Thursday, camp just out of the pinnacles that night, and that gives us a single day's walk on the Friday. OK, eh, Laurent?'

Laurent hesitated slightly and then smiled back. 'Yes, a long walk, but it is possible.'

Tim turned to me. 'Fine. Any objections, Henry?'

I shook my head. Then a question came to me. 'So what do we do tomorrow?'

There was silence for a moment. Something, probably a large moth, fluttered by overhead.

Tim spoke quietly. 'Unless anyone has a better idea I'd like to try to get a look into that area of deep pinnacles over there.' He gestured with a nod of his head to the south.

Laurent looked at me, caution and enquiry in his eyes.

'Well, Laurent and I figured it was pretty tough country, Tim. It's worse than anything we've been through so far.'

In the firelight I could see a look of vague disappointment on Tim's face. It seemed to be vaguely rebuking me, but he said nothing. Rather to my surprise I heard myself speaking.

'But I guess it could be done. We'd have to be slow and careful, but I see no reason why we couldn't explore the edges of it. At least we wouldn't have heavy packs with us. What do you think, Laurent?'

As I spoke I realised that given Laurent's congenital dislike of disagreement there wasn't really much he could say after what I'd suggested.

There was a fraction of a delay. 'It can be done, yes . . .'

If he was going to say anything else, he didn't get the

133

chance as Tim spoke: 'Good, we'll take care and travel light.'
His tone didn't leave much of an opening for dissent.

Shortly afterwards I decided that I couldn't avoid perform-
ing my allotted duty and took the dirty pans down to the
stream. In view of the fact that the main pool was used for
bathing, the agreement was to use the downstream end of the
pool for washing up.

As I slowly scoured the pans with sand, I reviewed, again,
the Cyprus decision. It seemed to be a measure of the problem
that I was always able to find some new angle to it. That night
I decided that although I didn't feel at peace about it I felt reasonably happy about calling George Roumian and saying no.
After all, I argued to myself, I can't spend my life jumping at
the whim of every well-meaning friend. The prospect of Tina's
disapproval still lingered threateningly. It was lifted slightly by
the thought that at least now I would show her that I was decisive. It even crossed my mind again that it was perhaps this
indecision that had put her off.

As I walked slowly back across the sand bar to the fire I
became aware of the conversation going on between Laurent
and Tim. What first struck me was not any actual words but
the tone; slow, serious and thoughtful. I slowed down and
gradually drifted into the arc of firelight.

'And you believe that, Laurent?' Tim's voice was quiet and
intense.

'Yes, I believe that it is demanded of men, all men, that
they make repentance and put their faith in Jesus Christ.'

'But why not believe and do what you like? That way you'd
get the best of both worlds.'

It was a question coolly put, with no aggression or malice.
Laurent was silent for a moment, and I wondered whether I
would have to try to bail him out. I hoped not; I wasn't sure I
had an answer. He spoke earnestly but slowly.

'That would not be true faith. I think the true faith is not
just a thing of the mind, but of the life.' He seemed to struggle
for a moment with words. 'For example here, in this place, you

might believe that I know the way out to Antsalova. That would be faith, I agree. But it would only be true faith if you followed me out. And that alone would save you.' I remembered he was a pastor's son.

I quietly sat down by the fire. Both gave me the benefit of a snatched glance of acknowledgement. The atmosphere was hushed, but there was a feeling of electricity in it, as though the air were charged with some hidden immensity. No one spoke. I looked at Tim's face; taut and shadowed in the fickering light. Yet it seemed to me too that what Laurent was saying seemed to apply elsewhere. For a fraction of a second I wondered if perhaps the words fitted me, then I pushed the thought aside and stared at Tim again. I felt as if some gigantic wave were poised overhead, waiting to break. Something indefinable seemed to be hanging, poised in balance, even imminent.

Then Tim spoke slowly, his tone sad and retrospective.

'Nice idea. Give your life to Jesus. But it's not on for me. Maybe once, but not now. It's not that I don't believe it. I guess I do; at least at one level. But I can't now.'

There was a hesitation, a suggestion of thoughts being marshalled. 'No, I've got goals and dreams of my own. I won't sacrifice them for anyone, not even Him. My heart wouldn't be in it. And that, it seems, isn't enough.'

There was the slightest of pauses. 'Sorry.'

Tim opened his hands wide in a gesture of hopelessness and finality. I felt a cool breeze across my face, and the tension evaporated.

It's curious. I now know that much of what Tim spoke to us was totally false. And yet I cannot get it out of my mind that in this one conversation with Laurent there was sincerity; that here there was the genuine Tim Vaughan speaking. The currency was for once real, not counterfeit.

As I think back over that incident in the light of all that followed it, I cannot avoid wondering if it could perhaps all have been different. Perhaps if I had thought more about my own state rather than Tim's, then things could have been different. Perhaps.

Tim got to his feet slowly. 'Welcome back, Henry. Laurent and I have been having a deep discussion.' Tim's tone carried the faintest suggestion that it was a matter now completed.

'Well, I'm tired. Should be a good day tomorrow. I'm going to turn in. Night. And thanks again, Laurent.'

I looked at Laurent, but he was staring at the sand between his fingers in some private and unfathomable reflection. I got up and moved to go to my tent, gripping his shoulder as I passed.

'Good night, Laurent. God bless.'

He spoke quietly as in a dream. 'You also, Henry.'

Despite a palpable tiredness I could not sleep for a long time that night. My mind went round and round in a half-waking dream. Pictures of Laurent, Tim and George Roumian fused and separated again in a wild mental tumult. All was instability and uncertainty. Time and time again I tried to wake up enough to drag myself out of the ceaseless whirlpool of images, but each time I slipped back. In the maelstrom, one stable feature appeared. It was the Hensons; and merged with them Laurent's family. I seemed to be tumbling eternally around them, and as I hurled past for the hundredth time I saw that their faces bore expressions of sternness and reproach.

22

There was an ill-defined but very real awkwardness about the party the next morning. As we walked over the rubble of the Cricket Pitch with our half-empty packs there was little conversation. Each of us seemed immersed in our own problems. Tim appeared slightly on edge, even jumpy. Laurent seemed withdrawn, and I felt tired and unhappy. Everything seemed unresolved.

We entered the pinnacles in the area that Laurent and I had surveyed. Whether it was the same avenue I wasn't sure. Certainly there was no trace of the earlier markings. In that area there were about a dozen openings, and all seemed similar.

We had not gone in far before it became apparent that this was indeed the deep pinnacles. The limestone here had some of the severest weathering effects of any area we had seen. The most obvious difference was depth. Here the height was often twice that of the crevasses that we had been used to. Despite the presence of these thirty- or forty-foot-high walls, the width was no greater than before. This had the effect of greatly increasing the gloom. The poor lighting was particularly awkward as the floors of the clefts were anything but smooth, having widespread angular protuberances that struck ankles and threatened to catch feet. The result was that we spent a lot of time peering downwards, a posture that not only slowed us down, but meant that we had little sense of where we were actually going.

More subtly, it seemed to me that as we moved further into

the zone of deep pinnacles, the rules that the rest of the region obeyed broke down. The crevasses here were not the straight linear features that we had seen hitherto, but curved and wiggled as if trying to break free of something. Junctions, often of considerable complexity, occurred more and more. Similarly, the convention that the crevasse floor followed a single level was also disobeyed with an increasing frequency. Related to this, and a source of mounting concern, was the presence of potholes on the crevasse bottom. They occurred without warning and dropped down into all-concealing darkness; some at least were more than ten feet deep.

It was hard not to think of this deterioration of the limestone as a stone cancer spreading out from some central tumour in the region into which we were heading. At every junction we were careful to mark our trail back. At one junction Tim rebuked Laurent, who was being parsimonious with the felt pen.

'For crying out loud, don't economise on that marker. We ain't needing it after today, and I don't intend flying any spares back.'

It was with great difficulty that I continued the effort of keeping up the sketch map in my notebook. We hadn't had to use it yet and I was tempted not to bother, but the complexity of the passages here forced me to maintain the practice.

Despite, or because of, its hostility to man there was no denying the majesty of the region. I found myself thinking that this was perhaps the finest scenery of its type anywhere in the world. As I sweated along in the shadows of the humid and airless corridors I kept reminding myself that it was a privilege to be there.

The day moved on, although there was little evidence of it from our vantage point, walking slowly along at the bottom of the colossal incised maze.

We stopped for lunch at a point where our crevasse, for once a rather shallow affair only three times a man's height, ended abruptly as it ran into another deeper corridor. We stood cautiously at the edge of our crevasse, peering down the sheer twenty-feet drop into the next corridor. Tracing that laterally we noticed that perhaps ten yards to the right it terminated as abruptly and dropped down into a still lower crevasse level. It was a sobering sight. The effect of adding a vertical dimension to our already tortuous horizontal maze pushed to the surface a question that had been around for the last hour.

'Say, Tim, after we've eaten why don't we wend our way back? At the risk of being accused of being chicken I think I'd rather play safe. I don't think we will see much more than we have done already. Just variations on a theme.'

Laurent nodded his head slightly in tacit but virtually subliminal agreement.

Tim looked at his watch and cast a glance at the sky. The little that could be seen of it beyond the needled ramparts high around us was unsullied by cloud. His voice began on a faintly irritated note.

'I read you, Henry. The whole thing is just variations on a theme. I don't suppose we are more than a few hundred yards from the Cricket Pitch . . . Aw, but heck, why not? No sense in taking risks. Might as well take it easy. I don't fancy spraining an ankle at this late stage. Anyway, I don't think I've taken enough photographs of this stuff yet.'

So after a leisurely lunch we headed slowly backwards, with frequent stops for photographs. Tim's photographic style seemed to be based on the concept that if you use a lot of film, some frames at least will be satisfactory. He seemed obsessed by strange angles and on one occasion got us to stand in a junction while he took a shot from a hundred yards away along a lateral crevasse. Eventually, near the edge of the pinnacles, he must have run out of film or something and we called it a day.

It was about four o'clock when we emerged tired and relieved out of the clefts. We stood for a few moments surveying the grand scene of the serried arrays of peaks and then turned for camp.

It was pleasant to be back at the camp with the sun still above the pinnacles. After taking my pack and boots off I just lay on my back on the warm sand and relaxed. It was a balmy afternoon, and the protected beach formed something of a sun trap. My mind was idling in neutral. Laurent had taken a towel and was bathing just out of sight on the bend.

Tim was pottering around camp and going in and out of his tent.

Suddenly he swore and came over to me. 'Henry, when did I last have my camera? It's not with me now.'

I sat up and looked around on the off chance it had been put down on the ground somewhere.

'I can't remember. Just as we came out of the pinnacles? We certainly stopped there and I took a photograph. Didn't you?'

'Aw, what a . . . Oh well, I must have left it there. My mind is going. Definitely time to go home. Well, I'll just have to run over and grab it.'

He moved as if to go.

'Say, Tim, do you want me to come?'

'Naw, I guess I can find it easy enough. I'd better go now anyway or the light will have gone.'

Before I could say anything else he turned and walked off. As he passed his tent he stopped and, almost as an afterthought, picked up his half-empty pack.

I lay down again and tried to think about Yugoslavia. Perhaps I'd put an extra week into the trip and do some lying around on beaches. It was something one could acquire a taste for, and it might help me forget about having said no to George Roumian. I developed the idea a little further; perhaps that was what I needed to do—to look beyond the present crisis. By September my problems with Cyprus would be history.

Laurent came up from the river carrying his towel and dirty clothes. As he walked to his tent he went past our neat lit-tle rubbish pile. With a quick motion he stooped and picked up something. I renewed my idle meditations. A few minutes later

Laurent came out of his tent and started sorting out things for the evening meal. His action prodded my conscience, and I got to my feet and went over to help him. Laurent was rummaging through the small pile of silver foil-wrapped packages.

'What did Tim want us to eat tonight?'

'I don't know. He's just gone back to pick up his camera. He left it where we stopped last, just out of the pinnacles.'

Laurent stopped abruptly and looked vaguely surprised. 'I hope he finds it.'

'Incidentally, talking of Tim, that was an interesting conversation you were having last night.'

Laurent looked sheepish and stared at the burner for a moment. 'Ah, my friend, I have a confession to make. You see until last night I do not think that I really . . . cared for your friend. Perhaps it is not easy to explain, but I found him a bit of an offence. He has come here just for a holiday. He spends enough on this pleasure to pay for a new school building. He seems to have no interest in Malagasy people; only their rocks. Even then he seems more interested in his machines. So I am afraid I found him difficult. Perhaps too I was envious.'

There wasn't much to say. Eventually I asked him what had happened to change his mind.

'Ah, then I realised the obvious. I realised that he too was human. He has a heart which needs Jesus. His money has not cured that. He knows that he needs something, but he still hopes that what he has is it.'

He stopped and looked at me. 'Henry, last night did you not feel that he was pulled? I felt that he nearly gave in. He has a burden, a demon. Something drives him. Poor man.'

That cast an interesting perspective on Tim. I had been so involved with my own problems that I had failed to consider those around me. I suppose of the two I had assumed that it was Laurent who had the problems, but somehow my vague envy of Tim's freedom had blinded me to his needs. But as I thought about his problems it came to me that at depth I was not greatly different from him.

I was trying to shift my thinking back to the sun-drenched blonde-draped beaches of the Adriatic when I felt a slight chill. There was a breeze getting up off the water, and the sun was well down in the sky. Suddenly, I felt vaguely alarmed.

'Talking of Tim, where is he? He should be back by now.'

Laurent looked at me and something crossed his face, doubt or fear. He glanced at the sun and made some mental calculations.

'Henry, I agree. There is less than an hour of light. Let's go and help him look.'

The mood of unease acquired a life of its own and began to grow. I grabbed my boots and pulled them on. As I did so I tried to argue myself out of the vague alarm that had surfaced. There was surely no danger in Tim's trip to the edge of the pinnacles. The concern was doubtless due to the fact that we had been completely together over the past week, so that now being a twosome instead of a threesome was slightly unnerving. That was all, I told myself. The worst thing that could have happened was that Tim couldn't find his camera. Yet as I said all these things to myself I realised that he had been gone nearly an hour.

I paused briefly to empty my pack and to collect a torch, first-aid kit, and a spare pullover. I looked up to see that Laurent was off the sand and already up the slope into the scrub of the Cricket Pitch. His shadow was long.

It took us ten minutes to make it across to where we had stopped on our way out. No faster speed was possible without a real risk of twisting an ankle on the loose stones underfoot. The wall of rock was a golden grey in the fading light. It was the crevasses, however, not the stone, that seemed to catch the eye, like knife slashes across a painting.

There was no sign of Tim. I called out his name half a dozen times. The words echoed back mockingly from the rocks. A disturbed kite circled curiously above.

I looked at Laurent for reassurance. His worried face gave none. 'Henry, you look over there. I'll try over here.'

There was an edge to his voice. I tried to suppress the worries that came to mind and agreed in an automatic manner.

A minute later Laurent called out. I ran over, getting the worst of a thorn bush to see that he was holding a piece of paper. I all but snatched it off him.

'It was stuck on this rock pile here. I couldn't miss it.'

The note was pencil-written in a tight neat hand. The piece of paper looked as if it had come out of Tim's diary.

'Realised I left camera at last stop in the pinnacles. Can do it in time. Cheers, Tim.'

'The idiot,' I heard myself mutter.

Laurent shook his head, his lips pursed.

'Now what? Follow him? In there?' As I spoke I stared at the ominous gashes. They seemed to dominate the scene. I could easily imagine that the shadow that infilled them was due to some flowing tide of gloom that emanated from beyond in the deep pinnacles.

'The heart of darkness.'

'What?'

'Sorry, Laurent, it's a book you wouldn't enjoy.'

Reluctantly I moved to the nearest crevasse. The ones five yards either side looked identical. 'Is this the one we went into?'

As I raised the question, an ill-defined flicker of doubt rose and crossed my mind. There was something obvious that I had overlooked, but what? Then whatever it was fled my mind before I could catch it.

I made as if to go in. Laurent grabbed my sleeve. 'Careful, my friend. Let us not get lost.'

'It's OK, Laurent. We will just go to the first junction.'

The sun was only a small way above the pinnacles as we entered the fissure. Instantly, all around our feet was darkness. At first we stumbled along with hands out against both sides before our eyes became accustomed to the gloom. Even then progress was slow and the first junction seemed ages in coming.

When we got there, there was not much to see. Further corridors ran off either side and ahead. The tops of the pinnacles still gleamed in the dying light. Along the crevasse bottom a charcoal blackness ruled.

I called out Tim's name as loudly as I could. The effect was horrible. The word bounced around the rocks becoming ever more distorted. Then silence prevailed. After my last shout, something seemed to answer in a distant raucous cry, but it was not human.

Laurent was as close to me as he could get without actually touching me. 'Now what, Henry?' He spoke in little more than a whisper.

'Let's just check which way he would have gone.'

I turned to look for the red slash on the rock to my right. It was there, just visible in the gloom.

'Good news! We were on the right crevasse but . . .'

In an instant my earlier ill-defined flicker of doubt returned as a solid stab of alarm. 'Oh no! Laurent, what an idiot I am. The marking system. It never occurred to me. Do you see?'

He was silent for a few seconds. Then he spoke in a quiet puzzled voice. 'But how do we know which way the route is?'

I found myself spelling it out, as much to clear the muddle in my own head as to explain it to Laurent. It was difficult to avoid sarcasm.

'My system was designed to allow us to retrace our steps, so at every junction all we did was mark the right hand side of the crevasse we'd just come along—like this. When we returned and we came to a junction we'd just go anticlockwise round all the crevasses until we found the one that started off with an arrow on its side. Dead easy, simple, and it works. Marvellous, eh? Oh yes, I thought of everything.'

I paused for a second. 'What I never thought of is what happens if, having got safely out along your route, you decided to try the route again. You do what we've done; assuming you've picked the right crevasse to start with, that is. At the first junction you can't tell which of the three or four or five avenues you are to take, because the wretched marking only shows you the way out. So what do you do?'

It was a half-rhetorical question, but Laurent answered it slowly. 'You would have to try each one in turn. Eventually you would find the marker at the end of one. And you would know it was the right one you had come along before. So in time you would find your way through. It would be slow but possible.'

He looked uncertain. I went on with only the briefest pause. 'Oh yes. Slow and possible, but not fatal. Not, that is, unless you were a proud man in a hurry.' I paused for effect. 'Then you might be tempted to guess, eh Laurent? And if you ended up in a corridor which was the wrong one, then you might feel like trying to take a shortcut through to the next one. And that might be just about the last thing you ever did.'

I glared around at the great slabs looming over us, dark grey against a rich blue-black sky. I felt failure, bitterness and anxiety.

'I can see it all now, Laurent. A nice little trap, just ready for one foolish act, one moment of overconfidence. God help him, Laurent, if he is stuck in here, because I don't know that we can.'

Laurent grabbed my shoulder. 'It is not your fault, Henry. If this is what happened it was his foolishness that caused it. Look, we can do nothing here. Let us go back. Perhaps he may have come back out of one of the other crevasses.'

I called out his name again. Called it out again and again in the darkness.

There was nothing. Nothing.

We turned and began the trip back. In front and behind us there was near-total gloom. The black walls rose above into a brief band of indigo. High above us the stars were coming out.

We hadn't gone far before I bashed an ankle. 'This is stupid. Laurent, reach in my pack and get out the torch, please.'

The very act of talking was disturbing. The muffled, trapped echoes were a reminder that rock, not open air, surrounded us. Laurent got out the torch and passed it to me in silence.

I switched it on and angled it so that the yellow beam pointed vertically down. It helped both of us that way, but the fashion in which the shadows moved around our feet was unnerving. For the first time I began to feel that the pinnacles were not just neutral objects, but genuinely hostile towards us. I could almost believe that we were intruders into a world with a deep antipathy to humanity. A kingdom far older than warm flesh and blood, a world at enmity with us; a place perfectly capable of silently swallowing up a man on his own. The shadows closed behind us like the doors on a private club.

Then abruptly the rock walls ended and we stumbled out into the glorious open. We were no longer enclosed in rock. True, a hundred yards ahead the pinnacles began again, but here at least there was something which could vaguely be called a horizon. Here a faint breeze blew and voices didn't reverberate endlessly.

In the west the embers of the sunset were fading away behind the stone needles. Above, the stars were clear.

'Tim, Tim, Tim, where are you?'

We called and cried out. But there was nothing other than an echo ringing back from the rock.

We sat silently for a few minutes. Laurent began to shiver, so I lent him the spare pullover. As I dug around inside the pack I noticed that the torch batteries were fading.

'I wish I'd put new batteries in, Laurent. These are on the point of going.'

Laurent stirred himself and spoke in a thoughtful tone. 'I thought you had done that today. That is curious.'

I paid no attention to his comment because the idea had struck me that however unpleasant it was here with a fading torch it was infinitely better than being in that ghastly rock maze with no light at all. Nothing but the light of the stars and silence. A silence broken only by the rustling and slithering of animals.

'It must be horrible in there.'

'Indeed, but if Tim does not panic he is probably in no danger. Not tonight. If he stays where he is, then we should be able to find him tomorrow.'

'I guess you've put your finger on the critical issue. Did he panic?'

And as to that, there was no answer, but the memory of the incident with the spider wasn't encouraging.

We stayed there outside the mouth of the crevasses for an hour. Then we gave up and headed back to the deserted and silent camp. We forced ourselves to cook some food and ate it with no appetite.

After eating, we reviewed the situation in as cold and rational a manner as possible. Vaughan, it seemed certain, was lost in the pinnacles. He possibly had some water and perhaps some emergency rations, but little else. We both agreed that it was perfectly likely that we would find him tomorrow. But despite that, we found ourselves discussing what would happen if we didn't.

One thing became distressingly clear in our discussions. Laurent and I were on our own on this. There was no possibility of getting any help. It would take a good day's walk to get to Antsalova, and it was difficult to see what could be done there other than fill in the appropriate forms. Even if there were volunteers to go and look for Tim, which seemed hardly likely, did we have any right to hazard their lives? As Laurent ruefully commented, any search of the pinnacles would probably lose more people. Besides, if he had gone running off, then a hundred people wouldn't be enough to find him.

On the outside chance that the phone lines out of Antsalova worked it might be possible that there was a helicopter within flying distance. But then what? I remembered clearly the dry, weary voice of the pilot I'd flown with last year, laying down the rules before the first flight.

'I guess it will not have escaped your notice that your precious pinnacles aren't exactly overflowing with landing zones?

Well I've got a single turbine. So that gives me a problem if we get an "engine-out." I've got to auto-rotate—glide, to you—out of trouble. And to do that I need height or speed. If you want to go low that's fine, but I'll be going fast enough so that if I get an engine-out I can still get out. If you want to go slow, I'll have to be high enough to get clear. So I can go either low or slow. But not both, OK?'

The chances of spotting Tim in the darkness of a deep cleft at either height or speed would be virtually zero. Ultimately, even if against all the odds Vaughan was found, there was a final cruel twist. There was no way to pick him up. The helicopter couldn't land, and even a perilous hovering with a twin-engine machine wouldn't be of any help if he was in a crevasse.

In the background lay the further problem of the flight back on Saturday. To catch it we would have to leave the pinnacles at first light on Friday. If Vaughan was still lost, then possibly the best thing to do would be to report it directly to the authorities in 'Tana. Although what they could do to help was difficult to imagine. At the end of our gloomy review we resolved to get up early the next morning and try to scour the pinnacles systematically for the whole day.

After that Laurent prayed that Tim would either be found or find his own way out, and I gave a troubled 'Amen' in assent. That done we crawled wearily into our sleeping bags and slept.

23

Laurent shook me out of a deep sleep just before dawn. After a brief cheerless breakfast we walked over to the crevasse entrances. There was no sign of life, and my heart sank. We called again and again for Tim, but there was no reply. The stone walls just seemed to isolate and trap our voices.

I looked at Laurent.

'Do we have any choice?' There wasn't much expectation in my voice.

'No, none I think. We must go in again.' He spoke wearily.

So picking up our light packs we set off down the most northerly of the six crevasses that Tim might possibly have gone down. I knew, I suppose we both did, that basically it was a hopeless business. The sheer size of the crevasses reduced the chances of stumbling across Tim to a very low level indeed. If he stayed in one place, there was a fair chance that given enough time we would run into him unless he had fallen down a hole. However, if he was lost and moving around in an attempt to get out, then the probability of finding him would be extremely small. Even if we had had a dozen men the chances wouldn't have greatly improved.

Every route branched and rebranched. Every corridor looked familiar, an endless multiplication of the same few basic patterns. As we moved down them, once or twice I felt sure, against all reason, that the branch we had followed had doubled back on itself. In the absence of any fixed reference point it was difficult to disprove this. The paths we took were confusing. And the confusion was dangerous.

Our preoccupation became to ensure that we did not go the way of Tim and find ourselves lost. I did my best to keep a spidery sketch map of the path taken, but it was difficult. The bare rock retained no trails or footprints. It was almost as if we were too insubstantial to register on the pinnacles.

By midday we were tired and bruised and very depressed. It was becoming a real but unmentioned possibility that Tim Vaughan would never be seen again, by us or anybody. We snatched a bite of food and some drink and kept going. By restricting the distance we had gone into the pinnacles, we were able to swing round to the middle crevasses by early afternoon and found ourselves checking the area near the track we had taken the day before. This had to be considered the prime area for Tim to be in.

As we walked wearily down one crevasse I looked up to see something white in the greyness ahead. As I stumbled towards it I saw it was a piece of paper held down by a small stone. I grabbed it and scanned it, with Laurent peering round my shoulder.

The writing was in the same pencil as the earlier note. The hand, however, was markedly changed. It didn't need any calligraphic analysis to see that whoever had written it was under stress. It was dated 7.30 pm the previous night. The message started terse and rational, but soon deteriorated.

> No food or water. Position uncertain. Missed the arrows. Must get out of this place soon. Will try to travel west as fast as I can out of the pinnacles. In the event you get this note, please leave a food cache at camp and the pinnacle edge. Sorry, my stupid pride. Not your fault, Henry.
>
> Sorry,
>
> Tim R Vaughan.

There was a scribbled last line: 'Laurent, I should have listened to you.'

I felt myself shaking and sat down against the rocks. Tim's plight came over me in a wave of raw feeling. What a terrible situation to be in; what an appalling, horrible mess he had got himself into. All over a stupid camera.

'What a ghastly business. To be lost in here. It's awful. I had really hoped he hadn't got stuck in here.'

It sounded empty and futile.

Laurent had his head in his hands. He said nothing. The reality of it all came to me. That last night, after three hours of being lost, a battered Tim had come struggling through here and had, in the torchlight, scribbled this forlorn note.

Laurent shook himself in an apparent attempt to pull himself together. 'Henry, if he goes west is there any hope?'

As he said it my heart missed a beat. I pulled out the tattered enlargement of the French 1:50,000 map and marked on it our position. The conclusion wasn't a difficult one. There wasn't much point in being melodramatic, and I tried to keep my voice as cool as I could when I spoke.

'It is about as hopeless as can be. Five kilometres of pure pinnacles. Other than to go due south he couldn't have picked a worse route. There is no water that way, and it could take a fit man a week.' I paused, trying to correct a tremor in my voice.

'Assuming, that is, that he could keep a straight path and not go in circles. No, Laurent, I'm afraid he has signed his own death sentence.' If only Vaughan had paid more attention to the maps, I thought. Why due west? I could only conclude that he thought he'd hit the bend in the Beboka. Unfortunately, that now lay to the north of where we were.

'We should follow him?' Laurent's voice came almost as a surprise.

'We could try, but not for long. We must be able to get out ourselves. Besides, unless he has marked his track, it will be hopeless after the first turnoff. We can't even be sure that he will keep going west. After all, his sense of direction isn't good. Still we must try and follow. But, Laurent, it is impossible.'

'With God nothing is impossible. Let us pray that we may still find him.'

We didn't find him. An hour later we had to admit defeat. We had walked continuously and were exhausted. There was nothing. The crevasse walls loomed above us; it was hot and humid, and the sweat kept running into my eyes. The likelihood that we were on Vaughan's track was laughably small. There had been at least twenty junctions since we picked up his note. If I had had the energy or the time I could have worked out the probability to a fair degree of accuracy. Increasingly, I was worried about getting back safely ourselves. We could have been anywhere in the pinnacles. Our only hope of getting out was to follow those faint red arrows back. After the usual futile callings we turned around and set off back.

It took us an hour to get out of the pinnacles, and a horrible hour it was too. At one point I was convinced we had taken the wrong route when we could find no markings at a particularly complex junction. Then, as I was trying to decode my sweat-stained notes and straining to suppress a feeling of mounting panic, Laurent checked again and found the arrow.

The pinnacles had become hateful to me. I was now coming to terms with the fact that they had killed Vaughan. Half of me felt that they probably wanted to do the same to us. If anyone had told me a month earlier that I could attribute malevolence to a limestone landscape, I would have laughed at them. All my science and my vestigial theology combined to make them inanimate parts of creation. Yet that afternoon, with Vaughan's loss hanging over us and after nearly ten hours of nothing but bare rock, my feelings overrode my reason.

The sun was setting as we arrived back at the deserted camp. I did not know what Laurent was thinking; he was silent and withdrawn. My own feelings were in turmoil. It may sound callous, but it would be untrue to say that I felt pure unalloyed grief at Tim's plight. In truth, I alternated between anger and pity for Vaughan and anger and pity for myself. Whenever I felt angry about Tim for getting us all into this awful mess, I realised that he was paying a heavy price for it. The feelings for myself were less clear and didn't reflect well on me. Part of them hinged upon annoyance at having been so stupid as to walk into this mess, particularly in view of all the various warnings I'd received. The pity I didn't rationalise, but the thought crossed my mind that this was going to be an appalling blot on my career. Ever after my name would be associated with the doomed Vaughan. I could hear a mutter emanating from a deep armchair in the Senior Common Room.

'Ah yes, Stanwick. A promising career, but got into a nasty mess in Madagascar. Got an American killed, I believe. No real fault of his own, of course, but you know how these things are.'

But then whenever I felt sorry for myself I would suddenly realise with a pang of guilt what I was thinking and try to come up with ways in which I could constructively help Tim. Only I couldn't think of any.

After the meal, Laurent spoke in a deliberate tone. 'Henry, I am thinking. We are short of food—especially as we are now to leave a food supply here and at the edge. Also, our flight leaves the day after tomorrow. What do we do?'

'Well, what are our choices? We could stay here trying to pursue him in the pinnacles. But the odds are awful. The more we do that, the more we risk losing ourselves. We are both very tired, and today we nearly slipped up.'

I paused, trying to think clearly and to make the right decision. Finally I spoke.

'The other alternative is to try one more time tomorrow by cutting in south from here. Then we leave tomorrow lunchtime and keep walking. Out of here. Out of this place and out to Antsalova. On that basis we may be able to make it for the flight back on the Saturday morning.'

'And what do we do about Tim?'

'Call the Embassy and get them to do something. Perhaps they could get a helicopter . . .'

I thought about it. 'Laurent, I think we have to be realistic. It is just possible that Vaughan may come walking out; either here or more unlikely still on the other side of the pinnacles. It is *much* more likely that he will not make it. In fact, to use the military term, we are going very soon to have to say he is "missing, presumed dead." Whichever way, I doubt there is much we can do here.'

Laurent was silent, evidently thinking hard. 'Yes, that is probably best; every way is difficult. Certainly let us search tomorrow. At lunchtime we will decide.'

And shortly after that we went to our tents. Despite the turmoil and anguish in my mind I had barely taken my clothes off before I fell asleep.

The next morning Laurent seemed terribly preoccupied with something. The search went badly. We tried to cut in from near the camp southwards, in the hope of intercepting a possible westward movement by Tim. It was a continuous struggle; wearisome to body and mind. Well before lunch we had given up any hope of finding him. A silence that seemed to mock us reigned throughout the realm of stone. Where we were searching was a bleak area, even according to the exacting criteria of the pinnacles. A few trees clung impossibly to the tops of the needles above us. There was no water. A few brown lizards ran across the rocks and I wondered, with a shudder, what they would be like to eat. The landscape seemed to be accursed.

At twelve o'clock I was ready to stop looking. Laurent, looking tired and under stress, merely nodded agreement. Back at camp he spoke.

'I think we should take our tents and leave Tim's. Should we see if there is anything of his that we must take back?'

'You mean papers, letters and so on?'

'Perhaps. I am not sure. There may be something we should leave behind, beside food.'

So I crawled in and pulled out what was there. There wasn't very much, and it was all either in nylon bags or plastic containers. There were some run-of-the-mill pharmaceutical products, like mosquito lotion and mild painkillers. There were spare clothes and a pair of expensive training shoes. One box contained film, and elsewhere there was a long telephoto lens and a tripod. There was a notebook of neat jottings in a computer language I didn't recognise and Vaughan's little short-wave radio. And that was about it.

I didn't think much about it at the time, but the whole thing was rather impersonal. In a sense it was a relief. There were no photographs of a wife or girlfriend, no children's letters, no cherished reminders of home and family.

'I suppose all his papers were in his pack as usual. At any rate there is nothing here that I would think we should take with us. I suppose it will be safe here for a long time.'

Laurent agreed. I pushed it all back into his tent, thinking that despite ransacking his personal belongings there was still virtually nothing that I knew about Tim Vaughan. He remained as insubstantial as an image on a computer screen.

It took only another half an hour to pack up the camp. We reduced our packs to the minimum. Finally, we left a package for Tim just inside his tent. It included the spare food, which was surprisingly little, and some extra medical supplies. On top of it I had written a note:

Tim,

We have tried to find you in the pinnacles. We are going to Antsalova and will inform the police there and the Embassy in 'Tana. If you read this, try to head northwest out of the pinnacle exit. That will bring you to a small village very quickly. Attached to this is a note in Malagasy saying who you are and requesting all assistance, etc. If they can't read, try pronouncing it. It's phonetic enough.

Good luck.

Henry and Laurent.

Good grief, I thought to myself. Isn't that typical of the academic approach? After you let them get themselves killed, you write them a little letter which includes clauses on phonetics. Perhaps I should have included it as a footnote. Stanwick Tours—they may kill you, but by golly they think of everything afterwards. Ignorant of my bitter thoughts, Laurent wrote out his note in bold capitals. We wrapped the notes in a clear plastic bag and placed them on top of the medical kit in the tent. That done we picked up our packs and walked down to the stream bank, where we took our boots and socks off. As we stood at the water's edge we turned and looked back. The solitary tent appeared desolate on its own in the middle of the camp now marked by dozens of footprints. Behind it all, everything was still and quiet in the warmth of the afternoon. I looked at Laurent for some encouragement. He gently took my elbow and led me round.

'Let's go.'

We turned our backs on the campsite and the Cricket Pitch and walked into the cool stream. As we waded downstream the rock closed behind us.

Following Laurent's suggestion I marked our path as we went so that if we did by some miracle get a search party we would be able to get back. We had been walking for perhaps ten minutes when we came into a corridor that had sand on the floor.

Abruptly, and with a curious decisiveness, Laurent stopped and looked round carefully. He then motioned me to be quiet. He calmly took his pack off and sat down, patting the ground next to him. With a good deal of puzzlement I followed his gesture and sat down beside him.

'Henry, my friend, I want to discuss something with you.'

I looked at my watch meaningfully. We were pushed for time, but then Laurent knew that too.

'Go ahead.'

'Last night I was praying about this matter, seeking guidance. In the middle I had a picture. A picture of two torch batteries.'

I doubt I would have laughed anyway, but my mood then was so black that it would have taken something much stronger to move me to laughter. He looked slightly guilty, but continued. 'You know that Malagasy people do not waste things. They cannot. So I have been collecting the batteries that you and Tim have thrown away from your torches. So far I have six. They are heavy, so I check them to be sure they are worth carrying back. I put them in the torch to see how bright the light is.'

Half of my mind was saying, what on earth is he talking about? We have miles to go and he is telling me about his recycling programme. At another level there was a growing flicker of interest.

'The day before yesterday—when Mr Tim vanished—I picked up two batteries that puzzled me. They were almost totally new. They were thrown away after we got back from the pinnacles that afternoon. Now I have spent last night and today wondering about this. Why did Tim throw away two good batteries just before he got lost? Would you ever do such a thing?'

I felt disappointed and my response came quickly. 'No way. I don't have the money.' I stopped and then went on. 'Except that, say before I was coming to Madagascar, I might be sure only to put in brand-new batteries because they are heavy and you can't get them here, but I don't see what that has to do with anything . . .'

Somewhere in my neural circuits some connections were being made. A monstrous idea crossed my mind. I got to my feet in agitation and walked up and down the sand a few steps.

Suddenly I stopped and stared at Laurent. 'You think that Vaughan replaced his batteries because he knew he was going to get lost?'

Laurent paused and motioned me down again. 'Yes. Truly

I do not believe that he got lost. No, I am definite; he is not lost now. That is why I waited till we were here to talk to you. No, I believe that Tim had need of his torch. So he put in a new set of batteries.'

The implications of the idea were flooding into my mind. I tried to treat it calmly.

'Interesting. But that is surely the only odd thing. Perhaps there is an explanation for that. Is there any other evidence?'

'Nothing big, but I am unhappy about the food we have left. I checked it very carefully from Antsalova to the pinnacles. I know how much was left at the edge of the pinnacles. I was surprised when Tim showed me what we had left at the camp-site. There seemed less than I had thought.'

'You are suggesting that he hid it in some way, I suppose in the pinnacles while we weren't looking?'

'Maybe closer. Remember that he had a whole day at camp when we were not there, when he had the leg injury—the one that appeared and disappeared in a day.' There was more than a hint of scepticism in his voice.

'Laurent, I'm sorry. I'm tired and this is all a bit much. What do you think happened?'

'I think, more and more, that Tim never went into the pinnacles at all. He hid somewhere to make us think that he is missing.'

I thought I had him there. 'Ah, but we have evidence that he was in the pinnacles. Two notes, which I have with me. And I cannot believe he would take the risk of going into the pinnacles on his own without marking the way out. No, Laurent, your story is interesting, but I think I believe the original version.'

He looked vaguely disappointed. 'Perhaps so. At times I think it is difficult to believe. But, Henry, remember where we found the last note. You have it in your mind, yes? Good. Now remember when Mr Tim took the curious photograph of us. The one where he walked up the crevasse at the side a long way. You remember that?'

'Yes, it was a funny shot. I remember saying. So?'

'Henry, can you be sure that they were not the same place?'

I thought hard about it. 'Yes, possibly they were, now you mention it. So the note would have been left in the early afternoon. But, Laurent, the whole plot would have to have been worked out in tremendous detail. It would have to have been set up a week ago at least . . .'

And yet as I thought about it, was that so odd? Patient, logical Tim Vaughan was capable of handling all the subtleties of computer communications. A painstaking plot like this might be just in his line.

'But, Laurent, the obvious thing—why?'

He shook his head in confusion. 'Ah, that I leave to you. I agree it is a problem. I cannot imagine an answer. Can you?'

I sat there for a minute, eyes closed, thinking.

'If I accept your idea—*if*, that is—I think I can answer at least part of it. He must want to appear to be dead. If we go back to 'Tana and tell our story then they will assume—I think—that he is dead. Now that raises an interesting point. It would only work if our testimony that he had been lost under these conditions could be trusted. So we would have to be above suspicion. Which, by and large, we are. Honest Laurent, son of universally respected local pastor and Dr H Stanwick, modestly respected (within confined limits) British academic.'

The idea gathered momentum, and I heard myself speaking faster. 'Perhaps that explains why we were chosen. At any rate it raises another question. Why want to be thought dead? And why here? Why not just drown in a boating accident?'

'There is a more serious question, Henry. What do we do now?'

'Yes. You have been thinking this out a lot. What do you suggest? My brain is reeling.'

'I think if we go back quietly now we will find Mr Vaughan at the campsite. There is his tent and sleeping bag. He has probably seen us going. He must also want to see if we have left a note.'

It was an attractive thought. It would allow a partial testing of Laurent's increasingly appealing hypothesis. If Tim was there, he was right; if he wasn't, then he was probably wrong. Either way it wouldn't take more than half an hour. I could hardly refuse.

'So we sneak up on him and say "Boo!" and ask him what he's up to?'

'Perhaps, something like that. Perhaps it can be sorted out.'

The long and short of it was that we turned round and walked back to the entrance of the pinnacles.

We tried to sneak out cautiously, but it was difficult with the packs and the water. I waded out first from the crevasse, trying to keep an eye on my feet as they slid and sank in the sandy bottom.

I peered round the corner and looked towards the tent. There was nothing. I moved further out and looked for any sign of life and at that point there was a faint noise behind me. I spun round, splashing heavily. On the river bank opposite the camp, braced against a rock, was a man. Unshaven and dirty, but definitely Tim Vaughan.

That much was a surprise that I was at least partially prepared for. What I wasn't prepared for was that he was carrying an object in his right hand which he levelled at me. I was just on the point of deciding that it looked rather unpleasant and disturbingly familiar when he fired it.

24

I hadn't time to do more than flinch before the shot went over my head. Its shattering noise echoed and reechoed round and round among the rocks. As it died away Tim spoke.

'You aren't welcome. I hope you get the message.'

In retrospect I think the voice was nearly as scaring as the shot. There was a flat chill edge to it, but the most striking thing was the apparent absence of anger; indeed any discernible emotion.

In fear and consternation my mind began freewheeling crazily at the turn of events. Vaughan seemed to have no such uncertainties.

'You, Stanwick, get out of the water, onto the sand there and put your hands in the air. Move slowly. You, Laurent, get over there. Stand next to him. Face away from me. Total silence or I'll shoot to kill next time.'

I couldn't think straight. I rarely can in crises. Vaughan was alive, but what was going on? It crossed my mind that he was mad; then I realised that he was absolutely rational.

Laurent was right. He must have smuggled the gun in. He had cheated us ever since we got here; possibly before. I began to get angry. He had tricked us and was now trying to kill us. I spun round and snapped at him. I felt like swearing, but I'd got out of the habit.

'Vaughan, you're a psychiatric case. Loony, crazy and the rest. We've spent the last two days risking our necks hunting for you. Now drop that toy and give us an explanation. You could try apologising, too.'

I hadn't been that angry with anyone for a long time. Vaughan stopped on the edge of the stream bank and gave me a look of such cold ill-will and contempt that I stepped back.

He raised his gun again. The words came out as bleak and cold as before. If I'd tried to make him angry, I'd failed miserably.

'I thought you'd seen these things before, Dr Stanwick. They make a nasty mess of people. As your mind seems to be wandering, perhaps you could concentrate on this single statement. The simplest and most logical thing for me to do right now would be to kill you both, straightaway.'

As he spoke my anger evaporated, to be replaced with that sick visceral feeling that I always get when faced with the wrong end of a loaded gun barrel. Not that it's happened a lot, but as events go, they do tend to stick in the mind.

'Now turn round and do as I say from now on. Drop your packs on the sand, walk two yards forward from them, and stand up facing towards the tent. Let me warn you again, I'm in a mind to kill. Oh, and as a special consideration, Stanwick, if you try to jump me or do anything silly I'll put a bullet in your sidekick's head. And you, Laurent, you move out of turn and I blow out your Henry's precious brains. Savvy?'

Pretty neat. A little voice in my head observed that at least he had learnt something about Christian ethics. I flicked a quick glance at Laurent, whose face was frozen into an attitude of dull puzzlement. He walked woodenly out of the water until he was nearly level with me and dutifully dropped his pack.

Vaughan called out again with measured and controlled words. 'Slowly and carefully put your boots back on. You may yet be doing some walking. If you are lucky. Then stand up and face away from me. No talking, no nonsense. Do you read me?'

We obeyed. Well, what else could we do?

Vaughan moved up behind. I tried to work out what he was up to. I tried to turn my head slightly, but all I got was a curt order to face front. It was difficult to avoid the impression that Tim's military career had been much longer and more recent than he claimed.

A coil of nylon cord was thrown at Laurent's feet. It looked as if it had been cut from one of the tents.

'Stanwick, hands together behind your back. You, tie his hands together. Make it tight. I'll check it afterwards. Do it in silence.'

Laurent did as he was told, and it felt uncomfortably professional. I doubted if I could get my hands free very easily. Vaughan then tied up Laurent's hands in the same way. He kept the gun in his hand as he did it. It was an odd-looking, light-weight contraption with a grip that certainly wasn't metal. I wondered if he'd fired it to demonstrate that it was indeed a killing weapon.

Vaughan then came up behind me. I felt like cringing, expecting him to hit me or worse. He just checked Laurent's knots and with a mutter ran a couple more loops round my wrists. My hands didn't hurt much at the moment, but I was under no illusions about what they would feel like soon. He then carried out a very thorough search which cost me a penknife.

Vaughan walked round in front of me and looked me in the eye. His blue eyes were accentuated by the shadows under them. He didn't look mad. But then the really dangerous ones never do.

'I've got to decide what to do with you guys. You're threatening a lot. Part of me says wipe you out and get it done with. The other half is trying to be kind. I need an hour to think. Sit down on the sand. Don't move, don't talk. Remember, I'm trying to save your skins.'

With that he went over to the tent and crawled in. Every few minutes or so his head appeared to check on us. There was nothing to do but sit quietly and try to think of a way out. I caught Laurent's gloomy face and tried to wink at him. He looked back and mouthed a single word, 'Sorry.' He obviously felt he was to blame for our plight. It wasn't a perception that I could share. However you looked at it, it was me who had got us all involved. And at that I felt embarrassed. What was it that

Laurent and Tina had seen in Vaughan to worry them that I hadn't? Why had they suspected what lay behind the facade when I hadn't? How could I have been so blind? 'Pride,' said my little voice and I had to concede that for once it might be right. The thought of Tina and Grantforth seemed to heighten the anguish further.

The afternoon wore on. My wrists ached. I tried wriggling in the hope that the bonds would give, but it was futile. The way Vaughan had us sitting, it was very difficult to be sure that you were not being observed from inside the tent. What was he up to? I had no idea. I did decide, however, that if Laurent and I could get free I would be happily content never to know. I reviewed all I'd ever heard about being held hostage. It all seemed to revolve around making friends out of the kidnappers. There wasn't much about what happens when it's a friend doing the kidnapping.

After what was probably about an hour, Vaughan emerged from his tent. The pistol was held carefully in his right hand, while in his left he clutched a plastic-wrapped package the size of a thin paperback. Some slight weight seemed to have been lifted from him, but he hardly looked carefree.

'It's your lucky day, guys. Answered prayer, Laurent. There may be a way out. I want to show you something first. We are going upstream, to where the water goes through the gorge. Slowly. Henry, lead the way—silently. Take it carefully. It's a conditional reprieve.'

It took twenty minutes to get to the point where the stream wound its incised way through the limestone. As I stumbled through the prickly bushes, I tried to remember everything about the place from my reconnaissance there with Laurent ten days ago. What stuck in the mind was not encouraging. The dark swirling waters, the precipitous sides and the razor-edged rock didn't reassure me. The afternoon was coming to a close rapidly.

When we got there the place didn't seem any better than memory had suggested. I was worried that Vaughan was going to make us sit on the edge of the sheer drop. He spared us that, granting us a relatively smooth spot a couple of yards away from the edge. But given the way the rocks sloped rapidly I'd have been happier to have been even further away. I couldn't see the water, but its muffled turmoil was clearly audible. The rocks faintly seemed to transmit the vibration.

Laurent was ten yards from me and he looked very uneasy. Vaughan made himself comfortable about the same distance away, to form a neat equilateral triangle.

As I sat down I groped slowly and carefully with my tied hands, feeling the rock behind me inch by inch. I soon found what I wanted and began slowly rubbing the nylon against the raised rib of limestone. To my knowledge, most of the practitioners of the 'and with a single bound he was free' school of escape have never tried abrading strong nylon under the watchful eye of captors a few yards away. It did fleetingly cross my mind that if I ever did free myself this way, it would be the ultimate riposte to the 'What on earth is the use of knowing about limestone weathering' type of question that I habitually received during every course. But then it crossed my mind that if I didn't do precisely that there might not be another Limestone Geomorphology option at Grantforth University next term. At least not one given by me. Then Tim started talking and I had to think of other things.

'OK, I'm giving you a chance to come with me. But before I do that I guess I'd better fill you in on what I'm doing. Possibly then you won't think I'm too bad.'

He paused, stretched his arms behind his head and then, his thoughts apparently collected, began.

'Firstly, I guess I was, well, not technically correct about my military connections. They are kinda stronger than I have suggested. One time I held a considerable rank for my age. Some years ago I was involved in a project. An "Ultra-Black" project. Its name, for reasons I've forgotten, was Jezreel. They got a bunch of us boys together and a lot of flash computing gear. At least for those days it was red-hot. Even now it wouldn't be bad. They also gave us access to any data we wanted. The first and last time that's been done. The purpose was to predict the future. You'll have seen the civilian stuff, Henry. Climatic, eco-logical and geopolitical trends to the year 2000 and beyond. That stuff's rubbish. We neutered it. Besides, they never got half the data we had to start with. Now you must understand that our data was good and our techniques the best that were around. I've been keeping tabs on them since and they haven't falsified our methods. Do you believe me?'

He looked at me acutely. I reviewed it all in my mind. It sounded all too probable, although I'm pretty cautious about the results of these fancy projections.

'I'll accept it. I'm hardly in a situation to evaluate critically your methodology.'

'True 'nough. Now about halfway through the program we got results that we didn't expect and didn't like. The results began to pan out with a very high probability of global collapse within twenty years. We fiddled the figures, and we could stretch it to thirty years—at the most.' He paused for effect, and I broke in.

'The civilian versions were not that bad. They implied a certain hope.'

'After what happened to Jezreel, steps were taken to ensure that they said that. No, we had better data. The problem is simply put: as the developed world becomes more complex and interlocking it becomes more vulnerable. It's like a machine. The more complex it gets, the more easy it is to put a spanner in the works. Like, you wouldn't believe how much all the financial systems of the world depend on transferring money as packets of electrons. No, the system is getting too complex. In fact sooner or later it will collapse. And it may not be easy to rebuild.'

He paused. It was a new Tim, or at least one of whom there had previously been only faint hints. There was a note of the visionary in his voice. A secular prophet, perhaps. Then he started again in his cool quiet voice. It was still passionless. On some people's views of knowledge he would have made a good academic.

'And, of course, just when we need greater global stability we get less. Have you tried plotting the power of the weapons used by terrorists in terms of time? A nice curve, Henry—real neat—and easy to extrapolate. On our predictions, someone somewhere in a terrorist group is working on the plans for a nuclear weapon right now. You can't go on increasing your weaponry on a finite and vulnerable earth. And that's just one fragment of the modelling. Then there is all the ecological and financial side as well. Fundamentally, you just get the two curves. The margin by which the global system stays stable continually decreases and the destabilising forces continue to increase. We were the first to quantify it, and to see when the curves would cross.'

There was a lot of grim logic in the views he was propounding. On their own they weren't new. I'd heard similar ideas kicked around, even in Grantforth Staff Common Room. Here it seemed pretty compelling. Presumably Tim believed it enough to base this whole trip on it.

He began again. 'One image has been used by a friend of mine. The earth is like a ship in the middle of an ocean. In the old days the thousand petty states acted like watertight compartments. Sure, they had wars, ecological collapse and economic anarchy. But their fragmentation minimised damage. Kept it isolated. Besides, they didn't have the mechanisms for doing real damage. What we have been doing in the past forty years is smashing down the bulkheads and at the same time using our technology and numbers to knock holes in the side of the ship. The water's coming in real bad in a number of places. Madagascar is one of them. I guess we're fortunate it's a long way from the engine room. But there are leaks occurring in some critical places. From the right perspective you can see that our ship is developing a nasty little list and there's a few warning lights flashing on the bridge. But there's no captain: the crew are split into two main factions who spend their time fighting each other. And everybody else is too busy enjoying the party and listening to the band.'

He paused and stared at me. 'Oh yes, and we don't have any lifeboats. At least not yet. But there are a few of us who know what's happening and who are trying to do something. Before it's too late.'

The light was fading rapidly now, and the crevasses either side were deep in gloom. I had been so taken with Tim's narrative that I had almost stopped trying to wear away the cord tying my wrists. I tried again, hoping Tim wouldn't see what I was doing. He began again abruptly.

'Well, let's drop the model. The conclusion we came to was simple. If the world continued to be dominated by two bickering superpowers then disaster was inevitable. A real mother of a disaster, with no reasonable hope of recovery. Not in our lifetime, or even your children's lifetime. No, the system must be brought under control, the world made more stable and the disruptive elements eliminated.'

I was still thinking about his previous point. 'Just a minute—I don't see how an economic crisis could trigger the sort of catastrophe you are talking about.'

'Ever tried not paying an army? When states collapse, their armies disintegrate and they take their weapons with them. You saw it in Lebanon, I'm sure. With tanks and rifles it's a nuisance. But with thermonuclear weapons? Anyway, let me continue. With the two chief powers perpetually impotent because of being locked in this ceaseless rivalry, then it would be only a matter of time before disaster occurred. So we concluded that there were only two alternatives. Perhaps you could supply them, Dr Stanwick?'

Vaughan smiled in a manner that was almost pleasant. I forced my mind to think for a few moments.

'Get the US and the Soviets to get their act together? Stop fighting and jointly man the pumps? That'd be one option. The other might be to get Uncle Sam to wipe out the other side pretty smart and then get on with saving the world.'

'Exactly so. You're a natural, Henry. As you might expect, they didn't like either. Jezreel was scrapped before the results could be formalised. Those of us involved were posted as far away from each other as they could put us. They erased all the files; even the project name was forgotten.'

A pause. The setting sun was gleaming orange on the tops of the pinnacles. It was difficult to think about dawn. Even whether there would be one.

'But I never forgot the conclusions. There had to be another way. And now I've found it.'

Vaughan pulled out his thin plastic-wrapped package and held it delicately in his hands. 'As I said, only if one side had total power—the power to rule unchallenged—only then could disaster be averted. I've thought and agonised over it, but I believe the only answer is to let it be the Eastern bloc.'

'So you are defecting. But how does that help?' I was anxious to show that I was listening. I didn't want him to think that I was preoccupied. But the nylon cord still seemed to be intact.

'This is the answer. It is a series of communications circuits.'

He opened the package and carefully pulled out a circuit board. I recognised little more than a collection of diverse silicon chips.

'It's the oldest truth in the book that communications are critical in warfare, and keeping one jump ahead of the opposition is a permanent nightmare. Every innovation—every new code—has a short life before it is cracked. And a cracked code, as any history of wars will tell you, is the most powerful of all weapons for the other side. This is a partial answer. This little box is going to be installed in a few main military centres. A dozen in fact. It sits there and does precisely nothing. In fact it is forgotten about. We call it a twenty-three fifty-nine, because that's when it's switched on. At a minute to midnight; on the brink of a nuclear war. It is then switched on and suddenly the critical communications links become unintelligible to the enemy. It codes and directs signal transmission in a novel way. Sure, they can crack the code. They can break any code, but only with time. It will allow the uninterrupted and tight transmission of signals in the vital moments before a nuclear attack. Very neat.'

Why was Vaughan coming clean? Things were beginning to fit together. If these were indeed the size of the stakes in the game, then the scale of this whole Madagascar charade began to fit into place.

'I have nearly reached the end of my story. Tomorrow, according to prior arrangement, a helicopter lands to pick me up here. I travel with it and with this device. It provides a weapon that will allow the Eastern bloc to win any East-West confrontation. In a year's time there will only be one super-power. And we will be able to set to work to avert the disaster.'

'But why all this game with us?'

'Isn't it obvious? I couldn't just defect. The slightest hint that my disappearance wasn't what it seemed and there would be investigations. Even the possibility that I had defected would cause them to recode the entire twenty-three fifty-nine project. The whole defection would be worthless. No, I've been setting this up for the past two years. There were other localities, but Madagascar just clicked the moment I saw your article, and you and Laurent would have satisfied the most suspicious coroner. A pity, yes sir, a real pity. Still, the rule in communications is to make sure you always have a back-up—especially when whatever you are doing mustn't fail. And this isn't going to fail. For your sake, for your children's sake, it mustn't. I won't let it.'

Here comes the bill, I thought.

'So I'm not an ideological spy. I'm no commie. I just want to save the world. Kinda naive, eh? So I'm giving you two choices. Join me—I think I can swing it for you to come along—and leave with me tomorrow. In a year you will be able to surface again—as heroes probably. If not then, certainly to your grandchildren when they see the disaster you saved them from. Or . . .'

There was a pause.

'Or what?'

I didn't really want, or need, to ask.

'Or else I kill you here. The reason why we are here is that I don't want any bodies around. If the three of us vanish without trace that might just warrant a search party and I really wouldn't want them to find any bodies. They won't, down in these crevasses. I just shoot you and slide your bodies down into the stream. You have five minutes to decide.'

He took his watch off, pressed a button on it, and lay it on the limestone. Then he rose, stretched his arms, yawned, and walked to the edge of the cliff where he stood staring at the sunset.

25

For a few seconds sheer mental panic set in. I wanted to try and run away or crawl over to Tim and gibber for mercy. Then somehow something cooler took over. To my surprise I heard my voice speaking quietly, although it was shaking badly.

'Well, Laurent, what do we do?'

There was silence for a second. Then Laurent spoke slowly and hesitantly. 'I think you know what my answer is, Henry. You know the history of our church. If I went with Mr Vaughan I would not want to call myself a Malagasy Christian again. And you?'

Indeed, a very good question. What options did I have? Then I suddenly realised that I had stopped rubbing the cord. Vaughan was still apparently gazing abstractly at the sunset. I found the edge of the limestone and pressed down hard on it. It slipped, and I felt it gash into my wrist. I pressed down again and rubbed.

'Laurent, is there no other way out?'

There was a beep from the watch. Four minutes left.

'Not honestly, Henry. Besides, even if we gave in and followed him I am not certain that I would trust our friend's promises. The devil is the father of lies, not just one lie.'

I tried to lower my voice to a level that Vaughan couldn't hear. 'There may be another way if I can break this cord. Then we must get his gun.'

But the bonds seemed as tight as ever. Or weren't they just a bit slacker?

Laurent just nodded slowly. Neither of us spoke. The angle of my wrists as I tried to flex the cord against the rock was agony. Laurent was silent, although I could see his lips moving faintly. He was praying. It struck me that that was what I should be doing. I tried to pray, but it seemed to me empty words. I felt that I heard a little voice saying to me that it was a bit late now. It was my stupidity and pigheadedness that had put us in this spot in the first place.

Beep. Three minutes.

If I couldn't break these cords, what would happen? I couldn't let Vaughan shoot me. Not here, not in this stupid place. I had a life to live, things to do.

Everything seemed very distant, unreal. This was all a dream. Yet surely this wasn't going to be the end of everything? There must be a way of cheating death. But how? Only by giving in. I suppose if I had been on my own I might have done it. But in the face of Laurent's example how could I?

Beep. Two minutes.

The bonds were still holding. My wrists hurt, and there was the sticky feel of blood around the point where the cord cut in. Vaughan turned round and walked slowly towards us. It was difficult to see his face, silhouetted as he was against the dying sun. I tried not to think of the people I'd seen dead of bullet wounds. It was stupid when I largely agreed with Vaughan anyway. It was only the means that I objected to. No, I'd have to give in. Sorry, I wasn't going to be on the honourable list of martyrs.

But if he then shot Laurent? I couldn't really follow Vaughan then, could I?

There was a waiting silence.

Beep. One minute.

Vaughan turned to look at us, then looked back at the view. I found myself thinking that it was the most beautiful sunset I'd ever seen; that life was worth living; that I really couldn't be expected to give it up. Everything started to become muddled and choked by anger, fear and guilt.

Beep Beep Beep. Time.

Vaughan picked up the watch and switched it off. Then to my surprise he went over to Laurent.

'Laurent, you understand the issues. Your country needs your help. Will you come with me?'

'*Tsia*, no. I will not. I do not believe that the way to help this world is by lying and stealing.'

Vaughan nodded his head slowly. 'Very well. I'm sorry.' It came out mechanically.

He turned to me and took a step towards me. 'Well, Dr Stanwick? Will you then come and help me?'

For a second or two no words would come. Vaughan was on the point of saying something. Then, as if in a dream, I heard myself talking. 'No, I too will not. Sorry, Vaughan, no deal.'

I wasn't at all sure that that was what I had meant to say. He paused.

'Henry, I don't think you believe me. Very foolish.'

He turned and took a pace over towards Laurent. There could be no mistaking his actions. He held the gun in both hands and moved his legs apart as if bracing them; but in doing so he had turned his back on me. In desperation, I jerked at my wrists as hard as I could.

The cords snapped. I lunged forward and sideways in a clumsy move that was half a roll. I hit the rock on my shoulder. It hurt horribly. Vaughan spun round, but I had kept moving and before he could do anything I had collided with him. He went down onto the rock. My aching hands went out towards where his right hand and the gun was. Suddenly, Vaughan rolled and pinned me under him. He was strong, terribly strong. I was conscious of Laurent getting to his feet and coming over. Vaughan's hand—it must have been his left hand—had encircled my throat.

I released one hand and tried to prise his fingers off my neck. My other hand was around his wrist, and I was trying to move upwards to grab the gun. I couldn't breathe. It was dark and suffocating. Something swung in over my head to hit Vaughan. He rolled and took it on the shoulder with a grunt. I realised dimly that Laurent was kicking him. A hard sharp object was pressing into my chest, forced down by the weight of Vaughan's body. My lungs ached. The thin angular block slipped down between us as we rolled. I vaguely realised what it was and, without thinking, left his gun hand alone to grab it. It was the circuit board, coming free of its plastic cocoon. I think I had some idea of using it to hit Vaughan with. Suddenly, his left hand released my throat and he made a grab for the board.

What happened next I cannot be sure. In an uncontrollable reflex I gulped in a lungful of air and my grasp on the board temporarily slipped. I felt it being torn away by his strong fingers. Suddenly, in a crashing, aching blow a booted foot swung in and hit my hand. I was conscious of pain, and the board seemed to be flung free. There was a cracking sound, then a slithering noise, followed by two rattles; the second fainter. Finally, there was a quiet splash. Its meaning didn't register. Nothing registered other than pain and despair.

Vaughan, however, seemed to freeze in his grapple and with a yell of 'No!' broke free. Laurent, hands behind his back, was just flung aside. I had half got up to a sitting position when a bunched fist hit me in the stomach. Sickness, breathlessness and searing pain struck me instantly, and I collapsed in what felt like a terminal agony.

Everything was a dark blur for moments or possibly minutes. I felt like death. A shapeless mass, rimmed by fire, resolved itself into the figure of Vaughan in the dusk. He was standing over me, and the gun was extended.

We had lost. This was it. My mind was a whirl of despair.

He was speaking. The gun looked funny. Something was wrong. Or was it right? Vaughan was extending the gun towards me. A hand was lifting me up. Vaughan's hand?

Oh, my stomach.

He spoke again and this time I caught the words, although it took forever for me to understand them.

'Henry, I'm sorry. I've lost. You've won. I surrender.'

175

26

'I'm sorry, Tim. I thought you were going to kill us.' My words came out painfully, but it was very good to be able to say anything.

'I was certainly thinking about it. In fact if it wasn't a futile exercise I'd shoot you both now for fouling things up.'

'Sorry.'

I was checking myself over to make sure there wasn't any major damage that I was unaware of. There seemed nothing but very painful bruises and scrapes.

Tim began again. 'I'm afraid you, or perhaps we, dropped that neat little device down the cliff. So I'm left without my trump card and I have to rethink it all now.'

There was a curious flat note in his voice.

'So?'

The new situation was beginning to register with me.

'That's it. The whole point of my defection was to take that board over with me. Or didn't I make myself clear? Without it I have nothing to offer.'

He didn't seem to be talking to anyone in particular. I got to my feet unsteadily; nothing seemed to be broken. In fact I was more or less intact. I felt distinctly better, and I knew I had to try and take charge.

'That, as they say, is your problem. Now where is the safety catch on this wretched thing?'

He showed me; it was already on. I thought about throwing it into the stream or at the very least unloading the magazine, but I wasn't that trusting. I'm all in favour of forgive and

forget, but it takes longer than ten minutes to forget that someone has just been trying to kill you.

'Now, let's sort Laurent out. Vaughan, stand well clear. My
nerves aren't what they were. Second thoughts, pass us your
knife. Slowly.'

I hate guns. I could feel the effect of simply holding the thing.
Already I had the feeling of possessing power over Vaughan.

It was getting very dark. It occurred to me that we must
get off these rocks. Everything on the ground was shades of
grey and black. I went over to where Laurent had fallen, but I
was careful to keep half an eye open for motion from Tim.

Laurent was trying to free himself from his bonds near
where the rock passed into coarse grass. I bent over him, found
the nylon, and cut it through.

'Well, your prayers were answered, Laurent. How are you
feeling?'

'I am alive. That is a mercy I did not expect.'

He rubbed his wrists.

'What happened?'

'Your misspent youth paid off. Your karate kick sent his precious box into the river. Our friend has decided that having lost
it, he isn't in quite such a strong position as he was. In fact he
seems to think he has lost.'

There was a moment's silence. 'Very strange. I will not
argue with him.'

It was getting very dark. I decided that some positive
action was necessary, so I ordered us all back to the campsite.
Tim acquiesced without a murmur.

An hour later we were sitting round the fire at the campsite, although there was only one tent standing. I had made a
relatively rapid recovery, helped doubtless by the realisation
that a premature death was not now imminent. Vaughan was
quiet and subdued; if not a broken man, at least a bent one.
The gun resided in my pocket with the safety catch very firmly
on. I thought it most unlikely that I would ever bring myself to
use it, but nevertheless I hadn't felt it wise to empty the mag-

azine of bullets. We had just finished a session of bandaging up wounds. This was tricky by torchlight, but the fact that it had to be a team operation had a beneficial effect. None of the bruises and gashes appeared to be serious, although Vaughan had a nasty cut on one arm due to hitting a limestone edge in the struggle. In civilisation it would have been given stitches, but he seemed happy enough with some careful bandaging. Laurent and I had got off with little more than some cuts and bruises, although my throat and stomach felt particularly sore. My hand wasn't feeling too good either from the bruise I'd received from Laurent's kick.

Outweighing many of these aches and pains was the feeling that we had come off well. Vaughan had been beaten and his stolen circuitry destroyed. His plans lay in ruin. Laurent, however, seemed depressed and uneasy. If we had indeed won, he was very cautious in believing it. It crossed my mind meanly that he was peeved at missing the long and honourable list of Malagasy martyrs. Of course there were problems ahead. I wasn't sure what we were going to do with Vaughan, and something had to be decided before the arrival of the helicopter tomorrow.

Laurent finished putting a large plaster on a gash on Tim's wrist.

'Thanks, Laurent. A neat job. I don't know about anybody else, but I could use some food. Any objections?'

It sounded like a good idea, so I just gave assent. In fact it turned out to be very much what we all needed.

There was, however, no denying that it was a very curious meal. I tried to pretend that everything was what it had been a few days ago in this very spot. But as hard as I tried, Tim's despondent look, my aches and pains, and the pressure of the gun in my pocket reminded me otherwise. We ate largely in silence.

After we had finished, Tim turned to me, his face visibly dirty, even in the firelight. His eyes seemed sunken. 'Well, I guess apologies are in order, if hardly adequate.' He paused.

'Although I'm pretty mad about the whole business, Henry, you jumping me gave me an excuse. I mean, I didn't actually want to kill you, but I couldn't reckon on any other way out. Well, I guess you found one for me.'

He didn't sound pretty mad at all. He stooped and picked up a handful of sand and let it dribble through his fingers. 'It still leaves me in a mess. But at least I'm not guilty of murder. Treason to a state, maybe. But then doesn't duty to the whole Earth override duty to a small part of it?'

I shrugged my shoulders and regretted it instantly. That was a nasty bruise. Laurent said nothing. He just sat there watching Tim. If any expression could be seen in the firelight it was that of mildly sorrowful disapproval.

Tim spoke again. His voice was quiet and betrayed little emotion. 'Well, you guys hold the cards now. What happens tomorrow?'

'I haven't really given it much thought, Tim. You kept me rather preoccupied over the last few hours. Laurent and I need to discuss it together.'

Laurent nodded slightly. His eyes did not, however, leave Tim's face.

I continued, 'I guess we will plan to leave here together, well before your friends arrive in their helicopter. I've no desire to be on the wrong side of a gunship.'

Tim shook his head. 'Hardly that. No hammer and sickle flying boldly either. No. I guess it will be some third-party deal. That's the way these things work.'

'I wouldn't know. Treachery isn't my line.' As I said it I regretted it.

'Touche, as they say. But when one day you're stopped at some militia checkpoint in the centre of Grantforth, or when you're sitting in some basement hearing them firing 155 mm artillery rounds into the heart of Oxford, I hope you'll realise what I tried to stop. It was Oxford, wasn't it, Henry?'

I didn't answer for a moment. Tim's words had produced a powerful superimposition of images of Beirut and the two

English cities. Besides, I'd realised I wasn't holding the credentials to pass moral judgements.

'Yes, Oxford.'

It seemed a universe away. I shook myself clear of the nightmare.

'I don't suppose you can call this helicopter and tell them no deal?'

'We discussed communication beforehand, but on your information I assumed that it would be too difficult to get a signal out of here on a low-power transmitter. Probably correct, incidentally. Besides, with the twenty-three fifty-nine, and other things, I was carrying all I could.'

'Well, tough on them; they will just find nothing.'

Vaughan spoke very quietly. 'They may not like that. Not at all. They have set up a deal that is costing a lot to pull off. There could be repercussions.'

Out of the corner of one eye I saw Laurent stiffen.

'Sorry, Tim, I'm out of my depth here. Try to be a bit clearer.'

'I'll spell it out. They arrive here. No one, nothing. They know the names of the party. The next step is to put out a general search enquiry for you. Hotel rooms, passenger lists. I would expect that you would have an interesting interview very shortly after returning to 'Tana. If they thought you had the device you could be, well, under some pressure to give it up. On the other hand, if you convinced them that you did not have the device, then they might decide to tidy up some loose ends on this failed project. Professional pride.'

He paused briefly. Any residual euphoria from the events of the early part of the evening evaporated rapidly into the darkness. The circle of flickering firelight seemed small and threatened. I'd have given a lot for the crowds and noise of the pub I'd been in with Jim Barnett. Tim continued, 'Look, I'm sorry about this. You've got involved in this innocently, but that is irrelevant. You are now involved. I'll do what I can to see that you get out of this in one piece, but the point is, from the moment Laurent kicked that thing over the cliff, we had a problem. Not just me, but we. Do you read me?'

'Point taken. But let's get one thing straight. I mean, why can't you reconstruct this thing yourself?'

Tim shook his head violently.

'I guess I didn't explain the board properly. Custom-built chips. Give me a break! Each one is the complexity of the street map of the whole of LA. No, that's gone. No one could reconstruct it. Besides, the main point of the twenty-three fifty-nine was that it kept shifting variables like pitch and coding in a non-predictable manner. Trying to decode anything in the twenty-four hours or so it was to be in operation would have been hopeless. Like hitting a target moving apparently randomly in three or four dimensions. All those changes were controlled by a single chip. Without that, even knowing the other chips is useless.'

'So what do you suggest? That you meet them empty-handed?'

Tim sighed and rose to his feet. My hand slipped towards the gun.

He caught the gesture, and I caught a flicker of amusement on his face in the gloom. 'Just remember to take the safety catch off first. Oh, and aim before you pull the trigger. A hole in your foot would be painful.'

I pulled my hand away.

Then his face changed to pained concentration. 'No, we are in a mess. Me in particular, but it's still tricky for you. We don't have much time. And I'm tired.'

He stretched and gave a slight groan. I wasn't the only one with bruises, then. He turned round and sat down. He sounded depressed. 'Try this as an idea, both of you. Suppose I met them alone, and I said, well, that I'd lost it; that it had fallen out of the pack into the stream? Something like that. Also, that you guys had left, assuming I was dead. No, even better, forget the dead business. We'd all got out of the pinnacles and then split. I'd hung around on my own. Last you saw of me I was alive and well on the pinnacle edge. Yeah, that might work. That way they'd have nothing to say to you.'

'And what would happen to you?'

He shrugged dismissively. 'That's my problem. I guess I'd put a case that I was still worth dragging along. However, they're more likely to suggest I walk home.'

'Or worse?'

Tim answered hesitantly. The glow from the embers of the fire was enough to illuminate a frown. 'It sure can't be ruled out, but I don't see how any other way will work. I'm reluctant to go back to 'Tana because I think that this would mean a death sentence for all of us.'

There was silence. I ached all over and felt that I could just topple over and sleep where I fell. I couldn't see any way forward, either.

The silence was broken by some animal rustlings in the bushes. A pair of small red eyes glowed in the dark and then moved away.

Tim spoke again. 'At any rate I've had it. I'm going to crash out. See you fellows in the morning. Sorry again for all the excitement. Don't worry about mounting a guard. I've got troubles enough without jumping you and making my own way back. Night.'

With that he turned and disappeared to his tent.

Laurent and I set to work putting our tents up. I was tempted just to lie out on the sand, but the nylon afforded some protection against mosquitos and the possible scorpion. We did a terrible job, but at last they stood up. I motioned Laurent away to a point well out of earshot of Tim's tent.

'What do you think, Laurent? I mean, about what we do tomorrow?'

'I'm not sure, Henry. It is difficult. Do we believe him?'

'Mmm, I think you have put your finger on the problem. Still, there is no doubt that he was waiting back here for something. It could only really be a helicopter. But certainly I want to see that tomorrow before I believe him completely.'

I fondled a bruise on my arm for a moment while I tried to think. 'As for the story he tells, well, it seems to fit. Where I know enough it sounds reasonable. He certainly had some sort of circuit board with a complex chip arrangement on it. And you did kick it into the river. So it sounds plausible, believable.'

I paused and thought further. 'Nothing else makes sense. At least not to me at the moment.'

'Perhaps,' said Laurent with a definite air of doubt. He went on hesitantly: 'I think that we should take him back to someone who can sort it all out. His Embassy, perhaps. However, I see a problem. What if he does not want to go?'

'Aren't you forgetting that I have his gun?'

There was a slight laugh. It was too dark to see his face, but I knew that Laurent was grinning. 'I have not forgotten that. But what will you do with it? Shoot him?'

'Drat, I'd forgotten that. That explains why he gave it to me. He knows I won't use it. A smart boy. Oh well, that problem will wait till tomorrow. Anyway, I'm too tired to think. I'm nearly falling asleep on my feet.'

We turned to walk back across the star-lit sand. The fire had almost gone out. A silly thought struck me.

'Incidentally, Laurent, that was a good kick. How does it feel to have saved the West with a single kick?'

'Perhaps I could believe that, Henry. But if I believed Tim I would also think that I had put the world at risk at the same time. I prefer not to have the blame for either.'

And with that we went to our tents. As I lay down a thousand things—problems, questions and incidents—seemed to flood into my mind, every one clamouring for attention. I ignored them all and fell asleep in moments.

27

Light was coming in through the tent when I woke up, aching and stiff. For a moment I panicked, thinking that I'd overslept and the helicopter had landed already. In fact I had indeed overslept, but not by that much. Laurent and Tim were sitting around the fire drinking coffee. The atmosphere appeared to be awkward.

I walked over testing my limbs. They seemed to be in some sort of working, if painful, order. Vaughan spoke first, looking up from his plastic mug.

'Everything still in one piece, Henry?'

Despite having washed and shaved he still looked rough. The plasters and bruises didn't help. He had on one of his long-sleeved grey shirts which hid the large bandage on his arm.

'No thanks to you, but I'll live.' It was an attempt at joviality.

Tim gave a sour smile. 'Sorry. But you gave as good as you got. Breakfast will help. There's plenty of it because whatever happens we don't need to take any food away with us.' He paused and turned to Laurent. 'Incidentally, Laurent, you had me worried when you checked the food supplies here. I thought you might have actually counted all the packages and figured I'd hidden away enough for myself. Was that what put you on to me?'

Laurent looked embarrassed. 'It was one thing. There were others.'

There was an expectant silence, but he said nothing more. Tim gave the faintest shrug and looked away.

I sat down, grabbed some food, and checked my watch. Seven thirty.

'Tim, when is the earliest we can expect your friends?'

'Two hours from now. The planned time is ten-thirty, plus or minus an hour.'

'So we need to decide what we are going to do.'

It was stating the obvious, but I wanted to get the debate rolling.

Tim shifted his position on the rock that passed for a seat. 'Henry, let me give you my proposal. You may not like all of it, but I think you should consider all the other alternatives before rejecting it.'

I looked at Laurent. He was watching Vaughan's face with total attention. 'Go ahead, Tim. We're all ears.'

'I'm anxious to talk to the contact on the helicopter—to tell him that there is no deal; that I've lost the device. I may simply tell him that in a fit of conscience I destroyed it. But I think it is vital that Moscow knows about the Jezreel Project. They can rerun it; perhaps they will get better results; perhaps they will be able to put pressure on the US to act together; perhaps they may be able to contribute to another solution—one that does not need that device. I will also say nothing that will put you at risk. I will simply say that we separated outside the pinnacles and that you believed I was going to walk along the edge on my own. In fact I told the Embassy that I might stay out here a bit longer on my own, so it would square with the official story. I'd say, of course, that you have no idea about the device.'

He gestured to the point where the Beboka came out of the cliffs. 'Perhaps losing it was providential. It will allow me to go with open hands. Perhaps they can be persuaded. So I'd prefer to wait here for them, but I want you guys to stay around.' He seemed uneasy. 'It is possible that they will just fly off in a huff and leave me to walk out. I'd rather have company in that case. If that happens I'll go with you to 'Tana.'

I wasn't sure what to say. For one thing I was vaguely

peeved that he was taking the initiative. I felt out of my depth. Laurent's face was impassive—so much so that you could even believe it was carved.

'How do we know we can trust you? Maybe the helicopter will unload a squad of soldiers.'

There was a faint look of annoyance and impatience on Tim's face. 'Henry, give me a break. If I meant you harm, then I would hardly have given you the gun.'

I said nothing. He had a point. After a minute Tim ended the silence. 'So I'd prefer to take my chances with the other side. It's better than the alternative for me, and it also involves less risk for you.'

I said nothing and looked at Laurent and caught a flicker of his eyes. 'Tim, I think Laurent and I need to discuss this.'

'OK, but time is passing.' He looked round the horizon to the east as though expecting the helicopter to appear at any moment.

Laurent and I walked down the sand, already warm to the bare foot, to the verge of the stream. The sun had beaten off the early morning mist, and it was the start of another bright day. A parakeet flew downstream.

'Well, what do you think, Laurent? I have my own ideas.'

'Henry, my view is that we should ask him to come back with us. Perhaps wait, hidden I think, for this helicopter to see if that part of his story is true. But . . .' His voice tailed off in indecision.

I cut into the pause. 'I think we should give him the benefit of the doubt. Let him meet this helicopter. I don't think he will do any more harm.'

'I am not so sure.'

'But we can't have nobody here. Vaughan is right that it would be asking for trouble. Big trouble. For all of us.'

Laurent's face was unyielding.

He could be stubborn. It crossed my mind though that in this case he was probably right. Perhaps I should just acquiesce and like good schoolboys we should drag Tim along to the

Headmaster's study. But I felt myself rebelling. The real world wasn't so neat. I could well believe that if this thing was big enough for someone to lay on a helicopter in and out of here, along with the rest of the charade, then they might well want to make a few enquiries of their own. They might indeed want to tidy up the whole mess. I didn't particularly care either for having come into the possession of two separate confidential defence secrets, Jezreel and the twenty-three fifty-nine. It was the sort of thing that was likely to get your mail steamed open for a long, long time.

As I thought about that side of things a vision of being pursued came upon me. I'd forgotten what it was like. The scars heal and you forget the sweating terror of it all. The fear of every solitary place that possessed you. Forever looking over your shoulder until you walked straight into their arms. The discreet, scared whisper from a friend: 'Henry, someone was looking for you last night. You understand?' Everywhere dark shapes blocking gloomy alleys. The quiet persistent knock on the door. I felt my stomach turn over. No! That had to be avoided. By whatever means.

In something like desperation I played my last card. The one, possibly the only one, that Laurent might listen to. 'Besides, Laurent, if we drag him back to 'Tana what do you think would happen to him?'

There was no answer. 'At best, they'd put him in jail—for a long time. Alternatively, they or his dissatisfied clients might arrange for him to have an accident.'

I paused briefly and then, feeling like a tired boxer throwing a last desperate punch, I spoke again. 'Laurent, I do not want that on my conscience. Do you?'

It was shameless manipulation, and I cringe at the remembrance of it. At the time, all I could think of was whether or not it would work. It did.

Laurent looked anguished. He knew I'd punched him below the belt.

'Very well.'

He turned around and walked back to Tim.

I strolled over, feeling relieved, but as though I had cheated. 'Tim, OK, stay and talk to them. We'll wait it out. If they don't take you we'll escort you back to 'Tana.'

That was all I had intended to say. Yet I kept on talking; something else came out unbidden. 'And if this is another one of your tricks, don't expect any mercy, from me or anybody.'

The words seemed threatening. I realised that basically I was still very angry.

Tim's eyes, cold and serious, stared at me. 'I've given up expecting mercy from anybody. I gave up a long time ago. But thanks.' There was an awkward silence.

We all seemed to stand frozen for a moment.

Suddenly Tim broke it by bending down and reaching into his rucksack. 'I'm intrigued that you guys have forgotten that I owe you money.'

He was right; I certainly had. He pulled out a plastic-wrapped brown envelope. 'Laurent, this is yours. I think you will find it's the right amount.' Laurent paused. For a moment I thought he would reject it. He looked at me.

'Take it, Laurent; the labourer deserves his hire.'

He shrugged his shoulders slightly, took the packet off Tim, and put it carelessly in his back pocket. I thought to myself that I wasn't sure I'd be able to be that careless with a year's salary.

Tim seemed to think the same thing.

'Perhaps you'd better check that it is not forged.'

Laurent looked at Tim curiously and then spoke quietly. 'Thank you for whatever you have given me.' It came out rather formally.

'Henry, I think I owe you something too.' He pulled out another package and handed it to me. It felt like a lot of notes. I clumsily tucked it in the top of my rucksack. Laurent was right, this wasn't the time or place even to look at it. When I looked up, Tim was reaching deeper into his sack.

'You might as well take this. Under no current scenario will I be needing it.' It was his camera bag.

'I can't, it's worth an awful lot.'

Tim gave me a weak smile. 'There is a certain justice, Henry. It was your photographs that got you into this mess.'

It seemed oddly funereal. There was a pause. 'In fact, Henry, if you promise to give your binoculars to Laurent, you'd better take these. I'd rather you have them than some gook in the Red Army.'

I was speechless for a moment. 'Come on, take them. Probably your last chance to acquire a West German pair of binoculars in your job.'

'Thanks, Tim, but well—what's the word—it feels like looting.'

'I'm not a corpse—at least not yet. Anyway, I think you've earned them. If you guys hadn't tried so hard to save my life we wouldn't be in such a mess now. There's a nice irony there too somewhere.'

He handed them over to me. I shrugged and put them in my bag and muttered something about generosity.

Tim looked at his watch again. 'They could be here in less than an hour. We'd best get your tents down and clear up any evidence that more than one of us has been here recently. Then I guess you need to find somewhere that you can see from but not be seen.'

Half an hour later we had packed everything up and were ready to go.

Tim casually strolled over to me as I tightened the straps on my rucksack. Laurent was out of earshot. 'If they do take me, what are you going to tell them in 'Tana?'

I thought for a moment. 'The truth, Tim, what else?'

As I said it I wondered if it was a lie.

'I had guessed as much. Well, if that happens then I guess that's it. I suppose I'd prefer to be thought safely dead. I have a few aged aunts and some old college friends who would put the worst possible construction on it.'

He scraped a groove in the sand with the toe of his battered training shoe.

'I suppose it's never crossed your mind, Henry, that defection is like death? You don't get to answer your critics.'

'Well, if it's any consolation, Tim, you're the only example I heard of where it was possibly defensible.'

He thought briefly. 'Thanks. That means a lot. If you do tell them I crossed over, and I can see your point of view, be careful what you say. You could still end up in big trouble with one side or the other. Keep an eye open. Remember, I'll cover for you from my end. I guess it's the least I can do.'

'Well, we'll see what happens,' I said, trying to be non-committal.

He looked hard at me. 'Just think carefully before you open your mouth. I shall do *all* I can to avoid trouble for you. And I mean all I can.'

He looked around at the sky briefly. 'Incidentally, Henry, if there *is* any rough stuff, don't bother weighing in with the gun. They are probably better armed, and certainly better shots. Besides, I guess I deserve whatever comes my way.'

I didn't have time to say anything in reply before Laurent had strolled over with his pack. He looked strained.

Tim cocked an ear skywards. 'We'd better all be getting in place. I need to be up there with a signalling mirror.'

He turned and picked up his rucksack. From the ease with which he picked it up there seemed to be little now in it. Then he hesitated. His face seemed full of tension. He stood tensed for a moment, looking across to the landing spot.

'Nope, it's got to be done.' He seemed to be speaking to himself.

He turned to us. He was abstracted, somewhere else in thought. 'Well, so long, fellas. Probably be seeing you in ten minutes.'

He held out a hand. I hesitated a fraction of a second and took it.

'Sorry it ended up this way, Henry. Thanks for trying.'

'Sorry too, Tim. I suppose I wish I had had time to talk the whole thing over with you.'

He turned to Laurent. 'Laurent, I'm sorry. I hope you'll understand one day.'

He held out his hand. There was a definite pause and Laurent took it, correctly and courteously, but with no obvious warmth.

'Well, let's do it. Let's hope it works out for you. See you guys.'

With that he turned and set off across the sand towards the top of the Cricket Pitch.

I watched him go with a definite unease. Something was all wrong. He had lost last night, yet there was no impression of a thwarted man. On my reading of the circumstances there seemed to me a reasonable chance that Tim would have to come back with us. Yet he seemed fairly certain that he wouldn't. But if that was so, why was there this curious attitude of resignation; resignation to what? He seemed to sense some impending doom hanging over him. Yet surely if he thought the risks were so great he'd volunteer to return with us? I felt totally out of my depth, even afraid.

'Laurent, I'm horribly worried I've done the wrong thing.'

'Perhaps.'

It was a formal comment. There was no doubt what Laurent thought, indeed knew; that it was indeed the wrong decision done for the wrong motives. I thought about trying to justify myself, but it seemed pointless. It was all too late.

There was something in the air. A faint noise. Laurent heard it too and stiffened. I yelled to him, 'Come on! Let's get out of here.'

We ran heavily across the sand, down to the rocks, and started scrambling carefully up the flanks of a fallen, sloping block. It provided a scaleable pathway to the top of a block where we could sit under the trees and keep a lookout across the Cricket Pitch. Halfway up the slab I stopped to listen. It was unmistakably an engine noise, but it didn't sound like a helicopter.

Suddenly I had a thought. 'Laurent, no hurry, it's the plane coming in to Antsalova.'

He grinned, 'Of course! I think we will be missing it today.'

We continued at a slower pace and within a minute had made it to the foot of the trees. It was a good spot for our purposes. We faced due eastwards, although there was a good view to the north as well. In the foreground we could see the disturbed sand of the campsite and beyond it the grass and stones of the Cricket Pitch. Further still, and swinging round to the north and south like a stockade, ran the ramparts of the pinnacles. Behind them the lines of teeth stretched as far as the eye could see. The figure of Tim could be seen standing around on the top of the gentle rise in the centre of the Cricket Pitch. From our angle he was partially silhouetted against the grey of the limestone. I supposed we must have been at about the same level. The Beboka could be traced upstream until it vanished into the rock wall at the point where we had had our fight the night before. Behind us a thick forest cover had developed on the top of these pinnacles, and we were hidden from overhead. I checked the ground for spiders, scorpions, and the seed pods of an irritant vine and sat down behind a bush. It seemed a safe spot from which to watch everything; it would be virtually impossible to see us from where Tim was.

It was getting hot. I opened my rucksack and pulled out my old binoculars. 'These are yours now, Laurent.'

'Thank you.'

'Thank Tim.'

I adjusted Tim's binoculars for my eyes and focused on him. They were good. He was sitting on a rock picking up small stones and throwing them half-heartedly at an unseen target. He seemed slightly stooped and vaguely dejected.

The air was humid and had a vague vegetable smell to it. It was warm, and my hands were sweaty. There was silence. Time passed. We heard the plane noise again very faintly; it had now taken off from Antsalova, and the sound faded away to the northeast.

We lay there silently, hidden by the bush. The minutes went slowly. A few brown lizards scuttled past on their inscrutable purposes. I felt in turmoil. I knew that I hadn't done the right thing. I felt like apologising to Laurent. But every time I thought of that, I thought of the impossibilities of any other course of action. Then when I thought of that, the feeling would come to me that Vaughan, a proven liar, had manipulated me. To add to the misery, it came to mind that I now had only a few days left to make a decision about my future. The events of the past few days had pushed it to the back of my mind, but it would not go away. In my present frame of mind there was no question but that I would turn down George's offer; nevertheless I still felt it was wrong to do that. Thinking about Cyprus didn't leave me feeling any happier. I was making a mess of everything and seemed incapable of doing what I knew to be right.

Suddenly Laurent touched my hand. 'Listen!'

There was a faint disturbance in the atmosphere. It was barely a noise, but it was unmistakable. It grew till a faint beat could be distinguished. With the naked eye I could see Tim standing up. I scanned eastwards with the glasses.

Laurent saw it first. 'Over there, just south of Tim.'

The dot grew in size as it moved northwards. It seemed to be going past us when it banked and came straight towards the landing site. I turned the glasses down to where Tim was. He was moving a hand-sized signal mirror in small arcs. The helicopter came on. I tried to focus on it, but it revealed little from its head-on attitude. The beating noise increased. Birds rose out of the trees. Near the Cricket Pitch it swung southwards and banked round steeply. It was a large machine painted in a bright yellow. The speed dropped slowly, the pilot clearly taking a good look at the terrain.

Tim was gesturing with his hands to outline the landing zone. The yellow machine continued to move slowly round on its axis and at one point seemed to be coming overhead. The branches swayed, and leaves and small twigs blew everywhere. Laurent and I cowered for fear of discovery.

Then he circled northwards before completing the circle. Losing height rapidly he ended up hovering just a few feet beyond Tim and then with some delicate shuffling movements gently lowered himself down. The skids gradually spread out to take the weight.

The helicopter was virtually face-on to us. I tried to think of the name of the type. It certainly wasn't one of the Soviet Mils that you'd occasionally see in Syria. Rather it looked like one of the larger Bell models, the sort that crop up in all the Vietnam clips. I couldn't read the registration number from this angle.

There were two people in the front of the machine. The pilot on the left wore a tinted perspex face plate. As I watched, he nodded towards Tim in a clear signal to come in under the rotors. Of the passenger I could see little. Vaughan ran up, crouching low under the tips of the blur of the blades, to the passenger's door. There was a bit of theatre as he gestured for—and was given—a headset. Tim then unclipped the set and the passenger turned to the pilot before unstrapping himself and getting out.

The passenger had less cause to worry about the rotor blades than Vaughan. He was a squat, stocky fellow with a small dark moustache. I couldn't see much of his face, but it seemed to remind me of someone.

He certainly didn't seem European. The two of them walked some way from the machine and began talking. After a few minutes the pilot shut down his engine, and the blades began their declining arcs.

It seemed to me that the ensuing silence was even more ominous than the beating of the rotor blades.

28

I looked at Laurent. He was watching the scene intently. He spoke softly without looking at me.

'I do not like this at all, Henry.'

It crossed my mind that he had been saying that since the start of the trip. I supposed that he could readily claim that events had vindicated him. Fortunately, he wasn't the sort to say, 'I told you so.'

'Tim's business is pretty serious, Laurent. You don't hire one of those things for nothing.'

The financial side of the operation was indeed sobering. To have set up the whole deal with me couldn't have come cheaply, but to rent the helicopter must have cost many thousands of dollars. I wasn't even sure that they might not have brought it in from outside the country for the job. There's not a lot of profit to be made in sitting on the runway at 'Tana waiting for business. Having spent that much, they were really not going to be pleased about losing what they had come for.

The pilot came out and took his helmet off, revealing unkempt straw-coloured hair. He checked his landing site and called something to the passenger, who was deep in conversation with Vaughan. The reply the pilot received didn't seem to please him. He went over, and the three of them talked for a few minutes. Eventually, with a shrug of his skinny shoulders, the pilot walked back to the helicopter. He opened the side door, and pulling out a towel set off down towards the sand of the campsite. As he neared it I held my breath for fear he would examine the footprints or, even worse, decide to climb up to where we were. In fact he did nothing of the sort, but pulled out a cigarette and lighting it with fluent motions strolled on down to the stream. He was barely a hundred yards away, and his presence made us hug the rock.

However, after a few minutes it became apparent that he was not at all interested in his surroundings. Rather, he walked along the water's edge and finding a smooth rock sloping down to the water took off his faded T-shirt. Putting on dark glasses, he lay down and stretched himself out on his towel to sunbathe.

I looked back to where Vaughan and the passenger were. The conversation was clearly animated. The passenger pulled out a handkerchief and wiped his forehead, demonstrating a receding hairline. He gestured towards the machine and Vaughan, clutching his rucksack, went over. They went to the side that was slightly away from us and were lost from sight.

I glanced at Laurent. He was missing nothing. 'What do you think?' I hissed.

'I think we will lose him. I think he will go.' Then he paused. 'But I am not sure.'

I watched the pilot for a bit. He got to his feet and stared at the water as if wondering whether to go for a swim. He looked to be in his late thirties, his stomach beginning to show the ravages of a largely sedentary job. His arms were tanned and showed a couple of tattoos. He idly threw his cigarette butt away and looked apathetically up the stream. A great yellow butterfly flew past, and he rather half-heartedly raised a hand up towards it. It gracefully gained a bit more height and flew onwards. He stood watching it flutter slowly away, as if with professional respect, and then lay down on the towel again, seemingly intent on getting a suntan.

Time passed, and I began to feel hungry. What was going on at the helicopter? I was just wondering whether to risk trying to get some food out of my rucksack when Tim and the passenger came out of the helicopter. Tim carried his bag. There was a purposeful progression over to the stream edge where we had had our fight. For a moment they were out of sight beyond the grey boulders and the tall grass. Then we could see them again, peering down into the waters of the Beboka.

'So he has told them where he lost his package,' Laurent whispered.

I nodded assent. 'I just hope he hasn't told them who kicked it in.'

Laurent gave me a quick glance. For the first time there was a faint brief indication of something like fear.

They must have spent ten minutes there, but eventually they turned round and started to walk back to the helicopter. Something seemed about to happen. I felt my sweaty hands tighten round the binoculars.

'Laurent, are you watching?'

'Yes.' His voice was tense.

Suddenly, halfway back to the helicopter, Tim and the passenger stopped. There was the rapid movement of arms in gestures, and I felt I could faintly hear the sound of raised voices.

I refocused on them. There was no doubt about it: an argument was taking place.

Tim sat down suddenly on a rock and put his head in his hands. I was on the point of saying to Laurent that it looked like he was going to have to walk back when everything happened.

The passenger reached inside his safari jacket and pulled out something grey and metallic. In a practised slow movement he swung it up behind Tim's head. He held it there for a fraction of a second, then there was a faint flash. As Tim slumped forwards the noise of the gunshot reached us and echoed round off the rocks.

'He's killed him!' said a stupid voice which I realised later was mine.

I dropped the glasses and turned to Laurent. He was looking at me with wild eyes, and his face was pale. I began to feel sick. I started to my feet. Laurent grabbed my arm and pulled me down.

He was speaking Malagasy. Then he switched to English. 'It is no use, Henry. No use. Too late. Tim is dead.' There were tears in his eyes.

'Damn, damn, damn.' I hit my fist on the rock.

I peered over the edge, suddenly scared that the pilot had seen us. On that account I shouldn't have worried. He was running up towards the passenger and the still form that lay on the ground. What was happening there?

I picked up the binoculars and forced myself to focus on the passenger. The image swam drunkenly. I braced myself on the rock and for a second was able to see clearly before the image slid away into a juddering blur.

The passenger stood lighting a cigarette. With his foot he seemed to be carelessly poking the dark object below as one might tentatively try to roll over a piece of flotsam on the beach.

I thought again that I was going to be sick, but it passed. Then I realised that I had the gun. A raw heady vision of running out and shooting dead Vaughan's killer flashed across my mind, but I rejected it as soon as it came to me. I'd only make a mess of it.

The pilot was now standing next to the body, and there were words being exchanged. Eventually the pilot shook his head and turned to go to the machine. He was stopped by the passenger who carefully stubbed out his cigarette. Then together they picked up the body and carried it, head lolling, over to the helicopter.

They put the body inside. The passenger walked back to where Tim's bag lay, picked it up, walked back to the helicopter, and threw it in. I expected him to close the door, but he didn't. The pilot got in and began the scrutiny of the dials that precedes take off. The blades started swinging round, and in a few seconds the turbine fired and the noise of the engine became an ever-faster beat. I realised that the passenger must be sitting in the back. The engine roar increased to a fierce whine and then slowly the helicopter lifted itself up off the ground. A few feet up it moved towards us rapidly, almost as though it was sliding off the Cricket Pitch down to the river. For one ghastly second the machine looked as if it was going to crash into us. Then it seemed to rise vertically, and in a steep bank it swung away eastwards. There were swirling leaves, dust and sand everywhere.

I began to get to my feet. I was shaking with rage, fear and sorrow.

'Look, Henry, look!' There was a curious note in Laurent's voice that stopped me still.

I turned. The helicopter had slowed and was at a virtual stop about a mile away. It hung sideways on to us, perhaps five hundred feet up above the grey needles of stone. The large cabin door was open.

A sudden horror grabbed me. I picked up the binoculars and, hands shaking, focused them. The image swung crazily about. The passenger could be clearly seen at the cabin door. He bent down and began pulling and pushing something. Then as I watched he stood up and braced himself against the door frame. He pushed with a foot.

In a moment of sickening horror something large and grey slid out. It struck the skid limply and tumbled out falling spread-eagled downwards. It spun slowly, grey-clad arms flapping, down, down to the cruel blades of stone below.

I wasn't watching when it hit them.

Slowly the machine turned round and gained speed. It turned southwards and soon disappeared from sight.

Silence enveloped us.

29

I remember little of the journey back through the outer pinnacles. I have merely a blurred recollection of stumbling onwards with looming stone walls all around and Laurent leading on doggedly in silence. What distinguishes it from the memory of the other journeys through those terrible rocks is a permanent tinge of sorrow and despair.

Only when some two hours or so later we were out of the pinnacles did the horror begin to lift even slightly. The effect of being able to lie down on grass—however coarse—with an open horizon stretching for miles in front of us was therapeutic. Behind us, in a physical sense, lay the broken rock wall, grey and malevolent. But it also seemed in another sense that the violence of what we had seen was isolated back there. This, however, only slightly lifted the agony.

As I lay there I tried not to think of what had happened. It was, of course, a futile exercise. As soon as I relaxed I was suddenly watching Tim being shot again. I tried to stop it, but it was like a loop in a computer program. I found it hard to break out. I tried to talk about it.

'A mess, Laurent, a real mess.'

'Perhaps we expect too much from the world, Henry?'

I was silent, staring at the uncaring blue sky above. 'I'm afraid I'm largely responsible for Tim's death. I know he started it; that he got messed up with these people; that he cheated and lied and tricked and . . . who knows. But I feel that I'm somehow responsible. Am I?'

I turned to Laurent who was looking at me, his brown eyes filled with concern. He didn't answer for some time, but sat up and hugged his knees. His face was deep in thought. 'I think you are not responsible for his death. No, I am certain not. There is a justice here, my brother. He set a trap and fell into it himself. But perhaps, perhaps we might have been able to stop him from falling into the trap.'

I could think clearly enough to appreciate what Laurent was carefully getting at.

'A cruel justice.'

'So it seems to us. But if he had been successful, perhaps it would have been cruel for many more.'

'I can see your point. He sowed the wind and reaped the whirlwind. But it still feels lousy. And that passenger—the murderer—gets away scot-free?'

'Scot-free? Sorry, you mean without punishment? In this life perhaps. I have heard that Queen Ranavalona died quietly.'

He had a point; Ranavalona the First is a hot candidate for one of the ten nastiest females of all time. I said nothing. I tried to concentrate on the blue nothingness overhead. I couldn't. The images kept coming back. After a few minutes I sat up and looked back at the rocks. It occurred to me how I had seen this point in our journey in my imaginings. A bold final retreat from my subject. A heroic turning around from my academic success to a sacrificial career abroad. What an awful contrast the reality had become. A debacle ending in a horrific death. And now lying ahead of us a whole ghastly business in 'Tana that I didn't even dare think about. Physically, mentally and spiritually I felt a wreck. The whole thing had become a nightmare; worse than a nightmare because here there was no waking up. I almost felt like crying—for Vaughan and for myself.

Laurent offered me some food. We had picked up the cache at the pinnacles' edge. I thought about refusing it or throwing it away in some gesture of futility, but common sense prevailed and I ate it morosely, gazing at the stone walls. It helped though and after I'd eaten, the stone walls seemed merely impassive rather than malevolent.

'How do you feel, Laurent?'

'Sad, very sad.'

I ran over the whole thing again for the hundredth time. This time a different angle came to light. I sat up.

'You know, Laurent, thinking about the last things Tim said, I reckon he had a good idea what was going to happen to him. Yet he went ahead with it. I'm not sure we can rule out the possibility that he decided to do it to clear us.'

Laurent didn't answer immediately. When he did, it was in a thoughtful tone. 'Perhaps you are right. If so then I owe him an apology. As you say, it is possible.'

I felt a faint lifting of my spirit. 'I think it's true that at the moment we have nothing to fear. They must think that the whole matter is over.'

'Yes, my friend, but for how long?' Laurent's voice had a hint of weariness in it.

I was suddenly seized by concern. 'What do you mean?'

'I think we must still say something to the authorities in Antsalova or 'Tana. It was a murder.'

The prospect of walking away from the whole thing without any further trouble disappeared in a flash. Laurent wanted to bring everything out into the open, heedless of all the risks involved. I began to speak and then thought better of it. I needed time to think. I looked at my watch. Two o'clock.

'I want to think about this, Laurent. In the meantime, shouldn't we keep going? I feel like lying down and sleeping, but I think we should get going on to Antsalova.'

Laurent got to his feet by way of an answer. 'Yes, you are right. If we can get to Antsalova by early tomorrow then we may get a taxi to Maintirano. And late on Sunday afternoon there is a plane.'

It seemed a tall order, but we decided to try, and so cut our packs down to the minimum. Soon we had accumulated a small pile of things we would not be needing again. Laurent suggested we leave them together. 'If we leave them in a pile someone will pass by fairly soon, and they will be very happy.'

He paused. 'Henry, I think perhaps you should get rid of Vaughan's—of Tim's—gun.'

'As usual you make sense, Laurent. But are you sure that we might not need it?'

As I spoke I knew the answer. I managed to eject the magazine and threw it upstream. Then I took the gun and hurled it as far as I could downstream. I was glad to get rid of it. It certainly hadn't brought me any good fortune. Nor Tim for that matter. That done, we picked up our bags and set off over the plain towards the distant smoke of Antsalova.

The action of walking was helpful in one sense. Every step was one further from the pinnacles and the dreadful things that had happened in them. But in another it was worse. For every step forward brought us closer to the crisis looming ahead. Was I really going to put my head in the noose as Laurent seemed to want to do?

I tried to concentrate on actually being out of the pinnacles. I tried to enjoy the feeling of space that the distant horizon gave; almost a feeling of being out of prison. It was also good to have one's back to those dreadful rocks. It was in there that the nightmare happened, not out here in the bright sun among the grass and the clumps of trees. However, no matter what I did, the shadow only lifted temporarily before it returned again.

It seemed almost by mutual agreement that we spent little time in conversation. There was a definite and growing difference between us.

Every half-hour we stopped for a few minutes and a mouthful of water. The sun gradually got lower. At about five o'clock we stopped near an isolated clump of trees and wearily put up the tents.

We didn't bother cooking anything, but ate the emergency rations that were left. They were better than expected, although the meal was a silent one. I remained deep in thought. The ghastly events of the day still hung over everything. Every few minutes an image of the gun being raised and the collapsing body, or the spreadeagled silhouette tumbling groundward would flash back into my mind. But in between came a concern for what happened next. What was going to happen tomorrow? It wasn't all over by any means. The whole thing was like some great juggernaut, swerving and crashing downhill out of control. Tim had already been crushed under it and it had still not stopped. I looked well placed to be the second victim.

I tried to think through the issues. If Laurent had his way, there had to be a meeting with some authorities of some sort. The first priority was to avoid this. If it couldn't be avoided I had to think what to say, to sort out a strategy for Antsalova, or even 'Tana. 'Tana was surely preferable. It could take months to sort anything out with the gendarmes here. No, far better to keep on to 'Tana. But where in 'Tana?

Part of me wanted to discuss the whole thing with Laurent. The other half told me to hold on until I had sorted out a plan. Without it, a little voice said, that boy can get you into trouble. So I kept quiet and ran over the various possibilities. It had to be 'Tana, but I really didn't fancy the central Gendarmerie or whatever it called itself. That sounded easier to get into than to get out of. Besides, only one Malagasy had been involved in the whole incident and then as an eyewitness. No, the most obvious place was the US Embassy. There at least I would be able to speak my own language.

As I rehearsed the conversation, the whole thing assumed a rather alarming character. It was going to cause a lot of trouble, and we were going to become marked men. A clammy chill seemed to settle. Every way seemed full of problems.

I looked at Laurent, almost totally hidden in the gloom. He was sitting in an odd slumped fashion. I spoke his name, and he started upright.

'Time for bed, Laurent; there is a lot to do tomorrow.'

'Yes, yes, you are right.' He spoke as in a dream. After a few seconds he stiffly got to his feet and went over to his tent. I somehow found the energy to brush my teeth. It's funny how even in the presence of death and with a wrecked career ahead of me it was something I felt I ought to do. That done I crawled into my sleeping bag.

As I lay there I kept reminding myself that some way out of the various problems of tomorrow had to be sorted out. But try as I could no answer came. So I tried to go to sleep, but every time I relaxed for a moment the vision of a falling, tumbling body came back in an endless awful rerun. In my mind it fell and rolled for ever.

Next morning Laurent woke me while it was still dark. As I put a pullover on, it seemed that in the night the answer had come to me. It was clearly the only solution. But would Laurent buy it? It needed proposing carefully.

It was dark and chilly outside the tent, with mist hanging in a depressing shroud over our silent, hurried breakfast. It was only just lifting when we set off on the road to Antsalova.

After half an hour's walking I decided that I had to grasp the nettle. 'Laurent, we must decide what to do. Are we going to see the police in Antsalova?'

He looked troubled and pursed his lips. 'Perhaps it would not be best to. I think it might be easier in 'Tana.'

I breathed a half-sigh of relief. 'And in 'Tana, who do we go to? The police or the Embassy?'

He looked searchingly at me, as though trying to read my mind. 'What do you say?'

'If we go anywhere, I think the US Embassy.'

He gave me a hard, curious look, but said nothing.

At that point we rounded the top of the gentle rise, and through the clearing mist we could see the thatched roofs of Antsalova. A thin column of smoke rose above the huts. Now for the first step.

'The question is, what story do we give? I mean, we need to think about it carefully.'

'I don't understand what you mean, Henry.'

'Laurent, what did Tim say about the story he was going to tell his visitors?'

He shook himself slightly as if shaking sleep away. 'I'm sorry?'

'I mean what did he say he was going to tell the people who were meeting him about us? What was he going to say about us?'

'That we had split up outside the pinnacles and had left him, left him on his own.'

I said nothing for a minute. Surely he must see it? Then weighing my words I spoke slowly. 'Laurent, we are both tired, but think this through. Follow me carefully. What do these people who killed Tim . . .' I hesitated. 'What do they believe about us?'

'I suppose that we know nothing; that we think Tim is still walking here on his own outside the pinnacles.'

'Exactly. Now follow me carefully. Suppose we walk into the US Embassy in 'Tana and say, "Hey, that Tim Vaughan was a traitor. He had some electronics he shouldn't have, and the Reds came and killed him. We know because we were there." Now that sort of news isn't going to stay a secret, is it?'

Silence.

'Well, Laurent, my dear friend, what is that nice friendly man who put a bullet in our ex-colleague's head going to say when he hears about that?'

I meant it to come over as a cold clear logical sequence of deductions. It didn't. You could hear my fear, the suppressed hint of panic.

Laurent said nothing, but there was a look of unease on his face.

'He's going to say that we are hiding something. Maybe even that we have the precious box of tricks ourselves.'

Laurent spoke quietly but firmly. 'I see your worry. But I do not see what we can do other than tell the truth.'

He spoke in a determined impassive way, almost as if I had

been talking about the weather. My fears began to turn to anger.

'Is that all you can say? This guy is a killer. Tim knew it. He risked it to give us the opportunity to get out of here in one piece. We're about to walk in to 'Tana effectively shouting to this guy, "Hey what about us? If you've reloaded, us next please."'

I paused to take breath. My anger was mounting. I put on a turn of speed and walked ahead, but I soon realised that getting angry with Laurent wasn't going to help. I cooled down a bit and let him catch up. 'Sorry, Laurent, I guess I'm worked up.'

He nodded. I tried another tack. 'Look, our safest bet, the best thing for all concerned, is to say nothing. If we are ever asked, we just say we left him at the pinnacles' edge. We were low on food, and he decided to scout around on his own. The beauty about that is that it's what he told them he might do.'

Laurent looked horrified. I spoke again before he could say anything. 'Look, I'm suggesting we take the line of least resistance. The easiest way. The best way for Tim, poor fellow, for you and for me and for your family. It's not a total lie. We say we—well, just left him, if we're ever asked.' I paused as I tried to think.

'Look, it's not as though anyone is going to avoid judgement, is it? Tim's paid the price, hasn't he? "A sort of justice" you said. Let the dead bury their dead. He's hardly escaped justice, has he? This way he is not disgraced as well. The matter ends. It's finished. We just tidy it up. What is there to be gained by bringing it up?'

There was no answer, just a look of hurt perplexity in his face.

'Look, I'm just trying to save us a lot of danger, and Vaughan's memory any more shame. Basically he meant well, he just went about it wrongly. This way he gets to be remembered as a man who just had an accident. A tragedy not a villainy. Besides, it's more modest for us. None of this "and with one kick Laurent saved the west" nonsense.'

The emotion was visible on Laurent's face. 'But, Henry, it isn't true.'

'Laurent, it's the lesser of two evils. By talking about the whole helicopter business we put so much at risk. A diplomatic incident at the least. Us under investigation. Someone will probably choose to get rid of us. I mean, what about your family?'

He said nothing, but chewed his lower lip. We walked on for a minute, then he stopped.

'No, Henry. You do what you must, but I have no choice. I'm sorry.' The tone of his voice left no doubt about his intention. It was pointless to try and change his mind.

I sank into despair. This was awful. The whole thing had become a quagmire and just as it showed a chance of clearing, Laurent was going to drag me into it again. Beyond all hope of recovery.

At length the miserable journey was marked by our arrival into Antsalova. The children came out to greet us, and for once Laurent was almost terse with them. He turned to me.

'There is a taxi in the town. They think that there may be room.'

There was indeed a taxi. A battered Peugeot 504 that looked like a scrap heap on wheels. Whether there was room was a matter of opinion. In the end I got squeezed in against the window by a man who seemed all elbows and baskets. We set off to the accompaniment of noises that I don't ever want to hear from a vehicle again. I've had some awful journeys in my time, but this ranks up with the worst. The combination of fumes and stale sweat and animal smells was very powerful. The odours seemed to be of such a variety that you never completely adjusted to them. Something somewhere always seemed to smell horribly. I tried to open the window, but found the dust that blew in intolerable. Then the track gave up any pretence at being a road and disintegrated into a thousand ruts. It was a constant battle to avoid my head being knocked against the roof. This agony of smell, sound, heat and motion, superimposed on my mental turmoil, filled me with an awful feeling of despair. I felt like an animal being dragged to slaughter.

It was midafternoon when we drove into Maintirano. The driver dropped us by the glorified hut and grass strip that passed for the airport. I felt ghastly. I pulled out my rucksack, forlornly tried to shake the dust off, and looked at Laurent. The gaze he returned was distant. He spoke, correctly and coldly.

'I will see if there is any possibility of getting on the flight. It may cost money.'

It was the tone that he had used with Tim at the end, except here there was a tinge of sorrow in his words.

'Pay it.' I pulled out my wallet and threw it to him. I was gradually succumbing to a slow steady flame of anger.

He caught it and discreetly pulled out two large-denomination Malagasy notes before handing it back.

I found some shade by the building and sat down. Some children in their tattered shorts and T-shirts came over. I glared at them and they ran off.

After half an hour Laurent came back. 'Done. The plane arrives in an hour.'

I just nodded at him and took the proffered change.

After a few minutes of silence Laurent pointed out a tap, and I took the opportunity of getting washed and shaved. I dug out some relatively clean clothes and changed, swapping the boots for training shoes.

And so I sat there in my self-pity and misery until the plane arrived. It was a twin turboprop of some sort. I didn't even care enough to try to identify it. Somehow I got a window seat beside a clearly nervous Asian businessman. Laurent sat on the other side of the aisle, which suited me. I didn't want to talk.

We took off over the sea and swung back eastwards over

the brown and burnt grassland. After a few minutes we crossed the thin band of limestone which is all that is left of the pinnacles that far north. The faint lines of the cross-cutting fractures could be seen etched in the shadows of the declining day.

What a mess it all was. Calamity lay in every direction. Vaughan was dead. Not—it was true—because of me, but I hadn't exactly helped. My relationship with Laurent was in ruins. Sometimes part of me acknowledged it was my fault, but most of the time I was filled with quiet fury at the risk he was throwing us both into. I labelled it as a 'martyr complex,' as though labelling it helped. The time-honoured method of trying to put it all into a proper perspective really didn't help either. The disaster was total. On the further horizons, my relationship with Tina was broken, and I was hardly going to be taking up George's offer either.

Night fell outside, and as it did something else began to surface in the dark turbulence of my mind. It was a feeling—growing into a certainty—that my personal religion had failed me. Here I was in a crisis and there was no help, no comfort, no strengthening to do good. Just a vague nagging rebuke. Yes, Laurent was being a stubborn fool, but there was at least integrity there. He was making a stand on what he believed. I ruefully realised that what I had was too insubstantial to stand on. In fact as I thought about it I realised that my Christian faith was nothing of the sort. It was neither a faith nor Christian; simply an accretion of words, concepts and culture I'd picked up in my youth. There was no foundation there, no true faith as Laurent had outlined it to Vaughan. Nothing, just empty words.

We began the slow descent, and I forced myself to concentrate on what was going to happen in 'Tana. Laurent seemed bent on spilling the whole mess. However one looked at that it seemed desperate; at very best it would be a scandal, with me at the centre. At worst, the fate that had befallen Tim. Only slower, probably. I was heading into trouble, and there seemed to be nothing I could do about it. Soon my train of thought became locked into a wild circle of recrimination and anger, of guilt and self-hatred. The bumpy descent continued. As I looked out I could see the lights of 'Tana glowing faintly. A final rolling jar and we were down.

The cool of the night woke me up as we climbed down the steps and began the walk over to the terminal building. Then where?

As I walked across the concrete with Laurent a few feet behind, I noticed the great bulk of an Air France jumbo jet almost dwarfing the terminal. They were loading it up. It suddenly gave me a terrible desire to get out of there; to leave this ghastly island with its dirt, rock and primitive fauna. To go to Paris on a clean friendly jet, with a charming stewardess and food that wasn't rehydrated. To listen to Bach and Mozart on the headphones or see a movie. To be in a sanitised world of newspapers and television. To be in a world where I would be safe.

The longing obsessed me as the airport terminal doors approached. A policeman stared at me. I ignored him and walked in. Pale fluorescent lights lit the building. There was a sea of people milling around the desks, generating a great cacophony of noise. Suitcases, rafia bags, bundles, people and more people were everywhere. It was chaos.

'Must be the Paris flight,' I thought idly. Suddenly an idea hit me with a force that literally stopped me in my tracks. I stopped so suddenly that Laurent walked into me. I dropped my rucksack and stood staring.

The Paris flight! It was my flight. I tore open my rucksack, my heart beating crazily, and pulled out my passport pouch. There was the ticket. I didn't need to look. There were only three Air France flights out a week. It was my flight, and it left in an hour's time. They would be boarding now. I was booked on this flight.

Carefully, slowly, deliberately I folded the ticket away. Although my hands were trembling and my throat was dry, I felt coolly in control. I went over everything in my mind. There was no earthly reason why I couldn't simply go through the crowd to that counter over there and get on that plane. And when the sun rose I would be over France.

Everything seemed to stand still. Laurent was staring at me as though aware of what I was thinking. What about him? I thought. He'll have no option, said a little voice. He'll have to be realistic now and just say nothing. They won't know who he is anyway. He'll be all right. I took a single step towards the counter. I could almost feel the sterile comfort of the plane seats and hear the stewardesses. I couldn't stay, I could be here for weeks.

A party of burly and bronzed Anglo-Saxons made their way through the melee. The noise of them could be heard over that of the crowd. Many wore the baseball cap and thin nylon anorak uniform of the oil rig worker. A number had the big Malagasy beer bottles. They were all in high spirits.

The leader, with a face of a pirate heading for shore leave, squeezed his way past a frail little Malagasy nun. "Scuse me, luv.'

I stared at him, transfixed by the accent, memories flooding over me of childhood, the crowds at the market, Mum holding my hand, the high brown moors in the summer sun. Home, certainty, security.

As I stared, the roughneck caught my stare and grinned back amiably. He waved the bottle at me. 'Come and join t' party, lad. Four weeks on a dry rig. Paris, here we come.'

'Perhaps,' I muttered back.

'Suit tha' sel.'

It was almost the last straw. They were going home, and I would go too. Home to Grantforth.

But it would be wrong, said something in my mind. I'd be betraying a friend. Then I realised the implications of what I'd uncovered on the plane. I was barely a Christian; so why should I be bound any longer by that code of behaviour? I had discovered that all that was a sham, at least as far as I was concerned, and right now I was all that mattered. Surely it was now time to break out of those bonds, to stand free of all those entanglements? Now a double freedom seemed to beckon. From now on I would look out for myself and no one else.

I picked my bag up from the floor. I've got to go. Must run. Sorry, Laurent, this is where we split. Wish I was made of better stuff. I began to move and paused, in doubt.

The pirate stopped at the check-in desk and was counting his band of followers. He saw me looking. 'Come on, flight's aba't to leave.' I started walking towards him.

And then I stopped as my mind was suddenly flooded by an image. I seemed to have been walking, to have left the path and to have got badly lost. Now it seemed that I was perched on a ledge halfway down a cliff. It was desperately plain that I had just two alternatives. One choice was clear: to swing myself over the ledge and let go. Gravity would do the rest. It would be simple and easy. But it came to me that although it was an easy route, there was no promise of any safe landing below. Indeed, below there seemed to be hidden dark immensities and some sort of assurance that once beyond the cliff there was no road back.

The other choice seemed to be to try to go back up and start again, to climb up a hard route clouded in difficulties and dangers and over which there was no guarantee of success. But over it hung a suggestion that this way at least I might find the path.

I felt myself shaking; the pull both ways was enormous. Everything seemed in flux. How long I stood there in irresolution I cannot say. Perhaps it was less than a minute.

Then, all of a sudden, I was able to decide. Or perhaps the decision was made for me. I would try to go back up.

'So help me, God,' I said aloud. Suddenly I felt like crying. I turned round and walked to Laurent. 'I'm sorry, Laurent. I've been a fool. Forgive me.'

I put my arm round him and gave him a hug.

The pirate gave me the sort of look they normally reserve for cockroaches.

'Laurent, let's go.'

'Where to, Henry?'

'The US Embassy—to tell them the truth—then the Hilton. I have a telex to send. There's a job I'm supposed to take up.'

30

With hindsight it was stupid of me to have thought that it would all be over speedily. It wasn't. It took a long time for the wheels to turn, but at least Laurent was able to go home that Sunday night, although it was nearly eleven when they let him go and he had to make lots of promises. I could hardly complain about my own treatment. They ended up giving me a room of my own at a villa that seemed to be the off-duty quarters for the Embassy's Marine contingent. It was a classy sort of cell. I think they locked the door on me, but I was past caring by midnight.

Wayne Harris didn't much care for my story. He was a pallid-complexioned man with a vaguely worried look and a moustache that looked as if it was sickening for something. I felt that he'd spent the ten years since he left college trying to keep himself out of trouble. If so, he may have felt that in 'Tana he had the perfect posting because nothing ever happened. I hadn't got too far into the story before he started to fondle his moustache in a disturbed manner. His worried look had lost any sense of vagueness.

Wayne didn't say much. He didn't even say he believed me, but he advised me strongly about leaving his care and protection and was reluctant to let Laurent out. So in the end they drove Laurent home and me to the villa. In the car I noticed I had a locked door on one side and a big black Marine by the name of Thompson with a face of stoical impassivity on the other.

The next morning they woke me up at nine. I could easily

have slept later. When I got down it looked like Wayne had had me roused out of pique. He didn't look like he'd had any sleep himself.

He shook his head sorrowfully when he saw me, the way the mechanic usually does when I take the car in for its service. 'This better be the real thing, Mister Stanwick, or Washington is gonna bust me.'

I grabbed some breakfast and decided to try and ask to leave. I should have known better.

'You wanna leave? Well sure, but there's one thing ya' orter know.'

'What's that?'

'Well, you said it was OK to check your bags last night, right?'

'True enough. You had a right to know that I'm not carrying any explosives.'

Wayne gave his moustache a careful stroke of peculiar intensity. 'You're carrying ten thousand dollars, right?'

'So? I told you the late Tim Vaughan gave them to me as salary.'

'Sure, sure. But then you don't have a customs declaration for them. Or for that fancy camera gear. And you failed to report a murder.'

I said nothing. This was a whole new aspect.

'Look, Stanwick, I'm kinda new here. Dave Moss gets cerebral malaria all of a sudden and they ship him out PDQ and get me in from Kenya. But I guess I could find out real quick what the going rate is in Madagascan law for illegal currency dealing, smuggling and, what shall we say—conspiracy? But I guess I don't really need to go to that trouble. I think you'd prefer to stay with us.'

I didn't take too long to think about it. 'OK, you win. But let me send a telex out. And I'll need a reply to confirm that you really have sent it.'

He looked at Thompson, got no help, and thought for a minute. 'OK, if I can rewrite it. Wouldn't want any code words, would we?'

So eventually I was allowed to send off a cable to Abie which read, 'Please start resignation procedures and confirm acceptance with George. Confirm receipt of this telex.'

That done I settled down for a long stay. As hotels went it was one of the better sort. The food was excellent and entirely unreconstituted. The attempt to duplicate an American home had been done fairly effectively, so that sometimes it was hard to remember you were in Madagascar. The Marines were good sorts. They were careful to watch what they said in front of me and somehow I was rarely alone, but it wasn't oppressive. It was good, too, to catch up with a couple of weeks' worth of world news. There was also a swimming pool and a small, very enclosed garden to sit in.

The physical surroundings were not the best of it. Above all I felt curiously relaxed, even light-headed at times. I had decided what I was going to do and I felt that it was all going to work out. Perhaps, above all, I was glad that things were now out of my hands, at least for the moment. All I had to do was endure. In fact, as I thought about it I decided that in many ways I was more at peace with myself than I had been since the night of the Hensons' party when the first hint of the job offer had come up. That set me thinking about Tina, but it was a fruitless set of thoughts. Doubtless she would be pleased about my going to Cyprus, but that would be about it. She had no interest in me now, and anyway it wasn't her part of the world. She'd probably melt in the heat. A real shame.

So Monday passed. Wayne scurried around looking increasingly unhappy. Thompson kept a lazy half an eye on me, chewed gum, spoke a dozen words and watched Malagasy TV, a pastime for which he received a lot of jokes from the other Marines. I read and went to bed early.

Tuesday morning Wayne caught me at breakfast. He had a telex for me. It was short and to the point. 'Telex received and implemented with regrets. Shalom, Abie.'

So that was that. Good-bye Grantforth. Then I realised Wayne was speaking.

'This guy, this friend of yours, an Israeli?'

'Sorry? Who . . . Abie? No.'

Then I caught the look of quashed hope in his eyes. 'Sorry, Wayne, no Middle East connection on this problem; at least not the way you think.'

'Thought not, but you never know.'

'Any progress? What does Washington say?'

He shook his head. 'It's a mess, Stanwick. Sure there is a Tim Vaughan. He came in through 'Tana, left us a note. Seems like Dave Moss saw him. He was going into the bush with a Brit and a Malagasy. Trust Dave to jump before the job gets sticky. Anyway, so far no Tim Vaughan has exited the country. Yeah, he works with the military.'

He paused and took a sip of coffee. 'That much adds up. The rest is either being checked or can't be checked. There are a lot of phone lines very busy, and that's all I can tell you.'

The morning was quiet and I spent a lot of it reflecting on my new future in Cyprus. I lay by the side of the pool and stared at the water. If only I'd taken up the offer when it had come, Vaughan would probably be alive now. But surely it wasn't as simple as that?

Late in the afternoon Harris called me in from the shade of a jacaranda tree where I was half-heartedly playing with the pet ringtail lemur. He seemed in a lighter mood.

'Thought you'd like to know, we've just heard from Washington. They're sending a man.'

So that explained his mood; someone else was going to be the scapegoat.

'Who are "they"?'

'Aw, come on, Stanwick, we don't answer those questions, right?'

'Sorry, I'll eventually learn some manners. So the buck is now going to stop somewhere else?'

'Right first time. Trouble is, with your tale I daren't put it at the bottom of the filing tray. It just may be true.'

'Thanks. Anyway, who's the lucky man?'

Thompson had drifted over.

'A guy called Lemaire, JP Lemaire. Never heard of him myself.'

If it had been anybody else the expression on Thompson's face would have indicated no more than mild surprise and dislike. Given his normal lack of emotion it indicated the news was similar to finding a rattlesnake in your bed.

'Friend of yours?' I asked rather naughtily.

'No way. He's trouble that man. JP. They say it stands for "Just Poison."' It was quite a speech.

Wayne looked troubled and felt for his moustache. 'That right? Well, the man'll be here tomorrow, so I guess we'll all see.'

Wednesday morning was misty and cold. It reminded you that you really were in a southern hemisphere winter. I was sitting in the lounge flicking through old copies of *Time* and thinking that I should go and do something useful when there was the sound of a horn outside the high brown laterite compound walls. The gates swung open, and in rolled a big long station wagon. It stopped, and a bulky silver-haired man clambered stiffly out of the back. He looked as if he had found the cavernous vehicle too small for him. Harris and a Malagasy followed, carrying aluminium suitcases.

In a few seconds he was standing in the lounge door. My first reaction was that I wouldn't have called him 'Just Poison.' It wasn't the toxicity that I was dubious about, but that rather he didn't look as subtle as poison. The resemblance to an implement of murder was more to a sledgehammer, or the legendary blunt instrument. He seemed to block the door. JP had once had the build of an American footballer, but the muscles had long since sagged and flowed. As you looked at his face, you realised that he was very much the ex-footballer. His face was hung and lined and had suffered a lot of use. His hair had been red, but was now a dirty streaky silver. Small blue eyes above dark bags scanned the room and caught mine. He walked over slowly and steadily. The two Marines engrossed in their chess game stopped suddenly, one with a piece in midair, and stared.

Lemaire stood over me, and I half got to my feet.

'Stanwick?' The voice fitted perfectly: worn, harsh and rough. He stared at me with a cold critical look. I suppose I nodded some sort of acknowledgement.

'Stanwick, this better not be some sort of joke. I've come halfway round the world for you.'

Then he gave a half-snort and turned to the door where Harris stood, trying not to cower visibly. Behind him stood Thompson. JP walked over to the Marine and stood facing him for a moment. Then he turned to Wayne.

'I'm gonna crash for a few hours, Mister Harris.' He turned to the black Marine. 'You, Thompson—see, I remember your miserable name—you pick up my bag and be careful. I didn't bring decent bourbon all this way just to have you drop it.'

Then he turned to me and gave me a stare. 'And, Stanwick, see you later.'

Then he was gone. His words hung on the air, and it was only after the sound of the heavy footsteps could be heard receding up the stairs that the Marines shrugged, gave each other knowing looks, and went back to their chess.

31

The summons to Lemaire came mid-afternoon. Thompson called me upstairs to the bare, shuttered room that did as an office. Harris was sitting on the edge of a chair looking ill at ease, while Lemaire sat behind the desk and dominated the room. He had a sheaf of papers in front of him and a small glass of what I assumed was bourbon. The sleep didn't seem to have greatly improved him.

'Sit down.' He spoke without looking at me.

I did, reflecting that graciousness was obviously not JP's strong point.

'OK, let's take it through from the beginning.'

At this point he rather self-consciously pulled out a pair of gold-rimmed spectacles and perched them on his nose. He pulled a sheet out of a folder towards him.

'Henry Thomas Stanwick, eh? Doctor of what? Espionage?'

I wondered what sort of an answer he wanted from a question like that. Well, I wasn't going to be needled.

'Geography.'

'Where from, or did you get it mail order?'

At this rate I was going to be answering in like manner soon, which wouldn't help anybody. 'Oxford. That is, Oxford, England.'

'Well, la-di-da.' It was a barely disguised sneer. He paused and peered over his papers. 'For an academic, a don I think is the word, you've got a nasty little file.'

I tried to give a disarming smile. 'Just accident-prone, I'm afraid.'

JP didn't seem too easy to defuse. 'Damascus, Lebanon, wrong places, wrong friends. Tripoli, Bourj el Barajneh, Hama, Ain-el-Hilwe, Kurds, Shiites, Palestinians. Nothing sensational—it just adds up. Cumulative. And now this.'

My heart began to sink.

'I've always tried to be sociable.'

Lemaire paused, leaned back a fraction, and then swung forward till he was staring low over the desk at me. It was a vaguely reptilian move and full of menace. I could see the small broken capillaries on his cheeks.

'Cut out the funny stuff, Stanwick. This story of yours doesn't wash. Doesn't at all. It's got more holes than a fishing net. Let's go through the impossibilities first.'

He sat back and glanced at his notes. 'Firstly your "twenty-three fifty-nine" quote unquote, never was, never is, never will be. Kid, I checked it out at the highest levels. They made me look pretty stupid. JP doesn't like being made to look a fool, Stanwick. Rule one. Don't play games.'

I decided I might as well try and defend myself. 'Vaughan said it was secret. They might have been covering up.'

'True 'nough. But think about it. Boris gets it, eh? How is it going to be useful? He's gotta get World War Three on the boil. Then, and only then, would it be of any use. Until then he doesn't even know if the circuits are for real. I can really see him selling it to the Politburo, gambling the fate of the Soviet Union on a handful of stolen silicon chips that they don't even know work.'

Put like that he had a point. 'All I'm saying is what Vaughan told me, and he did have a circuit board of sorts.'

'Huh. Next, "Jezreel." Kid, too much Bible reading can fry the brain. Nothing. Silence. We went to the top. We even asked Mossad. They'd never heard of it, but were very interested. Said, "It's a nice place, but we call it something else now." Incidentally, they didn't give you a good character reference.'

I decided I might as well go down fighting. 'Vaughan said

it was an ultra-black project, by which I assume he meant that it was so secret that only a handful of people knew. He also said that all references to it were destroyed.'

'Kid, the only thing ultra-black around here is your chances.'

He paused to let it sink in and then began again.

'Point three. Your Vaughan wasn't, maybe isn't, much. Sure, a promising start, but the wrong sort. He's been in no position of importance for five years. If he was that bright, what were we doing sentencing him to Diego Garcia?'

It wasn't really worth answering, but I tried rather feebly. "He said it was to get him away from the rest of the people on this "Jezreel" thing.'

Lemaire didn't even answer. 'Finally, you identify the helicopter as a Bell 212 or similar from the picture books. We have an up-to-date listing of all helicopters in the country. No yellow Bell 212s. No green, blue or purple ones either. A shame you got no registration number. Convenient again. Mystery chopper with mystery pilot and mystery assassin. Kills your buddy, disposes of the body and vanishes.'

This time I didn't even think of answering. I know when I'm beaten.

JP yawned, revealing crooked, yellowing teeth and pulled out a cigarette which he lit in silence. He leaned back and dragged on it.

'Four impossibilities, Stanwick. What really happened?'

I gave a silent sigh of relief that I wasn't hiding anything. 'No change, I'm afraid. You have it there in triplicate. There is also a Malagasy witness who confirms it all.'

There was silence as Lemaire stared at me. It was a gaze of puzzlement and of hostility. 'He doesn't count. He's probably desperate for money, and you probably persuaded him to lie.'

'Rather the contrary, I'm afraid.'

Lemaire looked annoyed. He got up clumsily, downed the bourbon and put the glass back on the desk too heavily. Then he closed the folder and picked it up.

'Ten minutes, Stanwick, then I want the truth. You sit here with Sergeant Thompson while I go and get some air.'

He got up and walked to the door. Harris got up as if to follow. Thompson looked awkward, stood up, and tried to catch Lemaire's eye.

'What's up, Thompson? Scared to stay alone with the Brit?'

'No, sah, but I've got some information, sah.'

It came out like a forced confession. As he said it he looked hard at me. JP caught his glance. 'OK, for what it's probably worth, spill it to me in the corridor.'

He motioned Thompson out and Harris followed behind like a gatecrasher sneaking into a party. The door clicked firmly behind them.

There was talking just beyond the door. I could make out nothing except that Lemaire seemed to be speaking in a threatening tone. Suddenly, the door opened and Thompson came back in. He just shook his head slowly as if regretful over something and sat down in silence.

I said nothing. I wanted to know what he had had to say, but it didn't seem right to ask. The whole thing seemed to be out of my control. Curiously though it wasn't terribly alarming; possibly because I knew there was nothing I could do now.

The silence in the room was broken only by the buzzing of a fly and the faint sound of rock music from a room below. We waited.

Ten minutes or so later there was the sound of heavy footsteps on the stairs. There was a whisper.

'Good luck, kid.'

I turned, surprised. It was Thompson. Well, it felt good to have someone who wasn't against me.

Lemaire came back in on his own and resumed his seat. 'Right, let's have the story.'

'I've nothing to say.'

'OK, let *me* say it. You fell out with Vaughan. A mean place; you got irritable. We understand. Maybe he said the wrong thing. You hit him, too hard perhaps. An accident. Maybe he banged his head. So you made up a little story.'

It was difficult to believe he was being serious.

'A story guaranteed to attract attention? You must be mad. If I'd killed him I'd have just got on the plane out.'

It was like water off a duck's back.

'I guess one of us would have to be mad, and it ain't me.'

He stared at me and sighed. His tone changed slightly. I think it was meant to be softer and conciliatory. It was hard to tell.

'Look, Stanwick, Henry, I want to get back home, but I need this solved. I don't want a worldwide conspiracy. I don't want to bust open the KGB. Give me a break; I need one. Just a little successful case. I just want to fly off this little pile of brick dust with its mutant fauna. I'll come back here when evolution's caught up with the rest of the world. Just help me, please.'

I said nothing. This was getting irritating.

We faced each other across the table in silence. Lemaire spoke again. 'Stanwick, what's your price?'

I thought for a moment. 'I don't have one.' As I said it I thought that at the moment that was probably true.

'Everyone does. Sure, you've got to know the currency. Sometimes you even have to know the slot to feed it into. But everyone's got their price. Money, sex, drugs, power, whatever.'

I was beginning to feel angry. We were getting nowhere. I had to speak. 'Look, Mr Lemaire, I want answers too. I get dragged halfway round the world here by someone who was trying to vanish. Then he gets killed. There's one planned crime there and one very real murder. So far nothing you have said has shed any light on this business. Someone committed murder, and it looks as though he's going to get away with it on present progress.' I stopped suddenly. Lemaire glared at me.

'Getting worked up about it doesn't make it any more probable. I'm not even convinced that anything in your story is true. For all I know Vaughan may just walk in the door now.'

At that point there was indeed a knock at the door, but it was Harris who entered. He looked agitated. He walked over to the desk, clutching a piece of paper in his right hand and stabbing at it with the index finger of his left.

Lemaire leaned over and grabbed it. A flicker of some emotion crossed his face, and he turned to Harris.

'Where did it come from?' His voice was gravelly and full of anger.

'Mozambique. We're checking up. I don't understand. It wasn't registered; wasn't on my list. Moss made it up just before he got sick. It's two weeks old.'

Lemaire glowered. 'Let's get this straight. I ask you to check up on whether there is a helicopter that Stanwick here identifies as a 212. You consult the lists and say no. Then Thompson tells me—not wishing to contradict "Intelligence," of course—that the local TV station has shown the President of the country flying about in something pretty darn like it, and you kindly check up again with the airport, that flea-ridden pile of shacks. Lindbergh took off from a bigger one. They say, "Why yes, sir. They're using one on seismic near Morondava."'

Lemaire's face was growing red. He stood up and seemed to tower over the unfortunate Harris. 'What sort of two-bit operation is this? Get out of my sight and get me a written report on it. Tomorrow noon. No later.'

Harris turned pale, visibly trembled, and then left. To say he fled would be only a very slight exaggeration.

Lemaire looked at Thompson who was staring into space. 'You, wipe the grin off your face and get downstairs. I want a plane to take us out to that seismic camp tomorrow. You, me, Stanwick and his sidekick. Call the camp up and get them to ground the chopper and the pilot until further notice.'

Thompson got up, saluted, said 'Yes, sah' and left. I think he winked at me as he passed. If he did, he was jolly careful not to let JP see it.

Lemaire sat down heavily and pulled out a cigarette. He

offered me the packet. 'Thanks, but I don't.' It was a small token of a diminution of hostilities.

'Wish I didn't.'

He leaned back and stared into the air for a minute. When he spoke, his voice was slightly quieter and more reflective.

'You're not off the hook, boy. By a stroke of luck, though, your story is only stuck with three impossibilities instead of four. I guess that's progress.'

32

Eight o'clock next morning saw us standing in the mist at the end of one of the side runways of the airport. The pilot of the Twin Otter was making last-minute checks.

'Call this a side runway? They're all side runways.'

Lemaire was feeling morose and seemed ready to savage anything or anybody. He looked to be in possession of a hangover. Thompson chewed gum a few yards away, trying not to look as if he was standing guard over two large holdalls. From the bulges and evident weight of one I suspected it held weaponry. Laurent was rubbing his hands in the chill air. Lemaire's caustic remarks apart, it was a quiet party.

Soon, however, the mist lifted and we took off. As we flew westwards the cloud quickly broke to give a view of the rolling baked hills of the plateau. The visibility was good and I felt positive. I almost began to dare to hope that within a few hours the problems that enveloped me would be resolved. I kept telling myself just to hang on and persevere. It would be good to get out of this crazy environment of suspicion and intrigue to the real world. I realised that the evening with Laurent's family had been the last time that I had had any real external peace and tranquillity, and that precious memory seemed very dated now.

Lemaire sat at the front of the passenger cabin, following the journey on an aeronautical map. As we came to the edge of the plateau I went over and sat next to him. He grunted something that might have been a welcome.

'Well, Professor, tell me what I'm looking at.'

'We're dropping off the Basement, that's the really old

rocks, now. We've got a sandstone plain ahead of us now and you should just be able to see it rising up ahead, yes over there, the Bemaraha Plateau.'

'You don't charge extra for the guided tour? No, I guess I shouldn't complain, kid. It's what I asked for. I guess it's what Vaughan paid you for.'

'Possibly. Anyway, you should be able to see the Manambolo River down to the south now. No, Laurent and I reckon that Vaughan hired us as witnesses to his disappearance on account of us being trustworthy. It's a pity that's a minority opinion.'

'You can say that again.' But it was said in a voice that could have been described as being of low toxicity.

There was silence for a minute or so. The plane began to lose height slowly. I thought I might as well try to point out the view in front of us.

'OK, we're going to fly over the pinnacles. You can see them over there, the grey-looking stuff with the criss-cross fractures. That's it.'

'Can't say as I'm impressed.'

'You would be if you could see them low down.'

'Maybe, but I'd rather find Vaughan.'

I was going to say that I thought that was wishful thinking, but I was interrupted as the co-pilot stuck his head out from the doorway of the crew section.

'Belts on and hold on. It's a short strip.'

I went back to my seat. As we came in to land I caught a glimpse of a seismic line running due west in an almost impossibly straight line. Working along it was a stretched out convoy of dusty seismic vibrator trucks.

Then we were down on the strip, which proved to be not only short but bumpy, and the red dust blew up in great clouds behind us. Lemaire was first off, and the three of us climbed down the step behind him. The first thing that caught my eye was the helicopter parked at the end of the runway next to a pile of fuel drums and some dusty tents.

Lemaire caught my eye and I nodded. 'That's it.'

He looked at Laurent who just spoke quietly. 'Yes, it is the same.'

'OK, let's talk to the pilot.'

First the camp boss had to be placated. Clearly deficient in placatory skills, Lemaire chose to do this by plain intimidation. There was a lot of arm waving and then JP came back to us, shouting over his large shoulders as he did. 'Sure, sure, complain all you want—in writing, to the Embassy. And don't expect that 'Tana will overlook you buying your food in from South Africa when they find out.'

Then he turned to us. 'Idiot. Must be to work in this armpit of a place. Thompson, bring the gear, and keep an eye on this pilot. You, Stanwick, and you, whatever your name is, just say nothing, right?'

Thompson shrugged and picked up his bags. I looked at Laurent, whose face seemed vaguely strained. We set off towards the helicopter and the tents and trailers behind it. To one side of the helicopter stood two large, garage-like tents separated from the main sleeping and eating quarters; a wall of red fuel drums lay to one side. Beyond the helicopter tents lay a dozen more tents and four large air-conditioned trailers. Somewhere nearby a generator roared. A Malagasy labourer was watering round the helicopter to keep the red dust down.

As we came to the tents, two figures could be seen. One, in dirty shorts and shirt, was tuning a radio transmitter in the back of the tent, while the other, dressed in neat white clothes, lay out on a camp bed reading a novel.

As we approached he put it down, got up carefully to his feet, and came over to us. He was a tall dark-haired man with a vaguely Gallic look. He extended a hand to Lemaire. 'Good morning. Antoine Masson; how can I 'elp you?'

The accent was North American, but to my ears odd. I guessed at French Canadian. Lemaire ignored the proffered hand.

'You fly the chopper?'

'That is my job.'

My heart sank. This was certainly not the man I had seen in the pinnacles. Lemaire stared at him a second, then he glanced at me. I said nothing, and he turned back to the pilot.

'So you can tell me where you were flying last Saturday for a start.'

Masson gave him a curious look. 'But yes. The North Atlantic; specifically from Montreal to Paris, prior to taking the Air France flight down 'ere on the Sunday.'

Lemaire flushed slightly, stared, and then fired back belligerently, 'Whatdyamen?'

'I arrived 'ere in Madagascar on Sunday. I 'ave been 'ere precisely four days at the camp. I replaced the previous pilot, Steers.'

Lemaire swallowed. 'Who is where now?'

''Ow should I know? 'E's back on leave. Let me ask Dave.'

Dave was the engineer. In his early thirties, he had a freckled, good-humoured face with protruding ears. He came over with a grubby circuit diagram and shook hands all round. Then he waved everybody into one of the tents.

'Come in outta the sun, fellas; fry yer brains. Chairs we're short of, but I can fix you a couple of crates. Coffee? Coke? Beer's off till after six o'clock. Camp rules. Tony, go and get us some coffee, while I chats to the gentlemen, will yer? Cheers, pal.'

Antoine left with a faint dismissive shrug.

'Right, what can I do yer for as they say?'

Lemaire lost no time. He pulled out a scrappy notebook and a ballpoint and sat cautiously back on his crate.

'Steers. Tell me about him.'

'Thought as much. Mikey Steers, eh?'

He spoke in a tone that seemed to convey slight relief. 'Fer a minute I was worried you was coming about my tax problem. Anyway, who might you be, like?'

'That's neither here nor there, but let's say US Government.'

The engineer looked oddly at Laurent and me. 'Suit your-self. Now, Mikey Steers. Company 'ull give you all the date of birth stuff, I suppose. That's Steers without an "a." What do you wanna know? Medium height, yellow hair, forty next year. A sort of a Brit; I mean he was born there like me, but had been around a lot. I think he had a Canadian passport.'

'Could he see his belt buckle?'

Dave looked blankly at JP. 'Sorry, better translate.'

'I'll spell it out. How was his waistline?'

'Oh, I see. Yeah, he had a beer gut: not that he drank a lot. The food's good here. Not a lot to do for a pilot. Lunch in an hour's time. Antoine brought in some lobster yesterday from the coast—before he was grounded, like.'

The conversation had lifted my heart greatly. Not only had Dave's description fit the pilot I'd seen, but Lemaire must have known it. I tried to catch Lemaire's eye, but he looked away.

'I didn't risk my neck to hear about the cuisine. Just tell us about Steers.'

Dave made a faint grimace and went on. 'Good pilot, good bush pilot—and that's different. Knew the machine and knew its limits. SS never complained, like.'

'SS?' Lemaire was attentive if nothing else.

'The seismic company, the client. they're a mean bunch; fired two chopper firms in Tanzania. OK, OK, you don't wanna know that. Yeah, just tell us about Steers.'

It was hard not to like Dave. He seemed to have Lemaire sized up.

Lemaire interjected before Dave could continue. 'First, where is he now? He left on Sunday, right?'

'Sure . . . I dunno. He said he was going to stop off in Paris and have some fun. Then I'm not sure. He seemed to think he mightn't do another tour.'

'Interesting.'

Dave thought for a few seconds and picked up a screw-driver off the bench. 'Not really. Most pilots and engineers say that, at least at some time. Then the money runs out. Still,

Steers was a bit weird. He'd have a beer or two in the evenings, maybe watch a video. Sort of quiet. No trouble really, never got drunk or fooled around chasing the camp girls. Well, mostly no trouble.' He paused and fiddled with the screw-driver.

Lemaire hadn't written much, but he stopped and looked up in expectancy. Dave shrugged.

'OK, 'cept one night, a Friday night. The crew were ahead on the lines, it's a tight schedule. Camp boss donated a couple of boxes of beer. Well, it got a bit loud and someone said to Mikey it was a pity about his name as they didn't like being called "Steers' Queers." Something along those lines. Anyway, they got to making a few comments about whether he was a man or not. Anyway, Mikey stormed out saying he'd show 'em and came back with a pile of colour polaroids. What did he call them? "His war souvenirs"? Yeah, Mikey had flown in one of those African wars; Mozambique, maybe Angola, I forget which. A reprisal raid it was. So he just showed some of them. Some of his military buddies must have taken them for him, and he wasn't doing very nice things, was Mikey. Not the sort of things you want to see on a full stomach. These guys aren't exactly soft, but that was a bit much. The place just went quiet. Just like that. No one ever joked to him again about anything like that. In fact for the next couple of days no one sat next to him. I suppose I was pretty glad to see him go. There's always some sort of knife around here and you never know, like . . .'

There was an uncomfortable silence. Something unpleasant and foul seemed to be among us. Fortunately, at that point Masson entered carrying a tray of coffees. He passed them round and sat down nearby on a crate of helicopter parts. Lemaire added spoons of sugar to his mug and stirred clumsily.

'So why was he here?'

'Never talked much about it. I can guess it was money, same as us all. Why else come here? Not for the scenery or the company. Oh yeah, he did say about having messed around on the stock exchange and lost heavily. I think he needed the cash real bad like.' Lemaire tapped his pen irritably. He was beginning to sweat.

'OK, Saturday. What did he do? Take the machine anywhere?'

'Yeah, I'll check with the log, but it's easy to remember. It was a slack day. We've had a lot of them lately. In fact, sometimes I wonder why we need the chopper, but the boss makes the contract. Must be to fly the President around when he fancies a break. OK, yeah, Steers. We got a fancy location finder in Tango November.'

He nodded at the helicopter. 'Triangulates your position off radio beacons. Pretty neat, accurate to within a kilometre. Essential here, can't afford to miss your fuel dump when you're the only chopper around. Stupid, a single chopper operation, if you ask me. OK, OK. Well, Mikey the Knife, yeah, we never called him that to his face, spent the past month telling me that the thing was out. I stripped it twice. Nothing, but it's all chips, so how do I know? So maybe it's the beacons, or the maps, or this lump of brick of an island, he says. So Saturday he takes the machine off with the maps to "calibrate the malfunction," quote unquote. He wants to make sure the machine is just right for his replacement—professional pride and so on. So he disappears for five hours with one call to say he's shutting down and comes back with empty tanks. And missing a life jacket. And he says, "Well, maybe the box is right after all."'

This was marvellous news. I looked at Laurent and grinned. He smiled faintly back, but there was a note of concern on his face.

'A what? A life jacket? Had he been swimming?'

'Naw, he said he'd used it to lie on and left it. Nuisance. We don't use the things, but I've had to order a replacement.'

'So where did he fly to?'

'It'll be in the log book. Up north and west, I think. He wanted to hit precise landmarks. Stupid idea. These seismic boys know where they are to within a foot. See the satellite dish over there?'

He gestured beyond the helicopter and reached over to the table by the radio and pulled over the log book and opened it. 'He landed three times and shut down twice. Here's the co-ordinates for you, but I don't see the importance . . .'

He ran his finger over a page and then handed it to Lemaire. Lemaire fumbled for his glasses and, putting them on with his habitual embarrassment, looked at where the finger pointed.

'You're not supposed to see the importance, right? OK, let me copy these figures out and let's plot them up. Thompson, get those maps out. How do you know these figures are genuine?'

'We don't. Could check the fuel figures against distance, but that's only rough.'

Lemaire ignored him. He got Thompson to call out the figures as he plotted them up on the map sheets. I just sat there quietly rejoicing. It was all working out beautifully. The story was vindicated.

Lemaire called over his shoulder. 'He flew on his own?'

'Sure did. He invited me but, well, I don't care for bush flying and after those photographs . . . well heck, I had a lot to do here, anyway. Always write letters before a crew change, like.'

It was all I could do not to get up and look at the maps. Eventually, the strain was too much.

'Er, Mr Lemaire, can I see the co-ordinates?'

'Might as well.' Lemaire had ringed two places. One was where I knew it would be, on the Beboka as it twisted its tortured way through the pinnacles.

The other took a second to find as it was not on the map Thompson had brought. We found it on Lemaire's aeronautical map on the coast southwest of the pinnacles, near the mouth of the Manambolo. There was nothing special marked on the map.

'Comments, kid?'

'Well, it vindicates our story. He did fly there and he landed there when we said he did. Truth will out.'

'Will it now? I'm less confident. Anyway, who says this is truth? Your nice friend Mikey Steers? What about the first spot? What happened here?'

I was silent for a moment and then an idea dawned, but it was Laurent who spoke first. 'That is perhaps where he found the other man.'

Everyone turned to look at him.

JP picked the map up and turned to Masson who was sitting with his head resting on his hands in an attitude of rather tired puzzlement.

'OK, Mr Pilot. How soon can you be ready to take us to this point here? I want full tanks.' He gestured at the map.

Masson looked uncomfortable and then scrutinised the map. 'Well, the company says to afford you all assistance, so I guess we can do it, but that is a long way north. I 'ave not flown there at all.' There was little enthusiasm in his voice.

He paused for a moment and looked at the engineer. 'Ten minutes, Dave?' There was an affirmatory nod.

'Good, now if you will excuse us.'

Taking the engineer, he left and went over to the helicopter. Lemaire picked up the screwdriver, flicked it up in the air and caught it.

'So you're feeling good, Dr Stanwick, are you?' He spoke with a mock gentleness. Then his tone suddenly switched to one of harshness. He leaned over and glared at me.

'If you are, I don't see why. Maybe we *will* get some more light by actually visiting the scene of the crime. But one way of reading this is to reckon that you and your charming little fellow Brit were working together.'

And at that point he threw the screwdriver up in the air and let it drop. By some skill or luck it landed point down in the soil and stood there quivering, like some portent of judgement.

33

Masson and the engineer were over at the helicopter. The rest of us sat in the shade of the tents, staring out at the red dust of the landing strip. I was quietly fuming. In 'Tana, Lemaire's accusation wouldn't have been surprising, but to have come so soon after so much of our story had been vindicated stung. Exactly what he was playing at was a mystery.

After ten minutes Lemaire got up and, in evident impatience, went over to the helicopter. There was the sound of raised voices. Then he came back, followed by the pilot who had a look of cold anger on his face.

'And I'm the pilot of this machine, understand? I'll fly you where you want, but I'm taking no shortcuts for you or anybody. It's my skin, right?'

Lemaire twisted his face into a scowl, ignored him, and walked over to us. The voice of the pilot pursued him.

'And get this straight. That's my machine, and in the air I'm boss, right?'

Masson turned on his heels and walked back to the helicopter. Lemaire grunted, 'I only asked him to speed it up. You'd have thought I was asking him to fly blindfold.'

I got up from my crate and, steeling myself, went over to him.

'Lemaire, I want to talk with you.'

'Sure, kid, confession is good for the soul. Maybe we can do a deal before that jackass risks my neck.'

I snorted and walked out into the sun. It was hot now. Nearby, a pair of kites circled round what was obviously the camp rubbish dump. Lemaire followed heavily and when we were out of earshot of the tent I rounded on him.

'Listen, you're not crazy. You can't seriously believe that I'm in league with that knife man. How on earth . . .'

He waved a large hand dismissively. 'Stranger things have happened. Sure, I don't see you recruiting him, but maybe whoever you're working for hired him too.'

He paused for a few seconds. 'Kid, I don't know what I believe, but things don't add up. Your tale of Vaughan defecting to the Reds, that's not truth, that's trouble. And I don't like trouble.'

Lemaire pointed to a nearby tree. Directly underneath was a pool of shade. We walked over, and he squatted stiffly on his haunches. He spoke slowly, as if articulating something for the first time.

'Let me explain. I'm a survivor. Every Christmas I have a list of widows I send cards to. This is a mean business. Lost three colleagues one day in Beirut. Guess you were on the beach that day? No matter.'

He stared into the distance as if conjuring up their faces. 'Anyway, I've survived this long by picking my cases. I'm no idealist, I just want to retire. Maybe just a couple of years more. Maybe less. Florida I reckon. I've served long enough. Sure, I've missed promotion, but I've missed getting inside a flag-draped wooden box too.'

He looked at me. For the first time there was something that looked like a glimmer of sympathy. 'No, the first rule, Henry, is to keep out of the firing line, and that's what worries me about this case. If you're right, then this is big, and suddenly JP Lemaire is on everybody's list. I don't want that.' He picked up a fragment of stick and doodled in the sand.

'So you just want a neat story, irrespective of the truth?'

Lemaire gave me a sideways look. The hint of sympathy had vanished. 'Kid, save truth for Sunday. My job is to keep the world, or at least part of it, free enough for your sort to discuss truth. It's a luxury item.'

'I might differ on that.'

'Sure you might. It's not your skull that'll get holes put in it. Another thing. I couldn't say it in 'Tana, but we're fairly certain that Moscow hasn't got anything to do with this. I'm not telling you how we know, but we do. OK, that leaves a few other parties: the East Germans, the Israelis, the South Africans. It does put the skids under your story, though.'

I had nothing to say.

'Sorry, kid. Anyway, looks like that pilot has wound up the rubber bands. Time to fly.'

The interior of the 212 had started life as no more than basic, and long usage hadn't improved it. The paintwork had innumerable scratches, and the foam insulation was ripped in places. Lemaire sat up front to the left of the pilot. I sat with my back to him in the main body of the helicopter where the only concession to passengers was some worn, fold-down webbing seats. Thompson sat facing me impassively chewing gum, with one bag between his feet and the other loosely tied to some of the numerous lashing points on the floor. Laurent sat uneasily to my left.

Lemaire checked us out. His mood seemed to have hardened again.

'Stanwick, and you, what's your name, get this straight. No funny business. I've also survived to have grey hairs by taking precautions. Thompson may look stupid, but he's got orders to shoot you if necessary. And he obeys orders, don't you, Thompson?'

'Yes, sah.' Thompson spoke with a barely discernible tone of truculence. Lemaire glared at him.

'Stanwick, get ready to confirm the landing zone. And keep an eye on your friend. Him maybe not like white man's magic.'

I shook my head and caught a flicker of what might have been empathy from Thompson. Lemaire slid the side door closed on us and took his place up front. The engine started up. The blades began to turn and the cabin to vibrate with a thousand different roaring and throbbing bass frequencies.

Beyond the blurred arc of the blades the mechanic gave a cursory wave and turned his back on the rising dust.

Ten minutes later we had crossed the muddy Manambolo River and were flying north, parallel to the line of the pinnacles. Although we must have been only a thousand feet up, the pinnacles were little more than an irregular grey surface, broken by linear fractures visible through the door on Laurent's side.

'Stanwick, that your river coming up?' It was a distorted bellow. Masson interrupted in a cool flat voice. 'No need to shout.'

'Thank you, pilot.' Lemaire spoke only a fraction quieter, but with audible ill temper.

'*De rien*. The name's Antoine, by the way.'

I thought I'd better answer Lemaire. 'Roger. We entered the pinnacles at the point virtually underneath us now.'

'OK, pilot, I want to go due east at, say, 200 feet.'

Masson took the turn tightly, losing height as he did so. The result was that the window beyond Laurent was filled with grey spires and trees suddenly coming into focus. Thompson closed his eyes with a look of distaste. The loss in height suddenly brought the pinnacles into true perspective. Lemaire roared over the intercom.

'Will ya look at that! We still on Earth, pilot?'

'I 'ear you. Unless you fouled up on the map reading, yes. Where is your landing zone, please?'

The voice was unruffled. Up here Antoine was king, and he knew it. If I hadn't been so upset about the allegations Lemaire had made, I might have enjoyed the repartee.

I looked forward over Lemaire's broad shoulders. In the sea of spires a relatively smooth area of brown and green was coming up fast.

'Straight ahead. The high point is pretty free of large rocks.' My voice echoed in the headphones.

'Roger. 'Ang on in the back there. Don't unbuckle your belts until I say.'

240

Masson was careful and did a full circuit before coming down gently in a cyclone of leaves and dust.

We were back in the pinnacles again.

It took an hour for Lemaire to satisfy himself. He wandered around, prodded stones, and looked down at the river. I showed him where we had struggled with Vaughan and where I thought the shooting had taken place. Then he looked over the remains of the campsite where only faint human tracks could now be seen under numerous animal footprints. He looked inside and outside Vaughan's now dusty tent. Then JP left us under the shade of the helicopter while he walked slowly and aimlessly around.

Eventually Lemaire motioned me over from under the shade of the helicopter. He gestured at Laurent. 'You too, I guess.'

There was a note of decisiveness in his voice. Thompson caught it and stiffened slightly. His hand moved towards the heavier of the holdalls.

We walked out of earshot of the helicopter.

'OK, Stanwick, I've made up my mind.' He paused, perhaps for effect.

'I can't charge you. I've no body, no witnesses. But I don't want to let you go. The story stinks.'

My heart sank. 'Hang on, though. You've got to do something. You can't just leave the thing as it is. You can't do nothing.'

Lemaire sighed. 'Kid, your chances would be helped if you didn't tell me my business. "Nothing" is precisely what I am going to do. I'm going to let you go. The investigation will continue. We'll keep a small, intermittent watch on you. We'll do a little bit of digging around, check on your friends, watch your bank accounts. Eventually something will surface. Maybe you'll crack. Someone will slip up.'

I was speechless for a moment. 'But . . . but that's marking

241

me as guilty. I mean, how can I clear my name? I'll be followed.'

Lemaire seemed vaguely amused. 'Think of it as fishing, Henry. We've got you on the end of the line. Maybe at the end of the day we'll have nothing else, so we'll haul you in and be content. On the other hand you might just act as bait.'

I sat down. The implications of it all sank in: a semi-perpetual surveillance and the hint of worse. I felt as a fox must when he hears the sound of the hounds. A storm of bitterness blew over me; I felt angry with myself, with Lemaire and—most especially—with God. Since the airport I felt I'd been playing things His way, and instead of it all working out I looked to be in even bigger trouble.

'There are times when you live up to your nickname.' I shouldn't have said it, of course, but I did.

Lemaire coloured slightly. 'Professor, go easy on me. I don't entirely disbelieve you. Vaughan is missing. This Steers flew a chopper a long way on a bad excuse. But I can't entirely believe you either. There's no blood, no shell case, no motive, above all no body. What can I do?'

Suddenly Laurent spoke. 'Perhaps if we find the body?'

'Bravo! Sure, find me a stiff. That's what I want. That's why Thompson has lugged a body bag here. Maybe you've got some ideas?'

There was a moment's pause, and then Laurent spoke quietly. 'I think I know where it fell.'

He pointed into the pinnacles. Lemaire followed his gesture and then turned to me expectantly. I didn't rush to answer him, but eventually I spoke.

'It's a very long shot, but Laurent is right. If you fly low and slow we might see something. But collecting . . .'

It was more than a long shot, but what else was there to do? Laurent must be playing for time.

Lemaire walked on ahead back to the helicopter and started to talk to Masson. As we followed I turned to Laurent. 'Laurent, this is impossible.'

'With God all things are possible. Is that not so?'

'Well, yes . . .'

Lemaire waved a big arm at us.

'OK, you've got ten minutes over this pile of rubble. No longer.'

34

Masson flew the helicopter slowly eastwards. He'd allowed us to have the doors open to see better. My mind was locked in a reverie of deepest gloom as I stared downwards, concentrating on the unrolling landscape. The emotion was hardly surprising, given that my only hope hung on the discovery of a corpse. I concentrated again on the surface below. The stone teeth seemed to be reaching up at us like waves of a frozen sea. The wasteland scrolling by underneath us was broken only by dark crevasses full of gloomy shadow. Only the occasional fragment of green from a tree indicated life. My heart was cold and full of foreboding. It seemed a landscape made of ground bones, the charnel house of the world. We were hunting for the dead in the dead lands. Even the blobs of the precarious trees seemed simply to highlight the desolation, as the memory of health sharpens the sorrow of illness. Here Vaughan had met his end. In its way there could be no more appropriate place for such a death. Here, in the pure lifeless sterility of the bare rock, Vaughan, so mechanical and cold himself, had met the ground.

My thoughts were broken by Lemaire's bark, made distant by the intercom. 'Take her down lower, pilot.'

There was silence. 'Do you read me, pilot? I want lower . . . lower. Please.'

'Perhaps you'd like the stewardess to serve you a Scotch as well?' Masson's voice sounded strained. I don't think he liked the terrain either. Even with his twin engines, low slow flying was no joke over this. However, the helicopter gradually descended till we must have been no more than a hundred feet up. Now the peaks of the pinnacles against the sky could be clearly seen. Seeing those hundreds of acres of stone, it all seemed utterly hopeless. The body must have fallen into a crevasse. The pinnacles would not yield up the dead.

Then suddenly the shapes were changing; becoming smoother and softer as the stone teeth gave way to low rounded boulders separated by strawy grass. That was it. We were out of the pinnacles. There was silence for a few moments.

Lemaire's voice came over again. 'Do a 180, pilot. South or north of that line, you two? Your very last chance.'

I looked round at Laurent whose eyes were closed. I guessed he was praying. It occurred to me that that was what I should do. He fumbled for his intercom button and spoke firmly.

'South, I believe. *Deux kilomètres.*'

'Two kilometres, pilot.' Lemaire had his microphone too close to his mouth again.

'So, you're a French scholar as well. OK, 'ere we go.'

The clockwise turn was vicious; doubtless deliberately intended to give Lemaire the worst of it. It was just unfortunate that I was sitting behind him. Thompson looked very uncomfortable. When we had settled down straight and level the pinnacles were underneath us again. Nothing, absolutely nothing. More grey broken tormented rock. The seconds ticked away. Just more of the same. I flicked a glance up. The edge of the Cricket Pitch was coming into view. That was it.

Then there was a noise over the muffled roar and thudding of the engine. It was Laurent shouting, trying to find the microphone button. 'I see it, him. Over there, a kilometre to the south. Now behind us.'

My heart missed a beat. Could it really be?

'180 turn, pilot, and lower still.'

The turn was less violent this time.

The needles came closer.

'OK, I see you. Something there. Can you swing us round it, pilot? On my side.'

'Roger.'

Down still lower. As we went into the turn, it felt as though only the seatbelts were preventing us from sliding out of the door. I could see only rock. Laurent had been mistaken; a trick of the light. The clouds of gloom began to descend again. Then something came in to view, lying on the edge of a pinnacle. Its form and colour were ill-defined, as if smeared. It lay draped against the side of a molar-shaped crag and half-hung above a crevasse deep with shadows.

'Thompson, you read me?'

'Sah?' There was a worried note in his voice.

'Get that body bag out. Looks like we may have a stiff after all.'

The helicopter started to gain height in a gentle spiral.

Masson spoke in a cold voice. 'Mister, 'ow are you going to get that thing?'

'Get you to fly down and Thompson'll grab it. No sweat.'

A glance at Thompson suggested he thought otherwise.

'Can't get near it. I'd blow it over the edge if I brought the machine close.'

There was a moment's silence. I looked again at Thompson. He looked very uncomfortable indeed.

'How much flying time have we got here?'

'Fifteen minutes, then we must start back. Just as well we filled the long-range tanks. But no more.'

'OK. Stanwick? If we hovered over the end of the rock Vaughan's on, Thompson could crawl over and get the body, right?'

I could see Thompson's lips move. I pressed the transmit button. 'It might be possible—risky, though. The grip is good, but it's painful.'

'OK, Mr Masson, a favour, please. See the edge of the rock away from the body? Can you put Thompson down and pick him up in ten minutes?'

246

'You're asking much. Per'aps too much. Maybe. But I give the orders now.'

He began a steady descent. Lemaire began to speak, but Masson overrode him. 'You in the back . . . Thompson. Get ready to get out. You done this sort of stunt before?'

'Yeah.' Thompson looked unhappy. An idea was stirring in my mind that I didn't like, but it wouldn't go away.

Masson continued. 'Rest of you guys, don't move when I put a skid down. Thompson, you move slow, real slow. Same about getting back on. Slow; preferably don't breathe.'

Another voice could be heard. 'Masson, I'd like to go with him. It's safer with two.' It was my voice.

Thompson looked up from unstrapping one of his holdalls. He said nothing, and it was Masson who spoke next.

'OK, it's your life. Get off one at a time and make it slow. Don't transfer your weight all at once. Don't move until I say.'

'Stanwick, you don't need . . .' It was Lemaire, but he didn't finish.

'You shut up. One more word from you and we go 'ome. Both of you wait to come on board until you see me nod. I need both 'ands for the controls.'

Down, down. The pinnacles seemed to loom up on every side. I undid my belt and clutched the seat with my hands. Why was I doing this? I asked myself. There was no answer. It wasn't as if it was a live person I was trying to save; just a dead body. At the thought of it my stomach churned.

'Good luck. Don't move when you're on the rock until I'm well clear. I'll lift off straight away. Then move as quickly as you can. I'll come in for the landing after ten minutes. Exact. That's all you've got unless you want to walk 'ome. 'Ere we go.'

Stone and more stone. Dante would have loved this. Who would he have put here? The answer seemed plain: the unrepentant, those who would not turn to God. Those of the hardened heart. But was I free of that? We descended further.

I peered forward over Masson's shoulders. The grey block was ahead and below us. Masson was approaching from the opposite direction to the body to protect it from the down-draft.

The helicopter began to settle slowly, almost inch by inch. I peered out. The skid was a foot, now six inches, now an inch above. Then it scraped with a judder that rocked the machine. Masson lifted the machine again and came down more gently. The skid touched and slid outwards.

'Go! But slowly.' The unhappy thought struck me that Masson was only doing this to show Lemaire that he could. The note of tension in his voice was strong enough to indicate that he clearly had his doubts about it.

Thompson pulled the holdall to the edge of the compart-ment. He then slipped off the headset and fluidly lowered him-self down onto the skid. He gently put one foot on the scalloped rock surface and slowly transferred his weight. The machine swayed nervously. Then he had the second foot down and was reaching the holdall down.

I followed as if in a dream. Slowly does it. Take the head-set off first. The beat of the blades like some winged demon above. Everything blowing and flapping in the roaring gale. One foot, slowly two. One little movement, down onto knees, hard rock digging in. The body of the helicopter was hung over a crevasse many tens of feet deep. I looked away in fear. Then there was a roar and a great gale and the helicopter went straight up. A few moments, then peace.

'Thanks.'

'No sweat, Thompson. I owe you a favour.'

I looked around. Here was a different perspective of the pinnacles. Although around us the peaks rose high and jagged, here what caught the eye was the snaking dark thin crevasses. Fortunately, this particular pinnacle was more gentle than most, but its surface still sloped downwards into the fearful dark.

'Gotta move.'

'Let me lead, Thompson. I'm more used to this surface.' I set off. The route ahead was tricky as it went around the crest of the molar. The only way to the body was to straddle the side of the central peak. If you slipped you might have stopped yourself from sliding into the crevasse below, but it would have been at the expense of your hands. I tried not to look down. The sweat was pouring off me. Thompson was moving carefully behind, pulling the awkward bag. Every so often it caught and it took the two of us to free it. As we approached the point where the body was, my will failed me. This was going to be horrible. We rounded the crest. I kept my eyes on the rock and tried not to look forward. I caught a glimpse of cloth just ahead and stopped. Thompson carefully edged round me. I nerved myself to go on and look, but there was a funny noise from Thompson. I swallowed and looked. Everything blurred for a second. Then I saw Vaughan's jacket and trousers; a black mass for the head. But had he been wearing a bright yellow shirt?

Thompson leaned forward and prodded at the chest. A yellow mass fell out. I gasped. Thompson was making more funny noises. It took a second to register before I realised what the yellow object was and another to realise that Thompson was laughing.

'Lost a life jacket, huh?'

I couldn't say anything for a second. I prodded what was left of the dummy to be sure. There was no doubt. I found myself shouting.

'He's not dead at all. He did it again. He pulled the same stunt again. He's not dead!'

35

Thompson spoke slowly. 'Sure as anything it ain't your Vaughan, but I guess we better take it back anyway.' He paused. 'We don't, and JP ain't going to believe us.'

I nodded. It was about all I felt able to do. Thompson unzipped the thick silver grey plastic bag and we stuffed the dummy inside. It was a cunning device given the limited resources and time available; the arms and legs had been padded with spare clothes and the whole thing weighted with stones. The head was a sheet of black plastic wrapped around an old shirt of Vaughan's. Presumably they'd cooked it up in the hour or so they'd been inside the helicopter.

Time was running out. We hastily zipped up the bag and began to drag it with us back to where the helicopter could land. The surface was no easier with the bag. I tried not to think about the consequences of a single slip. Already I had cuts on one hand just from steadying myself. Above us the helicopter had started a slow descent. Thompson turned and shouted above the rising beat, 'Say nutten, Henry. We got to think this one out with JP.'

'I'll try, but it's going to be a bit difficult to disguise.'

'You'll do it.'

The helicopter came in ahead of us and touched down gently on a single skid with a great noise some ten yards away. After a second or two Masson nodded urgently, and we half-walked, half-crawled under the beating rotors. It was a delicate business getting aboard, and the helicopter rocked badly. Once strapped in I put on the headset and, pausing for Thompson to fasten his seatbelt, pressed the transmit button. I swallowed hard.

'OK, Antoine. Mission accomplished. We're ready to go home.'

I had barely finished before he took the helicopter up and swung her southwards. I turned away from Laurent and stared into the receding pinnacles. That this was going to be my last view of them was a thought that dumbly registered through the avalanche of other emotions.

Lemaire's voice came over the intercom. He was trying to speak softly, but it still hurt the ears. 'Well, I guess apologies are in order. Vaughan must have been dumped out of the chopper.' He cleared his throat. 'Nice work anyway.' He paused briefly. 'Couldn't have been pleasant Sorry but . . .'

I was thinking of something to say, but Thompson saved me. 'No problem, sah. Just obeying orders.'

There was silence on the intercom if nowhere else. I sat back in my seat and tried to think straight. I glanced out to see that we were now leaving the pinnacles. Below us the cold grey rock ended and the brown green of the rolling grass plains filled the view. Suddenly I felt a growing urge to grin. It was partly based on the realisation that there had been no murder and our story had been totally borne out by events, and the other part was irrational, bubbling up from deep inside. I made the mistake of looking towards Laurent, who was gazing at me with solicitous concern. Suddenly he caught my grin, which had escaped without warning, and his face paled. He snatched his eyes away and for the rest of the journey fixedly stared out at the landscape. Only the restless motion of his fingers betrayed his desperate unhappiness.

Then we were descending towards the tents and the trucks at the airstrip. The Twin Otter stood on its own, a white cross against a brick red soil. Then we were down with ribbons of dust the colour of dried blood snaking away from the helicopter. Antoine began switching off various instruments. Thompson got out of his seat and leaned over me to speak into

Lemaire's ear. After a few moments Lemaire's voice, quiet and thoughtful, came over the intercom.

'Well, many thanks, Antoine. Neat flying. I won't forget it. I'd be obliged if you'd allow me and the boys to have a little chat in the back.' He paused. 'I guess too it might be kinda helpful if you didn't mention what we picked up. Sorta bad taste.'

It sounded remarkably feeble. But I had misjudged the man. There was only the slightest of pauses before Masson replied, 'OK, but no autopsies back there, right? Not in my helicopter.'

The blades whistled to a stop, and a welcome silence descended. Masson stretched his arms and got out. 'Just don't touch no switches, right? And, Mr Lemaire, I trust you will inform the company of my co-operation with you? And also that the ban on my flying is lifted?'

Lemaire muttered, 'Sure, sure—many thanks.' Masson, apparently satisfied, turned and walked away.

Lemaire climbed heavily out and came round into the passenger compartment. He and Thompson slid the doors closed. JP sat down heavily on a webbing seat which creaked. He looked tired.

'So what's up? You got him, didn't ya?'

'You better take a look, sah.'

I glanced at Laurent. He was staring ahead as rigid as a statue. As I watched, a muscle twitched in his neck. Lemaire looked around, shrugged, and pulled out a handkerchief and held it clumsily across his nose. With his spare hand he reached down and unzipped the bag, then peered in.

His face paled. 'What in heaven! Thompson, if this is your idea of a joke, then . . .'

He stopped. 'No, it isn't, is it? At least not yours, anyway.' He stared again. 'Yeah. Neat and perfectly adequate for its purpose. Heck, he even made sure both you guys had binoculars.'

Laurent suddenly leant forward and looked in. His mouth opened, and he said something in Malagasy. He shook his head and stared at me. 'So where is Tim?'

'Oh, I can guess.' Lemaire was zipping the bag back up. 'On a boat somewhere. Steers picked up the gunman on the coast, probably a small island; flew him over and took them back there.'

He rubbed his jowls and then shook his head, flicking his fine silvered hair up. 'What a mess.' He relapsed into thought.

Laurent spoke. 'So at least there is no murder.'

'True 'nough, I suppose. No murder, but most everything else. Yet it makes sense. Vaughan had to be thought dead. When you found him, his original scheme was blown, so he made up a replacement story. Very neat. But why go to so much trouble?'

'Hang on, JP. He had the circuits and we fought him and . . .'

Lemaire laughed. It was a cold cynical sound. 'Oh yeah, that explains a weak point in your story, Henry. That stuff about you overpowering him. It may have convinced you, but it didn't wash with me. Vaughan wasn't fool enough to let you get close unless he wanted it.'

Puzzlement, confusion and anger came over me. 'So it was all a scheme to make us think that he was defeated and to make his subsequent murder look realistic. But the circuits?'

'No problem, kid. Remember his short-wave radio? Bet you never heard it again after your little fight, did you? I'll guess that's where he got the circuits from.'

I began to feel that I had been the willing victim of a cruel trick. I looked at Laurent who was shaking his head slowly. He said nothing. I turned on the attack. 'Now you mention it, we didn't hear the radio after that. But what's the motive, JP? The motive. Answer me that.'

'True. Yeah, you put your finger on it. Insurance scam maybe. But it's odd. Anyway I need a smoke. Not a word of this to Masson.'

He pulled himself out of the webbing seat and opened the door. As he did I could see that Dave was running up towards us, his expression strained. Over by the tent Masson had come out and stood, tall and suave, staring at us. His face seemed pale and foreboding.

As Dave ran up to the helicopter he shouted, 'It's Steers! Mikey the Knife. He got it.' He stopped and leant against the fuselage.

'It's awful. We just heard from Montreal. Steers is dead. Paris police just contacted the boss. Some sort of fight in a club on Monday night. Hell. He wasn't a nice fellow but . . . you work with a guy . . .'

Lemaire opened his mouth as if to speak and closed it again with a shake of his head.

I thought back to the brief glimpse I had had of Steers, the man with the towel on the Beboka, the man who had watched the yellow butterfly, the man who now was no more. The tentative idea that I had been starting to form of the whole thing being a bizarre game suddenly and chillingly evaporated.

36

Twenty-four hours later Laurent, JP and I stood just in front of the old palace looking down over 'Tana. Several hundred feet below us the sprawl of the city seemed to be lapping up against the near vertical edges of the hill we stood on. In the distance the sun had broken through the clouds, sending shafts of light over the green plain with its whale-like islands of rock. In places there was a glitter of silver as the sun caught the water in the rice fields. Three small boys in ragged shirts stared brown-eyed at us from a safe distance.

Lemaire turned to look again at the palace. His chest was heaving slightly and when he spoke he sounded slightly out of breath, as if the station wagon had been parked at the bottom rather than near the top of the hill. He didn't look like he'd had much sleep in the twenty or so hours we'd been back in 'Tana.

'Bizarre, eh? You say the architect was Scots?'

'It's authentically Scots in that he just built a stone surround around the old wooden palace. Evangelical economy. Still, it outlasted the French.'

'Amazing. May outlast us too. Very pretty, Laurent.'

'Certainly. But there has been much blood shed here. It is here that Ranavalona the First killed many who would not turn from God.'

'Just politics. Probably necessary in order for the state to survive.'

'Perhaps. But she did what was evil, and it failed and the church grew. Within a few years there was a queen who was baptised.'

Lemaire pursed his lips and said nothing. After a few moments he looked around idly. It was an apparently careless gesture, but I noticed that it took in a full 360 degrees.

'Hmm, well enough of the past. I need to talk to you both. Here is a good place. I'm not sure about the Embassy any more.' He yawned. 'I'm tired. Listen, I've been doing a lot of thinking. Sure, we've got problems, but Vaughan's got a lot more. Remember that, Stanwick. Everybody's got problems. Find 'em and exploit 'em. First things first: why did he do it? Sure he wanted to be thought dead, but this way is weird and expensive. Why not just go swimming and not come back?'

We said nothing and JP continued, 'What was his motive? Anybody got any ideas, please?'

Laurent shook his head. The whole thing seemed to be an alien concept to him. It occurred to me that in Madagascar most people would be more worried about staying alive than pretending to be dead.

I felt I ought to have a stab at an answer. I've always hated silences. 'Perhaps, JP, perhaps he was looking for a new way to be assumed dead. I mean, the drowning thing has been done so much, but, well, I don't know . . .' I tailed off into a shrug.

'Maybe. Anyways, I'm going to do some checking on deaths in our business. Deaths without corpses. Next question. Who was the contact man? We can guess what happened. Steers flew to the coast, picked up the contact, and flew on to the pinnacles. Vaughan told him there had been a foul-up and they went through with play-acting. I guess the contact fired just to the side of Vaughan's head. He knew the angle you were watching from, so he didn't have to be too close. No problem there. So Steers flew back to the coast, dropped off Vaughan and the contact and then back to camp. Vaughan and his contact in the meantime are out on the high seas on a ship somewhere. Too late to find them now.'

I turned on him. 'Come on, JP, surely your intelligence people could find them? There may be satellite images of the area for that day. Check possible ships. You sound pretty defeatist.'

Lemaire gave a little dry laugh. 'Stanwick, never play checkers when your opponent is playing chess. You'll be as dead as Steers soon. Truly dead, *vraiment mort*. They killed him to cover their tracks. How long would we last if we started asking questions openly? We know nothing about who they are.'

I looked around. I suddenly felt exposed. It was the feeling you'd get going through Beirut Port, driving across the Green Line, aware of those dead gutted buildings with their staring windows, any one of which could contain a sniper.

'Lemaire, I want out. This isn't my business. Can't I get off?'

'In a word, no. Jumping off moving vehicles kills.'

'Sure, but if the vehicle is going over a cliff it's the lesser of two evils.'

'Fair point, but just listen to me. That body bag never made it to the Embassy. Some Malagasy is now over the moon about his new soft suitcase. He's gonna look pretty silly wearing the life jacket though. No, the story is that there was no body, no dummy, no data. You are still under observation.'

'But that just is not fair.'

'Fair? Course not, but at least now I believe you. No, Stanwick, put yourself in the opposition's shoes. He knows—almost certainly—that you decided to tell the truth. An irrational, stupid move, incidentally. Actually, he probably had even that eventuality covered.'

'How so?'

'Dave Moss, I reckon. Wayne's predecessor. Something odd about the way that chopper record was missing. I would guess Dave or a colleague did your room over, too. Just checking.'

The last was a point I had virtually forgotten and as I thought it all over, I conceded that it made a certain sense. JP opened a packet of cigarettes and leisurely lit one, his eyes watching my face all the time. Then he continued.

'I guess according to the original plan, Dave would have dealt with your case when you turned up to say Vaughan was missing, or covered the tracks if anything else went wrong. No, our friend Vaughan has been unlucky twice—Laurent picking up the batteries and Dave catching cerebral malaria. Bad luck.'

He drew hungrily on the cigarette. 'Well, we may need all the luck we can get from now on. Anyway, if Vaughan and his buddy have any other contacts in our line of work he knows that I was summoned down here because of your story. Hence, probably, Steers' death.'

'You mean that because we came . . . he was killed?'

JP shrugged his big shoulders. 'He had it coming to him. Main thing to watch is that you are not next. Anyway, I suppose, Stanwick, you think I'm going to give Moss an interrogation?'

'Of course, he's your only lead, isn't he? Why not?' Then I stopped. 'Or wait . . . I can see a very good reason to leave him alone.'

'I should think so. Touch him and we ring the alarm bells. Remember, see the other man's problems. Vaughan's is that he doesn't know what we know. That will keep him guessing for a bit.' I looked around me again. I felt uneasy.

'So I'm going to do precisely nothing, Henry. I shall leave for Washington as soon as possible, deliver my verdict of an unproven crime, and leave the file open. When Vaughan and friends start getting worried they will try to check up on me. I reckon though I'll be safe there. In the meantime I'll start some cautious enquiries.'

'What about us?' I could hear the edge in my voice.

'Well, here's some news. I want you both out of here. I can't control things here. Moss may not have been the only bad apple.'

I looked at Laurent, who had clearly caught the meaning. His brow was furrowed in puzzlement. I spoke for him. 'I was going anyway, but how can Laurent get out?'

'What'd you like to do in England, Laurent?'

Laurent looked puzzled for a moment. 'Some travel, to see places, and to learn.'

258

'As I thought. Henry's buying you a plane ticket. Or rather I'm buying it out of that stash of dollars we are looking after for him. Don't worry, kid, I'll reimburse you. I might even forget to tell the local customs about your oversight on your currency declaration form. In the meantime we'll make sure you get the right travel documents.'

Laurent's face was a mixture of excitement and doubt. 'You mean, I will go to England?'

'Aw, don't get excited. It's not *that* great, despite what Henry says.'

'Er, JP, I don't want to interrupt the great American pastime of slanging the British, but what do we do in the UK? Besides, I'm supposed to be going to Cyprus at the end of the summer.'

'By then it should be a bit clearer. Do nothing. Just say you left Vaughan on his own. Well, it's true in its way. I don't think anything will happen. Probably oughta keep your eyes open—just in case. I'll give you a twenty-four hour phone number to call if you hear from or see Vaughan. Don't use it from home or work, use a booth. It's an extreme chance, but they may try to keep an eye on you. Nothing more, I'm sure.'

I looked hard at JP. From his expressionless face and the dry delivery, you could easily imagine this was some instruction to do the shopping.

'Great, superb, marvellous. In other words we are to be bait.'

'Kid, if anyone is risking his neck it's me. This whole stupid thing has got me deeper in this muck than I want. I'm breaking the habits of a lifetime to try to help you.' He threw the cigarette stub away with a gesture of impatience.

'Now, before we split I want you to tell me everything, every detail, about Vaughan's conversations with you after you discovered him in the pinnacles.'

'But I thought you agreed that it was all lies?'

'Sure, it was all lies, but he may have let slip some clue—something that will give me a lead.'

Two days later we were driven down to the airport. Thompson sat next to us, staring ahead and chewing gum. The trip was a silent one and Laurent seemed totally bemused. At the airport JP made the driver pull in to the car park and gruffly told him to go for a walk for ten minutes. Then he made us memorise a phone number and a name, 'Agravel.' Finally, he passed us the plane tickets. I checked them over.

'Hey, someone made a mistake. This is via Nairobi.'

JP stubbed out a cigarette before speaking. 'No mistake, Henry. We figured you'd better avoid Paris. You get off at Nairobi and pick up a direct London flight.'

There was nothing to say.

'Well, time for you fellows to get the flight. Thompson, get their bags out.'

We climbed out into the chill evening air and shook hands. JP said, 'It's probable that we won't meet again. I'd say that this is the end of this business for you. Perhaps you'll read about it in twenty years' time. Cheers, Henry. Sorry I doubted you. Laurent, thanks, and good luck with the studies.'

I muttered something and JP abruptly got back in the station wagon, waving us off. It seemed a bit unfair to expose Thompson to the mêlée going on in front of the check-in desks, so at the airport doors we relieved him of the bags he was carrying. He stuck out his big hand and gave what was a shadow of a grin.

'Henry, sure glad of your help out there. You watch your step now and don't trust no one—especially JP. Laurent, so long.' He turned and walked away to the station wagon.

On the long overnight flight in the twilight tunnel of the jumbo, I thought about JP's insistence on going over Vaughan's words to us after we had discovered him in the pinnacles. What had Lemaire said? 'Sure it was all lies, but he may have let slip some clue.' We had surprised Vaughan. Although tired, he had put together a convincing story in less than an hour.

Even assuming he was a master liar it was likely that he had simply altered the truth rather than create a new story from nothing. Perhaps in the tale about 'Jezreel' and its grim warnings, we had been given something more than fiction.

And what worried me, lying awake at 30,000 feet, was that the little we had been given might be altogether too much.

37

Laurent and I parted in London. He said he had some distant relatives in London whom he wanted to see. Although this was doubtless true, I suspected that the real reason was to let me get my affairs in order at Grantforth before he came up to stay. On the train going north I ran over things in my mind. Well, I was going to Cyprus and I had finally done the right thing in 'Tana. Now there wasn't going to be much time in Grantforth, perhaps six weeks, before I started to head southwards to Cyprus. Time just to pack things up and let the house. And to say farewell to Tina. Indeed more than farewells needed to be said, there were a lot of apologies to make. She had been right in her way about Vaughan. More seriously, I had also to admit that it was largely my refusal even to consider the Cyprus job that had driven me to Madagascar. Despite Lemaire's warnings there seemed no doubt that I had to tell her the whole truth. Telling her meant telling her parents too. Not that that would be any hardship for me; I had little doubt that Alec would be able to shed some light on the affair. But it would mean putting them into some sort of risk. As I thought about Grantforth the thing that did make my stomach quiver was the prospect of talking to Prof. He was bound to be furious. Well, it had to be done.

There was little in the mail at the house to detain me, so after a cup of coffee I drove down to the department. Miriam gave me a warm sun-tanned smile. 'Oh, welcome back, Henry. Have a good trip, did you, with that nice Mr Vaughan? Did he enjoy the scenery?'

'Er, yes, well, pretty good. I mean he enjoyed the scenery. It was, er, just what he'd wanted.' This was awful. I tried to change the subject. 'Nice suntan you've got. Spain, was it?'

'Canaries. Glad you like it. I thought perhaps I'd overdone it. You're sure the trip went all right?'

I was on the point of saying something when the door opened and a whiskered head appeared. 'Ah, Henry. Just the man I want to see. Come in, please. Welcome back.'

This was it. My stomach felt very unhappy. Funny, he didn't sound too displeased.

'Trip go well?'

'Er, yes. It allowed me to think a lot of things through.'

'Good, so more papers, eh? That's the stuff. The Principal has been on at us. Now what did I want to see you about?' He bent and rooted about in the debris of papers and folders on his desk.

'Er, Cyprus, Prof?'

'Cyprus? No, I don't think so. Oh yes, courses for next year. Spring. Morris is off to Toronto. Can you do his desert land-forms option?'

My mouth must have opened.

'Well, don't look so surprised. I know you can do it. Seen more desert than Morris, I'll bet. Probably won't miss as many lectures either.'

'Quite, I mean, well, possibly. Yes, let me think about it, Prof.'

What had happened? I ought to explain, I thought. Then I realised that if he didn't know by now, then it was too late. Abie Gvirtzman must be at the back of this. What was he playing at?

Prof was still talking. I waited until he had finished, then made excuses and left. It took only a few minutes to cross campus.

Abie's door was half open. I knocked, pushed the door wide and went over to his desk. 'Abraham Gvirtzman, what did you do? Where is my resignation? Why doesn't Prof know?'

Abie looked up from a thick volume and peered at me over his spectacles. He was silent for a moment. 'Let me preserve some civilities, Henry. Firstly, do come in; do sit down, and do allow me to say how delighted I am to see you back.'

He rose from his chair, walked over to me, and breaking out into a grin gave me a big hug. 'Henry, I've been worried about you. I nearly prayed for you once, but logic broke in.'

'Well, thank you, Abie, and I apologise for my rudeness, but what happened? You got my message and you telexed back to say you had implemented it, so why isn't Prof aware of it?'

Abie went back and sat on the edge of his desk. He was still grinning. 'Thereby hangs a tale. I sent the first telex to you and was about to send the one you asked me to send to Cyprus when I realised I'd forgotten the number. So I was walking back to my office past geography and I thought I'd check your mail. Don't ask why, I just did. There was a telex for you, so I read it. In fact I have it here.'

He reached down into his drawer and carefully pulled out an internal mail envelope. I read the enclosed telex hastily. 'Henry. Erickson's mother passed away last week. James feels he can now return in September. Thanks for considering the job. Keep in touch. Maybe some other time? George Roumian.'

I closed my eyes for a moment. I thought I was going to cry. I didn't have to leave at all. Abie spoke.

'Precisely so. So I just sent your friend an acknowledgement, and threw your resignation in the bin.'

He broke out in a fit of dry laughing. In the end I found myself joining in.

'Henry, I'm almost prepared to believe in the God of Abraham. You were finally prepared to put your career on the altar, but the Angel of the Lord has intervened. A substitute has been found. Go in peace and prepare thy lectures. But no—wait—tell me about your trip.'

'I'm too overwhelmed, Abie. I can tell you this has all been the most tremendous struggle and I nearly blew it. So it was all a . . .'

'A what?'

'I don't know, Abie. I'll have to think about it. I'm surprised and delighted, though.'

'Hmm. Incidentally—your American? It all worked out OK? Despite my fears?'

'Well, yes. It was tough, but really no problems.'

Abie's brow furrowed. 'Most unusual. Henry Stanwick lying through his teeth. Doubtless you have your reasons. One question: is it over? Is your matter finished?'

I breathed out heavily and stared at the ceiling. 'I have been promised that it is, Abie. I can but hope so. But I do have my reasons for silence.'

He shrugged. 'OK, but if you need me, you can trust me.'

I got up slowly. 'Well, maybe I should lie on the couch and tell you all. Sometime maybe. In the meantime I have to go see the Hensons.'

'Enjoy them, Henry.'

As I walked through the door I turned. 'Oh, Abie, I forgot to say thank you for checking up on that telex. Well done.'

38

To my disappointment there was no one in at the Hensons'. So I went back to the house and paid some bills. Then I sat down and tried to make sense of everything. I couldn't understand the Cyprus business at all; I'd been so certain that taking that job was what God wanted me to do. Yet in Abie's words I'd offered my career on the altar and it hadn't been required. Perhaps it was an offering that had been refused? A disconcerting thought that finally came to me was that perhaps more than the sacrifice of a career was needed.

As I thought through it all I came back to the revelation I had had of the shallowness, indeed non-existence, of my own faith. It briefly crossed my mind that I hadn't really straightened things out properly in that area. To be sure, since the airport I had tried especially hard to do what conscience told me was right. Yet somehow there didn't seem to be much progress in the area of my relationship with God. Then I realised that with the Cyprus question out of the way I had no great urgency to sort out that business. There would be time.

At six I called at the Hensons' again. Alec was prowling in the garden looking for the first signs of weeds. As I drew up he strolled rapidly over in almost unseemly haste.

'Henry, delighted to see you. Welcome back.' He gave me a hug and looked me over.

'Tina's out for another half-hour. Come and eat with us. In the meantime have a cup of tea. Viv, Viv! Henry's back!'

Viv came rushing out, trying to undo her apron at the same time. 'Henry dear.' A warm kiss. 'Lovely to see you. We've been so concerned. If we'd have known you were back today we'd have laid on a special meal. Really, we've been worried, and Tina . . .' She caught Alec's eye and stopped.

'Henry, come up to the study and tell me about it. Perhaps my dear wife could find time to manufacture a cup of tea? Excellent.'

In fact we didn't have much time. I had barely sat down before Tina's mini drove up. I went out to see her, possibly with more haste than I had intended.

It seemed to be the day for being hugged. Tina's was something special. 'Henry, I've missed you. We've all been worried, especially when you were overdue. It helped hearing from Abie that you'd telexed. And I was delighted more than you can know about you taking the Cyprus job. I must have been silly. I thought you wouldn't.'

'Hang on. Abie told you about my telex?'

She nodded, eyes brown and excited.

'Yes. Dad had been worried about the fact you were overdue, so he called Abie and he promised to let us know as soon as he heard anything. He called one day and said he'd just had this telex from you. I'm afraid he read the telex out over the phone. So we knew. Well done.'

'But didn't he tell you about the telex from George?' There was a blank look.

'Tina, they don't need me. James isn't leaving after all. The vacancy no longer exists. I'm staying here.'

Her mouth dropped a fraction. 'You're telling the truth? Oh!'

Her face twisted slightly, and the next thing I knew she had brushed past and run indoors crying.

I stood around for a few minutes, trying to look at the roses and feeling an absolute fool. Nothing seemed to make sense. Alec came out of the door and stood beside me. 'Poor Henry. I'm afraid your news was a bit much for Tina. She's been rather involved over this Cyprus job. She'll doubtless explain. Come on in and eat, anyway.'

Somewhat mystified I went in. Tina was still rather moist-eyed, but seemed radiantly happy. It made her look particularly appealing, and I began to feel in the sort of mood that has you looking for the flowery bits in the poetry books.

No sooner had we said grace when Alec looked at me searchingly. 'So it went according to plan, did it, laddie?'

I paused, spoon hung over soup. If there was a danger ('and Steers is dead,' said my little voice) could I involve these people? Surely the safest option was not to tell?

I put the spoon down. 'Look, it all went wrong—not according to my plans. I've got mixed up in something that is very big. I don't know if I should talk about it to you, because it will bring a certain risk to you. I should say there is one man dead already.'

Tina's lips moved.

'No, Tina, not Laurent, thank God. But I wish I could say it was all over.'

Everyone looked at Alec. He closed his eyes for a second and then turned to me. His face seemed concerned.

'Henry, we are your family. After the meal you can tell us all. In the meantime let us eat.'

The conversation during the meal was rather half-hearted. One thing of interest was a piece of news Tina had.

'Oh, Henry, your computer game can't have done Jim Barnett much harm. I've heard he's been attending St Paul's, Winscroft, lately.'

That was surprising news, although I knew little about the church. 'Really? Is that still Charlie Morris' church?'

Alec shook his head. 'No, he left a year ago. There's a new vicar. Evangelical—a sound man, I'm told. Ah, he'll be a sore trial to the Bishop.'

'Oh, Alec, you're mean. Give the Bishop the benefit of the doubt.' Only Viv would have stuck up for the Bishop.

'Doubt, my dear? That's not a scarce commodity in the cathedral.'

And the conversation drifted on to other things.

Twenty minutes later we were sitting down with coffee in the lounge. I told them the whole story, sparing almost nothing. They listened in silence except to ask for minor points of clarification. Alec listened intently, his eyes barely leaving my face. Tina sat on the edge of her seat, hands clasped, with an increasingly worried look on her face. Viv seemed ill at ease, wriggling slightly and frequently looking at Alec. She seemed to be hoping that he would say that it was just a plot of something I'd seen on the television. At length I came to the end.

'So that's it. Not a very honourable tale, I'm afraid. I don't come out of it very well. Disaster was averted by the very closest margin. Well, can anyone shed any light on this?'

Alec stretched his legs out. 'Hmm. Saved by grace alone. An odd story. But as my father would say of Walter Scott, "Not unedifying." Well, our prayers were needed and answered. A nasty business. I'd feel happier if I knew what lay behind it all. And happier still if I knew it was finished.'

Tina nodded. 'The key thing seems to be what Vaughan told you when you surprised him. This Lemaire man seemed to think so too. The bit about the "twenty-three fifty-nine" seems to be false, but the stuff about Jezreel seems, well, unproven.'

Alec jabbed a finger. 'Yes, there's something there that is odd. Codewords should never reveal the nature of the project. I remember that from my army days. But if you know what the project is, often you can see a relationship with the codeword. In its way Jezreel would be a fitting name for the sort of project Vaughan described, with its apocalyptic overtones. And it's the sort of link I can't see your man making up on the spur of the moment. Come on, Henry, you're the geomorphologist and you know your Bible; at least by today's poor standards. Significance of Jezreel?'

He had me there. 'It's the valley that cuts across Palestine. I've only ever seen it from the Jordanian side, of course. It's the site of lots of the great battles. But I don't see a link. Some Old Testament verse?'

'I think you'll find that from the valley of Jezreel rises the hill of Meggido.'

Light dawned. 'Oh golly, yes, apocalyptic is the word. "*Har Megiddo*," Armageddon. Yes, that is an oddity. Vaughan didn't exactly seem versed in Scripture. Maybe it was a genuine project, but I don't see how that helps us.'

Alec stood up. 'Nor I. Anyway, rest assured Viv and I will say nothing. It may be—as this Mr Lemaire said—all over, and then again it might not be. It would be as well to be as innocent as a dove and as wise as a serpent in this matter. We'll give it some thought and much prayer. Now Viv and I will go and do the washing up. I think you and Tina have a lot to talk about.'

They departed, leaving me facing Tina. I suddenly felt very much ill at ease.

'Tina, I've a number of apologies to make.'

'No, let me begin first. I'm awfully sorry to have burst into tears tonight. It's just that having, I mean seeing, you back was one thing and hearing about the fact that you are staying is another. This Cyprus business has been a big thing for me, I can tell you.'

It seemed a rather strong way of putting it, but I didn't query her phrase.

'Yes, but it had its uses. It allowed me to see that the job here had too much of a hold on me. Also other things . . .'

Tina's eyes glistened slightly. 'Henry, can I now explain something?'

I nodded for her to continue.

'This Cyprus thing was why I called everything off. You see, I had been uneasy for some time about how committed you were; whether your faith was genuine or just head knowledge. It was hard to tell. The Cyprus thing sort of focused it all. I felt that whether or not you took the job was a test. It may sound arrogant; it's just that sometimes other people's battles are clearer than your own.'

As she spoke a tiny feeling of irritation slipped into my mind.

'But why on earth didn't you tell me?'

Tina flushed faintly, and flexed her thin fingers together. 'But don't you see? It was your decision. You had to decide. I was scared I'd influence you. I was desperately worried that you might just decide to take the job to prove something. I wanted you alone to decide, so I tried to remove myself from the debate.'

My thoughts were not very happy ones. 'Or, you mean, the experiment. I see, or think I see. Your mind works differently from mine, Tina.'

It certainly did. To be able coldly and dispassionately to withdraw herself from a relationship she must have cared about was either a striking illustration of how she could keep her feelings in check or an evidence of a lack of feeling.

'That was a risky ploy, Tina. You must have known you would probably lose me completely.'

'Risk doesn't enter into it. It was right.'

'You sound just like Laurent.'

She smiled at me gently. 'From your tale earlier that sounds like high praise. No, I decided that I probably *would* lose you—either way. If you had stayed here, in spite of knowing that you should take up George's offer, I'm not sure I would have wanted to be involved with you. And if you went to Cyprus then, well, it's a long way away . . .'

She shrugged her shoulders.

'So now?'

She made a little face. 'Oh, really, Henry, do I have to spell it out? As I see it the problem between us is resolved. I was so delighted that you decided to take the Cyprus job; I mean . . . Well, I don't think that I have to say anything else.' Her smile was slightly strained.

I said nothing and looked at her, trying to think it all through. Tina sat in silence; elegant, delicate, beautiful and desirable. Of course at this point we should have kissed and made up. That we didn't was entirely my fault. I suppose all sorts of things went into what I did next. I think the main thing was pride. Despite the less than wonderful light the Madagascar story had painted me in, the act of telling it had given me a faint feeling of superiority. I think a part of me had rewritten what had happened so I partially believed that I had been leading a heroic battle against the forces of evil at the end of the world while Tina had been doing nothing more than shifting paper in a Grantforth office. In addition, the vision of my spiritual bankruptcy had become dimmed and there was a certain pique at Tina's moral supremacy. The final straw was the cold calculating logic that Tina had employed. While I could vaguely see the necessity of standing back and letting me sort it all out for myself, it seemed to treat me as some sort of experimental animal. If this forensic attention was the substance of her care for me, I wasn't at all sure I wanted it.

In the end I broke the silence. 'Tina, I don't know. I really don't. I need to think. It wouldn't be fair to start things up again suddenly without thinking it all through properly. I'm not sure I can do that now.'

A frown suddenly crossed her face. 'Yes, I'm sure that's right. I mean—yes—fine, let's think about it.' She sounded less than convinced.

I got up and went through to the kitchen where I said farewells to a thoughtful Alec and Viv. Then I walked down to the car with Tina.

'Henry, I'm sorry if I hurt you . . .'

'I'm sorry too, Tina. I guess it'll just take some time to sort it out.'

I squeezed her hand and drove home thoughtfully.

That night I couldn't sleep. It seemed clear that if I wanted it the relationship with Tina could be restored to what it was. Indeed I felt she would marry me given half a chance, and we would all live happily ever after. Or would we? I was still uneasy about how much she cared for me given the way she had dropped me over Cyprus. With that, a new doubt had crept in. Even if the question about the nature of Tina's affection for me was resolved, was she up to the big bad wide world that I seemed destined to live in? She had seemed overjoyed that I was not going to Cyprus. Yet was that because she felt she could stay here forever? True enough, today's news might mean that I was going to be in Grantforth for some time. But even if it was simply to do fieldwork I wouldn't stay around here forever. Sooner or later too I would leave Grantforth, possibly to go abroad. Would she survive uprooting? Could she handle the world where the milk wasn't delivered and the army announced the new head of government and the police didn't say 'Morning, luv'? Even her cool intellectual rationality that I so much admired seemed more suited to the delicate armchair discussion rather than the souk, the checkpoint or even the airport terminal. Was she really up to anything that wasn't as gentle and protected as her life here? How on earth would she cope with the likes of Vaughan or even JP? Those people played rough.

So the happiness produced by the news of my release from the Cyprus issue ended up being totally overshadowed by the problem with Tina. Why on earth couldn't my life sort itself out?

39

The next couple of days I found myself busy in the office, answering mail, correcting proofs and doing a variety of chores. The news that I could look forward to another year in Grantforth made me consider a number of ideas. One that seemed increasingly attractive was to go down to Yugoslavia in September. Vaughan's generous payment meant that my financial problems had gone. Perhaps I could even consider trading in the Beetle for a camper van. The problem over Tina I put out of my mind, although I made plans to take her out for a meal at the weekend.

On the Friday night I was working late in the office when there was a knock on the door. It was Jim Barnett. He looked a bit less scruffy, but he didn't seem very happy with life. After a few pleasantries I put on some coffee. As we chatted I began to feel increasingly uneasy about Jim's manner. I suppose I had been vaguely expecting some signs of a changed attitude to things. Instead there was something in his manner that was vaguely alarming and he seemed to be under stress.

'Hey, Jim, you look a bit uptight as the Americans would say. Are you keeping well?'

'Me? Yeah, sure, never better. No, just lots to do, and pressures at work. Something like that. Anyway, tell me about your Madagascar trip. Did it go well?'

Oh no, I thought, here we go again. 'It went just OK—lots of rocks, lots of walking.'

I wondered if I kept on like this whether I'd get better at lying.

'How did your rich American get on? You didn't leave him there, did you?'

I dropped the pencil I was fidgeting with and bent down rapidly to pick it up. This was getting a bit near the target. I straightened up.

'Actually yes, he had a few days to kill—I mean, to waste. So he hung around on the edge. We took the plane back. That is, Laurent and I. He's coming down here soon; just visiting London now. I'll introduce you.'

A flicker of interest passed across his face. 'Who's this? Oh, the guide you had. Heck, that must have set him back a bit coming to London, mustn't it? Where'd he get the money for that?'

Alarm bells were ringing. Jim had had no interest in Madagascar before I went. I tried to change the subject without lying further. 'Well, actually I gave him some. Vaughan was pretty decent about cash. These computer fellows seem to be rolling in it. Say, did you ever finish the game, the delta thing?'

Jim gave me a rather oblique look and took a sip of coffee. 'I did it. Just about when you left. Yeah, I saved the delta. The mainframe said only a dozen people had done it in the UK.' The pride in his voice seemed tempered by a certain something that might have been either regret or guilt.

'So there's a lot of copies about now. What's the secret? I've given up.'

'OK. As far as I see it the secret is to decide that saving the place is absolute priority and everything is subordinate to that. So all those little moral dilemmas get neatly solved. Actually, now you mention it, I can see your difficulty with it.' He seemed to be musing on something.

'So what was your strategy?'

Curiously, Jim seemed to be embarrassed. 'Well, it's only a game, isn't it? I made a deal with some of the rulers who were disaffected and stole a lot of blasting explosives and blew up the citadel with the remainder of the rulers.'

'Yikes! That was a bit ruthless, wasn't it?'

'Well, not entirely so. It killed about a hundred people, but I saved two hundred thousand. Some would call it surgical precision, but I do take your point. I really do. There are things about that game that make me very uneasy now.'

A moral concern in Jim was something I'd not seen before. I was tempted to ask him whether he thought the preaching at St Paul's was affecting him, but decided that that wasn't fair. Jim put his coffee cup down and seemed to brace himself. He spoke again.

'So that's that. Er, anyway, tell me about Madagascar again. You trekked through these pinnacles and back? Must have been tough, eh?'

There was no doubt this time. I know when I'm being pumped, especially when it's as badly done as this. 'No real problem if you take it carefully. Actually, Jim, I really must go; it's nearly ten. I'll tell you about it some other time. Perhaps when I get the slides back.'

I drove home in some consternation. What was going on with Jim? Someone was getting at him. But it didn't make sense, one second to be apparently shamelessly pumping me about Vaughan and the next to be expressing regrets about tactics on a computer game. It was almost schizophrenic.

Waiting for me on the doormat when I arrived home was a card from Laurent saying he was going to South Wales to stay with some friends of friends. He was hoping to go to the chapel where the first missionaries to Madagascar came from, but he couldn't spell it. Well, I sympathised—Neuaddlwyd rather lends itself to mistakes. Malagasy may suffer from long names, but at least you can pronounce them. After that he planned to join me towards the end of the following week. As a postscript he put, 'I hope you are making some progress.' Some hope, Laurent, I thought.

40

The weekend was a quiet one—at least until late Sunday evening. Saturday night I went out with Tina for a meal. By unspoken mutual agreement we had fenced off all the minefields and so the evening went well. The casual observer would probably have found it difficult to observe anything other than a broad affection and enjoyment of the other's company. My doubts were temporarily suppressed by her looks and manner, but later at home I wondered whether the matter was that she had an intellectual interest alone in me and that her tightly bound heart remained unengaged.

Sunday was a day for renewing friendships at church, listening to music and writing letters to friends; letters that were curiously vague about Madagascar.

The weekend was drawing to a pleasant close when at about nine o'clock the phone rang. I picked it up, gave the number, and the line went dead. Twenty minutes later there was an insistent tapping at the back window. I opened the back door with considerable puzzlement, as the only way round to the back of my end-of-terrace house is from a little-used access road. In the fading light stood a pale-faced Jim Barnett. As I opened the door he spoke urgently, the words tumbling over themselves.

'Quick, let me in, Henry. You're on your own? Good. Not a word. Don't put the light on.' He pushed past into the kitchen.

I was too surprised to say anything for a moment. Then I shut the rear door and after the briefest of pauses locked and barred it.

'Let me take your jacket, Jim.'

He shook his head nervously. 'Let's sit in your back room. No, leave the light on at the front. Keep it off here.'

He cocked an ear. 'Your radio? Good, turn it to a play or something with voices.' His hands twitched.

'Jim, would you like to smoke a cigarette? You look like you could use one.'

'No thanks, I've given them up. Well, three weeks now, at least.'

I went into the other room and put on some Sunday play about marital discord. If anyone was listening who knew my usual radio diet, then this would have been a sure sign something was wrong. When I came back Jim was perched on the edge of a chair looking very unhappy.

'Jim, just remind me. This is Grantforth in the latter part of the twentieth century, isn't it? Her Majesty's government still rules and there are still bobbies on the beat? Because you are acting as if this was Moscow or Tehran.'

To my surprise he put his head in his hands. 'Henry, please forgive me. I'm scared, but I had to come and see you.'

'Jim, I'm completely in the dark. What's up?'

'OK, I'll try and explain. I've been asked to spy on you. That's why I asked those questions about Madagascar.' His voice was uncertain.

The relaxing weekend disintegrated very quickly. 'You'd better start at the beginning.'

'Just after you left I was at a chemistry conference in Sheffield. Deadly. Anyway, I bumped into a girl.' He gave me a defensive look. 'We just talked. Anyway, she introduced me to some friends. A good crowd and we spent an evening chatting in a pub. Interesting stuff. At any rate, they invited me back up for a weekend.'

'What were they, some sort of political group?'

'Hmm, not sure really. Depends on your definition of politics. I suppose so. The way they said it was sort of like this: We always assume tomorrow is going to be like today, right? You know, spring, summer, elections, the Post Office, taxes, university committees. I mean, think of a world without mindless TV or newspapers or rain.'

'You mean that one day they might not be there?'

'Sure, except they said we'd better start living with the fact that one day they won't be there, unless something is done.'

I must have looked puzzled because he continued rather dreamily. 'It's like you drive in the motorway fast lane a lot. You've never had a smash, so you think they can't happen, at least not to you. Trouble is, chances are, when you do have a smash it'll be the last driving you'll ever do.'

'The horizontal learning curve thing.'

'Exactly. Well, they reckon the world is like that. We screw up the seas, strip away the ozone layer, burn off the forests and say, "Well, we've never had a smash, so we never will." We think the machine's invulnerable.'

There was the intimation of something in my brain. Jigsaw pieces seemed to be fitting together. 'So an ecological group, then?'

'No, at least not in the "Save the Seal" sense. That's just one side of it. See, the whole political thing is getting out of control. Everything has become interconnected. Half our food isn't from the UK, ninety per cent of the world's electronics is from a couple of small Asian islands. Your car's petrol is found in the Middle East by a firm from Dallas. The whole thing looks like some appalling building—absolutely unstable and just waiting for someone to hit it at the right point. Trouble is, everyone is still building on top of it. Probably collapse under its own weight eventually.'

The jigsaw pieces had fitted. 'But there's worse than that, isn't there?'

It was getting too dark to see Jim's face properly, but there seemed to be a look of surprise. 'Yeah, yeah. People are battering at the building. Last year they had gunpowder, today they have TNT, tomorrow nuclear devices, or chemical weapons, or something as nasty. Sooner or later the house will come down—at least that's their thesis. They put it neater; they've thought it all through. Do you understand what it's all about, Henry?'

'I understand.'

I nearly added that I'd heard similar stuff before, but I thought I'd better keep quiet.

'Well, basically the equation comes down to two curves. One curve is global stability—that's decreasing as complexity makes it more vulnerable. The other is destabilising forces, which are always increasing. Eventual result is a disaster. Inevitable.'

I wanted desperately to know where I fitted in, but there was one question I wanted to ask Jim first. 'Jim, if you had the computing power, could you ever quantify these curves? I mean, did anybody ever talk of when the curves meet?'

'Yeah, I heard it had been done roughly. But the thing is, you work out a best case scenario where everything goes right. That's the maximum you've got left. Chances are, it's much less. Figures I heard were twenty years.'

It felt like someone had opened the fridge door. I said nothing for a few moments. 'OK, so what does your group do and where do I fit into it?'

'Just kicks around ideas. Actually that's not fair. I mean, it sounds very low-key and free and easy, but it's pretty tight. They're going to link me up with a group on some of the chemical pollutants. A neat question. In an ideal world, what chemicals would we use?'

'What's the ideal world?'

'That's easy enough. One in which central decisions can be taken and implemented effectively across the globe. So we have none of this "I'll ban ozone-degrading chemicals only if you will" nonsense.'

'But you don't blow up fertiliser plants, or even nuclear plants?'

'Not yet. I asked that question myself, and I was impressed by the answer. Whatever action is taken must not cause a further destabilisation. Take out one nuclear reactor and it'd make no difference; take out a few and you'd cause such an energy problem that you might precipitate the crisis that would end it all. A careless attempt to dismantle the house might cause it to collapse. So it's data gathering, development of strategy, and then finally implementation. It also keeps the group within the law, for the time being at least. But there is a lot of urgency.'

'So you're not secret?'

'Of course we—well, they—are. This stuff is dynamite. If it leaked out, then it would cause such a panic that it would probably trigger the crisis.'

I wondered if I would have believed this if I hadn't been told something very similar by a man with a gun half the world away.

'OK, so where do I come in?'

'Yeah, well, one of the people said they'd heard that you might be interested in joining, that you might be "our sort of person," but that there were stories. You'd been up to something in Madagascar with a suspicious American. Could I find out? So I had a go. I wasn't very good, was I?'

'In a word, no. Grossly amateur. But then I've been gone over by professionals before now. So why are you telling me then, Jim?'

He didn't answer for a few moments. 'Well, it's odd. You know I started to go to church? I won't go into that. I haven't decided whether to become a Christian or not. Since I've been going, some things about this group stink. I mean, how can you disagree about saving the world? But it just doesn't seem right; I mean sneaking on you. I don't really want it. Sorry, but I felt I ought to tell you. Besides, you may be able to tell me what to do now. This thing feels evil.' He paused reflectively. 'Funny, evil's not a word I used to use. Anyway, what do I do?'

'Thanks. Can't you just say what you said now, that it isn't right?'

'No, that's why I'm scared. You see, Henry, one of the rules of the discussions is NHB. No Holds Barred. So if you're discussing, say, population control, then if you want to suggest that we let Africa starve, go ahead. Shouldn't dismiss an argument just out of sentimentality. Now I worry if the NHB policy might extend into other areas.'

'I can see that, but they don't sound worried about security. You weren't investigated, were you?'

'Yeah, I wondered about that too. I asked someone. She just laughed. "No need to worry about that," she said.'

'And had you?'

'Course not. Just met her at this conference, next thing we're averting World War Three. Henry, what do I do?'

I thought hard for a moment.

'Look, I'd tell them the truth about what I told you on campus—that I'm silent and uptight about it all. Then I'd find an excuse for a holiday and clear off until the start of term. Quickly. Don't attend another meeting if you can help it.'

'Yeah, sounds a fair idea. I've got relatives in the States I keep meaning to visit. I guess I can afford it. Look, I'd better go. Sorry to be so melodramatic with the back door stunt and making the phone call first to check you were in.'

He got up to go. I realised I had to say something to him. He was on his way out of the back door before I could nerve myself to do it.

'Jim,' I grasped his shoulder. 'Jim, I don't enjoy telling you this, but you had better be warned. There was someone in Madagascar who ended up knowing too much about a man who I now believe was a founder member of your group.'

'And?' His voice was almost a whisper.

'They had him killed. They play for high stakes.'

He stood there silently, his face silhouetted against the indigo of the night sky. When he spoke, his voice sounded firmer.

'Yeah. I should have guessed. Thanks for the warning. Pray for me, Henry. Please.'

Then he clasped my arm briefly and was gone.

41

I called Tina at work from one of the few call boxes at the university that had survived the weekend without becoming full of money or vandalised. Who vandalises university phone boxes when students are away is a mystery to me, but someone does.

'Can you see me tonight? I need to talk.'

There was a pause. I knew from that she had something planned. I hoped she could make it. My difficulties with Tina notwithstanding, it was her I wanted to talk to.

'Urgently?'

'You won't be disappointed on that score.'

'With you, Henry, I didn't think I would be. OK, any time after seven. See you then.'

The rest of the day I found work difficult. However hard I concentrated on the latest batch of journals, Jim's conversation seemed to sneak into my mind.

Prof called me in after coffee. 'Henry, how's your German?'

'Not quite non-existent, Prof. Some technical terms, that's all.'

'Oh well, anyway they all speak English. A letter arrived today . . . now where is it?' He dug under a pile of papers on his desk. 'Here, yes, I won't try to pronounce it. This German TV company is doing a documentary on the environmental effects of reservoirs. Gripping stuff, eh? But I suppose they don't have those war movies. Could we provide someone to talk to them about Thorpedale Water? Well, I thought it was more for the Botany people, but then it occurred to me that you'd done something on it. You have, haven't you?'

He peered at me as though expecting me to applaud his feat of memory. I nearly did. Prof's increasing absent-mindedness was a problem that we kept in check only with the aid of Ann, his excellent personal secretary, and a large desk diary.

'I'm surprised you remembered, Prof. I did one paper just as they were building the dam. First thing I ever wrote in fact. Then I did a follow-up last year. Strictly it's on the effects of the changing groundwater levels on the Carb Limestone below the dam. But yes, I know it. The details are all in my CV.'

'Ah yes, that's how Ann knew. Anyway, could you handle this one? Probably a few bob in it, I suppose. Better check with university accounts if it's very much. Thanks. I'm up to my neck with the Principal again. Couldn't find a cave for him, could you?' He winked at me.

'I'll do my best, Prof.' I took the letter and left.

As I was leaving he called out, 'Oh, use my line, they allow me to dial direct international calls. A great honour I'm told. I still end up paying.'

To my relief the Munich number was answered by a secretary with excellent English who put me on to the Herr Strauss who had written the letter. His English was the disgustingly efficient business sort, and the conversation proceeded without hesitation. He was passing through the area early on the following Friday morning and was scouting some locations for a possible programme. I knew the Thorpedale Water well? Excellent. There had been a dispute over it, yes?

Good. So could I meet him near the dam and talk about its effects on the landscape?

First rate. Nothing formal at this stage, but he'd probably tape the conversation and take some still shots. So could I meet him there?

Good. Did I mind early morning, as he would be on his way down from Penrith and had a ferry to catch. He wanted to see the area without too many people. Was seven-thirty too early?

Excellent. I waited a moment while he seemed to consult

a map. Was there room for two cars at Whale Force? Good. It did have a view over the area?

Fine. Then I would see him there, in a red Mercedes. Would I contact this number if there were any changes of plan?

Excellent. Very much obliged, Dr Stanwick.

I winced at the thought of the early hour. It was half an hour from Grantforth, but it would be a fine view if the present dry spell held.

Just before lunch I had a phone call from Brian, the Welshman who runs the local garage which specialises in old Volkswagens. In the manner of these things he is termed 'Brian the Beetle,' after the speciality that he resells at exorbitant prices. Brian had heard I was looking around and had a van for me. 'Real tidy, Henry, tidy it is. Norra scratch. New engine, the lot. Wouldn't mind it myself. Anyways, I need the space, you know, and I've a fancy to do up your Beetle. Could do you a good deal, I could. Tidy it would be. Come up by 'yur and see it before we close tonight.'

After lunch there was a note in my pigeonhole. It was from Jim. 'Henry, I've decided to go to the States for the next six weeks. Good luck, Jim. PS. Many thanks.' I screwed it up carefully and threw it in the overflowing office bin when no one was looking.

On the way back I called at 'Brian's' and checked the van out. It was indeed 'tidy' and looked to be a good buy. After a lot of haggling we ended up with terms that were mutually agreeable. There were a few things to be done on it, so I arranged for us to complete the deal on Wednesday. I drove home, ruefully reflecting that not even the prospect of buying such a prize camper could lift the unease that overshadowed me.

I picked up Tina just after seven, and we headed up onto the moors. I talked only about the German TV company and getting rid of the Beetle and buying the van. After a few minutes Tina looked at me. 'Henry, since when have you worried about looking in your rearview mirror?'

It's a standing complaint of hers that I drive in the best Arab tradition of ignoring everything behind me. I simply put a finger on my lips and said, 'It's a grand view.'

The evening was indeed a fine one, and there was a steady trickle of cars heading out into the country. After twenty minutes I pulled the car off the road into the car park at the top of Copplestone Edge.

About twenty yards from the car Tina spoke. 'OK, what's up?'

'I've never heard of a car being bugged, but I don't rule it out.'

'That bad?'

'What, my paranoia? No, there's been a rather odd development. It's important, but what it means I don't know. That's why you're here. You help me to think. Look, let's walk over to those rocks and I'll tell you what happened to me last night.'

I had virtually finished the story when we reached the rocks. I wandered round making sure that there was no one else there. We seemed to be on our own.

'So that's it. Now, I realise you have only heard my version of what was said and done in Madagascar and what was said last night in my back room, but does anything strike you?'

'Obviously the similarity of ideas. It sounds like Jim has met the son of Jezreel.'

'But how? What's the link between a Grantforth lecturer in Chemistry and an American computer expert, if that's what he was?'

'Henry, I wish I knew. Presumably Vaughan never met Jim. I mean, we have no evidence of that.' She fell into silence. I was about to say something when the peace was broken by the rising roar of three youths on motorbikes. They bounced along the path, cut across the scarred turf and careened past, heading on towards the main road.

I shook my head. 'Idiots! The damage they do to the

ground is enormous. There's no way grass is going to grow back with that sort of a stunt. They'll turn this place into a pile of dust within years.'

'Wasn't it you telling me about all the erosion caused by, what did you call them, "Off the Road" vehicles in the States?'

In that miraculous business of intuition, something was coming together in my mind. I nodded absent-mindedly. She began to say something. 'Hang on, Tina, I'm on the verge of something.'

'Sanity, I trust.'

I ignored her. 'Vaughan talked of that, ruining a park he'd known. He was really uptight about it, and it reminded me of that delta game.'

I lay down and looked up at the evening sky. It was coming together. It had to be the way it worked. 'Tina, I have the link! It's the game, but I don't know how it works. It's the third side of the triangle.'

Tina thought for a minute. 'Yes, in it you had to save the delta from destruction due to greed and stupidity. You mean the delta is the world? But how could that make Jim into an agent for Vaughan's group?'

'That's the problem. But Jim did do well at the game, you know. He was ruthless and committed enough to win. But how did they know that at the conference, which is where he was recruited?'

We said nothing for a few moments. Then Tina spoke, her voice hesitant. 'Henry, I think—yes, I'm certain—that I have the answer. Yes, it would work. Look, when you called the mainframe up it didn't modify the game, or at least if it did that was a minor aspect. What it did was report your performance.'

'Oh golly. Yes, that's it.' I paused to sort my thoughts out. 'It's not a game but a protracted series of tests of psychology and attitudes. And morality too. So they are looking for intelligent people, with commitment, but who don't care about the rules.'

Tina spoke again. 'Neat. It finds those who are idealistic but immoral and with technological ability too.'

Then a thought struck me. 'Nice, Tina, but sorry, it won't work. I mean, no one would give their name and address. You simply play under a codename. So how did they know it was Jim playing so well?'

'There must be a way round that. Phone number perhaps?'

'No, it's a university department. Jim could be one of a dozen people.'

Then I had the answer. 'Got it. The game includes a program that searches all the files on your hard disk for certain strings of characters—phrases like "Yours faithfully"—and it copies the next line of text. That would give you the name. The address would be trickier, but less critical anyway. Let me see . . . it would have to hunt for "Dear Sir" and it could copy, say, the five lines preceding. Eventually it would manage to get the address, unless you always used headed paper.

'So the mainframe, or its system operator, would say, "Hey, this man looks good, better find out his address," and on the call back it would trigger a separate program to find the name. Next time you called, it would give your results and the name and address. Smart.'

I got to my feet. It was getting cooler, besides which I was feeling threatened. I looked around. There was no one. 'So we can now see the picture. Vaughan is part of an organisation, originally set up by the Defence Department or whatever, that has taken on a life of its own. Their purpose is to steer things through the crises they see impending. Quite a tall order. To that end they are now recruiting, presumably only at a low level, by the game.'

'It's elegant, Henry. They avoid the one problem of being a secret organisation; that if you are secret you can't advertise for members. It's also a self-replicating recruiting device.'

'They are also able to screen potential members thoroughly. It minimises the risk of recruitment enormously. I was rejected without even knowing I was being assessed.'

Tina grabbed my arm. 'Henry, I'm scared.' She looked it too. Mind you, when I thought it through I wasn't too happy either.

'Yes, there's no getting out of it. We know far more than Steers knew. What we know is more than enough to get us killed.'

Tina was biting her lip. 'So what are you going to do?'

A good question indeed, but there was no point in panicking the poor girl. Although as I thought it, I realised she didn't act panicked. I tried to sound cool and in control. 'Nothing in a hurry. I need to think. I don't want to draw attention to us. I could call Lemaire, but, well, I don't entirely trust him. Besides, I'd have to bring in Jim's name and if Lemaire tries to squeeze him, then Jim's in big trouble with his friends. I have a niggling feeling that JP wouldn't bat an eyelid about sacrificing him if necessary.'

I stared around. The shadows were dark and long in the evening light. Everything else was fast losing any colour. Anything or anybody could be out there.

'Let's go back, Tina, it's getting dark.'

We strolled back and I took Tina's hand. For whose benefit or what purpose? I think we both needed the contact.

Just before we got to the car Tina turned to me and said, 'We must tell no one else, except perhaps Laurent, and Lemaire if you decide you must. It wouldn't be right to risk others.'

'OK, we're on our own.'

There was a faint smile on her face. 'Really, Henry, half your problems are due to the fact that you fail to apply your theology.'

42

I spent a part of that night wondering what to do about the game. The next morning I knew the answer. Just after nine I called the London number JP had given me. The phone number seemed to be that of an office complex, and it took some time to convince a frosty secretary that there really was a Mr Agravel there. Eventually, she relented enough to give me the address. I then scribbled a note of what I believed the game did and sent a copy of the original disk off by registered mail to the address.

That evening Laurent arrived at the station. He seemed to be enjoying his visit and had accumulated a couple of carrier bags of gifts for his family. Over a Chinese takeaway meal (with plenty of rice) I told Laurent what had happened with Jim. It was quite prolonged because most of the concepts were new to him. When I told him what I had done about the game he thought for a second.

'Why didn't you phone Mr Lemaire?'

'Good question. Partly to allow Jim time to get out of the country. I guess also because it was easier to explain the thing if he had the game itself. Also I suppose . . .' I pushed my plate aside as I tried to pull the words together. 'I want to get out of this mess, Laurent. I never want to see JP again, let alone Vaughan. Sending that disk to Lemaire was me signing off. *Khalas*! Oh, sorry, it's Arabic; it means, finished. I've got other things to do.'

'Like Cyprus?'

Then I realised he was still in the dark. Over coffee I outlined the change in plans.

'And Tina, what does she think?' Trust Laurent to put his finger on a nerve end.

'She thinks it's good news that I stick around. But what she thinks isn't the problem. Oh, Laurent, it's a mess.'

He grinned, but in affection, not malice. 'What can I say, my brother? These things are not easy.'

We left it at that. One issue we discussed was when Laurent would return to Madagascar.

'I must be back at the beginning of September. I have much to do.'

'Well, it should be sorted out by then. So you won't come with me to Yugoslavia?'

'I think not; there is much I want to see here still. Besides, I am sorry, but I have seen enough limestone.'

On Wednesday the van wasn't ready. I showed Laurent the sights of Grantforth, which didn't take long. In the evening I introduced him to a lot of people at the church mid-week meeting which I didn't normally attend. Although the Hensons were there, we spent only a brief time with them as they'd already given me an invitation to come round with Laurent for a meal on Thursday. Tina told me that she would like to come with me up to Thorpedale Water on Friday. It turned out that they were putting in new wiring in her office that day, and she thought she might as well use up a spare day's holiday she had.

'Only if the weather's nice, mind you. And afterwards would there be any chance of taking Laurent over the top of Thorpedale, over the fells? It's so bleak there without trees.'

I felt like saying that if she thought that was bleak she should see the Anatolian plain in mid-winter. But then I suppose that sort of thing is all relative.

Thursday I picked up the van. Laurent was most

impressed. He spoke only a few words. 'No rust!' and a bit later, 'These engine parts are original.' It was the tone of hushed reverence in which he said them that gave the game away. I'd never seen him like that with anything. He looked into every cupboard and into every niche. I began to feel as though I'd been given a Christmas present and he hadn't.

'I wish I could buy you one too!'

He pursed his lips and looked wistful. 'It would be nice, but I think I would worry too much about someone stealing the headlights. I have always wanted a new one, and now that we have a new road down to Tamatave there is something to drive it on . . .'

I kicked a tyre out of frustration. There are times when you feel the world is just too unfair.

To my relief the evening at the Hensons' went well. Given that I, despite my apparently covetable five-year-old Volkswagen Camper, sometimes felt awkward about my bank balance there, I was worried that Laurent would find it all a bit much. But then, I reflected, he wasn't thinking in terms of marrying one of their daughters. At any rate Alec and Viv didn't seem either embarrassed or defensive about the vast economic gulf between them and Laurent and neither did he. Much of the evening was spent in comparison and discussion about the respective church scenes. Tina and I sat rather outside it all, occasionally giving each other glances. Tina was at her best and also—with my present doubts—at her worst. She sat there composed and elegant, with her rather idiosyncratic beauty, while Laurent talked of dirt and poverty and riots. She seemed so detached and remote from it all and to belong in the genteel, polite civilisation of the Hensons' living room. I thought of the clamour of 'Tana airport and the raucous chaos of the market and the universal peeling paintwork. It was difficult to see her there.

In view of the planned early start in the morning we didn't stay late. Laurent listened to the engine note as we drove down to my house. 'Very nice, but I think it is not quite adjusted.'

'Tuned? Maybe not. It was supposed to be. Brian was in a hurry. Oh, we'll see tomorrow. It's a long climb uphill.'

I didn't really care very much. Tina was on my mind.

Despite an early night I couldn't sleep. The whole thing seemed hopeless. I would decide that I was being selfish, then I'd decide that it was simply that I didn't want to put her under the strain of something she couldn't take. Then that resolved, it would come to me that she probably didn't really love me anyway.

In a way it was a relief when morning dawned. Action is easier than thought. The forecaster on the local radio was positively exuberant; it was going to be another bright sunny day with just a faint breeze to keep the temperatures down. Tina was waiting for us when we arrived at the Hensons'. She looked a bit like they do in the fashion magazines that are the only thing to read in my dentist's waiting room. No makeup, but not a hair out of place. How she got the creases in her jeans I don't know. As she walked down the drive towards us I turned to Laurent. 'Laurent, there are times when Tina makes me feel a slob.'

'A what?'

'Tell you later, but you'd better pass me the comb out of my jacket. I'll try and look my best for the lady.'

Tina insisted that Laurent sit up front on the basis that she'd seen the view before. As we drove up out of Grantforth she made some general points about the interior decor. Eventually she said, 'You're going to drive this to Yugoslavia and back? It's a long way.'

'About three days solid each way. It's easier with a co-driver though.'

I gave her what I hoped was a meaningful glance, catching Laurent's eye in the process.

She looked rather dubious, and her answer was hesitant. 'I'm not sure I'd enjoy it. It looks a big thing to drive.'

My heart sank a little.

The road opened up as we came onto the moors and over the first cattle grid. Laurent had his head on one side listening to the engine. He turned to me. 'It is nothing serious, but there is something definitely not tuned in the engine.'

'OK, we'll have a look at it tomorrow.'

Soon we turned off the main road and began to drive up to the start of Thorpedale. The old stone-walled fields gave way to the forestry plantations. There was silence. A squirrel crossed the road. Then suddenly we were driving past the dam, and along the still water's edge. The water was low, and you could just catch a glimpse of the branches of dead trees surfacing a hundred yards out. A stone wall ran straight out down into the water. I kept on; we should just be in time at this rate.

Whale Force came in sight, a rather unprepossessing fine white streak of water, tumbling clear of a limestone rock ledge. The recent dry weather had reduced the flow greatly. The sign appeared for the road to the car park, revealing that it was a cul-de-sac, prohibited to all heavy vehicles, that it led to a pretty small car park, and that there was a much bigger one to be found by continuing along the main road. I ignored its veiled hints and concentrated on negotiating the steep bends. After the third bend we pulled above the trees, and Laurent made an appreciative comment about the view. I had to agree; Herr Strauss had certainly picked a good day and time. The highest fells beyond the lake and dam were clearly visible.

The car park at Whale Force is just below, and to one side of, the crest of the waterfall. From it one footpath goes up to the top of the waterfall and along over to Whale Fell. Another drops between scree slopes to the plunge pool below the waterfall and from there on down to the road along the reservoir edge. The size of the car park is restricted by the steepness of the slope, which allows it to be only large enough for a dozen cars.

It was exactly seven-thirty when we drove into the car park. The only sign of life was a red Mercedes with German plates parked flush with the slope dropping down to the lake and facing the entrance. I pulled straight in and stopped just inside the car park. Picking up a folder with a couple of maps and two reprints I said, 'Shouldn't be more than half an hour. See you then,' and set off to the Mercedes.

The occupant of the car was consulting a map, which he lowered as I got nearer to reveal a thin face with a neat moustache surmounted by a soft blue peaked cotton hat that looked very continental. He gave me a formal nod of the head and gestured to the passenger side.

I walked round the car, my mind half-full of Tina and half-trying to rehearse the various facts associated with the flooding of the valley. He had parked so close to the edge that it was quite a feat to get into the car without stepping onto the low cemented stone wall that hinders the careless—or alcohol-muddled—motorist from reversing off the car park and down the scree.

'Good morning, Herr Strauss. A lovely day.'

'Dr Stanwick, excellent. Please get in.'

I got in, observing the broad fine leather seats, the car phone, and the map on Herr Strauss' knees extending across the gear lever. I sank into the seat, pulling the heavy door closed behind me and looked at him, vaguely aware that the accent was wrong.

As I did, a gloved hand pulled the map back a fraction exposing a protruding polished grey metallic cylinder. It took me a second to recognise it, a second in which another gloved hand had pressed the central locking button. Anyone who has done time in the Middle East would recognise the barrel end of an AK47. I even got as far as deciding that in the confined space of the car it must be the version with the folding metal stock. I looked at the face again with a feeling of desperate certainty. Curiously, I didn't feel surprised.

'Vaughan.'

There was a fraction of a minute's silence. Then the cold voice spoke again.

'Exactly.'

43

'It's loaded and the safety's off. I'm not worried about holes in the door. Just talk. Who is in the van?'

I felt curiously detached. An external observer looking on, separated from the real world by glass. What did the books say? Evaluate. Look for weakness, anything that will help you. Keep calm. Eyes, voice, manner? Don't panic.

I looked at Vaughan's face. It was taut and drawn, the blue eyes slightly staring. The voice was flat, deliberate, and as emotionless as anything I've heard from flesh and blood. Any stress was well controlled. I flicked a glance at the hands. Not a tremor. Nothing to suggest any hope. Stuff the books.

'Tina and Laurent.' I spoke slowly. It came to me with an unequivocal certainty that there could be no trickery here. Not by me.

Tim was turned towards me, leaning back in between the seat and the door. His left hand must be on the trigger; awkward to fire, but he could do it. The fact that he would probably sprain his wrist wasn't going to be of much use to me.

'I may let her go. If you answer. He's dead. You too.'

A fraction of a pause. His face seemed thinner, hair and moustache dyed.

'What do you know?'

It was a funny gun for him to have; something smaller and neater would have been adequate. Something more hi-tech would have been more in character too.

'We found the dummy. We knew you were alive.'

The map slipped a fraction, exposing the left hand. There

was a fraction of movement in the trigger finger. It's amazing how threatening a millimetre or so of motion can be.

'We?'

'Someone in one of the American Intelligence services.' I paused for a second and looked Vaughan in the face. The frigidity of expression that I saw made me continue.

'Lemaire, JP. I don't know either his rank or outfit.' Sorry, JP, I thought, but I'm not going to lie now. Not when any second may be my last on earth. There was no reaction. Nothing. What could I do? I glanced at the van. Tina and Laurent were sitting up front, deep in conversation. How could I warn them? There was no way they could drive away without a three point turn.

Vaughan registered my glance. 'Act naturally, point out the scenery.'

So I waved my arms about in as natural a manner as I could.

'Lemaire. What does he know about the rest of us? The people that I work with.'

'He knows you killed Steers.'

I watched his face. It was a total blank. Nothing at all. Not a flicker of remorse, regret, or anything human. It crossed my mind that Vaughan wasn't alive, not in the real sense of the word. The blood still flowed, the nerve cells fired, but where it mattered he was as dead as stone.

'I ordered it. We have to minimise the possibilities of leakage. What else is known?'

'That it's all linked with Jezreel.'

I briefly wondered why I was telling him this. To appease him, to win a reprieve for Tina, to play for time, or simply because it was true?

'What does he know of that?'

'I don't know. I haven't seen him for ten days—since Madagascar.'

He was silent for a moment. I realised that I was facing imminent death.

'And the game?'

'It's not what it seems; it selects people.' I stopped abruptly. Tina was walking over, picking her way between the holes in the tarmac. I looked at Vaughan.

'Act naturally. Any foolishness and she's dead. Do you understand?'

He slid the map down over the gun. Hope stirred faintly. Perhaps she could say something, or do something like . . . like what? Tina came over to my side. Vaughan pressed a button and the window wound down.

'Good morning.' She nodded at Vaughan, who nodded mechanically back. 'I'm sorry to interrupt. Henry, Laurent wants to adjust your engine. I said I'd ask. That's all.'

That's all indeed.

'Yes, fine, Tina. Just fine.'

She smiled gently at me. 'Good, see you soon. Sorry to interrupt. Bye.'

She turned and walked back. The temptation briefly flickered across my mind to be angry with her for not doing something, but there was nothing she could have done. As I stared at her I realised that I'd got it all wrong. I'd tried to impose my terms; tried to mould her in my image. Why should she be anything other than the gentle person that she was? Why hadn't I just accepted her as she was? Tina, I cried out in my mind, there's a lot I want to say, but probably now never will. I love you; do you love me?

Vaughan was speaking again. 'The game—you told Lemaire?'

I came back down to earth.

'I sent him a copy. Yes, with a note.'

'When?'

'Tuesday morning. He'll have it by now.'

There was no change of expression. 'That's all I wanted to know. Thank you.'

There was the hint of emphasis on the word 'all' that struck home. A surge of panic rose up. I tried praying. 'Jesus, help me!' Nothing seemed to happen, but the panic subsided into a dull anger.

'You're crazy. You'll alert everybody if you kill me here. This isn't Madagascar.'

He said nothing. For the first time there was the faintest hint of something that might have been a vestigial emotion. An expression that could have been the precursor of a sneer crossed his face. With his right hand he reached under the seat and pulled out something heavy and metallic. It was a spare magazine for the Kalashnikov. Without moving his left hand off the trigger he prised a cartridge free and handed it over.

'Read it.'

I glanced at the end, rotating it to get the light right on the brass so I could read the tiny Arabic print stamped on the base.

'Recognise it?' Of course I did. Every kid in West Beirut has a handful of empty cases stamped with the same logo. The stuff's found its way into the hands of most of the leftist militias in Lebanon. I handed it back slowly.

'Syrian army issue. So?'

'Some time today Reuters in West Beirut will be handed a statement claiming responsibility for your execution for crimes against the Lebanese people. The usual thing. A lesson that distance and time are no barrier to vengeance for treachery, expressing regret about the innocent bystanders. It'll be signed by some suitable and hitherto unknown group. "The Guardians of the Revolution" perhaps.'

It was spoken flatly. No regret, no gloating, not even triumph.

He spoke again, slowly and thoughtfully. 'If you want to hide a signal, it is often sufficient just to increase the noise. You see, Henry, how efficiently we normally work. You had the misfortune to be involved in one of our few mistakes.'

I could just take it all in. A brilliant plot. Given my record it would be all too credible. I could visualise the press coverage tomorrow: 'Three years and three thousand miles away Middle East terror caught up with Dr Henry Stanwick.'

The engine on the Volkswagen turned over and started. Laurent was walking round to the back of the van.

'That's it, Henry. Open the door wide and step out very slowly.'

He released the central locking button. The van's engine was being raced. I slowly reached for the door handle. As I did so I tried to reassess the probability of being able to overpower him. Half of my mind screamed out to try and jump him. Yet something else said, hold on. As I considered the option, the map slipped away entirely; Vaughan had taken the gun with both hands and braced himself as if to fire. I'd lost that chance.

I opened the door a fraction. Presumably he'd shoot as soon as I got out of the door. It occurred to me that if I could get out fast enough I could be down the slope. But Vaughan's gaze was unflinching. 'Open the door wide.'

I swung it slowly open.

'Wider, and get out. Slowly or the girl's dead too.'

The van's engine was roaring. I started to lift myself out. Suddenly, the note changed as the gears were engaged. Tyres screamed. For a split second I stared at the van in bemusement before I realised it was accelerating at us. Vaughan, however, understood what was happening instantly. Out of the corner of my eye I saw that in a single move—without a moment's hesitation—he had swung round and was moving to open his door. The van had closed half the distance between us. I was still fixed to the seat, half in and half out of the car. Then the paralysis lifted. I half-pushed myself and half-jumped out of the car. I now realised what was happening. Laurent was heading straight at us and was going to smash into the side of the Mercedes.

As I tumbled out and turned to throw myself over the low wall I caught a final fleeting glimpse of what was happening. Then I jumped, and as I began falling I realised three things that ripped at my heart in a moment of savage, wrenching horror and dismay. The van was still ten or so yards away—the driver was Tina—and Vaughan already had the door open wide enough to fire through.

The next fraction of a second was agony as I hit the scree and slithered down. Firing, sharp and dreadfully loud, occurred above and behind me. Then there was a grinding crashing noise with the sound of metal being torn and glass being broken. The firing stopped, although the echoes continued to pound round the rocks. My sliding ended abruptly against a small limestone block. I was some twenty feet down the slope, and I hurt all over and most of all, inside. I turned to look up at the car. It hadn't moved; clearly the van hadn't hit it. I glanced down. Ten feet away was an accumulation of large boulders. In between them were cracks large enough to lie in. There was a noise above. I turned. Vaughan had come round to the edge of the car and was looking at me. He was holding the gun.

I didn't stop to watch, but flung myself down the scree again. It was pure pain. I tried to protect my face with my hands as I rolled and slid down, expecting to hear and feel the gunshots any second. I stopped, and opened my eyes. For a moment I was hopelessly disorientated. Then I realised that my feet were at the base of a lorry-sized block which was virtually split in two. With all my remaining strength I half-slithered and half-rolled across, coming to rest lying down on the floor of the fissure.

For a moment I was safe. I tried to get my breath back. There was blood dripping down my forehead. An ankle throbbed, and there were nerves screaming all over the place. I thought about Tina and it was almost unbearable.

There was a noise up the hill. I looked up. I could see nothing but the sky, the scree and the edge of the waterfall. The gash faced almost directly towards the waterfall. Unless Vaughan moved round that way, onto steeper slopes, he couldn't fire in at me. However, given time all he had to do was climb down and walk up to the crevasse and shoot me. That was the other side of the coin. I was trapped here. There was no way I was going to be able to make a break for it from here—not with an ankle that was at the very least badly sprained. Not that it all really seemed to matter now. It was just like one of those dreadful rugby matches at school where you were a full thirty points down, but the coach forced you to keep playing until the whistle blew.

And as I lay there waiting all sorts of things came to mind, and I realised that I had accused Tina of being committed to me with only her head and not her heart; an allegation that was now terribly disproved. But curiously my thoughts focused on the accusation, not on Tina, because I realised that what I had alleged of her was what I was guilty of. Not towards Tina perhaps, but—far worse—towards God. I had understood words such as 'atonement' and 'salvation,' I had assented to truth, and I knew that Christ had a claim on me, but had never truly yielded my heart.

And lying there in the fractured rock I heard myself say out loud, 'Christ, save me!' and it was a plea for the soul as much as the body.

Then there was the dreadful sound of a trickle of little stones on the scree. To my dismay Vaughan came into view. He was high up the scree, moving with ease towards the waterfall on the steep section. He stopped and turned, and I knew I had been seen. This was it. I looked around for some further shelter, but there was none. I had run as far as I could. The rock pressed against me on every side except the one that mattered. The only way out was forward. I pressed myself down as deep as I could and tried to present the smallest target possible. Vaughan took his time. I don't think he was sadistic; that would imply he felt pleasure, and I think that was beyond him. He was just doing it by the book. He wasn't carrying the spare magazine, and I was a good thirty yards away. Whatever its many virtues, the Kalashnikov isn't a sniper's rifle. He balanced himself carefully on the scree in a half-squat, braced himself and squeezed the trigger. It was a single shot. I heard it part the air and ricochet off the outside of the rock. He'd missed the crevasse. He paused briefly, fired again, and the second shot struck and whined away a few inches above my head. Pale, sharp stone chips flew around me. The echoes reverberated, slowly dying away into silence. I closed my eyes for the third, and probably the last, shot.

Instead, something very odd happened. Quite simply a phrase came into my mind with a quiet ringing clarity and definiteness. No voice, no lightning, no earthquake, just an unarguable statement of something that was inevitable.

'In due time their foot shall slip.'

For no obvious reason I opened my eyes. Vaughan was bracing himself carefully for the third shot. As I watched, a tiny piece of stone like a small grey mouse seemed to roll away from near his feet. Another, slightly bigger, followed it and a third after that. A larger slab slipped out from below Vaughan and slithered and rolled down the scree. As it did so, he lost his balance and leaned back, and as that happened the gun fell away from him. With a loud clatter it tumbled down the scree and rattled out of sight.

Vaughan regained his balance, stood up, and stared at me for a moment. The most chilling thing was that he said nothing. I could see his face clearly, pale and staring, like some kind of mask, and there seemed to be no trace of emotion on it. Then he peered down for a glance at where the gun had fallen and without a single further look in my direction, scrambled back towards the car and out of my field of view.

Instantly, I began to move out of the crevasse in a sort of crawl. I wanted just to lie down and pass out, but I knew I had to try to get back up. It was almost certainly too late, but I had to be up there with Tina. I had got out of the mouth of the crevasse when there was the sound of the Mercedes starting up. In a minute the noise of it was only faintly to be heard in the distance.

I tried to get to my feet. It was just about possible to stand, but walking wasn't on. However, the swelling now occurring in my ankle suggested that it was just sprained rather than broken. I set off up the scree, crawling.

It was a painful, bloody business, but I was driven on by

the thought of what might lie at the top. I had gone only a few yards when I heard a cry of 'Henry!' and Laurent slid down to where I was. He grabbed me and buried his head in my shoulders. I knew how he felt, but I had to know about Tina. I was just about to say something when below us we heard the noise of a car engine. There was no doubt from the tone and the way it was being driven that it was Vaughan going north along the dam road. If we had been a bit higher up we could have seen him. I looked in the direction of the sound.

Suddenly the trees became silhouettes against a brilliant white flash of light. The light turned yellow, then orange as the thudding roar of the shock waves reached us. The noise echoed and re-echoed round the scree. A boiling mass of smoke, dirty flame and spinning debris rose skywards above the green leaves of the trees and, as we watched, collapsed slowly inwards on itself into a single dying plume of brown vapour.

'Vaughan's car.'

Laurent looked at me. 'I don't understand.'

'Neither do I. Tina?'

He paled. 'She will be OK, I pray. Henry, I am sorry that it was not me. I didn't . . .'

I interrupted him. 'You're forgiven. Let's get up there. Give me your shoulder.'

Five minutes later we were on the tarmac.

The van was farther down the car park than I had expected. It lay on its side in a pile of glass. A front wheel hung in the air, the rubber hanging in shreds. Tina lay out beside the van.

'I pulled her out, Henry. I didn't know what to do. There is petrol around.'

I tried to sit down next to her and succeeded only in collapsing. She looked awful and seemed only half-conscious. There was a nasty bruise on her forehead. Laurent gestured to it. 'It is the only injury I can see. I think Vaughan missed her.'

I glanced at the front of the van; the windscreen had gone,

but most of the bullet holes were around the front wheels. Tina was saying something that I couldn't make out. I bent over and held her hand. I just wanted to collapse, to cry or to faint, but I couldn't yet. I tried to think hard.

'We've got to get help, Laurent.'

He looked at me and nodded. 'Which way do I go?'

I closed my eyes in despair, visualising the long road to the nearest farm. It was all too much.

There was a humming noise in the sky, rising to a roar. Laurent was saying something. It was only when the windscreen chips on the tarmac started sliding around and the dust began rising that I realised what he was saying was 'helicopter.'

I found myself crying.

44

They flew us back to a new private hospital on the south of town. No one said very much to me, and I didn't bother asking anything. The people at the hospital seemed to know what they were doing with Tina and made reassuring noises about her condition, so I reconciled myself to being patched up.

After they'd bandaged my ankle and taped over some gashes they put me in a white sunny room. On the door was someone who might have been a plain clothes policeman, but who wasn't unless Grantforth CID had been recruiting in the USA. So I lay on the bed and thought a lot. Gradually everything cleared up, and I was able to see how although the events in Madagascar had revealed the void at the centre of my life, my attempt to fix it with just trying my best had been a disaster. Indeed, it had taken that awful moment of revelation in the crack of the rock to show me that my heart had remained in rebellion. And so in that room I thought and prayed and progressively gave in till it was all done and everything was put right.

It was just after midday when Laurent came in. He walked in quietly and sat on the edge of my bed. He looked very subdued, and I feared the worst. He must have seen my face.

'No, Tina is fine. At least the doctors say so. I have not seen her. Her father and mother are now here. Henry, I have to tell you what happened.'

I was sufficiently relieved by the first bit of news to be able to tease him. 'Go on, Laurent, explain how you and Tina wiped out my new van.'

To my surprise he looked embarrassed. 'I'm very sorry. We were sitting in the van. Tina thought it was odd that you hadn't got out of the car. Suddenly, I had this thought that perhaps this man was Vaughan. Tina agreed when I said it. But how could we be sure? I remembered the scar he had above one eye. So we had to go and look.'

He paused for breath. 'She said that she would go as he would not expect her to recognise him. Otherwise—no I mean also—she said she was probably better at acting than I was.'

I interrupted. 'Well, that's probably true enough. She did a good job, Laurent. I'd forgotten about that scar, though. So she saw it and knew it was Vaughan.'

Laurent shook his head. 'No, she said the light was not right, and she didn't want to stare. She said as soon as she got there she realised that the ambience, the atmosphere, was all wrong. Also, she said the doors were locked. And she said you didn't look very happy at all. She had a great fear.'

'Golly, it was on that basis she decided to crash into Vaughan? Extraordinary.'

Laurent looked embarrassed again. 'Well, she said perhaps we should ram him. I did not like the idea. I tried to persuade her that we should wait. Perhaps it was not Vaughan, I said. I'm sorry, Henry.'

I suddenly saw the source of the problem. 'You didn't like the idea of wrecking my van and his Mercedes on a mere probability?'

He nodded faintly and looked down at his feet. I suppose in a society where used torch batteries were valuable, the idea of writing off two vehicles probably would meet with some resistance.

'They are just things, Laurent, big things, expensive things, but still things. Ultimately moth and rust get them too. Mind you, I sympathise. I'm not sure I'd have been prepared to do what she did.'

I nodded for him to continue. 'So she said, "OK, but pretend to tune up the engine." So I went back to do the acting of the tuning up. Then she shouted at me to stand back and just raced away. There was nothing I could do. Vaughan shot at the tyres and maybe at the windscreen, so she missed the car. I think she knew she had to turn to stop herself from going over the edge. So it rolled. I ran after her and decided to get her out first. I thought you might have escaped. I heard the shooting but . . . what could . . .'

He stopped. He looked very sad. 'Then the shooting stopped. Then Vaughan came back. I thought he would kill us.'

Laurent's face was filled with a look of awe and fear. 'When he came back he just walked past. He didn't even look at me. Henry, I have never seen such a thing. Right past. I almost thought he was a ghost.' He shook his head. 'And he is now dead.'

'Are we sure?'

He paled and nodded. 'Lemaire is here. He asked me to identify . . . Lemaire said you wouldn't believe unless . . . Truly dead.'

The words seemed to resonate in the sterile air.

'Don't say any more. Thanks for sparing me that. But what happened?'

Laurent shrugged. 'They do not know. Lemaire just said that they were investigating.'

I was going to make some apologies to Laurent when there was a knock on the door and without any wait for an answer two people came into the room. Leading the way was the bulky figure of JP Lemaire. He was dressed in a grey lightweight suit that looked creased and vaguely stained. The man behind was younger, thinner and more upright with a black blazer and a club or school tie that I felt I ought to recognise. He was unmistakably British and carried the sort of briefcase that meant he was either from the Ministry of Defence or the Inland Revenue. I didn't think it was the latter.

Lemaire grinned. He probably intended it to be an amiable grin, but he had lost the ability.

'Henry, good to see you.' He shook hands, heedless of the large plasters that covered my knuckles.

'I thought I'd better see you. I've brought along a friend. Charles Davis.' There was just the hint of emphasis on the first name which suggested a faint mockery.

'Charles is going to sort out some things with you. Over to you, Charles.'

'Er, yes. Mind if I sit down, Dr Stanwick? Good. This is your friend from Madagascar, yes?'

I introduced Laurent and even got his surname about right. I couldn't be too badly bruised.

'Good, well, let me first identify myself.' He presented his papers. Ministry of Defence.

He pulled up a chair alongside the bed. 'Right, now I'll be as brief as possible. As you can imagine I'm here about this morning. It was an American who shot at you?'

It seemed an odd way to view the thing.

'Yes, but . . .'

'In fact a member of that nation's military forces?'

'Well, he'd been working with them . . .'

'No, that's all we need to know. Had to confirm it. I mean ultimately we have to send the bill somewhere. Still, they tend to pay up quickly. Not that it will affect you, old chap. We pay you. Washington then pays us.' Lemaire nodded.

Perhaps I'd hit my head harder than I'd thought. 'I'm sorry, this isn't making much sense.'

'Charles, maybe you should just explain to the boy how you see the whole affair.' There was a suggestion of irritation in JP's voice.

'Right, yes, sorry. I thought you knew. Yes, we understand that this American soldier deserted from West Germany, stole a car and some weaponry, and ended up here, where he attacked you—as you well know. Probably some mental thingy. Drugs maybe. Anyway, after leaving you he accidentally or deliberately blew himself, and the car, up, fortunately with no damage to anything else other than the road, a wall, and some trees—all of which are the property of Grantforth Water Board whom I will see shortly.'

He gave me a guileless smile. I stared at him, only slowly understanding what he'd said.

'But it's not true! I can't support a tale like that. Vaughan was . . .'

Charles raised his finger to interrupt and flashed a glance at Lemaire. It seemed to convey acknowledgement of something.

'Ah, but you're not being asked to say anything. That's the whole jolly point. Just hear me out, please.' He reached into his briefcase and opened a folder.

'Your assailant was from a NATO force, so I am authorised under various reciprocal agreements to deal with you. Now, first of all, we handle compensation. No problem, I'll leave you the form. Afraid we need several copies, but I'll fill in all the tricky bits later.'

He handed me the forms, and I accepted them automatically. 'Now the dreadful word "confidentiality." In the wrong hands, Dr Stanwick, this could be trouble. The tabloid press would make a mountain out of this. The more serious Sundays might also. We can do without embarrassment at the moment, of course. The Arms Talks, you see. So basically we'd like it kept quiet. Now personally I'd take your word for it, but we'd like some legal safeguards.'

He dug out another sheaf of papers. 'It might also be in your best interests to sign this. You see, if any press chappy starts poking around, you just mutter something about having signed the Official Secrets Act and tell him to clear off.'

It was all very neat. First line of defence, Henry Stanwick's integrity. Back it up with an embarrassing, and hence plausible, cover story.

'So you see, Dr Stanwick? All we want is a promise of silence. And from Mr . . . Laurent, too, although we have no legal sanction there.'

There was a slight accent over 'legal' that I didn't much care for. 'No lies. Just sealed lips. I think you'll find it the only reasonable option. Just a signature.'

He looked at his watch. I thought hard.

'OK, I'll take a look at the form. Probably sign it too. Call back this evening. In the meantime I'll not talk.'

He looked very relieved. 'Splendid fellow. Excellent. You won't regret it. It'll work to your benefit.'

He got up and after getting a nod from Lemaire left after shaking hands. He had the grace to go easy on the knuckles.

As the door closed behind Charles, Lemaire spoke. 'I'm not stopping long, Henry. I've got a plane to catch. This whole thing is being rounded off nicely. You're even going to get a new van out of it.' My ankle was beginning to throb a bit.

'A pity about Vaughan.' I was surprised at the amount of anger in my voice.

'Yeah, kinda sad. Lotta talent but . . . least he didn't kill you.'

I felt my anger rising. 'Lemaire, I've got some questions I want answers to. Like where did you spring from?'

He looked a little discomforted. 'You're worried that we were prepared to sacrifice you to catch Vaughan?'

'I'm sorry, JP, but that unworthy thought had occurred to me.'

It's amazing how venomous I can become when I think someone's nearly got me killed.

JP shook his head slowly. 'No, we just blew it. I'm afraid we opened your mail and listened to your phone, but we hadn't a clue that you had this rendezvous. You didn't make our lives easy by getting rid of the Beetle. We didn't have time to put a location transmitter on the van. I'm ashamed to say we expected you in the office this morning at nine.'

I sat up in bed and regretted it. Lemaire continued, 'Budget operation. This morning I got a call at seven-fifteen from the guy who's been watching your house saying the van was gone. He'd gone for a paper he said and when he came back you'd left. So we panicked. We called the Hensons, and Alec said you'd gone to meet a German at Thorpedale. So then we knew we'd blown it. It was all we could do to get a chopper up in time. That's it. No trickery. Just an honest to goodness foul-up in the best tradition, but we did get your girl out. Could have been a long time otherwise. No, honestly, if we'd have known, we'd have cut off Vaughan. I genuinely wanted him alive.'

It sounded very believable too. I thought about getting annoyed over the phone lines, but it didn't seem worth it. Lemaire looked all set to leave the room, and I still had some more questions.

'So what happened to Vaughan?'

There was a flicker of something across JP's face. He looked at his watch again. 'We don't know. As Charles said, probably accidentally blew up. Bumpy road; unstable fuses. Maybe deliberate. Suicide perhaps. Anyway, it doesn't matter. Look, I must be off.'

I had a sudden intimation of what Lemaire was up to. 'Don't you want to know what he said to me? Or what I had to tell him?'

'Not especially. The guy's dead.' JP looked around the room as if to check he'd left nothing behind. 'Henry, the case is closed.'

'You're crazy, JP. He was part of something big.'

Lemaire looked at me intently. Then he spoke slowly. 'The conclusion of my investigations is that Vaughan acted on his own. He employed accomplices where necessary, but he was a one man band. There is no organisation.'

It all fitted. Just what I should have expected.

'Jezreel?'

'Doesn't exist on the files.'

JP began to get out of his chair. He looked tired.

'So his motive was what?'

Lemaire looked exasperated. 'That we don't know. Attempted defection maybe. It doesn't matter. He is dead.'

'The game then?'

'Neat, a curiosity. Propaganda maybe, no worse.'

He was moving towards the door.

'But I know someone who was enlisted through it.'

'Produce him then.'

I knew I couldn't bring Jim Barnett into it. And Lemaire knew I wasn't going to bring him in. Right now there were a lot of things I was thinking of calling him, but 'stupid' wasn't one of them.

'I won't.'

Lemaire paused by the door. 'Look, it's a textbook operation. The guy's dead, probably by his own hand. We have an adequate cover story. You three are alive. That's that. I'm off.'

I felt myself getting very annoyed. 'Now you listen to me, Lemaire. You've got what you wanted: a nice neat little case, neatly solved, nothing too big or too dangerous. Nothing life-threatening.'

JP moved a hand towards the door and then let it fall away. He looked hard at me. I didn't give him the chance to say anything.

'You really want the truth? I doubt it, but let me give you what I think happened—in fact what I'm virtually sure of. Jezreel did exist. The results were bad. The guys on it genuinely did believe that it was only a matter of time before the whole world system collapsed. In the end they decided they would rather put the world before the state, so your lot tried to abort the whole thing. But it's alive and kicking, isn't it, JP? And Vaughan was disappearing to join it. The Madagascar stunt was simply because so many other people have already dropped out elsewhere in other ways. They are too careful, they can't use the same method twice. Too many drownings with no bodies and people begin to get suspicious.'

Lemaire shrugged his big shoulders. I didn't wait for him to say anything.

'You know, Lemaire, I told Vaughan about what you knew.'

'He's dead.' There was a brief look of fear in his eyes. It wasn't much, but it encouraged me. I was on the right track.

'He had a car phone; but you know that. I have a hunch what happened after he left me. As he drove away he called his boss and told him what had happened. It was a stupid thing to do. Maybe he didn't believe he was disposable. Anyway, there was telecommunications stuff in the car with codes and frequencies that they didn't want to lose, so they probably had a self-destruct mechanism built in. Maybe he was too naive to think they might have wired it up to be fired by remote control.'

Lemaire was holding the door handle. He looked old, tired and vulnerable. How had I ever found him intimidating?

'Don't worry, I've nearly finished. Why kill Vaughan? Perhaps the boss knows you, JP. He probably knew that one dead body would give you what you want. He maybe reckoned it was worth losing Vaughan to get rid of you. A worthwhile sacrifice. So he decided to tidy up Vaughan's end of things and pressed a few buttons. I guess when you look at the remains you'll find the detonator was linked to the car phone.'

Lemaire's face had paled further. He turned the door handle and stood in the doorway. I thought he was going to walk away without saying anything. Finally he spoke, with slow, angry, scared tones.

'Stanwick, you're too smart, or maybe not smart enough. Supposing I did find that. Well, yeah, I'd probably see it as a deal; a trade off to preserve the peace. And maybe too I'd also see it as a warning: steer clear or it's you next. Are you listening? I'm not gonna say you're right, but even if you are, maybe especially if you are, the case would still be closed. You just sign that form and keep your mouth shut.'

At that point he seemed about to go, then suddenly he turned and, walking over to me, stood at the end of the bed. It should have been threatening as he probably meant it to be, but it wasn't at all. As he spoke, the whole veneer of bluster seemed to disintegrate.

'Look, let's assume your story is correct for the sake of argument. Then we have a deal, a truce with the Jezreel people. Don't break it, Henry. Please don't break it. Just don't break it. Promise me.'

I thought for a moment. 'The answer is no. I can't promise

315

that. I won't talk to the press, and I'm not going to gossip it about, but that's as far as it goes. They've made no truce with me.'

Lemaire stared at me for a moment as if hoping for a reprieve. Then he turned round and walked heavily away, head down, along the corridor. As I watched him I realised exactly how high the price of saving your own life can be.

Laurent got up and closed the door. He came over and sat on the end of the bed. His face seemed full of comprehension and sorrow. He said nothing.

'I'm sorry, Laurent. I didn't mean to get annoyed. I just knew that he'd got what he wanted. And I'm now certain what happened to Vaughan. It was no accident, no suicide.'

Laurent looked worried. 'Yes, I felt he agreed your guess was right. But, Henry, what do you do now?'

'You mean am I going to chase after Vaughan's killer? The answer is no. I've no evidence, no clues. Laurent, I can't even prove that it wasn't suicide. So I'm going to sign those forms. It's not my war. I don't see that I have got a mandate, an order, for doing that.'

He hesitated briefly. 'But you would do it if . . .'

'Yes, if I had to. That's why I wouldn't promise Lemaire to keep the truce. Yes, I've learnt that lesson. But right now I don't feel that calling. I've not been called up for that. Not yet.'

Laurent thought for a while and then spoke. His face seemed to show relief. 'Good. I think you are right at this moment.'

'Besides, I've got some more important things to do in the near future.'

A faintly quizzical look appeared on his face and slowly broadened into a grin.

'Yes, Laurent, like marrying Miss Henson.'

Half an hour later Alec came in without being announced, which I felt was just as well because I hadn't particularly relished the meeting. I felt there was quite a bit that I had to say to him. He looked tired but not anxious. Laurent got up off the bed.

'I will just go for a walk. If you need me I'll be outside.' He was having trouble hiding his grin as he left.

Alec nodded after him. 'A good fellow. Well, Tina's going to be just fine. The X-rays show nothing—just concussion. Viv's with her. They say she's in for observation and will probably be out within forty-eight hours, God willing.'

'Thank God.'

'Indeed and Amen. And yourself? I gather you have some striking bruising and the odd cut. A remarkably low toll of injuries all in all. You must both have been spared for something—hopefully less traumatic. Anyway, how are you feeling in yourself?'

I held his hand. 'What can I say, Alec? The better for hearing from you about Tina, but still rather full of sorrow and anger and the rest. Not as bad as I was earlier, and I've sorted a lot of things out, things that should have been cleared up years ago.'

Alec raised an eyebrow and sat down in the armchair. 'Well, you just tell me as much as you feel fit.'

So I told him the brief outline of what had happened and what Lemaire had said. I didn't mean to say anything about my misplaced doubts over Tina, but I'm fairly certain that much of it came out. Then I told him a little about what I'd found out about myself. Needless to say, Alec was the perfect listener. He sat through it all in near silence, with just the briefest of interjections and the occasional shake of his head. In the end I ground to a halt.

'So you see, Alec, I suppose above all I feel I've been spared.'

Alec looked at me. 'You mean it being such a near run thing?'

'No, not just that; not the dying business. No, Vaughan . . . what he'd become. It scares me. Do you think I was travelling the same road?'

Alec thought for a minute. 'It should scare us all, but you'd best answer that yourself.'

I struggled with my thoughts for a moment. 'I suppose Vaughan was a long way down that road when I met him, so it's hard to say. But how did he end up like that, Alec?'

There was a quiet sigh.

'I can only guess, of course. I'd imagine he started by forcing himself to believe that the value of what he was doing made a little lying and cheating right. It didn't, of course, but that deliberate suppression of his conscience, the wilful hardening of his heart, made it inevitable that he would fall ever deeper. So he did. Lies, ever grander lies, then the killing of yon pilot, and at the end he was ready for multiple murder.'

Alec stared silently at the ceiling for a moment, then continued, 'Aye, it's a road you could have gone on. A road that without grace we would all travel on. Vaughan just reached his destination faster and in more spectacular a manner than most.'

He shook his head sorrowfully. Then after a few moments' silence he turned to me with a half-smile.

'Enough! I think there's a time and place for discussing tragedies, and now is not it. I think we've talked quite enough about that. In fact, I really came to say that Tina's up to seeing you. Briefly, that is, and if you can make it over. I'm sure Laurent and I can lend you an arm or two—if I can find him.'

I got to my feet painfully. Walking was just about possible. Alec looked at me hard, as though evaluating me. What he saw didn't seem to displease him too much.

'She'll be very glad to see you.'

And she was.